Dangerous
bodies

~

MANCHESTER
1824

Manchester University Press

Dangerous bodies

HISTORICISING THE GOTHIC CORPOREAL

～

Marie Mulvey-Roberts

MANCHESTER UNIVERSITY PRESS

Published by Manchester University Press
Altrincham Street, Manchester M1 7JA, UK
www.manchesteruniversitypress.co.uk

British Library Cataloguing-in-Publication Data is available

ISBN 978 0 7190 8541 3 *hardback*
ISBN 978 1 5261 2718 1 *paperback*

First published by Manchester University Press in hardback 2016

This edition first published in 2018

FOR NIGEL

Corporeality is important to the gothic because it is, like the mode itself, caught up in a tug of war between its denunciation of the laws that govern the status quo and its exploitation of carnality and gore for affective or entertainment purposes.

Xavier Aldana Reyes, *Body Gothic* (2014), p. 8

Horror fiction is over and over again about the body.
Clive Barker, interview (1988) in Richard Lupoff
et al., 'A Talk with the King' (1992), p. 84

Gothic, then provides an image language for bodies and their terrors [...].
David Punter, *Gothic Pathologies* (1998), p. 14

Contents

~

Figures

❧

Figures 9 and 10 are screen grabs, reproduced here under
the fair dealing guidelines relating to criticism and review as
suggested by the Intellectual Property Office
(published 12 June 2014).

Acknowledgements

~

In the writing of this book, I have many debts of gratitude, which cannot, alas, all be accounted for. I would like to acknowledge the importance of the International Gothic Association, which has provided me with invaluable opportunities for networking with leading scholars, many of whom are listed below. Many thanks go to those who commented on draft chapters. These include Nora Crook, Madge Dresser, Bob Dumbleton, Alex Gilkison, Lesley Hall, Derek Hughes, Nicola King, Sarah Robertson, Dale Townshend and Lisa Vargo. Heartfelt appreciation goes to Nigel Biggs, Marion Glastonbury, Avril Horner and Gina Wisker, who read full drafts. The book has benefited greatly from their insights and advice.

I am grateful to the Faculty of Arts, Creative Industries and Education at the University of the West of England (UWE), Bristol, for granting me research leave for a semester to work on the book. Invaluable help was given to me by librarians, especially Amanda Salter, at our late Victorian Gothic campus, St Matthias, Ellen Reed at the Frenchay campus, Dawn Dyer at Bristol Central Reference Library, the library staff at Bristol University Library and at the Wellcome Library, London. I am indebted to the assistance given to me by the out-of-hours university IT support team for their invaluable help. Thanks are due to my Gothic literature undergraduate and postgraduate students on whom I tested out ideas over the years, as well as to my indispensable colleague and fellow Gothic lecturer Zoe Brennan. I am appreciative of those who gave me the opportunity of disseminating my research at conferences and during guest lectures. They include Bradford K. Mudge at the University of Colorado, Denver, Isabella van Elferen at Utrecht University, Tony Alcala at the National Autonomous University of Mexico, Kimberly

Coles at the University of Maryland, Gina Wisker at the University of Brighton, Catherine Wynne at the University of Hull, Sue Zlosnik at Manchester Metropolitan University, Ilse Bussing at the University of Costa Rica, Agnieszka Lowczanin and Dorota Wisniewska at the University of Lodz in Poland and William Greenslade, who runs the Long Nineteenth-Century Network at UWE, Joanne Parsons and Sarah Chaney, the co-organisers of the Damaging the Body seminar series in the United Kingdom and the Gender Studies Research Group conference at UWE, co-organised by Julie Kent, Helen Malson, Estella Tincknell and Margaret Page. In addition, there were those organisers of the International Gothic Association conferences who enabled me to give papers on areas relevant to the book: Fred Botting, Steven Bruhm, Justin Edwards and Catherine Spooner. I benefited from discussions with Elisabeth Bronfen, Carol Margaret Davison, Josie Dolan, Lesley Hall, Rehan Hyder, Karen Macfarlane, Paulina Palmer, Victor Sage and Dale Townshend, to name but a few.

I would like to thank Linda Friday for generously allowing me to make use of her research on *Dracula* and place and Nora Crook for her help with my Mary Shelley enquiries. Norbert Besch and Franz Potter very kindly helped with primary sources, Roger Evans with images and Glennis Byron and Dale Townshend for giving me the opportunity to blog on the Gothic Imagination website, run from the University of Stirling. I would also like to acknowledge the encouragement and inspiration of R. V. Bailey, Gillian Ballinger, Ross Belson, Kathryn Hardy Bernal (my companion in costume), Randall Bytwerk, Susan Chaplin, Carol Margaret Davison (whose first monograph has been an important source of inspiration), Sven De Hondt, Govinda Dickman, Brenda Duddington, Janet Evans, Sister Ruth Evans, Ann Finding, Peter Fleming, Paul Gough, John Granger, Jerrold E. Hogle, William Hughes, Tony Husband, Dan Jones, Frank Krause, LeAnne Kline, Anthony Mandal, Elizabeth Miller, Agnieszka Soltysik Monnet, Mowbray Publishing, Julie Peakman, Steve Poole, Anna Powell, David Punter, Peter Rawlings, Xavier Aldana Reyes, Catherine Rosenberg, Maria Santamaria, Andrew Smith, Sue Tate, Ardel Thomas, Sara Wasson, Marcus Wood, David Woolley, Colette Lassalle, my much-needed massage therapist, Christine O'Brien, the barista at Caffè Nero, Union Street, Bristol and finally my parents, Catherine and Emrys. The Catholic education I received at Dee House, the Ursuline Convent School in Chester, helped spark my Gothic interests, though the nuns may not have welcomed this outcome! I thank Matthew Frost at Manchester University

Press for taking the project on in the first place and for being so unfailingly accommodating. The sound advice given to me by readers arranged by MUP, the help of their team and assiduous Out of House editing has been gratefully received. My deepest gratitude goes to Nigel Biggs for inspirational insights, love and support.

Introduction

Where men burn books, they will burn people in the end.[1]
Heinrich Heine, *Almansor* (1821)

This investigation of dangerous bodies sets out to expose real-life horrors lying beneath the fictional terror and horror in Gothic literature and film. The ways in which the Church, the medical profession and the state have targeted dangerous minds and bodies will be investigated in a variety of historical settings that include the monastic community, slave plantation, operating theatre, Jewish ghetto and battlefield trench. The resulting body horror has been portrayed in Gothic fiction, which, as Dale Townshend observes, 'persists in representing a range of bloody rituals, gruesome tortures, ghastly punishments, and spectacular immolations'.[2] In this book, literary representations of the persecuted and the persecutor will be historicised through the Gothic body in the corporeal and corporate senses to encompass both monster and victim alongside the ogre of institutional oppression.

Our experience of the world is through the transitory experience of embodiment, which has been expressed in the more durable form of the written word. Text and flesh entwine within the semantic derivation of 'corpus', 'corporeality' and 'corpse'. The proximity of the body to writing also occurs in religious belief, which for Christians manifests through the corporeality of the Logos and for observant Jews in the phylacteries worn on the forehead during specified prayer time, containing scrolls of parchment inscribed with verses from the Torah. Jews are instructed to

1

bind the word of God onto their bodies, a correlation between body and book that has had sinister connotations. When Jewish sacred texts were destroyed in Nazi book burnings, as Heine's words so tragically remind us, Jewish bodies lingered not far behind.[3] Over the centuries, dangerous books have been imbricated on dangerous bodies. There are few more graphic demonstrations than those of Christian heretics burnt at the stake with texts strapped to their bodies. When victims and their writings are set alight, homicide is then compounded by bibliocide, so that 'In death, author and book became one.'[4]

As a body of writing, the Gothic has its own inherent dangers. Not only does it unlock taboos and collapse boundaries, but it can also generate and perpetuate negative stereotypes by stigmatising the inassimilable Other as dangerous body. The dread of difference is articulated through such bodies, particularly when seen as carriers of dangerous desires, inculcators for destabilising ideas or containers of counter-hegemonic ideologies, normally related to race, class, religion, gender or sexuality. Slavoj Žižek, in arguing that the Other is illusory and deriving its power (or lack of it) from the subject, claims that this very illusion actually 'structures our (social) reality itself'.[5] Which bodies are construed as dangerous and who should be deemed Other is subject to varying perspectives. David Punter's observation that 'Gothic is always that which is other than itself' does not preclude seeing otherness as an anxiety, not of difference, but of similarity.[6] Deconstructing categories between self and Other, as radical as that of victim and persecutor, is a profoundly subversive Gothic act whether brought about by author, film-maker, critical reader or viewer. Even when drawing on real-life horror, the non-realistic mode of the Gothic allows us to deflect or distance uncomfortable realities into a fictionalised imaginary 'safe' space and often at the cost of historical accuracy.

The opening chapter interrogates the Inquisition, the persistent monstrosity of which within Gothic fiction is invariably anachronistic. Indeed, the Inquisition has functioned less as an expression of the Gothic novel's supposedly anti-Catholic stance than as an imaginative construct set on foreign soil, which draws attention to issues nearer home. While the Gothic has provided writers with a vehicle for displacement, catharsis and reform, it can just as easily be harnessed by the forces of repression. Chapter 4, for instance, raises the disturbing question of whether the Nazis plundered Gothic Expressionist films for propaganda purposes to advance the horrors of the Holocaust. Martin Tropp argues that the modern tale of terror from Jane Austen onwards has run parallel with modern life to 'show us how literature and life create each other', for 'Horror stories, when they work, construct a fictional edifice of fear and deconstruct it simultaneously, dissipating terror in the act of creating it.'[7] He maintains that readers moulded by their expectations of popular fiction read real-life horror in a similar way, so that 'when the fears given form through fiction came up against the real horrors of day to day experience', as in, for example, the horrors of the First World War (discussed in Chapter 5), 'imaginative fiction helped shape the response'.[8] As Pierre Bourdieu argues: 'Reality, like freedom and identity, is retrospective' and 'all realities come from reflections on representations' that rest upon 'a consensus of subjectivities'.[9]

The making of the Gothic world, as for any repressive institution or state, depends upon the consensual formation of a monstrous alterity, whether it be vampire, ghost, demonic stigmatic or man-made monster. The existence of otherness in the world is most apparent through its corporeality. Monstrosity is invariably a perception relating to bodily confusion and the blurring of boundaries out of which liminality manifests as an object of fear. The monster refuses to be contained within the familiar taxonomies through which we organise the world. The shock effects of Gothic fiction can be the ricochet effects from a collision with epistemic comfort zones. Even though Gothic praxis achieves much of its sense of menace and drama from exposing anxieties arising from collapsing categories, it operates, nevertheless, within a universe of binary opposition. Without the polarisation of good and evil, darkness and light, self and Other, it is questionable whether the Gothic could continue to maintain itself for long. Furthermore, the Gothic can induce potential harm when received uncritically for, as Ruth Bienstock Anolik has indicated: 'The danger of the unresisted Gothic, then, is that it provides a cultural frame of reference to naturalize the demonization process [...] to encode what is unknowable, fearful and evil as the Other.'[10] Crucially, she adds, the recognition of Gothic as a non-realist genre can be an effective deterrent against allowing its demonised representations from escaping into history. But how hermetic is the Gothic container? Is there not a degree of leakage through which negative stereotypes and damaging images become superimposed onto a reality not seeking any kind of critical distancing? Indeed, Judith Halberstam argues in *Skin Shows: Gothic Horror and the Technology of Monsters* (1995) that it is the very idea of the monster that sustains social, economic and sexual hierarchies. The Gothic monster has been a rallying point for cultural, nationalist or religious hegemonies, seldom aware of how they too participate in the creation of monstrosity. Invariably the process of monsterising is born out of an abuse of power on a spectrum ranging from dictatorship to those who collude, albeit passively, with a repressive dominant ideology. As Michel Foucault indicates, Gothic narratives 'are always about the abuse of power and exactions; they are fables about unjust sovereigns, pitiless and bloodthirsty seigneurs, arrogant priests, and so on'.[11] He points out that where power resides, there will be resistance to it, though 'never in a position of exteriority in relation to power [...]. These points of resistance are present everywhere in the power network'.[12] The popularly perceived vertically hierarchical axis, along which power resides, often stacked top down, turns out to be an altogether more lateral beast. When traditional distinctions of up and down, inside and out are blurred, it is not always possible to distinguish self from monstrous Other. The identification between Victor Frankenstein and his monstrous creation is an obvious example.

Dangerous bodies come in many packages, from repressive corporate bodies, to the abject, sacrificial, blasphemous, suffering, wounded or rebellious body, capable of resistance, passivity, subjugation and subversion. The body has been subjected throughout history to barbarity, torture and destruction. Gothic novelists demonstrate again and again their capacity for breathing life into a body only to destroy it and sometimes quite savagely. All bodies, whether fictional or otherwise, are bearers of a politicised message. As the fleshed-out ghost of history, the body comes heavily laden. Theorised as ideally male by Sigmund Freud and Jacques Lacan, it is regarded by Foucault as a product of discourse and social construct which, as Elizabeth Grosz also argues, extends to the biological and supposedly natural.[13] Andrew Smith in *Victorian Demons: Medicine, Masculinity and the Gothic at the Fin-de-Siècle* (2004) questions ingrained assumptions about gender and the body, pointing out that during the *fin de siècle* it was not just aberrant femininity that was associated with pathologies, but heteronormative masculinities. Furthermore, he notes that the professionals dealing with deviant bodies were finding that the abnormal and the normal were becoming conflated. In the case of Jack the Ripper's Whitechapel murder victims, it was how 'a medical gaze seemingly encountered itself in the guise of a murderous autopsy'.[14] For Frederick Treves, the physician of the Elephant Man, John Merrick, there was the fear that medicine and its practitioners had become implicated in the production of pathology rather than serving as guardians of health.

The collection of dangerous bodies in this book will be traced to the effects of the English Reformation, Spanish Inquisition, the French Revolution, Caribbean slavery, Victorian medical malpractice, European anti-Semitism and warfare from the Crimean up to the Vietnam War. These forces of institutional terror have served as incubators for historical monstrosities, which will be mapped onto a number of literary and film texts. Chapters are organised around Horace Walpole's *The Castle of Otranto* (1764), Matthew Lewis' *The Monk* (1796), Mary Shelley's *Frankenstein* (1818), Bram Stoker's *Dracula* (1897) and F. W. Murnau's *Nosferatu* (1922). These texts, along with many others, will be explored in terms of how they mirror real human suffering brought about by the systematic violation of rights to freedom and humanity. In addition, some uncomfortable questions will be raised about the authors. For example, it will be discussed whether Mary Shelley used *Frankenstein* to explore the controversies around slavery, and how she may not have disapproved of the way it was used to oppose the immediate abolition of slavery. The possibility will be raised that Bram Stoker was aware of his brother performing clitoridectomy as a cure for both masturbation and lunacy and that this procedure was sublimated, along with other castrating operations, in *Dracula*. Was *Nosferatu* viewed in Weimar Germany as an anti-Semitic film and did it influence Nazi propaganda film-making thus paving the way for the Holocaust? Such iconoclastic approaches are part of a process for dislodging deeper disruptions quietly coiled beneath the very taboos that Gothic scholars so readily dismantle. It is surely the stuff of unease to consider how well-loved writers might be reinforcing negative stereotypes relating to the body, in regard to race and gender, that run counter to the liberal and humanitarian sympathies of modern audiences. Such a heretical approach could lead to seeing Murnau tolerating anti-Semitic perspectives or Mary Shelley holding some questionable attitudes towards race which were not uncommon at that time. By not countenancing such unpalatable thoughts, is there not a danger of imposing critical limits on our reception of Gothic texts and their authors? For the enlightened reader or viewer interrogating the threshold of representation and reality, an interpretation of 'ambivalence' might provide the necessary balm against venturing too far in the direction of a negative or politically incorrect reading of a classic text or film. Such considerations, particularly in the context of the relationship between body and book, invite us to consider Punter's conundrum: 'Is the Gothic [...] pestifugous, or is it a pestiduct? Does it spread contamination, or might it provide a channel for the expulsion of contaminating materials?'[15]

Dangerous Bodies will demonstrate how the Gothic corpus is haunted by a tangible sense of corporeality, often at its most visceral. Chapters set out to vocalise specific body parts such as skin, genitals, the nose and eyes, as well as blood, though hardly graphically enough for surgeon and writer Richard Selzer, who, in ruminating on the relationship between the body and writing, writes:

> Perhaps if one were to cut out a heart, a lobe of the liver, a single convolution of the brain, and paste it to a page, it would speak with more eloquence than all the words of Balzac. Such a piece would need no literary style, no mass of erudition or history, but in its very shape and feel would tell all the frailty and strength, the despair and nobility of man. What? Publish a heart? A little piece of bone? Preposterous. Still I fear that is what it may require to reveal the truth that lies hidden in the body.[16]

For the conveyance of bodily truths, the Gothic writer has resorted to more pragmatic means. In the hypertext, *Patchwork Girl* (1995), an adaptation of Mary Shelley's novel and James Whale's film, *Bride of Frankenstein* (1935), Shelley Jackson uses digital technology for enabling her heroine to enter her own body, and wander around her internal organs, as if in a garden of forbidden exotic fruits. Clive Barker literalises writing and reading the body for his *Books of Blood* (1984–5). In the first story, ghosts carve stories onto living flesh like 'grimoires that had been made of dead human skin'.[17] As Xavier Aldana Reyes explains, 'The gothic is experienced in the flesh, in its surfaces and crevices, and thus reveals its inherent and universal inscriptability'.[18] Barker's story is metaphorical of the tales told by the dead through Gothic writing. In *Harry Potter and the Chamber of Secrets* (1998) J. K. Rowling's hero discovers an undead book of surrogate flesh. While attempting to kill antagonist Voldemort, Harry Potter stabs his diary, which turns out to be the Dark Lord's displaced body, causing it to scream and the pages to bleed ink. In the light of Voldemort's candidacy for the anti-Christ, this neatly parodies the biblical Word made flesh, as well as trumping the body horror of that rather niche craft, bookbinding with human skin.[19] Writing the body is another means of aligning text and flesh, most commonly associated, at least in terms of literary theory, with the school of *l'écriture féminine*. Shelley Jackson has been more literal-minded in uniting the two by writing a living book called *Skin*, tattooed on the bodies of volunteers. For this ongoing project, subtitled *A Mortal Work of Art*, started in 2003, she uses for her paper – human skin. When the participants known as her 'words' die, so too shall the book. Since it remains unfinished, there is the possibility that the last word has not yet been born and that some words will outlive their author.[20] This is yet another variation on the word made flesh hearkening back to Christianity, which is where this book begins.

Chapter 1 revisits the orthodox position that Gothic literature is traditionally anti-Catholic. Horace Walpole, the author of *The Castle of Otranto*, which is widely considered to be the first Gothic novel, was a Member of Parliament, belonging to the Church of England, whose attitudes towards Catholicism were somewhat ambiguous. This is significant for a neglected reading of his novel, relating to the Henrician Reformation, which brought about the secession of England from Rome. The Catholic Church, once it came to be regarded as the Romanish enemy, was perceived as an institutionally dangerous body, associated with the intense and relentless persecution of its enemies, often involving torture and execution. The novel of Inquisition will be put to the question of whether its ostensible opposition to Catholicism masked different agendas nearer home.[21] The bleeding body, as a site of the sacred and profane, opens up a conduit for reassessing the religious attitudes of various Protestant Gothic novelists. In Matthew Lewis' *The Monk*, the character of the Bleeding Nun will be discussed as a parody of the mystical stigmatic within the Catholic tradition. Her bloodline of demonic stigmatics will be traced from Lewis and his imitators up to Bram Stoker's *Dracula*. Chapter 2 investigates the corrupting and corrosive effects of slavery. An association already exists between slavery and the rise of Gothic fiction through the West Indian connections of the major Gothic writers, Horace Walpole, William Beckford and Matthew Lewis.[22] Mary Shelley's new creation myth in *Frankenstein* draws not only on Prometheus and Adam but also, it will be argued, on the topical issue of the enslaved and the reluctance of many abolitionists to support the cause of immediate emancipation. Within this reading of *Frankenstein* as an allegory of slavery, the monster is considered as a demonised version of miscegenation and the fate of his female companion related to fears generated by rebel female slaves. Her resurrection in Whale's *Bride of Frankenstein* demonstrates how surgery can be used for sexual purposes in the creation of a female creature.

Chapter 3 looks at how surgical treatment was used to 'correct' women who had strayed from their traditional gender role. This forms a subtext to Bram Stoker's *Dracula*, a novel reflecting the social and political instability of gender during the *fin de siècle*. Several members of Stoker's family were doctors and surgeons, from whom he acquired clinical and surgical details for the writing of *Dracula*. Cases from the history of sexual surgery parallel readings from the novel, in which the destruction of the female vampire will be viewed as a deconstructed narrative of surgical horror and medical tyranny visited upon the female hysteric, along with other women deemed sexually perverse. As Andrew Smith expresses it, for the female hysteric, doctors were 'Gothic figures, inflicting pain and distress either through neglect or through a misplaced sense of surgical bravado'.[23] In Chapter 4, the vampire theme continues with a discussion of *Dracula*, Jewishness and blood. It will be argued that the early film version of Stoker's novel, *Nosferatu*, encrypts the ostensibly dangerous vampire body as a metaphor for the crypto-Jew. This approach reflects the interpretation of E. Elias Merhige's *Shadow of the Vampire* (2000) on the making of *Nosferatu*, which vampirises the earlier film. Besides looking back to the anti-Semitic imagery of *Nosferatu*, the film projects forward to the Jewish genocide perpetrated by fascist Germany, signified in a scene by a solitary swastika. This is an illustration of Jacques Derrida's hauntology, which paradoxically predicts the spectre, a thing of the past, returning in the future. Both films point to how Nazi anti-Jewish films had the opportunity to vampirically feed off the Gothic cinema of Weimar Germany.[24]

The most threatening collective of dangerous bodies is undoubtedly that generated by war, the supreme Gothic horror. The final chapter will conduct a wide-ranging exploration of the imagery, discourse and symbolism of vampirism in the context of warfare. Even though war is the ultimate blood-sucker, it has rarely been analysed as such. The metaphor is capacious enough to go beyond war in the abstract to accommodate most of the players and action involved. The vampire functions as a floating signifier moving across battlefields, as well as along the home front. This analysis seeks to demonstrate that the rhetoric and imagery of vampirism has a natural kinship with wars, ranging from the Crimean up to the Vietnam War. In 1879, Marie Nizet's *Captain Vampire* used the trope of the vampire to send out an anti-war message. I will argue that her fiction influenced the writing of *Dracula*, which will be read as another war novel, and revisit Jimmie E. Cain's argument that Stoker's narrative is a rewrite of the British defeat in the Crimea. The novel has also been linked to the Berlin Treaty and the Russo-Turkish war, in which Stoker's brother took part. A more recent example of the correlation between vampirism and war is Kim Newman's postmodernist intertextual pastiche, *The Bloody Red Baron* (1996), in which the First World War is reconfigured as a fantastical conflict within which vampires and humans are in combat. Between them, they convey the suffering and horror of war. As Martin Tropp points out, 'by the end of the First World War, history itself had become a tale of terror'.[25]

This story of corporeal repression and resistance builds on the work of scholars like Robert Mighall who treat the Gothic as a politicised art form rooted in history.[26] The subtitle of his book, *A Geography of Victorian Gothic Fiction,* brought out in 1999, is *Mapping History's Nightmares.* Derrida insists that we must listen to the ghosts of injustice, not only from the past but also from the future, 'be they victims of wars, political or other kinds of violence, nationalist, racist, colonialist, sexist, or other kinds of exterminations, victims of the oppressions of capitalist imperialism or any of the forms of totalitarianism'.[27] Due to its troubled relationship to social, political and religious forces, the body has been seen as a threatening bloody bag of unruly ideas. Even more than that, as Gina Wisker puts it: 'the state of rationality and the sense of the human ability to create order is threatened by the messiness of the body'.[28] While body horror represented through literature and film inevitably distances us from this physicality, it can still have the power to put us in touch with our own corporeality. The horror text functions as a rite of defilement that sometimes appears to collude with the forces of oppression and yet, at the same time, can be cathartic and transformative by collapsing the boundary between self and monstrous Other. Monstrosity derives in part from the Latin verb '*monstrare*' ('to show'). Its spectacular derivation points to how the monstrous functions as a looking-glass, permitting us to see our own inner monster and revealing the extent to which monsters are us. The act of reading can also make us complicit with voyeurism as we gaze helplessly at the Gothic excesses binding victim and perpetrator together. Yet this very feeling of helplessness can bring us to a realisation of victimhood. According to Angela Wright: 'In a sense, as readers, we also become victims as well as complicit literary voyeurs'.[29] She supports this point by quoting from Charles Maturin's *Melmoth the Wanderer* (1820): 'The drama of terror has the irresistible power of converting its audience into its victims'.[30] As a playwright of the Gothic, this was something that Maturin was in a position to appreciate. On the other hand, the spectator or reader can experience pleasure from the suffering body as theatre. In his *Romantic Tales* (1808), Matthew Lewis expresses outrage against torture when exposing its ineffectual nature as a method of reaching the truth.[31] Nevertheless, its graphic depiction in the Gothic is described by Dale Townshend as 'an experience akin to what Lacan and Žižek have termed *jouissance*, a pleasurable pain or pain in pleasure, the delightful *frisson* of unbearable suffering'.[32] As Steven Bruhm indicates, in many ways the history of pain can also be a history of looking.[33] For him, the Gothic body, with its 'violent, vulnerable immediacy', is one put on 'excessive display'.[34] He argues that Romantic sentimentalism can foster the illusion that pain can be transported beyond the pages of a book and be shared by 'the sentimental spectator' or reader in a spirit of empathy with a fictional pained body.[35] In his conclusion to *Gothic Bodies: The Politics of Pain in Romantic Fiction* (1994), Bruhm states: 'Pain forcefully returns us to that occluded body' and restores it to a forgotten mastery so that even subjectivity can be blotted out by its own physicality.[36] The publication of his book in 1994 proved to be a key co-ordinate in the mapping of the Gothic body for the late eighteenth and early nineteenth century. Another landmark text is Kelly Hurley's *The Gothic Body: Sexuality, Materialism, and Degeneration at the Fin de Siècle* (1996), which addresses the crisis of human identity around the advent of the twentieth century. This is fictionalised in the Gothic as the disintegration of the human subject, manifesting through the spectacle of the body metamorphosing into an undifferentiated state, marked by fragmentation and permeability. What arises from this ruination is the abhuman, the human unbecoming, which heralds a 'monstrous becoming'.[37] A critical text reading the physical surfaces of the body is Judith Halberstam's study of nineteenth- and twentieth-century Gothic bodies, *Skin Shows*, where she writes: 'Skin houses the body and it is figured in Gothic as the ultimate boundary, the material that divides the inside from the outside'.[38] The title evokes Jonathan Demme's film, *The Silence of the Lambs* (1991), in which a male serial killer becomes obsessed with sewing women's clothes for himself out of the skins of his victims. This resembles how the Gothic body is put together as a patchwork self, stitched together from discursive scraps and fabricated from race, class, gender and sexuality.[39] The deviant body is a monstrous proliferation 'as potentially meaning anything – it may be the outcast, the outlaw, the parasite, the pervert, the embodiment of uncontrollable sexual and violent urges, the foreigner, the misfit', so that, according to Halberstam, 'monstrosity has become a conspiracy of bodies rather than a singular form'.[40]

The production and consumption of monsters is what the Gothic does best, especially in recent years. Xavier Aldana Reyes, in *Body Gothic: Corporeal Transgression in Contemporary Literature and Horror Film* (2014), considers the Gothic's investment in the somatic as well as in the construction of corporeality. He defines Body Gothic as relating to the centrality of the body within Gothic fiction, incorporating a number of subgenres including: splatterpunk, the slaughterhouse novel, torture porn and surgical horror. Setting out to give priority to the body within the Gothic text, Reyes places it at the centre of the Gothic experience. He argues that the value and complexity of corporeal writing within the horror or Gothic tradition has often been underrated. At a time when notions of the body are under threat from decorporealisation in this digital and post-human age, Reyes has produced a counter-narrative stressing the importance of the corporeal and visceral, which acts as a bulwark against the possibility of Gothic becoming subsumed by the phantasmagorical or spectral. *Dangerous Bodies* builds on these scholarly works with readings from literary and film texts, demonstrating the violent collision between the corporeal and the corporate from the eighteenth to the twentieth century. This will reveal how the demonisation of the Other, as reflected in Gothic literature, may be traced to institutional persecution and acts of war. In historicising the Gothic body, this analysis points to the real-life narratives of fear, danger and persecution, which underpin the fictional terror and horror of the Gothic.

NOTES

1 Quoted in Haig Bosmajian, *Burning Books* (Jefferson, NC: McFarland, 2006), p. 3.
2 Dale Townshend, *The Orders of the Gothic: Foucault, Lacan, and the Subject of Gothic Writing 1764–1820* (New York: AMS Press, 2007), p. 265.
3 The epigraph appears in German at the Opernplatz in Berlin where Heine's books were burnt by the Nazis in 1933. It is taken from a play about the burning of the Quran by the Spanish Inquisition.
4 Bosmajian, *Burning Books*, p. 23.
5 Quoted in L. Andrew Cooper, *Gothic Realities: The Impact of Horror Fiction on Modern Culture* (Jefferson, NC: McFarland, 2010), p. 20.
6 David Punter, *Gothic Pathologies: The Text, the Body and the Law* (Basingstoke: Macmillan, 1998), pp. 1 and 219.

7   Martin Tropp, *Images of Fear: How Horror Stories Helped Shape Modern Culture, 1818–1918* (Jefferson, NC: McFarland, 1990), pp. 9 and 5.

8   Tropp, *Images of Fear*, pp. 5–6.

9   Quoted in Cooper, *Gothic Realities*, p. 19.

10 Ruth Bienstock Anolik, 'The infamous Svengali: George du Maurier's Satanic Jew', in Ruth Bienstock Anolik and Douglas L. Howard (eds), *The Gothic Other: Racial and Social Constructions in the Literary Imagination* (Jefferson, NC: McFarland, 2004), p. 186.

11 Michel Foucault, *Society Must Be Defended: Lectures at the Collège de France 1975–76*, ed. Mauro Bertani and Alessandro Fontana, trans. David Macey (London: Penguin [1997], 2004), p. 212.

12 Michel Foucault, *The History of Sexuality, Vol. 1: An Introduction*, trans. Robert Hurley (Harmondsworth: Penguin [1976], 1990), p. 95.

13 See Elizabeth Grosz, *Volatile Bodies: Towards a Corporeal Feminism* (Bloomington, IN: Indiana University Press, 1994).

14 Andrew Smith, *Victorian Demons: Medicine, Masculinity and the Gothic at the Fin-de-Siècle* (Manchester: Manchester University Press, 2004), p. 178.

15 David Punter, 'Introduction', in David Punter (ed.), *A Companion to the Gothic* (Oxford: Blackwell, 2000), p. xii.

16 Richard Selzer, *Confessions of a Knife: Meditations on the Art of Surgery* (London: Triad/Granada, 1982), p. 9.

17 Quoted by Xavier Aldana Reyes, *Body Gothic: Corporeal Transgression in Contemporary Literature and Horror Film* (Cardiff: University of Wales Press, 2014), p. 50.

18 Reyes, *Body Gothic*, p. 50.

19 See Steven Connor, *The Book of Skin* (London: Reaktion, 2004), pp. 42–7.

20 See Marie Mulvey-Roberts, 'The After-lives of the Bride of Frankenstein: Mary Shelley and Shelley Jackson', in Maria Purves (ed.), *Women and Gothic* (Newcastle-upon-Tyne: Cambridge Scholars Publishing, 2014), pp. 87–8.

21 This Gothic subgenre refers to novels dealing with the Inquisition.

22 See Candace Ward, '"Duppy Know Who Fi Frighten": Laying Ghosts in Jamaican Fiction', in Monika Elbert and Bridget M. Marshall (eds), *Transnational Gothic: Literary and Social Exchanges in the Long Nineteenth Century* (Farnham: Ashgate, 2013), p. 218.

23 Smith, *Victorian Demons*, p. 8.

24 Steen Christiansen is bringing out a book on hauntology in which he will be discussing Merhige's *Shadow of the Vampire*.

25 Tropp, *Images of Fear*, p. 6.

26 See Robert Mighall, *A Geography of Victorian Gothic Fiction: Mapping History's Nightmares* (Oxford: Oxford University Press, 1999).

27 Jacques Derrida, *Specters of Marx: The State of the Debt, the Work of Mourning and the New International*, ed. Bernd Magnus and Stephen Cullenberg, trans. Peggy Kamuf (New York: Routledge, 1994), p. xviii.

28 Gina Wisker, *Horror: An Introduction* (New York: Continuum, 2005), p. 178.

29 Angela Wright, *Gothic Fiction: A Reader's Guide to Essential Criticism* (Basingstoke: Palgrave Macmillan, 2007), p. 110.

30 Wright, *Gothic Fiction*, p. 110.

31 See Steven Bruhm, *Gothic Bodies: The Politics of Pain in Romantic Fiction* (Philadelphia, PA: University of Pennsylvania Press, 1994), p. 95.

32 Townshend, *The Orders of the Gothic*, p. 267.

33 See Bruhm, *Gothic Bodies*, p. xx.

34 Bruhm, *Gothic Bodies*, p. xvii.

35 Bruhm, *Gothic Bodies*, p. 115.

36 Bruhm, *Gothic Bodies*, p. 150.

37 Kelly Hurley, *The Gothic Body: Sexuality, Materialism, and Degeneration at the Fin de Siècle* (Cambridge: Cambridge University Press, 1996), p. 4.

38 Judith Halberstam, *Skin Shows: Gothic Horror and the Technology of Monsters* (Durham, NC: Duke University Press, 1995), p. 7.

39 See Halberstam, *Skin Shows*, p. 3, and Catherine Spooner, *Fashioning Gothic Bodies* (Manchester: Manchester University Press, 2004), p. 11.

40 Halberstam, *Skin Shows*, p. 27.

Catholicism, the Gothic and the bleeding body

The visions that proliferated in Europe during the thirteenth to fifteenth centuries became increasingly bloody [...]. Such intense visualizations of blood were also enacted in rituals and in bodies. Christ figures used in the liturgy to perform the events of Passion Week were sometimes outfitted with bladders of animal blood that could be punctured at appropriate moments to display Jesus' bleeding before the faithful; cruets for eucharistic wine survive in the form of Christ images with spouts where the wounds occurred. From the thirteenth-century on, bands of flagellants roamed Europe, tearing out of their own flesh the suffering and joy of union with Christ.[1]

Caroline Walker Bynum, *Wonderful Blood* (2007)

The wounded body is a leitmotif of the Gothic novel and central icon of the Roman Catholic Church, which has perpetuated images of crucifixion, martyred saints, bleeding statues and mystic stigmatics. Sacred art depicts an iconography of suffering, as in devotions to the Sacred Heart of Jesus in which Christ holds his fiery wounded heart wrapped in thorns, dripping blood and surmounted by a cross. His bleeding body has been emulated by penitential flagellants, stigmatics and martyrs. This *imitatio Christi* has a certain affinity with the Gothic. The Church has readily supplied Gothic novelists with cowled monks, lustful priests, immured nuns, confessionals and secret tribunals, while the Gothic settings of cathedrals, cloisters, convents and crypts evoke the medievalism of an earlier world view replete with superstition, feudalism and antiquity. This chapter will look at how Gothic literature has drawn not only on the repressions of the Inquisition, but also on anti-Catholic movements from the English Reformation to the French Revolution, with particular reference to Horace Walpole's *The Castle of Otranto* and Matthew Lewis' *The Monk*. Attention will be given to a neglected reading of Walpole's novel as a satire of Henry VIII, while Lewis' Bleeding Nun, who is resurrected in later works, will be seen to represent aspects of the Reign of Terror in revolutionary France.

Many critics regard the Gothic novel as traditionally anti-Catholic and even indicative of a deep-seated prejudice against the Vatican. The first critic to make this really explicit was J. M. S. Tompkins, who insisted: 'the prejudice against Catholicism, or, more particularly, against priests and monks, the "anti-Roman bray" ... is heard at its loudest in both the English and the German novels of terror'.[2] Voices dissenting from this creed include Montague Summers, who insisted that 'it is folly to trace any "anti-Roman feeling" in the Gothic novel'.[3] Mary Muriel Tarr has argued that the most important function of the Catholic materials she surveyed in 121 Gothic works was to serve as a source for the sublime.[4] Maria Purves, however, goes further by maintaining that the majority of Gothic novels, despite having been written and read by Protestants, are not actually anti-Catholic. She also points out that society during the eighteenth century was more sympathetic to Catholics than previously supposed, even though Catholic Emancipation did not come into force in Britain and Ireland until 1829. The eighteenth-century picture is complicated by the forces of anti-Catholicism that helped unify Protestants in the face of Dissent, as well as Catholics and Protestant Dissenters being 'uncomfortably allied' against the Anglican establishment.[5] By the 1790s, the Jacobin threat had supplanted anxieties targeted at the Catholic as 'the hated other'.[6] Within the Gothic novel, even overtly negative literary representations of Catholicism invariably prove to be less of an attack on the Catholic Church than a means of opening up subversive ways for critiquing secular hegemony and repressive governments.

There is no better expression of Catholic horror than the Inquisition. With its torture dungeons and black-habited Dominicans, the Inquisition was a thing of darkness waiting for the instruments of Gothic terror. Notorious as an organ of persecution in Catholic countries, the Holy Office is a familiar trope in early Gothic fiction, providing novelists with a hooded opportunity to portray the alien Other nearer home. The Inquisition's reputation for inflicting pain on its victims virtually institutionalised the Christ-like torment lying at the heart of the religion. The ingenuity with which many Catholics appear to relish suffering has been a mystery to their Protestant counterparts. The Passion of the crucified Christ and shedding of his sacred blood gave rise to a number of Catholic devotions. But it is how this veneration was inscribed on the bodies of devotees in the form of bleeding wounds that demonstrated for detractors the extent of the perversity and fanaticism of devotees. The holy stigmatic, through which the wounds of Christ manifest physically, mainly on the bodies of pious women from the Renaissance onwards, was a phenomenon that, it will be argued, has been Gothicised by novelists from Lewis' Bleeding Nun in *The Monk* to Bram Stoker's vampires. These demonic stigmatics are a sublimation of the horror and awe surrounding the crucifixion through which the bleeding body appears at its most sublime.

THE GOTHIC NOVEL'S CATHOLIC LEGACY

Catholicism is a living reminder of a medieval past. The verticality of the Gothic cathedrals rising up throughout Europe from the Middle Ages to the sixteenth century inspires awe and sublimity. Their pointed arches, ribbed vaults, flying buttresses and stone gargoyles furnished Gothic novelists with suitably atmospheric settings. These churches memorialise a pre-Reformation Britain, pre-dating Henry VIII's Act of Supremacy (1534), through which he established himself Head of the Church of England, but it was at an incalculable human cost. Monastic orders were left destitute. Rebellions against Henry's destruction of the Roman Catholic Church in Britain were ruthlessly suppressed. These included the execution of around 200 Catholics for treason following the Pilgrimage of Grace, a popular uprising in the north of England in 1536. Those resisting Henry's religious reforms were subjected to torture, beheading, hanging and burning, while some monks were hanged, drawn and quartered and executed by enforced starvation. In Raphael Holinshed's Chronicles (1577–87), estimates of the deaths run into the thousands. Even though the accuracy of the chroniclers was notoriously unreliable, such statistics served as a form of propaganda for anti-Catholic persecution, which lingered across the centuries. The horrors of this bloody episode in British history and the shock waves from the break with Rome vibrate through *The Castle of Otranto*, whose author, Horace Walpole, regarded Henry as a bloody persecutor.[7] Yet the novel's chief legacy has been in providing future authors with an urtext for the Gothic novel. Walpole was also a pioneer in the eighteenth-century architectural Gothic revival. His aspiration for Strawberry Hill, his Gothic home, was for it 'to have all the air of a Catholic chapel – bar consecration!'[8] As he explained, 'my house is so monastic that I have a little hall decked with long saints in lean arched windows.'[9] With its chapel proclaiming 'all the glory of popery',[10] Walpole's house was a veritable shrine to Catholicism, which he referred to as 'My gothic Vatican'.[11]

Walpole's admission that *The Castle of Otranto* was inspired by Strawberry Hill is not imparted to readers of his first preface.[12] He states falsely on the title page that it was written in Italian by Onuphrio Muralto, a Roman Catholic Canon, and translated by 'William Marshal, Gent.' The deception continued when he explained that it was printed in Naples and probably first written between 1095 and 1243. In his first preface, the accredited father of the Gothic novel has aligned himself with a fictitious Church father and adopted the false persona of editor. When the story 'first' appeared, as Walpole explains:

> Letters were then in their most flourishing state in Italy, and contributed to dis-pel the empire of superstition, at that time so forcibly attacked by the reform-ers. It is not unlikely, that an artful priest might endeavour to turn their own arms on the innovators; and might avail himself of his abilities as an author to confirm the populace in their ancient errors and superstitions. If this was his view, he has certainly acted with signal address. Such a work as the following would enslave a hundred vulgar minds, beyond half the books of controversy that had been written from the days of Luther to the present hour.[13]

The 'empire of superstition' under attack from the Protestant Reformation was the Roman Catholic Church. Walpole warns of how a wily Italian priest could succeed in undoing the effects of Martin Luther's reforms and turn his readers back into Catholics. Here a fake document of the Counter-Reformation is conflated with what would become a template for the Gothic novel. Walpole's criticism of the Church as a pedlar of 'ancient errors and superstitions' is ironic as he, himself, imparts, like an 'artful priest', such wares to his readers, with the mendacious assertion that 'I cannot but believe, that the ground work of the story is founded on truth' (p. 61). Like the writer of fiction for whom fabrication is an occupational asset, Catholicism, which prided itself on being the one true Church, was tainted by the misuse of casuistry.[14] In his second preface, Walpole con-fesses the deception to his readers.[15] According to Robert Miles, Walpole's 'imposture was meant to be transparent: as a pro-Catholic text *Otranto* is clearly self-subverting' and 'is not about, is not a defence of, or an attack on, Catholicism. It is really about legitimacy, or rather the lack of it.'[16]

While the question of legitimacy is central to the novel's main plot, it also informs a religio-political subtext relating to the Reformation. Luther's action in posting his 95 theses against Rome on a church door in Wittenberg was an affront to Catholic apostolic succession. In turn, he accused Rome of being the usurper of temporal rights. Walpole's novel revolves around the genealogy of an ancient Neapolitan line, which has been usurped by Manfred, who is now Prince of Otranto. Miles sees the plot and prefaces as a 'verbal fugue' on legitimacy.[17] This he believes to be intricately connected to the figure of the Catholic and the Glorious Revolution, which saw the peaceful overthrow of the last English Roman Catholic monarch, James II. The unsettling effects of the Act of Settlement of 1701, ensuring a Protestant succession to the throne, ripple through the inheritance-related plots of early Gothic novels. Walpole's condemnation of Manfred's usurpation and celebration of his overthrow at the end of the novel is read by Markham Ellis as tacit acceptance for the usurpation of Catholic James by Protestant William of Orange.[18] According to this royalist allegory, William of Orange, despite being a usurper himself, approximates to Theodore, Otranto's rightful heir. This apparent contradiction makes greater sense in terms of Whig ideology. The Glorious Revolution is described by Miles as 'the founding moment of contemporary Whiggism'.[19] The Whigs supported the Protestant Hanoverian succession, as opposed to the Catholic Stuart kings and pretenders, who were usurped by the Hanoverians. Walpole had in his possession a copy of the execution warrant, a souvenir relating to the deposing of the Stuart King Charles I.

Miles sees Walpole, a Member of Parliament and son of the first British Prime Minister, as being publicly unconcerned by accusations that his Whig father, Robert, had usurped the ancient Saxon Constitution, though he notes that this might not have been the case in private.[20] The constitution was figured as a Gothic edifice,[21] a metaphor not dissimilar to William Blackstone's famous comparison of English law to a 'Gothic castle'.[22] For Robert Walpole, the Glorious Revolution succeeded in banishing the Gothic darkness of absolutism and feudal subjugation. Rather subversively, Walpole used his considerable inheritance after his father's death to reinscribe the Gothic Catholic legacy erased by Anglicanism within both the interiors of Strawberry Hill and the pages of his novel. The ancient Gothic constitution, according to Maggie Kilgour, was 'a manifestation of a recurrent British argument that a better future is to be found by recovering the past'.[23] Unlike his father, it appears that Walpole saw the Gothic legacy as the continuation of a tradition of freedom pre-dating the Norman Conquest of 1066. Britain had restored some of these lost liberties through the Magna Carta (1215), a major stepping stone towards constitutional monarchy, established centuries later by the Glorious Revolution. Horace Walpole attached so much importance to the Magna Carta, also known as 'The Great Charter for the Liberties of England', that he hung a copy next to his bed. His father, on the other hand, due to the 'bribery and corruption' that he ran on 'an industrial scale',[24] was accused of nullifying the benefits of the 'sacred Covenant' when he 'rumpled it rudely up, and crammed it into his Pocket'.[25] Miles claims that Walpole used 'the qualities of political illegitimacy hurled at his father' for the character of Manfred who 'is, indeed, the usurper of an ancient Gothic house', and suggests that the Gothic genre was fed by the buried anxiety that the post-Glorious Revolution period was without legitimacy:[26]

> Horace Walpole was more than just the son of an influential Whig politician; he was also a zealous advocate of Whig ideology. For the enemies of the powerful Whig aristocrats, modern Britain was the product of serial illegitimacies: the Tudors ousting the Plantagenets; Henry VIII's divorces, from the true church as well as from his wives; and the usurpation of the Stuarts by the House of Hanover, the last battle of which had only recently been fought (1746). For ultra-Tories, 1688 was not a glorious revolution, but a thieves' charter. If Whigs could not appeal to divine right, what could they base their power on? Certainly not the people, who were mostly disenfranchised. The answer was to make a fetish of the Gothic constitution that glossed these multiple usurpations as evolutionary progress.[27]

The first of these 'serial illegitimacies' was carried out by Henry Tudor, who became Henry VII. Like Manfred, he too was a usurper. Both king and prince were determined to secure their dynasty and for that the heir was all-important, as the future standard-bearer of the family name. Walpole employs naming playfully and as a pointer to historical analogies. Conrad, Manfred's only son, shares his name, rather ironically, with that of an actual historical figure, who was a rightful heir and whose successor, Conradin, is denied his inheritance by another Manfred, the illegitimate ruler of Taranto, who was crowned king under false pretences. Walpole's *Gothic Story* (the subtitle of the second edition) concludes in accordance with the fictional convention of restoring the rightful heir. The usurper is punished by supernatural means, which is indicative of the kind of retribution exacted by the Divine Right of Kings, a belief upheld by the Stuart kings as opposed to the Hanoverians. Manfred is the grandson of a servant, Ricardo, who was chamberlain to Prince Alfonso the Good. In order to gain possession of his house and inherit the principality, Ricardo poisons his master and forges his will. As Jerrold E. Hogle points out in his discussion of the 'ghost of the counterfeit',[28] this fakery extends to the fraudulent first preface and the array of artifices, often involving the spectral, that litter the novel. As Walpole famously observed in connection with the poet forger, Thomas Chatterton: 'All of the houses of forgery are relations.'[29] The forfeit for Ricardo's forgery is a prophecy that should his family line run out of heirs then the inheritance reverts back to that of Alfonso. Working towards this is an ancestral curse afflicting the usurper's bloodline and causing Manfred's only son to die shortly before his marriage to Isabella. He is killed by a giant black-plumed helmet falling from the sky. Manfred's response to the disrupted wedding is to declare his intention of marrying Isabella, his son's former bride. His actions parallel a significant episode in Tudor history.

Following the death of Henry VII's first son Arthur, the king declared that his surviving son Henry should marry his dead brother's widow, Catherine of Aragon. Nearly twenty years later, Henry challenged the legitimacy of their union. Henry VII's match-making had inadvertently laid the groundwork for the severing of the Catholic Church in England from Rome. For Catholics, this could well have been one of *the sins of fathers* (p. 61), a phrase appearing in Walpole's first preface, echoing Exodus 20.5. Ironically, the true heir of Otranto turns out to be the son of a priest. This must have resonated with Walpole as the descendant of a Jesuit priest, Father Henry Walpole, who was tortured and executed in 1595 during the reign of Elizabeth I, a queen who had inherited her father's mantle as Head of the Church of England. Henry Walpole was drawn to the priesthood after witnessing the judicial murder and mutilation of the Jesuit priest Edmund Campion, who had advocated a return to ecclesiastical rule from Rome. When the blood from Campion's mutilated corpse spurted onto Henry's clothes, he took this as a sign to follow in the proselytising footsteps of the Catholic martyr.

Notwithstanding that his ancestor had witnessed religious persecution against a Catholic, Walpole regarded papists as an enemy to freedom, yet this did not detract from his deep appreciation of Gothic Catholic architecture. Clearly his antipathy towards Catholicism was more political than aesthetic. As Walpole revealed in a letter to William Cole, writing *The Castle of Otranto* had given him respite from politics, though critics have not necessarily agreed.[30] E. J. Clery sees Walpole as trying to exorcise his political demons in the novel, while Nick Groom traces the abuse of a sovereign power to Walpole's view that George III had over-used his Royal Prerogative.[31] A few years after its publication, Walpole wrote to Madame du Deffand on 13 March 1767: 'Let the critics have their say: I shall not be vexed: it was not written for this age.'[32] But well over a decade later, he declared in a letter to Hannah More on 13 November 1784: 'It was fit for nothing but the age in which it was written.'[33] Notwithstanding these contradictory statements, it would seem that the novel ranges from the medievalism of its setting through a sixteenth-century subtext up to the Walpolean period. Even though some critics are not convinced that the novel gave Walpole respite from politics, he seems to have relished engaging with the political and religious machinations of the Tudor period, as indicated in a letter written to his friend, the clergyman William Cole: 'I hope the satire on Henry VIII will make you excuse the compliment to Luther, which like most poetic compliments does not come from my heart – I only like him better than Henry, Calvin, and the Church of Rome, who were bloody persecutors.'[34]

The neglect of this interpretation of *The Castle of Otranto*, as a satire of the English Reformation, has obscured the extent to which this prototype for the Gothic novel was an aesthetic recreation of Catholicism rooted in the transition from a papal to a Protestant world view.[35] From the very start, a religio-political subtext, relating directly to the Henrician revolution, is signalled in Walpole's first preface, which is usually dismissed as little more than a hoax. It is here where Walpole notes that the work, printed in black letter or Gothic typeface, was originally published in 1529. This was the year in which Henry VIII summoned Parliament to deal with the annulment of his marriage to the Spanish Queen Catherine of Aragon. Known as the Reformation Parliament, it precipitated the separation of the Church of England from papal authority, triggering the English Reformation. An important clue in the first preface is Walpole's mention of the 'Arragonian [*sic*] kings in Naples' (p. 59), the very same dynasty to which Henry's Spanish wife belonged. One of her ancestors, Alfonso V of Aragon, was also king of Naples, where supposedly the story was originally published. Known as Alfonso the Magnanimous, he was an important figure of the early Renaissance. His portrait painted by Juan de Juanes depicts him wearing armour, with his large helmet and

Figure 1 Juan de Juanes' portrait of Alfonso V of Aragon (1557), also called Alfonso the Magnanimous in armour with his helmet in the foreground of the painting.

Note: The painter was also known as Vicente Juan Masip.

crown displayed in the foreground. Alfonso the Magnanimous provides a model for Walpole's armour-clad Alfonso the Good, whose portrait in the novel functions to help identify the true heir Theodore, whom he resembles (Figure 1).[36] The helmet in Juanes' painting may be the precursor of the gigantic helmet from Alfonso's statue that crushes to death the usurper's heir to the principality of Otranto.

After losing his only son, Manfred is anxious to secure another male heir, having been left with a daughter, Matilda. He laments that his wife,

Hippolita, has 'cursed me by her unfruitfulness: my fate depends on having sons' (p. 80). 1529, when Walpole falsely claimed that *The Castle of Otranto* had been written, was the year marking the start of the schism with the Church of Rome that had been triggered by Henry VIII's desperate need for a male heir. Like Manfred, Henry lost a son and, at that time, his only surviving child was a daughter, Mary.[37] Since his first wife Catherine of Aragon was over forty and unlikely to conceive again, Henry resolved to marry the younger Anne Boleyn and divorce his wife. This determination is reflected in Manfred's proposal to Isabella, when he declares: 'Hippolita is no longer my wife; I divorce her from this hour' (p. 80). His son's former bride shares a forename with Catherine of Aragon's mother, Queen Isabella I of Castile. Through his Papal Legate, Cardinal Wolsey, Henry tried persuading Pope Clement VII to grant an annulment on biblical grounds, contending that his first marriage was unlawful because he had married his brother's widow. The Pope refused. Not only was he unwilling to undo the dispensation made by Pope Julius II, which had allowed the marriage to go ahead, but he was also unwilling to offend Catherine's nephew Charles V, the Holy Roman Emperor, whose troops had sacked Rome the previous year. Even Wolsey's threats that Henry might divorce England from the Vatican would not sway His Holiness.

Similarly, Manfred appeals to Rome demanding a divorce so that he can marry a younger woman, but, as Father Jerome informs him, 'The church despises thy menaces. Her thunders will be heard above thy wrath. Dare to proceed in thy curst purpose of a divorce, until her sentence be known' (p. 147). Earlier, the friar ponders on what Manfred has said in regard to why he wants to divorce his wife, noting, 'if in truth it is delicacy of conscience that is the real motive of your repugnance to your virtuous lady, far be it from me to endeavour to harden your heart!' (p. 106). This echoes the argument regarding Henry's 'certain scruples of conscience',[38] and Manfred claims that he is prey 'to all the hell of conscientious *scruples*' (p. 121, emphasis added), asserting:

> It is some time that I have had scruples on the legality of our union: Hippolita is related to me in the fourth degree [of consanguinity] – It is true, we had a dispensation; but I have been informed that she had also been contracted to another. This it is that sits heavy at my heart: to this state of unlawful wedlock I impute the visitation that has fallen on me in the death of Conrad! (p. 105)

Hippolita's betrothal to someone else parallels Catherine's first marriage to Arthur. Henry blamed the death of his infant son and Catherine's many miscarriages on the fact that she had been married to his elder brother, despite the dispensation granted by the Pope. But this leviratic mishap did not deter him from marrying Catherine Howard, who was the first cousin of Henry's second wife, Anne Boleyn. Classified within the fourth degree of consanguinity, cousins fell into 'the forbidden degrees' (p. 122), the very grounds on which Manfred tried dissolving his marriage to Hippolita so that he could marry his dead son's bride. Father Jerome is compelled to denounce the proposition as an 'incestuous design' (p. 104). Catherine of Aragon tried to distance herself from accusations of incest by insisting that her marriage to Prince Arthur was never consummated. This was evidently the case for Isabella too since her fiancé Conrad is killed before his wedding night. A further complication to Manfred's matrimonial plans emerges in the form of Isabella's rival suitor, Theodore. In a jealous rage, the thwarted bridegroom attempts to stab his prospective bride, only to discover that he has murdered his daughter by mistake. The gruesome episode parodies Henry's role in the beheading of his wives, Anne Boleyn and Catherine Howard, who between them were charged with adultery and incest. The blood drops oozing from the statue of Prince Alfonso, above his tomb in St Nicholas' church, is an appropriate emblem for the bleeding victim. The statue dripping blood is where Gothic convention and Catholic superstition converge. As revealed in the title page of the first edition, St Nicholas is the name of the church at Otranto where the priest and supposed 'author' of the tale served as the canon. The name can also be related to St Nicholas I, who was the Pope (858–67) involved in the attempt by King Lothair II of Lorraine to divorce his childless wife, Theutberga, on the grounds of incest. Like Pope Clement VII, Pope Nicholas eventually supported the claim of the wronged wife. As drops of blood fall from the statue's nose, Hippolita falls to her knees vowing allegiance to her husband, in much the same way as had Catherine of Aragon in a series of staged appeals to Henry, affirming her loyalty as a wife.

Numerous similarities may be found between the long-suffering Catherine of Aragon and Manfred's wife Hippolita. Both were devout Catholics with personal confessors and a commitment to charitable works, an activity that greatly endeared Catherine to her English subjects. On first learning that her husband planned to divorce her, Hippolita is ready to comply with his wishes for the sake of their daughter and enter a convent. That was most certainly Henry's wish for Catherine. Her biographer Giles Tremlett speculates that had she agreed to retreat quietly into a convent, it is possible that the Henrician Reformation might never have happened and that England would have remained a Roman Catholic country.[39] While in Rome, Cardinal Wolsey spread a rumour that, after her divorce, Catherine, in her heart, wished to enter a nunnery, an urge that the queen stringently denied.[40] Walpole had his own way of bringing Henry VIII's former papal legate to life. He liked to greet visitors to Strawberry Hill while wearing a red cardinal's hat, boasting that it had once belonged to Cardinal Wolsey.[41]

Walpole had a collector's interest in Henry VIII, owning portraits, as well as a jewelled dagger that had once belonged to him.[42] Another of his prized possessions was a clock with an obscene pendulum given to Anne Boleyn by Henry as a wedding gift. Walpole's 'little Gothic castle', Strawberry Hill, contained a Holbein bedchamber, a fitting memento of Tudor marriage.[43] The bedchamber was a potent political site, having led to the secession from Rome and the excommunication of Henry, who previously had been honoured by the Pope in 1521 as 'Defender of the Faith'. In *The Castle of Otranto*, disapproval of Manfred's misdemeanours is signalled by the Catholic superstition of a statue dripping blood. When extended to Henry VIII, this omen is symbolic not only of the unwarranted disgrace brought to Catherine and her bloodline but also of the fractured family of Catholic countries and the damage done to the clergy and the Church's artefacts through his Dissolution of the Monasteries (1536–41).

Despite Walpole's political aversion to papists, his taste was decidedly influenced by the aesthetics of Catholicism. He described himself as a 'Protestant Goth',[44] and admitted to his friend, Rev. William Cole: 'I like Popery, as well as you, and have shown I do. I like it as I do chivalry and romance. They all furnish one with ideas and visions, which Presbyterianism does not. A Gothic church or convent fill [*sic*] one with romantic dreams.'[45] At the time of his Grand Tour of Europe in 1739, Walpole was exposed to countless examples of Catholic art and ecclesiastical buildings. It was during these travels that he started collecting art and antiquities. For Walpole, as it would be for the Victorian Gothic of Augustus Pugin, the Gothic style was a form of Catholic architecture. One can imagine that for an aesthete like Walpole, Henry VIII's real crime against the Church was not bigamy or even severing it from Rome, but vandalism. Through his Dissolution of the Monasteries, friaries, convents, monastic houses and priories were disbanded to fill royal coffers. Religious artefacts were melted down, confiscated and destroyed on a vast scale. Walpole's collection of antiquities and curiosities included

Catholic artefacts and paintings that had survived the desecrating purge. As Nick Groom has noted: 'As Catholicism venerated its saintly relics, so eighteenth-century connoisseurs and antiquarians valued artefacts with suggestive associations and *bona fide* provenance.'[46] In many ways, Walpole's hobby was a miniature version of the Counter-Reformation, protesting against the persistent destruction of the papal heritage. In a letter to George Montagu, he writes in panic:

> If I don't make haste, the Reformation in France will demolish half that I want to see. I tremble for the Val de Grâce and St-Cyr. The devil take Luther for putting it into the heads of his Methodists to pull down churches! I believe in twenty years there will not be a convent left in Europe but this at Strawberry.[47]

Many of the 800 religious communities closed down by Henry VIII were relics of the Middle Ages. Their buildings were converted into residences or abandoned, falling into ruin and forming part of an aesthetic of ruination.[48] As Groom puts it: 'A millennium and a half of culture and civilization was overthrown and the medieval world was literally left in ruins.'[49] Walpole was acquainted with Henry Spelman's *The History and Fate of Sacrilege* (1698), which describes what happened to those families who moved into former monasteries. These buildings were thought 'to carry God's curse' and had 'flung out their Owners with their Names ... by grievous Accidents and Misfortunes.'[50] Walpole's ancestors at Houghton, however, did not exploit or defame the ecclesiastical building they had come to occupy. The idea of a curse on those who were the usurpers of Church property is in keeping with the omens and usurper motif of *The Castle of Otranto*. Many of the desecrated buildings were believed to be haunted by phantom monks and nuns, which tied into the Catholic association of purgatory with ghosts. The Gothic novel, especially those with medieval settings or architecture, opened up a textual site for such spectrality. In Walpole's novel, Isabella's father Frederic witnesses the apparition of a ghostly skeletal monk with 'fleshless jaws and empty sockets' (p. 157), who had turned into a hermit, during his lifetime, on seeing his 'country become a prey to unbelievers' (p. 133).

Walpole's attitude towards Catholicism, which he referred to as 'Superstition's papal gloom', is equivocal.[51] There were times, he realised, when 'the interest of the monk plainly gets the better of the judgment of the author' (p. 61). While Catholic superstition is exploited in the novel for Gothic effects, the monastic life is presented as a route for Manfred's redemption at the end. Similarly, Anna Laetitia Aikin (later Mrs Barbauld) in her essay 'On Monastic Institutions' (1773) expresses scepticism of 'monkery', while singing the praises of the monkish life. The historical echo of the Dissolution of the Monasteries gives her pause for thought. Coming across a ruined abbey, she finds herself 'like a good protestant [*sic*]' starting to exult over the fallen 'proud priest and lazy monk fattened upon the riches of the land, and [who] crept like vermin from their cells to spread their poisonous doctrines through the nation'.[52] Nonetheless, she is also able to reflect on these monastic houses as charitable institutions and repositories of learning where the arts were fostered and preserved. She then presents the cloistered life as offering a welcome retreat for men and women in need of asylum (like Isabella) or for those (like Manfred) who fall from grace. The most vulnerable characters in Gothic novels find sanctuary in a church or chapel, for, as Father Jerome points out in *The Castle of Otranto*, that 'is where orphans and virgins are safest from the snares and wiles of this world' (p. 103). These structures would have been built in the Gothic style. During the reign of Henry VIII, Gothic architecture went into decline. Walpole not only captures this period in the sub-text of his novel, but was also a key figure in the revival of Gothic architecture.

In his first preface, Walpole claimed that the work had been found in the library of an ancient Catholic family in the north of England. For contemporary readers, the 'Old Religion' was redolent of the recent Seven Years War against Catholic France and Spain, which ended in 1763, the year before the novel was published. This reminder of the former national faith might have recalled the pre-Reformation heritage and stirred more recent fears of Jacobite invasion. Michael Gamer has identified the fabricated editor of the first edition, William Marshall, as a Tory, suggesting that he is likely to have been a Jacobite supporter of the Stuart line of kings. By translating a story about the restoration of a ruler who has been wrongly usurped and the downfall of the usurper and his line after three generations of holding power, Gamer points out that 'Manfred's position as the grandson of the usurper Ricardo corresponds nicely to George III's position as the grandson of the first Hanoverian king of Great Britain.'[53] As a staunch Whig, Walpole was hardly a Jacobite sympathiser, yet the parallel points towards subversion, while the novel imaginatively invokes the Old Religion.

In a tongue-in-cheek allusion to the First Roman Catholic Relief Act (1778) in a letter to William Cole, Walpole recreates a Catholic Britain: 'May not I, should not I wish you joy on the restoration of

27

popery? I expect soon to see Capucins [*sic*] tramping about the streets, and Jesuits *in high places*. We are relapsing fast to our pristine state, and have nothing but our island and our old religion.'[54] The political reality was very different. By the eighteenth century, the real presence of Catholicism, as the once-dominant religion, had been reduced to haunting its dispossessed ecclesiastical buildings in a spirit of *unheimlich*. Owing to their love-affair with the past, the Whigs were seen by some as nostalgic for a bygone Catholic age. In dismissing the priesthood as a relic of an earlier evolutionary stage of society, Mary Wollstonecraft rebuked the Whiggish Edmund Burke with the claim that 'you mourn for the idle tapestry that decorated a gothic pile, and the dronish bell that summoned the fat priest to prayer.'[55] Wollstonecraft criticised Burke's support for France's pre-revolutionary Ancien Régime with its clergy and hereditary privileges, asking 'Why was it a duty to repair an ancient castle, built in barbarous ages, of Gothic materials?'[56] Similarly, Burke's defence of the English constitution is attacked by Wollstonecraft when she enquired: 'Why were the legislators obliged to rake amongst heterogeneous ruins; to rebuild old walls, whose foundations could scarcely be explored'?[57] Here she targets Burke's lament for the Gothic constitution, which shared power with the ruler, noblemen, senior clergy and the common people, upon which it was claimed the British parliament had been founded. Its ancestor was the Anglo-Saxon Witenagemot, an assembly consisting of aristocratic and ecclesiastic officials, who advised the monarch. Their 'squabbles' were for Walpole 'another Gothic passion.'[58] According to his first preface, the story is set some time between 1095 and 1243, which coincides with the period of the Witenagemot and the Gothic constitution. Representations of monastic life in Gothic literature would go on to tap into a Burkean strain of sentimentality and Walpolean Catholic aesthetic.

Conflicted attitudes towards Catholicism were in evidence towards the end of the eighteenth century. Despite discriminating against Catholics, Britain provided a tolerant and sympathetic haven for thousands of clerical émigrés fleeing the French Revolution. Burke wrote an impassioned plea in *The Times* to raise funds for these refugees, victims of 'cruel and inhuman persecution' taking flight across the English Channel.[59] British Catholics helped many French clergy transfer to English monastic houses, thus helping reinstate a lost monasticism, not seen since Henry VIII obliterated the monasteries.[60] Protestants had once regarded Catholicism in Britain as a dangerous foreign influence. Absolutist in its institutions as opposed to British democracy and rationality, this 'alien' religion was perceived as secretive, conspiratorial, mystical and superstitious. The sacerdotalist reliance upon intervention by priest, saint or the Virgin Mary was contrary to the rational independent Protestant conscience, while the Church's asceticism and aestheticism in putting the suffering body centre stage made it resemble a religion of Gothic torment.

Anti-Catholicism is whipped up in the pages of John Foxe's *Book of Martyrs* (1563), a picture book of horror depicting the Inquisition torturing Protestant martyrs. According to Catholic convert John Henry Newman, a leading figure in the nineteenth-century Oxford Movement: 'we must have a cornucopia of mummery, blasphemy, and licentiousness – of knives and ropes, and faggots; and fetters, and pulleys, and racks, – if the Protestant Tradition is to be kept alive in the hearts of the population.'[61] Newman suggested that Protestantism needed the antagonism of Catholic-created horror in order to sustain the support of the people. But this should not presuppose that anti-Catholicism prevailed. Even though the Gordon Riots of 1780 were sparked by opposition to the Catholic Relief Act of 1778, momentum for the unrest was fuelled by poverty and urban overcrowding.[62] An economic downturn had been exacerbated by damage to trade during the ongoing American Revolutionary War (1775–83) in which Britain fought American rebels. Rising prices, falling wages and more frequent unemployment were all contributory factors. In pondering the causes of the Gordon Riots, Walpole concluded: 'Negligence was certainly its nurse, and religion only its godmother.'[63] In his landmark study, Victor Sage has argued that the Gothic novel reacted to the Catholic Relief Acts from 1778 to 1829.[64] He sees its rhetoric of horror underpinning a range of Protestant theological ideas. While Ann Radcliffe and Matthew Lewis are widely regarded as key figures in the promulgation of anti-Catholic sentiments to a receptive and sympathetic Protestant audience, their attitudes towards the religion are not without ambivalence.[65] While a balanced view of Catholicism can be found in the work of Radcliffe, this is hardly the case for Lewis' anti-monastic *The Monk*, yet even he may have been repenting for his overly damning portrayal of the Catholic Church in the novel through his drama, *Venoni, or the Novice of St Mark's*, first performed in 1808.[66] At the end of the rewritten final act, Lewis upholds the religious toleration of the Glorious Revolution by declaring in the words of a friar: 'Virtue and Vice reside equally in Courts and Convents; and a heart may beat as purely and as nobly beneath the Monk's scapulary, as beneath the ermine of the judge, or the breast-plate of the warrior.' In full agreement, Venoni imparts a final message to the audience to accept rather than demonise Catholicism, saying:

> let us scorn to bow beneath the force of vulgar prejudice, and fold to our hearts as brethren in one large embrace men of all ranks, all faiths, and all professions. The Monk and the Soldier, the Protestant and the Papist, the Mendicant and the Prince, let us *believe* them all alike to be virtuous till we *know* them to be criminal, and engrave on our hearts, as the first and noblest rule of moral duty and of human justice, those blessed words,
>   – 'BE TOLERANT!' –[67]

A novelist whose antagonism towards Catholicism was much less equivocal is Charles Maturin, an Irish Protestant clergyman of Calvinist leanings. As Chris Baldick puts it: 'To attack Catholicism was not for Maturin, as it was for Lewis in his prurient Gothic novel *The Monk* (1796), an antiquarian fancy-dress frolic. It was a very serious duty of his vocation, to which he was earnestly committed.'[68] Yet despite his willingness to exploit the terrors of the Spanish Inquisition in his novel *Melmoth the Wanderer*, Maturin's true concern was with Irish nationalism and the influence of the papacy on Catholic Ireland.[69] Daniel O'Connell's campaign for Catholic Emancipation started to gained momentum by 1824, the year in which Maturin's pamphleteering *Five Sermons on the Errors of the Roman Catholic Church* was published, in which he expressed his 'desire for the only true *Catholic Emancipation*, the emancipation of the intellect and the conscience' from the yoke of Rome.[70] In the same year, Maturin published *The Albigenses*, a novel set in twelfth-century France. Along with the Waldenses, the Cathars or Albigensians, pre-dated the French Huguenots from whom Maturin was descended. Outlawed as heretics by the Catholic Church, they were persecuted by the armies of Pope Innocent III and the Inquisition. For twenty years, it was said, Cathar 'blood flowed like water'.[71]

INQUISITION

Officially the Church, along with the Holy Office of the Inquisition, was not permitted to shed blood or mutilate the body when bringing about what Ariel Glucklich calls sacred pain.[72] For this reason, inquisitors substituted the *garrucha* or pulley, *toca* or water torture and the *potro* or rack for more sanguinary torments. In spite of this, there was little guarantee of a bloodless interrogation for those unfortunate enough to find themselves in the clutches of these secret tribunals. Gothic novelists portray a sadistic and bloody Inquisition, even though such representations have been scarcely applicable for most of its history. In Matthew Lewis' *The Monk*, the wicked monk Ambrosio, accused of rape, murder and sorcery, faces gruesome torture by the Spanish Inquisition and then burning at the stake, following an auto-da-fé (Spanish 'act of faith'). Through a pact with the devil, he manages to escape one set of flames only to discover, through a diabolical twist of fate, that he has been pardoned. The auto-da-fé was a rite of public penance for condemned heretics after which the judicial authorities carried out execution. The Catholic Mass formed part of the ritual in which the sacramental drinking of Christ's blood formed a grotesque corollary to the bloodthirstiness of the state, with which the Church was in league.[73] Although blood was not physically shed, since the punishment associated with the auto-da-fé was burning, it was invariably the real issue at stake. Due to anti-Semitic tensions in fifteenth-century Castile, race had become a legitimate target for persecution. Growing numbers of Jewish converts (*conversos*) to Christianity had provoked anxiety over the corrupting influence of crypto-Jews, suspected of still practising their old religion. *Limpieza de sangre* (purifying of blood) was a code under which statutes were passed to discriminate against those of Jewish ancestry.[74] In 1490–1, there was a show trial involving Jews and *conversos* accused of host desecration and the murder for ritual purposes of a Christian boy, who became known as the Holy Child of La Guardia. Even though no body was found, the accused were found guilty of removing the heart and using the child's blood for magical purposes to destroy Christians. In the Spanish town of Avila, they were burnt at the stake.

After the first two decades of its inauguration in 1478, torture and burnings were a relative rarity for the Spanish Inquisition. This was certainly not the case in England, France and Germany where such punishments continued for more than a century. In spite of this, Protestant countries perpetuated horror stories about the Inquisition, through anti-Catholic propaganda known as 'The Black Legend'. Foxe's *Book of Martyrs* subscribed to this political myth-making and provided Gothic novelists with a template of Catholic horror, in what can be seen as a competing work of fiction.[75] Matthew Lewis' unalloyed description of the mutilation and torture of Ambrosio near the end of the novel is a displacement for the atrocities Protestants imagined were carried out by the forces of the Inquisition. Even though he escapes their ultimate punishment, the reader does not escape a gruesome description of the bodily torments involved in the monk's torture and final damnation, leaving him 'bruised and mangled' as well as 'blind, maimed, helpless and despairing'.[76] Radcliffe's more psychological approach to Catholic horror appears in *The Italian* (1797). Her subtitle, *The Confessional of the Black Penitents*, refers to the Dominicans, who made up the majority of inquisitors in Northern Italy. Her hero, Vivaldi, is a prisoner of the Roman Inquisition, whose torment consists in listening to the agonised groans of other victims and the suspense of not knowing his fate. Unexpectedly, Vivaldi's interrogator turns out to be a 'just judge, whose candour, had it been exerted in his cause, could not have excited more powerful sensations of esteem and admiration'.[77] As Sage suggests, it is as if the tribunal has been transposed into that of 'a Surrey Assize Court'.[78] Indeed Radcliffe might have been responding to the Catholic Relief Act of 1791, which admitted Catholics to the practice of law in Britain, or may even have been preparing the national imagination for the first Catholic judge, who would not be appointed until the following century over thirty years after Catholic Emancipation.[79] Aside from Catholic inequality, her evocation of the fairness of the English justice system, with its equity and common law, contrasts with the injustices of the Ancien Régime and its imprisoning *lettres de cachet* by way of royal signature, which had flourished in Catholic France. On the other hand, Radcliffe's portrayal of the dungeons of the Inquisition invited comparison with the English penal system, which condemned prisoners to filth and semi-starvation, as well as condoning torture, albeit under a different name. From 1794 to 1795, the government suspended habeas corpus to facilitate imprisonment without trial rather like the French *lettres de cachet*. This had prompted William Godwin to raise the indignant question in *Caleb Williams* (1794): 'Is that a country of liberty where thousands languish in dungeons and fetters?'[80] He dated his preface 12 May, to mark the day in 1794 when prominent radicals, including the writer and orator, John Thelwall, and the novelist and pamphleteer, Thomas Holcroft, were arrested. They were accused of sedition in campaigning for parliamentary reform, including an extension of the franchise, and were charged with high treason and imprisoned in the Tower of London. *Caleb Williams* is Godwin's fictionalised version of his polemic, *Enquiry Concerning Political Justice* (1793), exposing the injustices of a tyrannical legal and penal system that could destroy individuals, however innocent, with impunity. Another fictional expression of this appears in his novel *St Leon* (1799), the publication of which coincided with another suspension of habeas corpus from 1798 to 1801. Godwin's eponymous immortal wanderer is taken prisoner by the Spanish Inquisition. The novel's political message goes beyond the religious persecution sanctioned by a sixteenth-century absolutist regime, to the more secular and immediate repressions of Britain in the 1790s. The radicals were put on trial and their acquittal by jury was a verdict reiterating the favourable judgment received by Vivaldi in *The Italian*. Radcliffe, like Godwin, may have been revisiting, through fiction, events at the Old Bailey. If convicted, the radicals would have been sentenced to being hanged, drawn and quartered. This was worse than anything associated with the Roman Inquisition at that time. The reason why the British authorities had reacted so harshly and suspended habeas corpus was to stem a potential mass Jacobin movement, growing out of the French Revolution. The Spanish Inquisition, however, had responded to the revolutionary events of 1789 by banning books and ideas originating from France, for by then it had reinvented itself as a torturer more of the book than of the body.[81]

BLEEDING NUNS AND THE FRENCH REVOLUTION

When Matthew Lewis' *The Monk* was published, the Holy Office had scaled the auto-da-fé down to book burnings and doubtless would not have hesitated tossing copies onto their bonfires. In revolutionary France, where Catholicism had been disbanded, readers had not been particularly offended by the novel.[82] Its anti-Catholic content, however, had angered Protestants in England, where it was threatened with censorship for its blasphemous and salacious content, giving Lewis little choice but to expurgate the fourth edition.

Such adverse publicity did nothing to lessen the appeal of *The Monk*, which ran into numerous editions. In a letter to his mother, Lewis explained that the novel was written in the style of *The Castle of Otranto*. He also made use of Walpole's Catholic setting in his story of the downfall of Capuchin superior Ambrosio, who is corrupted by a fiend in the form of a woman called Matilda, disguised as the male novice Rosario. Her name evokes that of Manfred's daughter in *The Castle of Otranto*, but she bears no resemblance to her in character having been recast as a villain, rather than as a victim. While Walpole's Matilda falls in love with the original of an image in a portrait, her namesake in Lewis' novel becomes the object of adoration in a painting. When Ambrosio wearies of her worldliness, Matilda obligingly uses witchcraft to enable him to rape the virginal Antonia, who turns out to be his sister. He later kills her and thwarts her mother's attempt at rescue by adding matricide to his repertoire of criminality. For his crimes, the monk is captured by the Inquisition. The novel concludes with him being dropped in an abyss by Satan. For six days, he is physically tormented, dying on the seventh in a diabolical reversal of the six days of creation in the Book of Genesis. An interpolated narrative relates to a nun called Agnes, who is in love with Don Raymond. She plans to escape from her convent by disguising herself as the ghost of Beatrice de las Cisternas, the ghostly Bleeding Nun who haunts the Castle of Lindenberg. The attempt goes wrong when Raymond 'rescues' the spectral nun by mistake, who is unrelenting in her sexual overtures to him. Thanks to the intervention of another liminal figure, the Wandering Jew, the Bleeding Nun is laid to rest and Raymond is finally left in peace. When Ambrosio discovers that Agnes is pregnant with Raymond's child, he passes the information on to the Abbess. As a result, Agnes is cruelly punished by being incarcerated in a dungeon where she gives birth to a baby, who dies a few hours later. Eventually, she is rescued by her brother Lorenzo and then reunited with Raymond, whom she marries.

The success of the novel stimulated imitations and redactions including Gothic bluebook versions, a genre that, as Franz Potter explains, has been unfairly marginalised as 'merely the undergrowth of legitimate novels or literary mushrooms'.[83] Since Gothic fiction is believed to have had a largely female-dominated audience, this may be why some adaptations render Lewis' Bleeding Nun a pale imitation of her debauched self, either as victim or helpful premonitory spectre.[84] For his play *The Castle Spectre*, which opened in 1797, Lewis resurrected his Bleeding Nun. Reappearing as a secular version of the original sexually rampant and mouldering skeleton, she is portrayed in almost beatific terms as 'a tall female figure, her white and flowing garments spotted with blood; her veil is thrown back, and discovers a pale and melancholy countenance; her eyes are lifted upwards, her arms extended towards heaven, and a large wound appears upon her bosom'.[85] This apparition manifests in a small chapel and looks as though she is about to administer a benediction, followed by a nun-like chorus of '*Jubilate*'. Less sanitised versions may be found in the highly plagiarised, anonymous *Almagro and Claude; or, Monastic Murder; Exemplified in the Dreadful Doom of an Unfortunate*

Nun (1810) and *Juliette* (1796) by the Marquis de Sade. As he famously stated in his 'Reflections on the Novel' (1800), the emergence of the genre of Gothic horror 'became the necessary fruit of the revolutionary tremors felt by the whole of Europe'.[86] It will be argued that, through her revenancy, Lewis' Bleeding Nun and her imitators replay the horrors of the French Revolution, including its anti-clericalism. Angela Wright shows how Lewis was influenced by the anti-monastic drama, Jacques-Marie Boutet de Monvel's *Les Victimes cloîtrées* (1791), and explains how a libertine priest, who immures a young woman in a convent for sexual pleasure, inspired Lewis' account of Ambrosio confining Antonia in the crypt of a convent, where he rapes her.[87] Edmund Burke, the author of the anti-Jacobin *Reflections on the Revolution in France* (1790), was concerned that the destruction of Catholicism in France could jeopardise all religion. This is demonstrated by the Bleeding Nun who, abandoning the religious life for debauchery and murder, professes herself to be an atheist, taking 'every opportunity to scoff at her monastic vows, and loaded with ridicule the most sacred ceremonies of religion' (p. 166). Her carnality, to a Protestant way of thinking, was confirmation that celibacy for religious reasons was unnatural and could lead to its opposite extreme. Matilda, the other recalcitrant female in the novel, has no such excuse, for she enters the monastery of the Capuchins in Madrid cross-dressed as the novice Rosario, for the express purpose of seducing Ambrosio. Lewis' depiction of women defying religion points towards Catholicism as a potentially destabilising influence on traditional femininity in Britain.

Matilda and the Bleeding Nun are forerunners of the Marquis de Sade's heroine in *Juliette*, who also cross-dresses and murders. After being raised in a convent, Juliette goes on to attack religion, in a way that faithfully embodies the doctrine of Enlightenment. According to Max Horkheimer and Theodor W. Adorno, 'she demonizes Catholicism as the latest mythology, and with it civilization as a whole. The energies previously focused on the sacrament are now devoted, perversely, to sacrilege'.[88] Juliette is a lover of system and order. In Sade's earlier *Justine, or The Misfortunes of Virtue* (1791), a love of systematisation is reflected in the Comte de Gernande's mathematical and almost ceremonial blood-letting of victims, a forerunner of the regularity and ritual of the guillotine. For Juliette, reason holds sway over virtue and selfhood prevails over social good. Denis Diderot, the philosopher and author of the erotic novel, *The Nun* (1796), laid the foundations for a materialist individualism in which personal gratification prevailed over morality or religious duty. Mario Praz describes him as 'one of the greatest exponents of that *Système de la Nature* which, carrying materialism to its logical consequences [...] paves the way to the justification, in the name of Nature, of sexual perversions'.[89] After leaving the convent, Juliette's sister, the heroine of *Justine* (1791), is sexually tortured by a frenzied monk at the monastery of Sainte-Marie-des-Bois. Within its walls, the communion wafer is anally desecrated and an image of a crucified woman displayed. But Justine still manages to retain her faith and dogged pursuit of virtue. In this respect, she resembles the much abused heroine of Sarah Wilkinson's bluebook, *Priory of St. Clair; or, Spectre of the Murdered Nun* (1811). This imitation of Lewis' novel tells of a nun abducted from her convent, where she was confined against her will. Even though she is freed by the wicked libertine, Lewis Chabot, Count de Valvé, the fair Julietta insists that she would rather return to the cloistered life than marry him. This illustrates how Gothic fiction is more than capable of espousing positive representations of the convent, which here provide a refuge from unwelcome suitors. Refusing to release her, Lewis imprisons Julietta in his castle. Rather aptly, she tries escaping through a Gothic chapel, but he manages to thwart her plan by stabbing her to death at the altar. Six months later, at his wedding to a less reluctant bride, Lewis sees the spectre of the murdered nun. The name of Wilkinson's villain is undoubtedly a tongue-in-cheek allusion to Matthew Lewis. A quotation mentioning nuns used for the epigraph of the novel has been taken from *Tales of Terror* (1801), a work ascribed to Lewis, though recently doubt has been cast on his authorship.[90]

Another imitation of *The Monk* is Sophia L. Frances' *The Nun of Misericordia* (1807), whose Bleeding Nun is also murdered by a male seducer for choosing the convent over him. Clearly these Gothic nuns prefer the constraints of religious life to the patriarchal controls of marriage. By contrast, Lewis' Bleeding Nun is prepared to kill to secure a husband. For Wilkinson and Frances' bleeding nuns, despite their virtue, there is no happy ending. For that, the reader must turn to *Juliette*. Here, Sade's heroine finds happiness with her lesbian lover, Durand, described by Angela Carter as being 'as destructive as Kali, a sumptuous infecundity whose masterpieces are plagues'.[91] Such lesbian contentment is certainly not the case for the convent-enclosed heroine of Diderot's *The Nun*, who resists unwelcome sapphic advances.

Amongst Lewis' litany of anti-Catholic stereotypes, which includes a wicked abbess and licentious monk, the Bleeding Nun stands out as a more innovative figure, even though she is not entirely original. Lewis identifies her as having originated from a spectral nun who is not bleeding. So where, one might wonder, did the blood come from? In the 'Advertisement' to the novel, Lewis points out that traditions of the Bleeding Nun existed in many places in Germany and that her ghost continues to haunt the ruined castle of Lauenstein. The story that he claims was related to him concerns a 'Spectre Nun'.[92] It has a remarkable similarity to the German tale, 'The Elopement' (1782–6) by Johann Karl August Musäus, in which a young officer, Fritz, elopes by mistake with a ghostly skeletal-looking nun, instead of Emily, the heiress of Lauenstein.[93] To his horror, the spectre visits him every night, declaring: 'I am thine – thou art mine, with body and soul.'[94] It seems almost certain that Lewis used this story for his Raymond and Agnes sub-plot in which the Bleeding Nun appears. In Musäus' version, to which he appears to be alluding, Lewis notes that there is 'a spectre habited as a nun (but not as a bleeding one)'.[95] For the bloodiness, Lewis might have drawn on the superstition of ghosts of murder victims displaying a fatal wound. In *The Italian*, seen as a reply to *The Monk*, Radcliffe's hero Vivaldi refers to this folklore belief, after witnessing the apparition of a supposedly ghostly monk. Lewis' Bleeding Nun received her wound after being stabbed by her lover Otto. Her now spectral wounding ghosts the mortal wound that she delivered to her previous lover, Baron Lindenberg, at the instigation of his brother Otto. As the giver and receiver of a wound, this might have sufficed in the novel as a blood stain, but instead it actively bleeds. Ann Williams ruminates on the possible implications of this:

> The hints of physicality and process suggested by the present participle may be a Kristevan example of 'poetic language,' in which this word 'bleeding' implies the horrifying disruptiveness of 'female' materiality. Certainly the nun, who has sworn to renounce sexuality and motherhood, does, in breaking her vows and murdering her lover, embody such a horror of the dangerous female.[96]

Another explanation is to consider the Bleeding Nun in the light of the bloodiest episode in recent history, the Terror of the French Revolution. This is relevant not only to the graphic horrors of bloodshed but also to one of the primary causes of unrest, which was the profound dissatisfaction with the Church of the Ancien Régime, seen as greedy, corrupt and harbouring amorous clergy. The profligacy of Beatrice, the Bleeding Nun, also unveils Catholic hypocrisy around celibacy. Anti-clerical propaganda played an important role in dismantling the power of the Church and accelerating the revolutionary de-Catholicisation of France. Lewis, who spent the summer of 1791 in revolutionary France, finished writing *The Monk* in September 1794, just two months after the end of the Reign of Terror. The Marquis de Sade, in linking the Gothic novel to the French Revolution, gives 'pride of place' to *The Monk*, which has been interpreted as a deconstructed allegory of its atrocities.[97]

In Lewis' poem 'France and England in 1793', Marie Antoinette is represented as a Gothic heroine. Attempts to rape and murder her are described in Burke's *Reflections on the Revolution in France*, would have provided Lewis with a model for the crimes committed by Ambrosio towards Antonia, named after the queen.[98] The savage murder of Marie Antoinette's close friend, the Princess of Lamballe, in the September Massacres of 1792, also finds parallels in *The Monk*. Following her attack by a brutal mob, she died from blows to the head after which her body was mutilated. The bleeding corpse was paraded through the streets.[99] Similarly, Lewis' wicked prioress of the Convent of St Clare is set upon by rioters who 'tore her one from another' and 'dragged her through the streets' before she is killed by a blow to the head, causing her to fall to the ground 'bathed in blood' (p. 302).[100] Lewis' description of how the prioress' body was pulped to 'a mass of flesh' (p. 302) grotesquely parodies the Catholic Mass's doctrine of transubstantiation, whereby bread and wine are miraculously changed into the body and blood of Christ. The sacrament was abolished in France by the anti-clerical forces of the revolution. Perversely, the sans-culotte were rumoured to be indulging in secular versions of flesh-eating and blood-drinking.[101] Allegations of cannibalism were linked to the grisly death of Lamballe. This spectacle of horror heralded the coming Jacobin Terror of 1793–4. With reference to Marx's famous image in his *Communist Manifesto* (1848), 'A specter is haunting Europe',[102] Jacques Derrida sees in the spectral not only the past, 'a *politics* of memory', but what is yet to come.[103] The horrific image of the bleeding head of her dead friend stuck on a pike was intended to haunt Marie Antoinette, in advance of her impending fate. Mercifully, she never saw the head held up to the window of her prison in the Temple fortress, but its unseen horror must have imprinted itself indelibly upon her traumatised imagination. As Burke points out, obscurity seems necessary for making something very terrible.[104]

Edward Montague's *The Demon of Sicily* (1807), described by Montague Summers as 'infinitely more extravagant than *The Monk*',[105] provides further parallels with the atrocious fate of Lamballe. In this Lewis imitation,

Montague describes how Ugo De Tracy, having returned to his castle after a pilgrimage to the Lady of Loretto, is approached by the ghost of his wife, Isabella. She leads him to a headless woman, lying on the ground, which turns out to be her own lifeless corpse. Although decapitation occurs in pre-Revolutionary Gothic fiction, its most recent impact, for Lewis and his contemporaries, was in having ended the lives of countless aristocratic men and women during the Reign of Terror, most notably Marie Antoinette. Montague's fair Isabella meets her bloody fate for rejecting the sexual advances of 'the gloomy' Leonardi di Vicensio.[106] Her severed head is put on display, as was that of Lamballe. But while Lamballe's heart was torn out, Leonardi is prevented from doing the same to Isabella's body by her husband. After saving his wife's corpse from mutilation, Tracy kisses the dead lips. The depraved revolutionary mob had wanted the queen to plant a kiss on the lips of the horror head of her friend, whom she used to address as 'my dear heart'.[107] Political pamphleteers describe Lamballe being raped and forced to kiss bloody corpses, after which her body was sexually mutilated with its breasts and genitals displayed on pikes and her heart cooked and eaten.[108] Next to Montague's 'headless trunk of a female', a spectre utters the words 'revenge the deed' (p. 11). These decapitated corpses sent out a message, condemning the kind of barbarism that characterised the Terror of the French Revolution.

The apparent corporeality of Lewis' Bleeding Nun, to which Raymond initially responded, belies her spectrality. The apparition wears the habit of a religious order and 'her dress was in several places stained with the blood which trickled from a wound upon her bosom' (p. 140). On the political stage in France, her murder can be seen to represent the massacre of nuns, monks and priests for having colluded with a callous and decadent aristocracy. Beatrice's fate has some similarity with that of the Princess of Lamballe, even though the latter was martyred for the privilege and abuses of her class. Like the Bleeding Nun's bloodied attire, Lamballe's blood-stained chemise, mounted on a pike, is on public show.[109] Obscene libels accused the prudish princess of being the lesbian lover of Marie Antoinette. Her loyalty to the queen in front of a revolutionary tribunal infuriated the mob, for whom she became a royal surrogate.[110] Enlightenment Libertine writing satirising the aristocracy and the Church revealed the extent to which pornography and political radicalism had become entwined. Anti-clerical erotica was nothing new, as indicated by the lewd French text, *Venus in the Cloister or the Nun in Her Smock* (1683).[111] The increasing appetite for lurid details of flagellants in monasteries and convents also situates the Bleeding Nun in an anti-monastic and libertine context. During his visit to revolutionary Paris in 1791, Lewis read accounts of monastic orgies and eroticised cruelty in *Justine* by the Marquis de Sade, impresario of the bleeding body. There can be little doubt that the novel influenced the writing of *The Monk*, which in turn inspired Sade's rewriting of *Justine*.[112] In the light of this, the wound that the Bleeding Nun receives on her bosom corresponds to the bleeding breast of Justine after she has been whipped by the corrupt monk Clément. The rape and sexual torture of women by Benedictine monks in *Justine* forms an obscene parody of the interrogations carried out by the Holy Office. The novel reflects a culture of anti-clerical political pornography, in which Marie Antoinette was seen to be having consensual sexual intercourse with a priest. She was also accused of being 'a profligate dripping with French blood',[113] an image tallying with the murderous concupiscence of the Bleeding Nun, for whom Marie Antoinette as Bleeding Queen served as regal equivalent. The assertion that the Queen's 'impure blood will not suffice to wash out all her wickedness' points to the dual purpose of blood to purify and pollute.[114] The other kinds of blood with which Marie Antoinette has been associated relate to the racial otherness of her Austrian bloodline, the brutal manner of her death by guillotine and the menstrual excesses she suffered in the days before her execution that visibly stained her chemise.[115] Reports of this express what Williams describes above as the 'horrifying disruptiveness of "female" materiality'.

Theological misogyny dates back to at least the fourth century when St Jerome declared: 'Nothing is so unclean as a woman in her periods; what she touches she causes to become unclean.'[116] The Bleeding Nun serves as a metaphor for menstrual impurities for, as Diane Long Hoeveler explains, 'the sheer profusion of bleeding nuns who inhabit these convents [...] suggests that there is no final haven, no escape from the realities of the physical female body. Women will always bleed; they will always be unclean in the eyes of the patriarchy and finally in their own eyes'.[117] In the anonymous Gothic bluebook, 'The Bleeding Nun of St Catherine's' (1801), another imitation of *The Monk*, a ghostly nun takes revenge against her treacherous lover for her death and that of her prematurely born child. Her bleeding is suggestive of blood that has been shed in childbirth.[118] In Lewis' novel, the onset of Beatrice's libertinism would have been marked by an erotogenic wounding, the tearing of the hymeneal veil causing the shedding of virginal blood. Another veil with bridal connotations was the one covering the nun's cadaverous face. The association between whiteness and death ties into the ghostliness of the Bleeding Nun, whose long veil is especially apposite as she has taken the place of Agnes on her wedding night with Raymond. Beatrice's amorous after-life pursuit of Raymond signals an extreme reaction against the vow of chastity, especially for those forced to 'take the veil' as brides of Christ. The black habit worn by holy orders is a sartorial signifier of how professed nuns entombed within the convent are dead to the world.

The divine effluence emitted by the saintly stigmatic, as a vessel of the sacred blood of Christ, was seen not only as life-giving but also as capable of sanitising all types of impure female blood. The bodies of such holy women cross the divide between the spiritual and material. In *Powers of Horror* (1982), Julia Kristeva locates abjection in corporeal functions marked by the ambiguous status of being both inside and outside the body, as in an open wound and menstrual blood. Her ultimate example is the corpse 'seen without God' through which death infects life.[119] As an embodiment of the wound, menstrual blood and the corpse, Lewis' demonic stigmatic is truly abject, yet her corporeality is compromised by her spectrality. There is an uncanny disjuncture between her face of death in an advanced state of decay and a body exuding fresh blood. This unruly bodily fluid, by continuing to defy containment, even that of the grave, represents the transgressive nature of the leaky female body. In *The Nun of Misericordia*, Frances produces a composite of Lewis' Bleeding Nun and his Gothic nun Sister Agnes, who is imprisoned in the dungeons of her convent. Kneeling before the image of her patron saint, torrents of blood pour from the wound in her bosom, staining her white robes. Sister Agnes visibly out-bleeds the Bleeding Nun. She too had received a stab wound from a malevolent lover. But any similarity with Lewis' unholy nun ends there, as her kneeling posture in church situates Sister Agnes more closely to a Renaissance tradition of devout stigmatic.

The blood of the mystic stigmatic constituted a public, authorised bleeding, as opposed to that of the private and taboo menstrual flow. The wounds were perceived as sacred portals to a life within the risen Christ. Conversely, Lewis' demonic stigmatic and her vampire sisters in Stoker's *Dracula* are resurrections of the profane rather than of the pious body. Instead of being redemptive, they reinforce the blood curses visited upon Eve and her daughters. By contrast, the religious stigmatic invariably acquired reverence, authority and even canonisation in the Church by professing to bleed, not her own blood, but the sacred blood of Christ, with its power to wash away sins.[120] For some stigmatics, this was linked to the monthly cycle. Accordingly, the reclaiming of the power of female blood had radical implications, for, even up to the late seventeenth century, menstruating women were discouraged or forbidden to receive Holy Communion and, in some cases, barred from entering a church, prohibitions that still apply to the literary vampire.[121]

In 1897, the year in which Bram Stoker published *Dracula*, the Roman Catholic Church was figured as a female vampire. The image appeared in Walter Walsh's attack on the Oxford Movement for 'Romanising' Anglicanism: 'The "woman drunken with the blood of the saints" (Rev. xvii. 6) has not lost her cruel nature ... Her persecuting laws are still the same as when in the Dark Ages her infernal Inquisition performed, unhindered, its bloodthirsty work.'[122] In *Dracula*, Catholicism can be seen as a perverse feminising process. In order to repel vampires, Stoker's characters draw on the rosary, crosses and consecrated communion wafers. Solicitor Jonathan Harker is persuaded by an old woman in Transylvania to wear a crucifix for his protection, even though, as an English Churchman, he was brought up to regard such items as idolatrous. By making use of this sacred paraphernalia in the fight against supernatural evil, Stoker was reinforcing the Catholic Church's association with superstition. The novel also exploits similarities between Catholics and vampires. The rite of transubstantiation at the heart of the Catholic Mass and the act of vampirism in *Dracula* precipitates rebirth into eternal life. Dracula himself represents a quasi sacramental host for whom 'the blood is the life', which is the refrain of his disciple Renfield.[123] Mina Harker, when forced to drink from the bleeding body of Count Dracula, resembles a Catholic communicant kneeling before a priest clad in black.[124] The count slitting open his chest for her to drink has been linked to the traditional iconography of Christ as the legendary pelican feeding its young from a self-inflicted breast wound.[125] Stoker, however, compares Mina's blood-drinking to a kitten licking milk from a saucer. These images of nurture feminise the count who, in many respects, is a Christ-like figure. In the Middle Ages, Jesus was represented as a mother and the spiritual practice of blood lactation was advocated by St Bernard. Calling his monks 'women', he exhorted them to suck the breasts of the crucified Christ, as well as his wounds for purifying body and soul.[126]

A major difference between Christ and the count is that Dracula's blood cannot purify, but only pollute. This is a further feminisation by association since, as indicated earlier, within theological misogyny the blood of women, particularly in menstrual, sexual and childbirth contexts, was regarded as impure.[127] Dracula is not only a procreator of vampires but also an imbiber of female blood, which makes him an even more harmful contaminant. Professor Van Helsing prescribes male blood as medicinal for Dracula's vampire victim Lucy, implying that it will compensate for the inferiority of female blood, saying: 'A brave man's blood is the best thing on this earth when a woman is in trouble' (p. 186). Accordingly, he arranges for Lucy to have blood transfusions and obtains donors from his band of male vampire hunters. Lewis' Bleeding Nun also has masculine blood mingled with her own when her lover plunges into her heart the very same dagger with which she killed his brother, still smeared with the victim's blood. The spectral version of the dagger carried by the ghostly nun is described vampirically as having drunk the blood of her paramour. This could be Lewis' way of mocking the body of the Church by satirising how its followers drink the blood of their beloved in the expectation of gaining eternal life.

Over the centuries, Catholics have invoked divine intervention through devotions to the sacred blood of Christ and cults of holy relics. Anecdotal accounts exist of devotees visiting preserved bodies of saints, miraculously exuding blood.[128] Stoker describes Jonathan Harker coming across Dracula lying in a 'great box' (p. 83), with blood trickling from his mouth. Similarly, Lucy's undead corpse, while resting in her tomb, is the dark doppelgänger of the saintly incorruptible body. Through these descriptions, the author may have been reliving the time, as a boy, when he visited the vaults of the church of St Michan in Dublin, which still has on display the mummified bodies of a crusader and a 400-year-old nun, whose heart and lungs are visible beneath her leathery skin. The vault could have provided Stoker with a prototype for the crypt, where the corpse bride Lucy Westenra tries to lure her fiancé into her deathly vampiric embrace. This eroticisation of the undead recreates Lewis' phantom Bleeding Nun in pursuit of conjugal consummation with her reluctant earthly bridegroom Raymond and in doing so continues the lineage of the demonic stigmatic and tradition of Catholic horror.

NOTES

1 Caroline Walker Bynum, *Wonderful Blood: Theology and Practice in Late Medieval Northern Germany and Beyond* (Philadelphia, PA: Pennsylvania University Press, 2007), p. 4.

2 Quoted in Maria Purves, *The Gothic and Catholicism: Religion, Cultural Exchange and the Popular Novel, 1785–1829* (Cardiff: University of Wales Press, 2009), p. 2.

3 Quoted in Mark Canuel, *Religion, Toleration, and British Writing, 1790–1830* (Cambridge: Cambridge University Press, 2005), p. 55.

4 See Mary Muriel Tarr, *Catholicism in Gothic Fiction: A Study of the Nature and Function of Catholic Materials in Gothic Fiction in England 1762–1820* (Washington, DC: The Catholic University of America Press, 1946).

5 Ann Radcliffe, *The Italian, or, The Confessional of the Black Penitents*, ed. Robert Miles (Harmondsworth: Penguin Classics [1797], 2000), p. xx.

6 Radcliffe, *The Italian*, p. xx.

7 See Walpole, letter to William Cole, 12 October 1771, *The Yale Edition of Walpole's Correspondence*, ed. W. S. Lewis *et al.*, 48 vols (New Haven, CT: Yale University Press, 1937–83), 1, p. 241.

8 Walpole, letter to Horace Mann, 8 July 1759, *Correspondence*, ed. Lewis *et al.*, 21, p. 306. Strawberry Hill eventually became St Mary's Catholic teachers' training college in 1925, where the Vincentian Fathers lived. In the vicinity is Pope's Villa, the home of the Catholic Alexander Pope. In 1914, the building was turned into St Catherine's convent school run by the Sisters of Mercy, where the author's aunt, Sister Ninian, taught for many years.

9 Walpole, letter to Horace Mann, 27 April 1753, *Correspondence*, ed. Lewis *et al.*, 20, p. 372.

10 Walpole, letter to Lady Ossory, 28 September 1786, *Correspondence*, ed. Lewis *et al.*, 33, p. 529.

11 Walpole, letter to George Montagu, 23 August 1765, *Correspondence*, ed. Lewis *et al.*, 10, p. 168. He is drawing here on Alexander Pope's expression, 'A Gothic Vatican!' in *The Dunciad*, Book I, l. 125.

12 Horace Walpole, *A Description of the Villa of Mr. Horace Walpole, youngest son of Sir Robert Walpole Earl of Orford, at Strawberry-Hill near Twickenham, Middlesex. With an inventory of the furniture, pictures, curiosities &c.* (Twickenham: Strawberry Hill Press, 1784), p. iv.

13 Horace Walpole, *The Castle of Otranto and The Mysterious Mother*, ed. Frederick S. Frank (Peterborough, Ontario: Broadview Press [1764 and 1768], 2003), p. 59. Subsequent references are made parenthetically in the text.

14 The casuistic method was used by early modern Catholic thinkers, but fell into disrepute after Blaise Pascal attacked Jesuits for misusing it in his *Provincial Letters* (1656–7).

15 The publication date given on the title page of the first two editions with their different prefaces is 1765, even though the novel was published on Christmas Eve, 1764.

16 Robert Miles, 'Europhobia: The Catholic Other in Horace Walpole and Charles Maturin', in Avril Horner (ed.), *European Gothic: A Spirited Exchange 1760–1960* (Manchester: Manchester University Press, 2002), p. 93.

17 Miles, 'Europhobia', p. 93.

18 See Markman Ellis, *The History of Gothic Fiction* (Edinburgh: Edinburgh University Press, 2000), p. 38.

19 Miles, 'Europhobia', p. 95.

20 See Miles, 'Europhobia', p. 94.

21 See Anon., *Common Sense* (1739), in E. J. Clery and Robert Miles (eds), *Gothic Documents: A Sourcebook 1700–1820* (Manchester: Manchester University Press, 2000), pp. 60–1.

22 Quoted in Sue Chaplin, *The Gothic and the Rule of Law 1764–1820* (Basingstoke: Palgrave Macmillan, 2007), p. 40.

23 Maggie Kilgour, *The Rise of the Gothic Novel* (London: Routledge, 1995), p. 15.

24 Edward Pearce, *The Great Man: Robert Walpole – Scoundrel, Genius and Britain's First Prime Minister* (London: Pimlico, 2008), p. 2.

25 Quoted in Ralph V. Turner, *Magna Carta* (Harlow: Pearson Education, 2003), p. 175.

26 Miles, 'Europhobia', p. 94.

27 Robert Miles, 'The Gothic Novel', in David Scott Kastan (ed.), *The Oxford Encyclopaedia of British Literature* (Oxford: Oxford University Press, 2006), p. 445.

28 Jerrold E. Hogle, 'The Gothic Ghost of the Counterfeit and the Progress of Abjection', in David Punter (ed.), *A Companion to the Gothic* (Oxford: Blackwell, 2000), p. 299.

29 Quoted in Robert Miles, 'Abjection, Nationalism and the Gothic', in Fred Botting (ed.), *The Gothic: Essays and Studies* (Cambridge: D. S. Brewer, 2001), p. 60.

30 See Walpole, letter to William Cole, 9 March 1765, *Correspondence*, ed. Lewis *et al.*, 1, p. 88.

31 See Horace Walpole, *The Castle of Otranto*, ed. E. J. Clery and W. S. Lewis (Oxford: Oxford University Press [1764], 1996), p. xxx; Horace Walpole, *The Castle of Otranto*, ed. Nick Groom (Oxford: Oxford University Press [1764], 2014), p. xxxiii.

32 Quoted and translated from the French in Horace Walpole, *The Castle of Otranto*, ed. Michael Gamer (London: Penguin [1764], 2001), p. xxvi.

33 Quoted in Walpole, *The Castle of Otranto*, ed. Groom, p. xxxviii.

34 Walpole, letter to William Cole, 12 October 1771, *Correspondence*, ed. Lewis *et al.*, 1, p. 241. See also Victor Sage, 'Roman Catholicism', in William Hughes, David Punter and Andrew Smith (eds), *The Encyclopedia of the Gothic*, 2 vols (Oxford: Wiley-Blackwell, 2013), 2, p. 565.

35 Anne Williams is one of the few critics to devote any discussion to *The Castle of Otranto* as an allegory of Henry VIII, though she does not take up the religious implications of his reign for the novel. See *Art of Darkness: A Poetics of Gothic* (Chicago, IL: University of Chicago Press, 1995), pp. 28–30.

36 Michael Gamer regards Alfonso the Magnanimous (1416–58) as the most likely model for Alfonso the Good, who was praised as a military leader and commended for his morality in personal matters. See Walpole, *The Castle of Otranto*, ed. Gamer, p. 112.

37 Amongst the failed attempts to produce an heir was Prince Henry, who died in infancy.

38 Quoted in Alison Weir, *The Six Wives of Henry VIII* (London: The Bodley Head, 1991), p. 69.

39 See Giles Tremlett, *Catherine of Aragon: Henry's Spanish Queen* (London: Faber & Faber, 2010), p. 427.

40 Earlier Catherine had begged her father, King Ferdinand II of Aragon, to allow her to enter a convent should she not find another husband after being widowed. See Tremlett, *Catherine of Aragon*, p. 147.

41 The memento was presented to Walpole by the Countess Dowager of Albemarle. See Strawberry Hill Residents' Association, 'A History of Roman Catholicism in Strawberry Hill', http://www.shra.org.uk/Catholicism%20 in%20Strawberry%20Hill.pdf. Accessed 3 May 2011.

42 See Walpole, *The Castle of Otranto*, ed. Frank, p. 40.

43 Walpole, letter to Horace Mann, 10 January 1750, *Correspondence*, ed. Lewis *et al.*, 20, p. 111.

44 Walpole, letter to Richard Bentley, [day missing] September 1753, *Correspondence*, ed. Lewis *et al.*, 35, p. 153.

45 Walpole, letter to William Cole, 12 July 1778, *Correspondence*, ed. Lewis *et al.*, 2, p. 100.

46 Walpole, *The Castle of Otranto*, ed. Groom, p. xxxvi.

47 Walpole, letter to George Montague, 23 August 1765, *Correspondence*, ed. Lewis *et al.*, 10, pp. 167–8.

48 See Nick Groom, *The Gothic: A Very Short Introduction* (Oxford: Oxford University Press, 2012), p. 28.

49 Walpole, *The Castle of Otranto*, ed. Groom, p. xv.

50 Quoted in Diane Long Hoeveler, 'Demonizing the Catholic Other: Religion and the Secularizing Process in Gothic Literature', in Monika Elbert and Bridget M. Marshall (eds), *Transnational Gothic: Literary and Social Exchanges in the Long Nineteenth Century* (Farnham: Ashgate, 2013), p. 93. Hoeveler's book, *The Gothic Ideology: Religious Hysteria and Anti-Catholicism in British Popular Fiction, 1780–1880* (Cardiff: University of Wales Press, 2014), came out as this book was going to press.

51 Quoted in Hoeveler, 'Demonizing the Catholic Other', p. 93.

52 Anna L. Aikin, 'On Monastic Institutions', in *The Works of Anna Laetitia Barbauld*, ed. Lucy Aikin, 2 vols (London: Longman, Hurst, Rees, Orme, Brown and Green, 1825), 2, p. 195.
53 Walpole, *The Castle of Otranto*, ed. Gamer, p. xxix.
54 Walpole, letter to Rev. William Cole, 21 May 1778, *Correspondence*, ed. Lewis *et al.*, 2, p. 79.
55 Mary Wollstonecraft, *A Vindication of the Rights of Woman, A Vindication of the Rights of Men, An Historical and Moral View of the French Revolution*, ed. Janet Todd (Oxford: Oxford World's Classics, 1994), p. 60.
56 Wollstonecraft, *A Vindication of the Rights of Woman*, ed. Todd, p. 42.
57 Wollstonecraft, *A Vindication of the Rights of Woman*, ed. Todd, p. 42.
58 Walpole, letter to George Montagu, 11 June 1753, *Correspondence*, ed. Lewis *et al.*, 9, p. 149.
59 [Edmund Burke], 'Case of the Suffering Clergy of France: Refugees in the British Dominions', letter to *The Times* (18 September 1792), 3. I am indebted to Dale Townshend for this reference.
60 See Purves, *The Gothic and Catholicism*, p. 43.
61 Quoted in Victor Sage, *Horror Fiction in the Protestant Tradition* (Basingstoke: Macmillan, 1988), p. 28.
62 For other theories, see Ian Haywood, *Bloody Romanticism: Spectacular Violence and the Politics of Representation, 1776–1832* (Basingstoke: Palgrave Macmillan, 2006), pp. 184–90.
63 Walpole, letter to Rev. William Cole, 15 June 1780, *Correspondence*, ed. Lewis *et al.*, 2, p. 224.
64 See Sage, *Horror Fiction*, pp. 28–9.
65 In Radcliffe's *The Mysteries of Udolpho* (1794), the horror lying beneath the mysterious black veil is that of a human figure depicted in a state of semi-decay, whose face and hands are disfigured by worms. This turns out to be a memento mori, devised as a penance for a previous Marquis of Udolpho, who had offended against the prerogative of the Church. See Ann Radcliffe, *The Mysteries of Udolpho* (Oxford: Oxford University Press [1794], 1992), p. 662.
66 See Radcliffe, *The Italian*, ed. Miles, pp. xx–xxi; Purves, *The Gothic and Catholicism*, pp. 93–118. Mark Canuel discusses Radcliffe, Walpole, Godwin and Clare Reeve's use of the Gothic in the context of Catholicism and religious toleration; see *Religion, Toleration, and British Writing*, pp. 55–85.
67 Matthew Gregory Lewis, *Venoni, or the Novice of St Mark's* (London: Longman, Hurst, Rees, and Orme, 1809), p. 86.
68 Charles Maturin, *Melmoth the Wanderer*, ed. Chris Baldick (Oxford: Oxford University Press [1820], 1989), p. xiii.
69 See Miles, 'Europhobia', p. 90.
70 Quoted in Niilo Idman, *Charles Robert Maturin: His Life and Works* (London: Constable, 1923), p. 283.

71 Quoted in B. K. Kuiper, *The Church in History* (Grand Rapids, MI: Christian Schools International, 1964), p. 143. Contemporary Gothic novelist Kate Mosse's Languedoc trilogy relates to the Cathars.

72 This is the title of his book, *Sacred Pain: Hurting the Body for the Sake of the Soul* (New York: Oxford University Press, 2001). In chapter 13 of J. K. Rowling's *Harry Potter and the Order of the Phoenix* (London: Bloomsbury, 2003), the eponymous hero has to write out lines in his own blood on parchment for a new headmistress, Dolores Umbridge, the High Inquisitor at Hogwarts School of Witchcraft and Wizardry. Magically, the words are painfully inscribed on the skin of his right hand, though the wounds disappear, leaving no trace. Websites have linked the Inquisition at Hogwarts to Ofsted, the unpopular official body for inspecting schools in the United Kingdom. Many of the historical inquisitors were black-habited Dominican friars resembling Rowling's hooded Death Eaters or Dementors, the supernatural guards of Azkaban prison, who bring soul-destroying misery to their victims.

73 See Joan Curbet, ' "Hallelujah to your dying screams of torture": Representations of Ritual Violence in English and Spanish Romanticism', in Horner (ed.), *European Gothic*, p. 164; Derek Hughes, *Culture and Sacrifice: Ritual Death in Literature and Opera* (Cambridge: Cambridge University Press, 2007), p. 172.

74 See Helen Rawlings, *The Spanish Inquisition* (Oxford: Blackwell Publishing, 2006), pp. 50–1.

75 In the book, John Foxe wrongly asserted that the Church of England was a continuation of the true Christian Church. Catholic detractors such as Thomas Harding alleged that the book was 'full of a thousand lies', quoted in John Mozley, *John Foxe and His Book* (London: SPCK [1940], 1972), p. 138.

76 Matthew Gregory Lewis, *The Monk*, ed. D. L. Macdonald and Kathleen Scherf (Peterborough, Ontario: Broadview Press [1796], 2004), pp. 362–3. Subsequent references are made parenthetically in the text.

77 Radcliffe, *The Italian*, ed. Miles, pp. 407–8.

78 Sage, *Horror Fiction*, p. 154.

79 This was William Shee, who was appointed a justice of the Court of Queen's Bench in December 1863.

80 William Godwin, *Caleb Williams*, ed. David McCracken (Oxford: Oxford University Press [1794], 1970), p. 181.

81 See Toby Green, *Inquisition: The Reign of Terror* (Basingstoke: Macmillan, 2007), pp. 340–1.

82 See Lewis, *The Monk*, ed. Macdonald and Scherf, p. 22.

83 *Literary Mushrooms: Tales of Terror and Horror from the Gothic Chapbooks, 1800–1830*, ed. Franz J. Potter (Fullerton, CA: Zittaw Press, 2009), p. 9.

84 In Charles Farley's version, *Raymond and Agnes; or, The Castle of Lindenbergh*, a drama produced in 1797, the Bleeding Nun does not pursue Raymond sexually but serves to warn him of danger. See Lewis, *The Monk*, ed. Macdonald and Scherf, p. 421.

85 Matthew Gregory Lewis, *The Castle Spectre*, in *Seven Gothic Dramas 1789–1825*, ed. Jeffrey N. Cox (Athens, OH: Ohio University Press, 1992), p. 206.

86 'Marquis de Sade (1800)', in Victor Sage (ed.), *The Gothick Novel* (Basingstoke: Macmillan, 1990), p. 49.

87 See Angela Wright, *Britain, France and the Gothic, 1764–1820: The Import of Terror* (Cambridge: Cambridge University Press, 2013), pp. 127–8.

88 Max Horkheimer and Theodor W. Adorno, *Dialectic of Enlightenment: Philosophical Fragments*, ed. Gunzelin Schmid Noerr (Stanford, CA: Stanford University Press [1947], 2007), p. 74.

89 Mario Praz, *The Romantic Agony* (Oxford: Oxford University Press, 1970), pp. 99–100.

90 See Douglass H. Thomson, 'Mingled Measures: Gothic Parody in *Tales of Wonder* and *Tales of Terror*', *Romanticism and Victorianism on the Net* (May 2008), http://id.erudit.org/iderudit/018143ar. Accessed 1 February 2014.

91 Angela Carter, *The Sadeian Woman* (London: Virago Press, 1979), p. 115.

92 Lewis, *The Monk*, ed. Macdonald and Scherf, p. 375.

93 For a reproduction of the story, see *The Monk*, ed. Macdonald and Scherf, pp. 369–79. See also Syndy M. Conger, *Matthew G. Lewis, Charles Robert Maturin, and the Germans* (New York: Arno Press, 1980), pp. 93–105.

94 Lewis, *The Monk*, ed. Macdonald and Scherf, p. 377.

95 Lewis, *The Monk*, ed. Macdonald and Scherf, p. 461.

96 Anne Williams, 'Lewis/Gounod's Bleeding *Nonne*: An Introduction and Translation of the Scribe/Delavigne Libretto', in Gillen D'Arcy Wood (ed.), *Romanticism and Opera*, Romantic Circles (May 2005), note 4, http://rc.ctsdh.luc.edu/praxis/opera/williams/williams_notes.htm. Accessed 12 February 2013.

97 'Marquis de Sade', in Sage (ed.), *The Gothick Novel*, p. 48. See also Ronald Paulson, *Representations of Revolution (1789–1820)* (New Haven, CT: Yale University Press, 1983), pp. 217–24.

98 See Lewis, *The Monk*, ed. Macdonald and Scherf, p. 16.

99 See Antonia Fraser, *Marie Antoinette* (London: Weidenfeld & Nicolson, 2001), p. 363.

100 See Haywood, *Bloody Romanticism*, pp. 71–2. Lewis could also have drawn on the medieval legend of Pope Joan, who was killed by a crowd when it was discovered that she was a woman.

101 James Gillray depicts the September Massacres in a cartoon of a cannibalistic sans-culotte family. See Haywood, *Bloody Romanticism*, pp. 73–4.

102 Quoted in Derrida, *Specters of Marx*, p. 2.

103 Derrida, *Specters of Marx*, p. xviii.
104 See Edmund Burke, *A Philosophical Enquiry into the Origin of Our Ideas of the Sublime and Beautiful*, ed. James T. Boulton (Oxford: Basil Blackwell [1757], 1987), p. 58.
105 Montague Summers, *The Gothic Quest: A History of the Gothic Novel* (New York: Russell and Russell, 1964), p. 236.
106 Edward Montague, *The Demon of Sicily* (Kansas City, MO: Valancourt Books, 2007), p. 13.
107 Quoted in Fraser, *Marie Antoinette*, p. 85.
108 See Fraser, *Marie Antoinette*, p. 363; Peter Wagner, *Eros Revived: Erotica of the Enlightenment in England and America* (London: Paladin, 1988), p. 98.
109 See Fraser, *Marie Antoinette*, p. 364.
110 See Haywood, *Bloody Romanticism*, p. 71.
111 Jean Barrin has been identified as the author by Julie Peakman, in *Mighty Lewd Books: The Development of Pornography in Eighteenth-Century England* (Basingstoke: Palgrave Macmillan, 2003), p. 17.
112 Noting that Lewis' novel was translated into French in 1797, Angela Wright argues that it appears highly probable that *The Monk* influenced Sade's rewriting of the third version of *Justine*. See 'European Disruptions of the Idealized Woman: Matthew Lewis' *The Monk* and the Marquis de Sade's *La Nouvelle Justine*', in Horner (ed.), *European Gothic*, pp. 39–54.
113 Quoted in Anon., 'Ristori as Marie Antoinette', in *McBride's Magazine*, 1 (February 1868), 175.
114 Anon., 'Ristori as Marie Antoinette', 175.
115 See Fraser, *Marie Antoinette*, p. 410.
116 Quoted in Marie Mulvey-Roberts, 'Menstrual Misogyny and Taboo: The Medusa, Vampire and the Female Stigmatic', in Andrew Shail and Gillian Howie (eds), *Menstruation: A Cultural History* (Basingstoke: Palgrave Macmillan, 2005), p. 153.
117 Diane Long Hoeveler, *Gothic Feminism: The Professionalization of Gender from Charlotte Smith to the Brontës* (Pennsylvania, PA: Pennsylvania State University Press, 1998), p. 110.
118 See Anon., 'The Bleeding Nun of St Catherine's', in *Romances and Gothic Tales*, ed. Franz J. Potter (Crestline, CA: Zittaw Press [1801], 2006), pp. 25–32.
119 Julia Kristeva, *Powers of Horror: An Essay on Abjection*, trans. Leon S. Roudiez (New York: Columbia University Press, 1982), p. 4.
120 See Mulvey-Roberts, 'Menstrual Misogyny and Taboo', pp. 156–8.
121 See Uta Ranke-Heinemann, *Eunuchs for the Kingdom of Heaven: Women, Sexuality, and the Catholic Church*, trans. Peter Heinegg (New York: Doubleday, 1990), pp. 24–5.

122 Quoted in Patrick R. O'Malley, *Catholicism, Sexual Deviance, and Victorian Gothic Culture* (Cambridge: Cambridge University Press, 2006), p. 130.

123 Bram Stoker, *Dracula*, ed. Glennis Byron (Peterborough, Ontario: Broadview Press [1897], 1998), p. 178. Subsequent references are made parenthetically in the text.

124 See O'Malley, *Catholicism, Sexual Deviance, and Victorian Gothic Culture*, p. 159.

125 See O'Malley, *Catholicism, Sexual Deviance, and Victorian Gothic Culture*, p. 159; Fred Botting, *Gothic* (London: Routledge, 1996), p. 150.

126 See Caroline Walker Bynum, *Jesus as Mother: Studies in the Spirituality of the High Middle Ages* (Berkeley, CA: University of California Press, 1982), pp. 144–5.

127 See Ranke-Heinemann, *Eunuchs for the Kingdom of Heaven*, pp. 25–7.

128 See Christine Quigley, *The Corpse: A History* (Jefferson, NC: McFarland, 1996), pp. 260–1.

2

Mary Shelley, Frankenstein *and slavery*

I saw the daemon obedient to my orders: I saw him trembling at my frown; and found that, instead of selling my soul to a master, my courage had purchased for myself a slave.[1]

Matthew Lewis, *The Monk* (1796)

O my lov'd bride! – for I have call'd thee mine,
Dearer than life, whom I with life resign,
For thee ev'n here this faithful heart shall glow,
A pang shall rend me, and a tear shall flow.
– How shall I soothe thy grief, since fate denies
Thy pious duties to my closing eyes?
I cannot clasp thee in a last embrace,
Nor gaze in silent anguish on thy face;
I cannot raise these fetter'd arms for thee,
To ask that mercy heav'n denies to me;
Yet let thy tender breast my sorrows share,
Bleed for my wounds, and feel my deep despair.[2]

Thomas Day, 'The Dying Negro' (1775)

The early abolitionist Granville Sharp regarded slavery as a form of civil death, which divests a person of their humanity, '*as if such person was naturally dead*',[3] while Alexandre Kojève equated the slave with a 'living corpse'.[4] In *Frankenstein*, in which ample use is made of the discourse of slavery, Mary Shelley's monster, like the slave, embodies the living dead, having been made out of corpses by Victor Frankenstein, her scientist narrator. As H. L. Malchow points out, Shelley's creature parallels nineteenth-century racial stereotypes in size, strength and skin colour. He suggests that its creation provides a fictional counterpart to the ways in which race and racial prejudice are constructed.[5] Building on his work, it will be argued that *Frankenstein* is a parable of the life cycle of a slave and, as such, a narrative embodiment of real-life terror and horror. Framed by a sea voyage, the story can be seen to evoke the horrors of the Middle Passage within the triangular Atlantic slave trade, slave riots, the vengeful fugitive slave and the plight of enslaved women and their offspring. The demonisation of rebel female slaves will be shown to partake in the monstrosity of Victor's inchoate monster's mate. Anxiety over miscegenation is one of the reasons why Victor Frankenstein decided to destroy her, fearing that she might procreate with man rather than with her fellow monster. Her subsequent fragmentation resonates with that of the famous Hottentot Venus, who was regarded by many as a female monster and whose body parts were exhibited after her death. Public fascination and scientific curiosity surrounded her sexuality. The equivalent for the black African male is the myth of black potency, which will be discussed later in relation to an early film version of Shelley's novel. It will be shown how the experiences of Frankenstein's monster resemble those of a black African slave, while its very hybridity is indicative of a Caribbean mulatto. Since Shelley's male and female monsters are as ideologically piecemeal as the various body parts from which they were assembled, it is inviting to see them as metaphors for mixed race. There was an erroneous belief that mulattos were promiscuous. The revulsion and fear felt by Victor towards his creatures may be seen as an expression of contemporary negative reactions in regard to race and miscegenation. In this chapter, the monstrosity of *Frankenstein* will be read as an extended analogy of those enslaved by a system liberally dispensing 'carnage and misery'.[6] The novel reads as a textual patchwork of abolitionist writing and pro-slavery propaganda, inscribed upon the body of the monster and, according to Allan Lloyd Smith, parallels a slave narrative.[7] The pursuit of the monster by his maker is analogous to an escaped slave being pursued by his master. After dispatching the *Frankenstein* manuscript to the London publisher John Murray, Mary and Percy Bysshe Shelley finished reading John Davis's travelogue, which included details of American slavery and fugitive slaves in the Deep South.[8]

At the time of writing *Frankenstein* in 1816, rebellion in Barbados was affecting both slaves and slave owners. As a consequence, Eliza Fenwick, the author of *Secrecy; or, The Ruin on the Rock* (1795), suffered financial losses at the school she had started there.[9] Fenwick had close connections with Mary Shelley's family and had been present at her birth. She went on to care for baby Mary for a short time, following the postpartum death of her mother, Mary Wollstonecraft, in September 1797. Ten years later, Fenwick ran the juvenile bookshop owned by Mary Shelley's father William Godwin, from November 1807 to early 1808, before starting a new life in Barbados. The rebellion there reignited the question of whether to emancipate slaves. Oscillating between those starkly in support and those against was a *via media*. This was the path taken by many ameliorist who, fearing social anarchy, resisted immediate emancipation, believing that the slave needed to be prepared for freedom with better treatment and education. *Frankenstein* can be read as a meditation on this ameliorist position, which in all likelihood was supported by Mary Shelley herself, as this chapter will suggest.

MARY SHELLEY AND EMANCIPATION

When she started writing the novel, the slave trade had been abolished less than a decade earlier in 1807. Slavery itself would continue for nearly thirty years more, until the Abolition of Slavery Bill in 1833 freed slaves in August 1834. This did not become truly effective until 1838, when interim measures of enforced apprenticeship ended. Between abolition and emancipation, campaigners on all sides of the debate bombarded the British public. On 16 March 1824, Mary Shelley was brought indirectly into the debate by the Foreign Secretary and Leader of the House of Commons, George Canning, an abolitionist and ameliorist, who used her fictional creation as propaganda against the immediate emancipation of slaves (Figure 2). With the Prime Minister, Lord Liverpool, he introduced amendments to a Bill for the gradual extinction of slavery, which effectively disabled its immediate progress by putting decisions in the hands of pro-slavery colonial governing assemblies.[10] As one cynic predicted: 'The word "GRADUAL" will cover a period of 500 years ... Depend upon It.'[11] Vehement opponents of emancipation were keen to throttle debate on the grounds that it was an incitement to slave unrest.[12] They were quick to draw attention to an uprising by slaves during the previous year in Demerara, part of British Guiana, involving 10,000 slaves and leading to the deaths of over 200 enslaved people. The catalyst had been the erroneous belief that slaves had already been emancipated by the British

Figure 2 Statue of George Canning, who became Prime Minister in 1827, Parliament Square, London.

Note: This photograph was uploaded by Prioryman on 27 January 2015, http:// en.wikipedia.org/wiki/Parliament_Square#mediaviewer/File:Statue_of_George_ Canning,_Parliament_Square,_London.jpg.

government and that settlers were withholding freedom from them. Equally troubling to some ameliorists was the fact that the leaders were Christianised Creole slaves, since this militated against the widely accepted view that Christianity was a benign influence.[13] John Smith, a missionary from London, opposed planters wanting to deny their slaves religious instruction, on the grounds that Christianity was dangerously antithetical to slavery. Smith was accused of promoting discontent and colluding with the rebels. He was put on trial, found guilty and sentenced to hang. While awaiting appeal, he died in prison in February 1824. His untimely death, along with the publicity given to the brutality of the plantocracy, caused a furore in Britain and fuelled the cause of emancipation. A month later, in a speech to Parliament, Canning cautioned against the dangers of freeing under-prepared slaves too quickly by conjuring up the spectre of Frankenstein's monster:

> In dealing with the negro, Sir, we must remember that we are dealing with a being possessing the form and strength of a man, but the intellect only of a child. To turn him loose in the manhood of his physical strength, in the maturity of his physical passions, but in the infancy of his uninstructed reason, would be to raise up a creature resembling the splendid fiction of a recent romance; the hero of which constructs a human form, with all the corporeal capabilities of man, and with the thews and sinews of a giant; but being unable to impart to the work of his hands a perception of right and wrong, he finds too late that he has only created a more than mortal power of doing mischief, and himself recoils from the monster which he has made. Such would be the effect of a sudden emancipation, before the negro was prepared for the enjoyment of well-regulated liberty.[14]

Canning's reference was highly topical. The first stage adaptation of Mary Shelley's novel, Richard Brinsley Peake's *Presumption; or, the Fate of Frankenstein*, had been performed the previous July and proved popular enough to continue to at least 1850. By then, the monster had come to resemble a semi-naked African tribesman (Figure 3). For this one-act burlesque by Robert and William Brough, *Frankenstein; or the Model Man*, first performed in 1849, the monster played by Paul Bedford is identified as 'The What Is It?', representing the polar opposite of 'the *Model Man*'.[15] At the time of Canning's parliamentary speech, the stage version of *Frankenstein* at Covent Garden was double-billed with a popular comedy by Richard Cumberland called *The West Indian*, whose eponymous hero, Belcour, has newly arrived in London. As a Creole, he found himself in an uncomfortable social position. Another of Cumberland's plays

SCENE FROM THE EXTRAVAGANZA OF "FRANKENSTEIN; OR, THE MODEL MAN," AT THE ADELPHI THEATRE.

Figure 3 Scene from the Extravaganza of *Frankenstein; or the Model Man* (1850) at the Adelphi Theatre. Here the Frankenstein monster is depicted as an African tribesman.

Note: This appeared in *The Illustrated London News* (12 January 1850), 27.

on a West Indian theme, *The Wheel of Fortune* (1795), performed in 1823, contained racist jokes, including one about putting 'sooty slaves' to death.[16]

We know that Mary Shelley was aware of the allusion made to her book in Parliament and its broad context, for as she explained in a letter to her friend Edward John Trelawny: 'They are introducing some ammelioration [*sic*] in the state of the slaves in some parts of the West Indies – during the debate on that subject Canning paid a compliment to Frankenstein in a manner sufficiently pleasing to me.'[17] A few years later, she found the praise even more gratifying in its retelling. In a letter written in Italian to Teresa Guiccioli, Byron's former lover, she enquired: 'Did you know that he [Canning] praised my Frankenstein in honorable terms in the House of Commons – extremely pleasing to me.' Mary Shelley had been reflecting on the death of Canning on 8 August 1827 as an 'irreparable misfortune' for England in 'the loss of this great man', saying that it 'weighs upon my heart – as if he had been a friend of mine'.[18] Her biographer Miranda Seymour claims that in using Frankenstein's monster to oppose the immediate emancipation of slaves, Canning had 'misread her intentions'.[19] In view of this, why then did Mary Shelley not baulk from the association? Instead she described the use made of her novel as having been couched in 'honorable terms'? The likelihood is that she was sympathetic to Canning's ameliorist position. This should come as no great surprise considering that no less a figure than William Wilberforce, the high priest of the abolitionist movement, had been swayed by Canning and his supporters to accept the ameliorist amendments as opposed to a motion for full emancipation that he had initially agreed to table in the House of Commons.[20] Nevertheless Wilberforce regarded Canning's announcement in the speech that amelioration would be restricted to Trinidad as reneging on a promise that it would be introduced throughout the West Indies.[21] With Thomas Clarkson, Wilberforce had been a founding member of the anti-slavery society founded in January 1823, officially known as the Society for the Mitigation and Gradual Abolition of Slavery throughout the British Dominions. The words 'Gradual Abolition' were not dropped until the 1830s, a time when there was a tidal wave of support to campaign for immediate abolition.[22] Even Mary Shelley's husband Percy Bysshe Shelley, an ardent opponent of slavery who had joined her in the sugar boycott, believed that the freeing of slaves from the West Indian plantations ought to be 'necessarily cautious'.[23] As he pointed out: 'Can he who the day before was a trampled slave suddenly become liberal-minded, forbearing, and independent?'[24] Mary's father, the philosopher William Godwin and author of *Enquiry Concerning Political Justice* (1793), in which he speaks out against slavery, was also of the opinion that slaves should be given instruction and guidance over a protracted period to prepare them for freedom.[25]

Many abolitionists had been unwilling to accelerate emancipation, not wanting to plunge themselves into a quagmire of conflicting interests. The churches were compromised by the threatened loss of patronage for missionaries funded by West Indian planters amidst a climate fearful of impending economic, national and colonial collapse. The most immediate concern was that the emancipation of slaves would precipitate mass slaughter on both sides. It never happened, but how, at that time, was anyone to know? In 1816, the year when Shelley started writing *Frankenstein*, there was an insurrection of Africans in Sierra Leone. The colony had been set up by British abolitionists for freed slaves, who had been returned to Africa. On 6 May, the London *Times* reported that the riot had led to the murder of many white inhabitants, initially seen as a horrifying consequence for pro-emancipationists until it was revoked the following day as wholly inaccurate. As Seymour indicates, there had been a readiness to believe the bloody rather than the bloodless version.[26]

This reflected an underlying belief that freeing slaves would not necessarily improve behaviour and, disappointingly, the free labour colony in West Africa proved to be a commercial failure. But an even more disastrous enterprise was the Nashoba plantation in Tennessee set up in 1825 by Frances (Fanny) Wright, with the support of her friend Mary Shelley. Wright bought slaves to educate and prepare them for the freedom that their own labour would eventually purchase. Even though there was less coercion, slaves were no more enthusiastic about their slavery in the 'New Harmony Colony' than under any other regime of enslavement. Their productivity was poor and, if disobedient, the slaves were treated more harshly, in line with punishments meted out by conventional plantations. This was hardly a recipe for harmonious race relations, particularly since parent was routinely separated from child and female slaves were refused locks on their doors against predatory males. Rumours that interracial marriage was tolerated provoked public outrage driving away financiers and bringing about its final collapse.[27] Eventually Wright bought her slaves their freedom and sent them to Haiti. One of her concerns regarding abolition was the possible danger of releasing uneducated and resentful ex-slaves in large numbers onto American soil. Manumission was widely feared as an incitement for increased rates of miscegenation with negative social results. For this reason, anti-miscegenation legislation, prohibiting interracial marriage, continued in sixteen states until 1967. *Frankenstein* can also be seen as a warning against miscegenation and the dangers of freeing slaves too quickly. Indeed, the word 'monster', which Shelley uses more than any other in referring to Victor's creation, has a derivation from the Latin verb '*monere*', to warn.[28]

The nearest we have to a public statement by Mary Shelley on slavery appears in a little-known reply to an argument made by J. P. Cobbett in 1831, the year in which the revised edition of *Frankenstein* was published.[29] Proving himself to be every bit as anti-Semitic as his well-known father William, Cobbett protested against Jews being put on an equal footing with Christians, prompting Shelley to respond:

> The very reasoning of all persecutors – Why? Because slavery makes them what they are, and liberty would render them just and virtuous. If that be not the case, liberty is an idol, unworthy of the blood shed at its shrine. More – it is not only that the Jews are enslaved, so also are the Catholics, but they are made aliens and outcasts, and no truth is more evident in morals or political

> justice, than that the branding and forcibly debasing a tribe of men, trans-
> forms them at once if not to villains, yet to be the natural enemies of their
> branders, and incapable of exercising towards them the social virtues.[30]

'Branding and forcibly debasing' are expressions applicable not only to ghetto Jews but also to plantation slaves. As Mary Shelley reasons, the enforced debasement of 'a tribe of men' makes them antitheti-cal to civilised behaviour, turning them into the 'natural enemies' of their oppressors. As demonstrated in *Frankenstein*, Victor's creature is transformed into a villain precisely because he has been debased as an outcast, rendering him incapable of exercising 'the social virtues'. The author conveys how understandable it is, even 'natural', for the monster to wreak revenge on his oppressor, his maker and his family, for, as he declares: 'My daily vows rose for revenge – a deep and deadly revenge, such as would alone compensate for the outrages and anguish I had endured' (p. 143). Towards his master, he has 'sworn eternal revenge' (p. 144). Vengeance was a driving force for many slaves. Many amelio-rists were hopeful that freed slaves would be deterred from this course of action by improved plantation conditions, education and religious instruction to school them in the social virtues as preparation for their release. Yet education, including exposure to Christianity, does not dis-courage Frankenstein's monster from violence and destruction. Mary Shelley may have been exploring the quandary facing ameliorists that it was usually educated and Christianised slaves who were the leaders of rebellion. So where did this leave liberal-minded thinkers like the Shelleys? Since Mary says nothing about where she stood on the ques-tion of emancipation, we must examine other contexts. These include connections with slavery made by her parents and P. B. Shelley, the abo-lition movement, the influence of Matthew Lewis, a slave-owning fellow author, and her own reading.

Mary Shelley's father, William Godwin, and mother, Mary Wollstonecraft, were abolitionists, who met for the first time in 1791 at a dinner held for Tom Paine, a prominent opponent of slavery.[31] Indeed an abolitionist stance is only to be expected from the author of *The Rights of Man* (1791) and avid supporter of the French Revolution and its Declaration of the Rights of Man in 1789, which proclaimed all men to be equal and free. This radicalised the slavery issue throughout the Caribbean, triggering the 1791 slave rebellion in the French colony of Saint-Domingue. This led to the establishment of the first Black Republic, renaming itself Haiti in 1804. John Thelwall, whose radical activities as a member of the London Corresponding Society had been defended by Mary Shelley's father, had an 'almost diseased enthusiasm'[32] for discussions on the slave trade, and describes the cruelties of planters in his anti-slavery novel set in Saint-Domingue called *The Daughter of Adoption* (1801).

Godwin reported on the slave trade for the Whig *New Annual Register* in the 1780s and 1790s and witnessed the defeat of Wilberforce's motion in April 1791 from the visitor's gallery of the House of Commons.[33] While Wollstonecraft famously compared the plight of women to slaves in her *Vindication of the Rights of Woman* (1792), it is less well known that her former lover Gilbert Imlay, the father of Mary's half-sister Fanny, had been involved in the slave trade, going on to reinvent himself from 'bungling slave-trader' to Jacobin 'champion of social and political reform'.[34] Whether they were aware of his dark history is not known, but certainly Mary Wollstonecraft never concealed her detestation of commerce as a force for corruption and her vehemence might have been heightened by this family secret. In a telling letter to Imlay condemning 'speculating merchants', she writes: 'These men, like the owners of negro ships, never smell on their money the blood by which it has been gained, but sleep quietly in their beds, terming such occupations lawful callings.'[35]

Growing up in a radical family, Mary Shelley would have been aware of slavery. After her mother's death, Godwin remarried and in 1807, he moved his bookshop and family to 41 Skinner Street in the east of London. Next door was another business run by Edward Wallis who, with his brother John, was the leading publisher of board games. In 1823, the year in which *Frankenstein* was staged, they brought out an illustrated juvenile pamphlet sympathetic to the plight of the Caribbean slave. Later it was marketed as a thirty-nine-piece jigsaw called 'The Progress of Sugar Neatly Dissected'.[36] This merchandise contributed to a flood of pamphlets responding to the fierce parliamentary debate on emancipation of 1823, which was when Godwin edited a second edition of *Frankenstein* for his daughter in an attempt to capitalise on the stage version that premiered in July. The combined effect of the reappearance of the novel and the stage play, may have prompted Canning to compare the Negro slave to Shelley's monster, the following year.

In 1800, there were around 20,000 people of African origin living in London, which, with Liverpool and Bristol, was one of Britain's main slaving ports. Shelley is likely to have come across former slaves working as sailors, dock-workers or domestic staff in London or Bristol, which she visited the year before starting *Frankenstein*.[37] A year earlier, in July 1814, the local press reported on a meeting held at the Guildhall, dealing with the campaign to halt the French slave trade.[38] Later that month, 13,000 Bristolians signed a petition, which was sent to the Houses of Parliament. A local newspaper reproducing at length the impassioned speeches made by the Dean of Bristol, Dr Beele, amongst others, on the cruelty of slavery, rather ironically also carried an advertisement for the sale of a plantation in Antigua with nearly three hundred slaves. In another column, Bristol's weekly imports itemised sugar and rum from Jamaica.[39] As the pro-slavery Member of Parliament James Baille declared: 'Bristol owes ALL her prosperity, nay, her existence to her commerce with the West Indies.'[40] Evidence of the wealth built literally on the proceeds of slavery is still visible through the city's Georgian architecture and is most apparent in the Clifton village area of the city where Mary Shelley stayed and which at that time housed the highest concentration of retired slave owners beyond the capital.[41]

Clifton was also where the Gothic novelist Sophia Lee retired with her sister Harriet and where, in 1824, she would be buried. After the death of her mother, Mary Shelley's father proposed marriage to Harriet. Her sister's popular Gothic novel is *The Recess; or a Tale of Other Times* (1783), echoes of which may be found in *Frankenstein*.[42] The story tells of the fictitious twin daughters of Mary, Queen of Scots, one of whom, Matilda, is forcibly transported across the Atlantic, where she spends eight years as a virtual prisoner in Jamaica, a fate not unlike that of a slave. Another novel set in Jamaica, where the daughter of a cruel plantation owner is surrounded by discontented slaves, described as 'savages driven to desperation', is Charlotte Smith's *The Letters of a Solitary Wanderer* (1800), which Mary Shelley read in 1816, the year in which she started work on *Frankenstein*.[43] The heroine's shock discovery is that some of the mulatto servants are her father's daughters, making her their half-sister. This revelation impacts upon her sense of identity and leads to the sobering realisation that she is little more to her father than another slave when it comes to the marriage market. It is possible that these novels influenced Mary Shelley and may have encouraged her to write about slavery in a less explicit way in *Frankenstein*, which would have allowed her to explore more deeply its complexities and controversies from different perspectives.

Questions that Frankenstein's creation asks about his origins and identity are not unlike those of a displaced person, especially one whose appearance clashes with the aesthetic values of his new environment, for, as he observes: 'My person was hideous and my stature gigantic' (p. 131). Slaves were often bred for size and strength in order to carry out back-breaking work. The creature goes on to ask: 'What did this mean? Who was I? What was I? Whence did I come? What was my destination? These questions continually recurred, but I was unable to solve them' (p. 131). This crisis of identity would have been familiar to an African abducted into slavery particularly as a young child, separated from family members. 'But where were my friends and relations?' (p. 124) asks the creature. As he recollects: 'It is with considerable difficulty that I remember the original era of my being: all the events of that period appear confused and indistinct. A strange multiplicity of sensations seized me' (p. 105). Millions of Africans were literally seized and taken to the Caribbean and North and South America by slave traders. As the creature dimly recalls: 'I walked and, I believe, descended' (p. 105). Might this be a reference to climbing down into the hold of a ship into stinking, fetid conditions of darkness? Many slaves were held below deck for months before a ship sailed, waiting for more human cargo to be loaded off the coast of Africa. Eventually, they embarked on the Middle Passage until, at the end of the voyage, a slave might experience that which the creature recollects: 'I presently found a great alteration in my sensations. Before, dark and opaque bodies had surrounded me, impervious to my touch or sight; but I now found that I could wander on at liberty, with no obstacles which I could not either surmount or avoid' (p. 105). This might be referring to the feeling of liberation after being confined in dark cramped conditions on board. As little as ten inches per person was the allocation on some slavers.[44] Not surprisingly, the mortality rate was extraordinarily high. As a living being made from dead bodies, Shelley's creature provides an apt metaphor for how the living and dead could sometimes be chained together in the hold of a slave ship. In view of the novel as a rewriting of *Paradise Lost* (1667),[45] this pandemonium, and prelude to a lifetime of enforced labour, corresponds to John Milton's description of hell as 'regions of sorrow, doleful shades' where 'hope never comes' only 'torture without end.'[46] Victor appropriates the language of slavery when describing a brief respite from his sense of enslavement to the monster he created, by confessing: 'For an instant I dared to shake off my chains, and look around me with a free and lofty spirit; but the iron had eaten into my flesh' (p. 166).

In October 1814, Percy Shelley sent Mary a long letter from *The Times* on the shocking conditions endured by captives on the slaver caravans in Africa, saying, 'See where I have marked with ink', and urging her to 'stifle your horror and indignation until we meet'.[47] The following winter, Mary and Percy started reading Jamaican planter Bryan Edwards' history of the West Indies. Edwards was a powerful supporter of the slave trade. His descriptions of slave rebellion contain gruesome details of vengeful slaves joining in the Jamaican revolt in 1760 led by Tacky, a former African chief:

> At Ballard's Valley they surrounded the overseer's house about four in the morning, in which finding all the White servants in bed, they butchered every one of them in the most savage manner, and literally drank their blood mixed with rum. At Esher, and other estates, they exhibited the same tragedy; and then set fire to the buildings and canes. In one morning they murdered between thirty and forty Whites and Mulattoes, not sparing even infants at the breast, before their progress was stopped.[48]

This was the most significant insurrection until that of the so-called Black Jacobins of Saint-Domingue, which Edwards goes on to describe. As the most profitable possession of the French Empire, the island was dubbed the 'Eden of the Western world' by William Pitt.[49] Some 100,000 slaves joined the colony's civil war (1791–1804), killing 10,000 blacks and 5,000 whites, often with great brutality. Never before had planters and their families been killed in such large numbers. In this terror of the Caribbean, nearly two hundred plantations were destroyed, many by fire. Likewise, Shelley's monster behaves like a rebellious slave in burning down the De Lacey cottage. After carrying out unpaid heavy work around the homestead with a physical strength characteristic of a slave, he kills members of Victor's close circle, including his little brother William, and pins the blame on a young family servant, Justine Moritz. As a consequence, she is judicially executed.[50] The monster goes on to murder Victor's best friend Henry Clerval and then the scientist's fiancée Elizabeth Lavenza on their wedding night. Her body, being found on the bridal bed, is suggestive of rape. In Thelwall's novel, the Creole, Seraphina Parkinson, who is modelled on Shelley's mother, narrowly escapes being raped by a slave in Saint-Domingue. This has been seen as 'an iconically racist moment, which reinforces the contrast of white morality and black savagery'.[51] Shelley's ravaging monster made out of dead body parts connects to further instances of horror described in Edwards' book of women being raped on top of their husbands' corpses.[52] With a trembling hand, he goes on to write about how the 'monsters' decapitated a husband and dissected alive his pregnant wife, throwing her unborn baby to the hogs. The rebels then inserted the head of her husband inside her belly and then sewed it up.[53] This gruesome conjunction of the living and the dead underwrites the monster's very existence as a suturing of different body parts. Horrific as these reports undoubtedly are, the extreme savagery of the rioters was retaliation for the systematic sadistic cruelties practised by the colonists of Saint-Domingue. In this context, the monster's mandate to his maker can be seen to be a voice declaiming on behalf of the mistreated subaltern slave: 'I am thy creature, and I will be even mild and docile to my natural lord and king, if thou wilt also perform thy part, the which thou owest me' (p. 103). Indeed, as the creature has already pointed out: 'Do your duty towards me, and I will do mine towards you and the rest of mankind. If you will comply with my conditions, I will leave them and you at peace; but if you refuse, I will glut the maw of death, until it be satiated with the blood of your remaining friends' (p. 102). Was this a reminder of past bloodshed and a warning of future insurrection?

The Saint-Domingue rebellion and its repercussions through colonial warfare led to the deaths of tens of thousands of French and British soldiers, who shed their blood in battle or through haemorrhages caused by yellow fever, known as 'Yellow Jack'. In addition to the rebel leader Toussaint L'Ouverture's mobilisation of largely African-born ex-slaves, there was also a mulatto army.[54] On the eve of revolt, slaves ceremonially drank the blood of a pig, swearing an oath to seal the uprising. One leader reportedly proclaimed: 'Throw away the image of the god of the whites who thirsts for our tears' and 'listen to the voice of liberty'.[55] These radical injunctions were inspired by revolutionary pamphlets from France. The image of a ferocious blood-drinking tiger served as a metaphor in anti-Jacobin writing for revolutionaries and republicans.[56] Edwards used this imagery in his description of enslaved Negroes as 'savage people, habituated to the barbarities of Africa' setting on 'the peaceful and unsuspicious planters, like so many famished tigers thirsting for human blood'.[57] Victor's fiancée Elizabeth makes a similar point, only applying this bloodthirstiness more generally when observing that 'men appear to me as monsters thirsting for each other's blood' (p. 95).

A greater humanitarian attitude towards race than that evinced by Edwards appears in the life and work of the explorer, Mungo Park, the author of *Travels in the Interior Districts of Africa* (1815), though Park's relatively liberal views may have been compromised in parts of the work that were edited by Edwards. 'Read and finish[ed] Mungo Park's travels', Mary Shelley recorded in her journal for 14 December 1814, 'they are very interesting and if the man was not so prejudiced they would be a thousand times more so.'[58] There are plenty of indications that her reading influenced the writing of *Frankenstein*.[59] In 1795, the explorer embarked for West Africa to trace the course of the Niger, a river in which he would eventually drown, while under attack from assailants. Park describes being robbed and imprisoned by a Moorish chief in Ludamar for four months, before making his escape with only a horse and a pocket compass. The account of his flight, detailing the lack of food and drink, is a mirror image of the famished monster hiding in the woods from his persecutors. Park experiences reverse racism as when a woman screams at the unfamiliar sight of a white man, which could fill Africans with horror. In Shelley's novel, the approach of the monster provokes similar reactions. On arriving at a village, Park finds himself to be an object of curiosity when several African women 'asked a thousand questions, inspected every part of my apparel, searched my pockets, and obliged me to unbutton my waistcoat, and display the whiteness of my skin; they even counted my toes and fingers, as if they doubted whether I was in truth a human being.'[60] Again Park finds himself subject to a racial gaze through which he is constructed as cultural Other. This is how the monster is received, only the latter internalises the oppression to which he is subjected and perceives his appearance as hideous. Such a reaction is analogous to the way in which racial hierarchy was naturalised by society and reinforced through education. When the monster encounters an elderly blind Frenchman, who is unable to judge by appearance, he is treated with kindness and friendship. An additional factor to consider when encountering the racial Other was that a fugitive slave was seen by white settlers as a dangerous threat, while harbouring a runaway was a punishable offence.[61] When other members of the De Lacey family arrive and catch sight of the monster, they react with horror. The daughter Agatha faints, while the old man's daughter-in-law, Safie, whose mother had been enslaved by Turks, runs out of the cottage, leaving the son Felix to beat off the creature with a stick. The family are French refugees, who had fled political oppression in Paris. Their nationality may be significant in the context of slavery since, during the writing of the novel, France had been refusing to abolish the slave trade, despite vigorous protests from the British public, combined with political pressure.[62] Mary Shelley's use of an old blind man's family in the novel may have been inspired by Park's description of meeting an old blind woman in the town of Jumbo and witnessing her reconciliation with her son, who had spent four years away from her. Her stroking of his hands, arms and face 'with great care' and her rapture over his return caused Park to conclude: 'From this interview I was fully convinced that, whatever difference there is between the Negro and European in the confirmation of the nose and the colour of the skin, there is none in the genuine sympathies and characteristic feelings of our common nature.'[63] Another cross-over between coloniser and colonised is when Park is mistaken for a cannibal by some of the Africans he meets. When Victor's youngest brother William encounters the creature, he assumes that he must be cannibalistic and exclaims: 'Monster! ugly wretch! you wish to eat me and tear me to pieces' (p. 144). Here he anticipates his brother's tearing apart of his female creation. William's own murder by the monster parallels the brutal killing of settlers' young children in the Saint-Domingue rebellion made all the more horrific by their bodies being 'transfixed upon the points of bayonets' as 'bleeding flags which followed the troop of cannibals'.[64] Many African slaves on being transported to the West believed that they were going to be cannibalised and served up to the colonisers. But as they would discover, their destiny was to be food producers, rather than the food itself.[65] Food, however, would be put to an altogether different purpose when deployed as a weapon of war by rebel slaves, who succeeded in firing cannonballs made from blocks of sugar at their oppressors.[66]

MATTHEW 'MONK' LEWIS, PLANTATION OWNER

A significant figure who came briefly into the orbit of the Shelley circle was Matthew 'Monk' Lewis. He was directly involved in the sugar trade, having inherited in 1812 two Jamaican plantations containing 590 slaves. Though he regretted the implementation of slavery and the degree to which it had become embedded within the British and West Indian economy, Lewis resigned himself to its inevitability, making no attempt to further the cause of abolition as a Member of Parliament. Between two trips to his estates, he visited Villa Diodati in Switzerland, from 14 to 21 August 1816. Lewis arrived two months after the ghost story entertainment conducted there by Byron and his guests, which had sparked the writing of *Frankenstein*. By then, Lewis had written his *Journal of a West India Proprietor* (1834) and failed to get the first half published in 1815. Here he registers his anti-emancipationist and paternalistic attitudes as a slave owner. During lengthy absences from his Caribbean estates, Lewis was concerned that his slaves were being deprived of his humane stewardship. As a slave waterman had once informed him: 'kindness was the only way to make good negroes, and that, if *that* failed, flogging would never succeed.'[67] *Frankenstein* can be read as a parable of the well-intentioned slave master, who abandons his slave. As such it is comparable to Lewis who, despite benevolent intentions, was nevertheless still an absentee plantation owner. The way in which Victor Frankenstein recoils in horror from his creation and then abdicates his paternal obligation is not dissimilar to the discomfiture of Lewis, a pro-abolitionist, on inheriting the horrors of slavery from his father. Whenever he visited his West Indian inheritance, he spent most time at his Cornwall estate in the west of Jamaica. His other plantation, Hordley, on the eastern end of the island, was more remote. On a rare expedition there, Lewis found it on the verge of anarchic collapse, due to neglect. As Ellen Malenas Ledoux points out: 'Finding his scheme to humanize Hordley impossible, Lewis abandons his abomination/creation, the plantation.'[68] Lewis expressed his wish to Bryon and his guests that a member of his family, interested in the welfare of his slaves, should continue visiting them after his death for the protection of their well-being. To this end, he signed a codicil in Geneva, witnessed by Bryon, his physician John Polidori and Percy Shelley, but never in fact added it to his will.[69] On returning to England, Lewis corresponded with Wilberforce over the issue. The dilemma facing him was, what if his successor, the new proprietor, turned out to be a tyrant? Manumission was an obvious solution, but Lewis feared that it might endanger the island and its white inhabitants.[70] The following day on 21 August, Lewis departed from Villa Diodati and Mary Shelley recorded in her journal: 'Shelley and I talk about my story.'[71] It is certainly plausible that Percy, who met with Lewis five times that summer, informed Mary of the discussion concerning the Jamaican slaves. Although she was never present at Villa Diodati at the same time as Lewis, key members of her circle were certainly in direct contact with him, which makes similarities between Lewis and Victor Frankenstein, as a representative of the conflicted slave master, worth exploring.

Fellow passenger, Mary-Ann Finlason, reflected rather idealistically on Lewis' voyage to Jamaica in order to visit his slaves, saying: 'His philanthropic consideration of their wants had endeared him to this simple-hearted race; and they regarded him rather in the light of a deity come to give laws, and make regulations for their happiness, than as a master whose property they were.'[72] Lewis' deification is comparable with Frankenstein's god-like aspirations, continued by H. G. Wells in *The Island of Doctor Moreau* (1896), where a mad scientist and God the Father figure is the self-appointed 'Giver of the Law' to his Beast People. There are parallels with the Atlantic slave trade since Dr Moreau imports animals from Africa for the purpose of enslavement. They provide him with raw material for his inhuman experiments, designed to create new beings. For the most part, slave masters were more likely to be experienced by their slaves as demonic rather than god-like. In Lewis' 1797 play, *The Castle Spectre*, an enslaved African called Hassan is so incensed by his slavery that he declares war on mankind and especially on the European race. He does this by serving his villainous master, Osmond, whom he describes as 'an avenging Fiend', saying: 'Oh! 'tis a thought I would not barter for empires, to know that in this world he makes others suffer, and will suffer himself for their tortures in the next!'[73] Hassan, like Shelley's monster, starts off with a good and gentle heart, but 'sorrows have broken it, insults have made it hard!' (p. 161). Like Frankenstein's monster, whose benevolence is rewarded with cruelty, causing him to vow 'eternal hatred and vengeance to all mankind' (p. 143), Hassan declares: 'I banish humanity from my breast' and 'vowed aloud endless hatred to mankind' (p. 161).

Performed in the wake of uprisings in Jamaica and Saint-Domingue, the play's sentimental representation of the humanity of a slave was controversial. Not only did the drama play a role in the debate over the abolition of the slave trade, as did *Frankenstein* in the debate regarding emancipation, but it was also used against Lewis as a politician. While critiquing the Atlantic slave trade through the play, it is ironic to consider that he was benefiting financially from its continuation.[74] Lewis probably tried to ameliorate the incongruity of being an abolitionist and slave owner by striving to be seen as a benign plantation master. In his journal, he expresses his willingness to listen to the complaints of his slaves, yet some of his fellow planters believed that giving slaves a voice was an incitement for disobedience, low productivity and even rebellion. In his account of the oratory of Negroes, Edwards notes how their use of figurative speech sometimes surprised him, since they were able to produce 'such pointed sentences, as would have reflected no disgrace on poets and philosophers'.[75] While listening to his creature's plea for a mate, Victor is swayed by the humanity of his rhetoric and use of a sentimental discourse. The speech is an evocation of the abolitionist medal depicting a kneeling slave, inscribed with the words: 'Am I not a man and a brother?' Victor yields to his monster's demands and embarks upon 'the filthy process' (p. 169) of making him a companion. Later he reneges on his promise and savagely rips apart the female, which he has partially constructed. In the context of slavery, this can be seen as retaliation for the punitive treatment of the black body by the powers of plantocracy, from lashings to mutilations, as when rebel slaves dismembered whites with machetes, the very tools of their labour. The brutality symbolised the fragmenting of colonial power. But not all vengeful slaves were represented as savage. In the painting, *The Negro Revenged* (1807), the artist Henry Fuseli, to whom Mary Wollstonecraft had been hopelessly romantically attached, 'had given the public a towering, elemental, and heroic black'.[76] The vengeance that the monster wreaks on Frankenstein, however, falls far short of this Romantic idealised representation. After witnessing his maker's barbaric act of unmaking, the monster relegates him to the status of a slave, declaring: 'Slave, I before reasoned with you, but you have proved yourself unworthy of my condescension. Remember that I have power; you believe yourself miserable, but I can make you so wretched that the light of day will be hateful to you. You are my creator, but I am your master; obey!' (p. 172). It is as if the power of the plantation master, with its cruelty and demand for obedience, had now been appropriated by the mutinous slave.

Lewis' most recidivist dissident slave was a Creole named Adam, whom he referred to as 'a most dangerous fellow, and the terror of all his companions'.[77] Adam was an obeah man, credited with the power to animate a corpse. It is tempting to see a link with Shelley's new 'Adam' (p. 103), who was himself animated from cadavers. When Lewis arrived at Villa Diodati, he would have regaled his companions with news of his narrow escape from a planned insurrection involving nearly a thousand slaves, intent on killing all the whites in Jamaica.[78] The conspirators had sealed their intentions by drinking human blood and eating grave soil.[79] Over the course of the novel, Victor not only identifies with a slave but also as a 'vampire [...] forced to destroy' (p. 78). Fortunately for the colonists, the plot was thwarted. Yet the last words of the ringleader about to be hanged, predicting that his followers would still carry out the massacre, must have brought little comfort to the recently reprieved. Lewis was amused by the rumour that planters were blaming the plot on his own mild reforms.[80] Leaders of the failed revolt were in fact slaves from a different plantation run by another benign planter. In his journal, Lewis glossed over the evidence that treating slaves better did not necessarily protect owners from rebellion, and continued to convince himself how much he was loved by his slaves. Nonetheless, Lewis does admit that they loved themselves more. Such a clash of self-interest might easily have led to his assassination. After Lewis died, the apocryphal story circulated that he had been poisoned by his slaves, after unwisely telling them that they would be freed after his death.[81] In actual fact, Lewis had written three codicils to his will and had specified in one that only a select number of slaves on the Cornwall Estate be freed. The third codicil, witnessed at '*Maison* Diodati', which contained instructions for the amelioration of his slaves, made no request that they be manumitted, though it was clear that Lewis had no objection to a future owner granting them their freedom.[82] The most likely explanation for him retaining an enslaved workforce was simply because he did not want to lose the revenue. Byron claimed that Lewis was greedy and, not content with making £3,000 a year from his estates, had wanted to increase it to £5,000 a year.[83]

Following abolition when slaves could no longer be bought or sold, slave births were vital for keeping up numbers on the sugar islands to maintain or even increase productivity. Lewis, like many plantation owners, was concerned that the death rate was outnumbering rates of reproduction. Edwards believed that the promiscuity of slave women was the chief cause of what he assumed to be infertility, as well as a propensity towards spontaneous abortion.[84] Before him, the influential polygenist, Edward Long, was convinced that mulattos, whom he described as 'mule-kind', were virtually incapable of breeding and that even when a baby was born, it could never reach maturity.[85] The most likely cause of the high mortality rate was not his racist fantasy, based on a pseudo-scientific theory of differing human species, but poor nutrition and overwork.[86] Another explanation is that slave mothers were aborting their unborn or committing infanticide in order to save their children from slavery. This hidden female history is one on which Toni Morrison draws for her novel *Beloved* (1987). The disposal of the remains of the female monster in Shelley's novel resembles a deconstructed abortion or infanticide. Victor conceals his murderous deed by submerging the body parts and weighing them down with a stone. Lewis designed an incentive scheme for successful childbearing by rewarding mothers with a girdle and a medal for each child. These tokens afforded them privileges, including the avoidance of punishment.[87] The idea of a mad scientist, who could create new beings from dead bodies, may well have appealed to Lewis as a fantastically pragmatic solution for keeping up his stock of slaves.

A more practical method for planters wanting to increase the number of slaves after the abolition of the trade was to father them themselves with a slave mother. Victor's description of his creation as 'a being whom I myself had formed, and endued with life' (p. 78) is a rather overblown way of describing parenthood. Familial imagery formed part of the paternalistic language of master and slave to help facilitate social control. It is ironic to consider that enslaved fathers were denied any rights of paternity, as these had been superseded by the slave master, who had ownership of their children. On the verge of giving life to his creature, Victor appropriates the discourse of fatherhood, declaring: 'A new species would bless me as its creator and source; many happy and excellent natures would owe their being to me. No father could claim the gratitude of his child so completely as I should deserve theirs' (p. 55). By contrast, the expression used to describe the relationship between father and son within the Frankenstein family is 'love', rather than 'gratitude', the latter being a sentiment that Lewis expected from his slaves. 'The Grateful Slave' (1804) is the title of a short story set in Jamaica by Maria Edgeworth, in which a cruel master is contrasted with a benign one. For many slave owners, paternalism was a prevailing ideology, to which Lewis subscribed. Even though he denied being a father figure to his slaves, he continued to infantilise them and was convinced that they saw themselves as his children.[88]

As the offspring of white men, mulattos expected preferential treatment and were sometimes released from slavery. Nevertheless, even after abolition, many were still denied these privileges and were relegated to working in the field, though this was less likely for slaves with lighter skins, who were usually assigned less arduous duties.[89] Victor's monster, deprived of the love of a father and cast aside by his master, parallels the plight of a plantation owner's 'natural' mulatto son, deprived of his rights and freedom. 'Mine', says the creature, 'shall not be the submission of abject slavery' (p. 148), while acknowledging: 'I was the slave, not the master' (p. 222). Rejected by both blacks and whites, the mulatto occupied an interstitial state, akin to the loneliness and isolation of the monster, who complains that even Satan had his devils for companions.[90] The monster's knowledge is derived from reading Milton's *Paradise Lost* (1667). Two conditions for the emancipation of slaves – education and religion – are imparted to him through this single poem, yet it also served to reinforce his sense of social inferiority. Even though he identified himself with Adam, the creature confesses: 'Many times I considered Satan as the fitter emblem of my condition' (p. 132). The perception of himself as a creature of darkness is reinforced by the way in which his maker refers to him as 'devil' (p. 102). Indeed Lewis, on observing the loud jubilation of his slaves, when responding to their head slave driver drinking a toast to the Duchess of York, compared them to Milton's devils on catching sight of Satan's standard. While mulattos usually received greater educational opportunities than black Africans, the downside was that they were tutored in self-contempt through their greater exposure to a culture systemising racial discrimination.[91] Furthermore, they were perceived as having a corrupting influence, partly connected to the nature of their illegitimacy. Mary Shelley refers in disparaging terms to the mixed race of Alessandro de' Medici, the Renaissance Duke of Florence, known as 'the Moor' who, she declares, was 'the natural son of Julius himself, by a negro woman' and 'a man bearing the stamp of a base origin and brutish race, frightful in person, and depraved in soul'.[92] Nora Crook finds this oddly reminiscent of the monster in *Frankenstein*.[93] The friend of Mary Shelley's father, John Thelwall, portrays mulattos as morally dubious in *The Daughter of Adoption*. Here Lucius Moroon, whose name echoes that of 'Maroon', is a plantation owner. The blame for his dissipated character is put on the mulatto servants who brought him up. Thelwall, who disliked mulattos for their 'hoggish voluptuousness', describes them in his novel as 'a set of people in whose composition vices the most atrocious, and virtues the most rare and disinterested, are frequently so confused and blended, that it is sometimes equally difficult to condemn with sufficient abhorrence, or applaud them with sufficient ardour'.[94] Mixed-race children were, to borrow Mary Shelley's expression, the 'hideous progeny' (p. 10) of colonial exploitation, since slave women were frequently the victims of predatory white men. Yet, far more attention was given to the racist stereotype of rebel slaves killing white men and raping white women. The year in which Mary Shelley started writing *Frankenstein*, rebels in Barbados were reported to have flown a flag with the picture of a white woman begging a black chief for mercy.[95]

Lewis writes about this very scenario, the plantation owner's secret horror, in a narrative Gothic poem called 'The Isle of Devils' (1834), written a few months before his arrival at Villa Diodati in 1816 and not published until 1834, the year of emancipation, along with his journal. A 'race of devils' (p. 170) is what Victor fears will ensue from the union of his monster and its mate. Lewis' poem tells of a beautiful Portuguese woman, Irza, and her lover and cousin, Rosalvo, who are shipwrecked on a fantastical island. The ruler of the island behaves like a rebellious slave by killing the man and raping the woman. His stature is in line with stereotypes of the African male: 'Gigantic as the palm, black as the storm, / All shagged with hair, wild, strange in shape and show'.[96] The diabolical nature of Lewis' iron-hoofed 'master-fiend' (p. 169), symbolising a thinly disguised black man, had already appeared in Charlotte Dacre's *Zofloya* (1806), about a Moor who turns out to be the devil. Dacre's novel was published shortly before the abolition of the slave trade in 1807. The relationship between Dacre's villainous heroine Victoria and Zofloya, the Moor, underlines the dangers of miscegenation. At the end of Lewis' *The Monk*, which Mary Shelley read before writing *Frankenstein*, Ambrosio is offered a chance of escape from the Inquisition by Lucifer, who again is represented as black: 'A swarthy darkness spread itself over his gigantic form' (p. 356). The price of Ambrosio's freedom, in exchange for his soul, is couched in the language of slavery: 'Answer but "Yes!" and Lucifer is your slave' (p. 357). In Lewis' poem, prefaced with an extract from *The Tempest*, the Caliban figure is consumed with lust for the fair, white-skinned and blue-eyed virgin Irza. Her 'savage lord' wears beads of shells, crystals and seeds.[97] Having saved Irza from being eaten by dwarfs, the demon monarch offers her marriage. After being forcibly impregnated by him, Irza laments that she is now 'A monster's mother, and a demon's wife'[98] in what must surely be a sublimation of the fear and horror surrounding miscegenation.[99] A repeat of her ordeal leads to another birth. This time she provides a human son, whose skin is so snowy white that the blood is visible beneath his skin. Not surprisingly, it is the child mirroring her own self-image who is favoured by Irza and subsequently cherished. As Ellen Malenas points out, this is comparable to the favouritism that a white planter might show towards his child of mixed race with light-coloured skin.[100] Irza's rejection of her other offspring forces the demon king into adopting a mothering role by breastfeeding the monstrous child himself. Mindful of the importance of suckling for ensuring the survival of babies born on the plantation, Lewis granted indulgences to nursing mothers.[101] The nurturing side of parenting is something that Victor

Frankenstein, as a single parent, signally neglects. In Lewis' poem, Irza eventually escapes and, like Victor, abandons her offspring, having been told by monks on the rescue ship that they are diabolical creatures. To her horror, she witnesses the demon killing her children and then himself. According to Lewis' biographer D. L. Macdonald, the demon king is 'clearly a black slave, as re-created by the guilty and fearful fantasy of a white slave-owner', whose 'suicide suggests that the slave, however savage and rebellious, cannot survive without his master'.[102] At the end of *Frankenstein*, the monster also sets out to commit suicide after witnessing the dead body of his maker/master. In a valediction to him, there is the suggestion that he would have continued to live had his maker survived: 'Farewell, Frankenstein! If thou wert yet alive and yet cherished a desire of revenge against me, it would be better satiated in my life than in my destruction' (p. 225). As Lewis indicates, the greatest fear of his slaves was to be without a master whom they knew, while to be accused of belonging 'to no massa' was considered shameful.[103] In spite of this, Lewis continued to be an absentee master. Indeed, his sustained intervention at the Hordley estate might have brought about a more humane regime. But it was not to be. During his second trip to Jamaica, Lewis visited Hordley, his real-life equivalent of his 'Isle of Devils', and admitted: 'I felt strongly tempted to set off as fast as I could, and leave all these black devils and white ones to tear one another to pieces'.[104] It was hardly a reassuring picture of inter-race relations.

The 'hideous progeny', resulting from the union between the demon king and Irza, consolidated anxieties surrounding miscegenation, for which Lewis appeared to have a 'loathing' and 'moral revulsion'.[105] Mary Shelley's monster, with his yellow skin, glossy black hair and black lips, bears the inscription of mixed race. She may have responded to Bryan Edwards' description of the African Eboe people as having a sickly yellow complexion.[106] In her biography, Miranda Seymour argues that Shelley's nameless creature's 'yellow skin, black hair and giant limbs allowed her to combine contemporary perceptions of the Eastern "lascars" with the African and West Indian', while Anne K. Mellor has looked at the creature's yellow skin as emblematic of the 'yellow peril', signalling alarm from the direction of China.[107] But by far the most common use of 'yellow' is to denote the skin colour of mixed race. Lewis refers to the inhabitants of Jamaica as black, white and yellow, a colour coding commonly used by ethnographers. He was familiar with Long's classification of race, which included his designation of 'black or yellow quasheba' for women whom he regarded as succubus-like in preying on susceptible European men who had succumbed to their 'goatish embraces'.[108] Their reputation as temptresses is picked up in the conversation of a dinner guest reported by Lady Nugent, wife of the Governor of Jamaica, in which 'black and yellow women' are referred to as serpents.[109] The overseer of her estate was a Scotsman, who had fathered 'three yellow children' with a black woman whose ebony skin was 'highly polished and shining'.[110] Edwards, like Long, was particularly preoccupied with distinctions of race, colour and caste and designated the original inhabitants of the Caribbean islands yellow Charaibes. That his work had engrossed Mary Shelley is evident from her journal.[111]

In 1819, the year after *Frankenstein* was published, George Cruikshank produced a scurrilous cartoon called *The New Union Club of 1819* in response to an anti-abolitionist pamphlet.[112] The print purports to depict a dinner at the African Club for liberal Europeans and liberated blacks. Abolitionists are caricatured, most notably Wilberforce, who lifts a glass to toast 'the black joke' in undignified proximity to a commode. Cruickshank's racist implication was that instead of blacks becoming more civilised through this interracial contact, it was whites who were turning into uncouth savages.[113] In the background, a picture entitled 'The King of Hayti and his Black-guards' serves as a sober reminder of what happens when blacks get the upper hand. Vituperative allusions are made to mixed race. From a Quaker's mouth streams, 'Hail! piebald pledge of Love', onto an anarchic scene in which black women are pouncing on white men to demonstrate the dangers of miscegenation. A black father and a white mother proudly display their mixed-race baby, whose body is vertically divided by two broad stripes, making it literally half black and white (Figure 4). By the 1820s, mulattos in Jamaica were more numerous than the white population. Their ringleaders were especially feared, like Edward Jordan, the leader of the free mulattos, who had called for an end to slavery. While the men were seen as potential mutineers, mulatto women were widely believed to be concupiscent.[114] In a patronising jingle, Lewis writes that to become a housekeeper to a white man (whose duties often extended to those of mistress), the mulatto girl 'directs her aim; / This makes her happiness, and this her fame'.[115] Similarly, Victor speculates that his female monster might reject her monstrous experimental counterpart for the 'superior beauty of man' (p. 170). For Charles White, a Manchester surgeon and lecturer, Europeans topped a hierarchy of racial aesthetics as the most 'beautiful of the human race', while at the opposite end lay

Figure 4 Detail from George Cruikshank, *The New Union Club of 1819* (1819). Here a mixed-race baby is satirised and William Wilberforce is seen rising from a commode as he toasts the assembly.

the Negro, whom he regarded as closer to 'the brute creation than any other of the human species'.[116] Mary Shelley's observations on foreigners during a tour around Europe are recorded in a vitriolic journal entry made on 28 August 1814, where she wrote:

> We stopped at Mettingen to dine and there surveyed at our ease the horrid
> and slimy faces of our companions in voyage – our only wish was to absolutely
> annihilate such uncleansable animals, to whom we might have addressed the
> boatman's speech to Pope – "T'were easier for God to make entirely new men
> than attempt to purify such monsters as these.'[117]

It appears that Victor's endeavour to build his new Adam and improve
on God's creation was to create an 'entirely new' man along the lines of
another species. This ties into the polygenic view that different races did
not necessarily have a common ancestry.

Victor was determined to eradicate disease and render 'man invulner-
able to any but a violent death!' (p. 42). Like those advancing civilisation
at the cost of slavery, Victor, in the name of scientific discovery, unleashed
destruction onto the world. He feared a further escalation if he created a
new Eve and even if the monster and his mate were to venture far from
Europe to the 'deserts of the new world', they could still propagate a 'race
of devils', who 'might make the very existence of the species of man a condition precarious and full of terror' (pp. 170–1). For pro-slavers, this tied
in with fears that escaped or freed slaves would turn on their former cap-
tors. There was apprehension concerning the return of liberated slaves
to the African colony of Sierra Leone and fears over the insurgents who
founded the Black Empire of Haiti. The fugitives joining Maroon communities of Jamaica precipitated years of warfare against the British. The
risk for Victor, in allowing his female creature to live and subsequently
breed, is encapsulated in his rhetorical question: 'Had I a right, for my
own benefit, to inflict this curse upon everlasting generations?' (p. 171).

Eventually he resolves the dilemma by tearing apart the female creature
he was creating, whom he refers to as the 'thing' (p. 171), a designation used
by Granville Sharp to denote a slave's lack of legal and political rights.[118]
Unlike his master, however, the monster, after receiving a cruel beating from
Felix De Lacey, the most common punishment for slaves, resists tearing his
assailant apart 'as the lion rends the antelope' (p. 137). Tellingly, this is an
image more commonly associated with the African plains than with the
European forest, where the monster is actually located. Victor destroys his
monstrous female companion because he fears that she will be 'ten thousand
times more malignant than her mate, and delight, for its own sake, in murder and wretchedness' (p. 170). At a time when tens of thousands of slaves
were nursing the grievance of slavery, the ripping apart of the female monster can be seen as emblematic of the tearing up of the immediate prospects

of emancipating slaves, in favour of the delaying tactics of many influential ameliorists.

FEMALE SLAVES AND THE *BRIDE OF FRANKENSTEIN*

Victor's specific concern with the dangers of the female might also be a sublimation of fears relating to women leaders of rebel slaves and the threat that their conduct posed for femininity itself. The escaped slave Nanny of the Windward Maroons was the most notorious female leader. She had taken part in the Maroon war against the British, which ended in 1739. According to Herbert T. Thomas, this 'Maroon Amazon' was of mythical proportions being 'ten times more ferocious and blood-thirsty than any man among the maroons', language that reiterates Victor's alarm that his female creature will be 'ten thousand times more malignant than her mate'.[119] Thomas gathered information from oral traditions while researching his travelogue, *Untrodden Jamaica* (1890), where he traces his journey from the Blue Mountains to Nanny Town. An earlier account of an old obeah woman widely believed to be Nanny was recorded by Philip Thicknesse in his *Memoirs and Anecdotes* (1790). As a lieutenant whose mission was to seek out Maroons, Thicknesse describes entering Quao's Town, where he discovers that a soldier has been beheaded. Quao, one of the rebel leaders, had wanted to spare the soldier's life, but was over-ruled by an old obeah woman wearing a girdle around her waist with 'nine or ten different knives hanging in sheaths to it [*sic*], many of which I have no doubt, had been plunged in human flesh and blood'.[120] Thicknesse was fearful for himself and his men that at any moment, 'that horrid wretch, their Obea [*sic*] woman would demand their deaths'.[121] Whites, terrified by her reputation, joyfully received the news that she had been killed by a loyal Negro.[122] As a co-operative Negro, Nanny's assassin was diametrically opposed to the 'wild negro'. This was how planters regarded the Maroon, whose name derives from the Spanish '*cimarrón*' for savage or wild. The return of these fugitives to an African culture, recreated illicitly in the Caribbean, effectively wiped out the initial three-year conditioning or 'seasoning' process carried out on the plantation. By rescuing a reported 800 slaves and integrating them into the Maroon community, Nanny was regarded by the plantocracy as instrumental in encouraging slaves to renege on their civilising influences, thus atavistically returning them to an earlier phase of bloodthirsty savageness.

Figure 5 *Love and Beauty: Sartjee, the Hottentot Venus* (1810). Baartman's association with the erotic is indicated by the cupid perched on her pronounced buttocks, who is saying 'Take care of your hearts'.

Note: This was published in October 1810 by Christopher Crupper Rumford. Westminster City Archives, Broadley, BP/2/361.

A female rebel in more recent memory, who was active during the writing of *Frankenstein*, is Nanny Grigg. She had worked as a senior domestic slave on the Simmons' plantation in Barbados and, in 1816, helped plan the slave revolt on the island. Grigg had actually set the date for the uprising against plantation owners and the First West India Regiment. What distinguished this revolt from others was that it aimed to influence the campaign for emancipation in Britain. It was not a spontaneous or hastily planned uprising, but a carefully orchestrated rebellion organised by elite slaves on a number of Barbadian plantations. While Frankenstein's destruction of his embryonic female monster was partly prompted by her potentially violent threat to mankind, which was akin to that of rebel female slaves, her inchoate existence was more in tune with the passivity of the Hottentot Venus.

This was the name given to a South African Khoisan woman called Saartjie, or Sarah, Baartman, who is another possible model for the female monster.[123] Brought over from Africa, she became a symbol of slavery, even though she was never an actual slave. Known as the Hottentot Venus, Baartman was exhibited as a freak show attraction in Europe and arrived in London in 1810. Like the Frankenstein creature's mate, she too was subjected to the scientific gaze. Baartman performed as a nude tableau, aside from the modest use of a handkerchief with which to cover her pudenda. But it was this very region that attracted the scientists' most intense interest, owing to its suspected abnormality. In common with Victor Frankenstein, they were eager to pursue 'nature to her hiding-places' (p. 55). Baartman's genitals, especially her enlarged labia, were studied as a marker of sexual difference and put on public display after her death, along with her brain, skeleton and body cast. Body parts of Khoisan people had been collected as exhibits by Europeans, who had even used women's breasts as tobacco pouches.[124] One member of the scientific team was Geoffroy Saint-Hilaire, who founded the science of teratology, the study of malformations in the natural world. Baartman was called a monster and, as her biographer Rachel Holmes pointed out: 'European racism made Saartjie a Frankenstein's monster of its own invention.'[125] After her death, in December 1815, she was dissected as an anatomical specimen to advance the pseudo-science surrounding studies of race and 'to reveal', in terms relevant to *Frankenstein*, 'the deepest mysteries of creation encoded in African female sexuality'.[126] Peter Kitson sees her mutilation as parodied in Victor Frankenstein's act of tearing apart his female monster.[127] In 1816, the results of Baartman's anatomical dissection were first published.[128] A later version was produced the following year by the French anatomist Georges Cuvier. His brother described him in terms foreshadowing Victor Frankenstein, as 'master of the charnel house'.[129] Cuvier, whose brother owned a zoo, compared Baartman to a monkey and an orang-utan. Her simian status formed part of his polygenetic quest to find the missing link between animal and human. An early pre-Darwinian evolutionist was James Burnett, Lord Monboddo, who is ridiculed as Sir Oran Haut-Ton, a civilised orang-utan standing as a Member of Parliament in Thomas Peacock's *Melincourt* (1817), a novel admired by Byron, Mary and Percy Shelley. Even the Shelleys' physician Dr William Lawrence entered into the debate on species versus race through a series of lectures, which he later published.[130] Percy Shelley went to consult him on a medical matter in 1815, around the time when Mary was staying in Bristol, where she may have encountered ex-slaves. Lawrence rejected the idea that there were different 'human' species, reasoning that theorists arguing to the contrary were attempting to justify the slave trade, which he opposed. Yet his critic, George D'Oyly, slammed his diatribes on the racial inferiority of blacks as likely to obliterate any qualms of conscience a slave driver might feel in the West Indies when herding slaves like oxen.[131] Despite blasting 'filthy Hottentots' and declaring that 'the Negro is more like a monkey than the European', Lawrence nevertheless condemned the identification of the African with the orang-utan, as 'shocking and detestable'.[132]

The Hottentot Venus personifies the nineteenth-century confusion between species and race, which generated the fallacy of biological racial difference. Although the Frankenstein monster, a combination of the animal and human, is conceived as a different species, Victor's creation also provides an effective metaphor of how mixed race was perceived at that time. The derogatory term 'mulatto' derives from the Spanish for 'young mule' and, through this etymology, has associations with colonialism, slavery and racial oppression. This semantic derivation is a reminder of how slavery not only reduced many masters and slaves to the level of brutes but also how it turned men, women and children into chattels, whose status Granville Sharp compared to that of a horse or dog.[133] Despite his liberal intentions, Lewis could not resist comparing his relationship with his slaves to that of a master and his dog.[134] This image of a domesticated trained animal, applicable to the seasoned obedient slave, contrasts with a metaphor used to describe the Saint-Domingue rebels: 'The Negro race … are but a set of wild beasts let loose.'[135] Shelley's creature uses similar language, comparing himself to a wild animal: 'I gave vent to my anguish in fearful howlings. I was like a wild beast that had broken the toils, destroying the objects that obstructed me and ranging through the wood with a staglike swiftness' (p. 138). He is also described as an animal and 'beast of prey' (p. 203), who is hunted and wounded by gunshot.

In line with the colonial pursuit of big game hunting, the Hottentot Venus represented a kind of living trophy. As a liminal figure, she was also a cross between ethnographical specimen and eroticised spectacle. The main attention of the viewing public was directed towards her extreme steatopygia, or protruding buttocks (Figure 5). As Sander Gilman points out, the black female during the nineteenth century was defined by her sexual parts, which were pathologised.[136] The buttocks were regarded as signifiers for anomalies of the genitalia. According to myth, Nanny of the Maroons resisted British military force by catching bullets in her buttocks and farting them out. This lurid depiction of a revolutionary black woman reduces the defence of her people to an undue emphasis on her posterior. For black men, white attention was on the penis. The myth of black men having larger genitalia than their white counterparts was bound up with fears of miscegenation. A belief in the greater potency, animal libido and physical strength of the black man was contrived by a racist society to pose a threat to white men and women. Their fears related to equality and assimilation, and culminated in the horror of black domination, all of which helped fuel the disturbing racial myth that black, rather than white men, are more likely to be rapists of white women.

James Whale's film *Frankenstein* (1931) and the sequel *Bride of Frankenstein*, which appeared four years later, have both been viewed as commentaries on racial issues arising from the legacy of slavery in America. As Elizabeth Young has argued, the monster's 'sexualized advances to the film's women encode racist American discourse of the 1930s on masculinity, femininity, rape, and lynching'. The first half of the 1930s, when the films were made, witnessed an increase in the lynching of young black men, along with a rise in the barbarity of such attacks.[137] Castration was the lynch mob's favoured form of emasculating black men accused of raping white women. Up to the turn of the twentieth century, there were attempts to legalise castration as a punishment exclusively for black men convicted of rape, and even for those attempting to carry out the crime.[138] A famous legal case spanning the 1930s was that of 'The Scottsboro Boys', in which an all-white Southern jury sentenced eight black teenagers to death for the alleged rape of two white women in Alabama. The verdict was widely seen as a miscarriage of justice and was indicative of the endemic racism within the court system of the Deep South. The National Association for the Advancement of Colored People campaigned for an anti-lynching bill but was defeated in 1935, the year that saw the release of *Bride of Frankenstein*. In the film, the monster, represented as sub-human, delinquent, brutish, criminal and mentally inferior, reproduced contemporary negative stereotypes of black men.[139] Film-makers were anxious to avoid inciting racial conflict with images that were too explicit, and Young cites an example of the restraint shown in an anti-lynching film.[140] Nevertheless, the scene in which the monster is pursued by an angry crowd resembles that of an American torch-carrying lynch mob.[141] As Michael Grant observed, the flaming sails of the windmill resemble the burning cross of the Ku Klux Klan.[142] One member of the crowd gloats over the monster's 'blackened bones' in language that, in the context of the times, is racially charged, especially as vigilantes would spend hours gazing at smouldering remains. A shocking image of the charred remains of Will Brown, lynched for the alleged rape of a white teenage girl in Omaha, Nebraska, was used as a postcard in 1919. Young sees the inscription of the racist myth of rape and race overlaying the scene in which the monster in Whale's earlier *Frankenstein* film enters Elizabeth's bedroom. Here he finds her moaning in terror: 'Don't let it come here' (p. 325). By contrast, in the casting of Nick Dear's fairly recent theatrical adaptation, the rape is enacted on a black Elizabeth by a white monster.[143] In *Bride of Frankenstein*, a racial subtext is apparent when the monster is rejected with horror by two white women, Elizabeth and his own reluctant monstrous bride. At the end of the film, the male and female monsters die in a fire in Henry's laboratory, along with his villainous co-creator, Dr Pretorius, whose yarmulke and alchemist's homunculi code him as Jewish. In the conclusion to the novel, Frankenstein's creature goes off into the Arctic wastes until he is 'lost in darkness and distance' (p. 225), in a final purging of the racial Other.

NOTES

1 Lewis, *The Monk*, ed. Macdonald and Scherf, p. 237.
2 Thomas Day, *The Dying Negro* (London: Flexney, Wilkie and Robson, 1775), p. 2. The spelling has been modernised.
3 Quoted in James Walvin, *A Short History of Slavery* (London: Penguin Books, 2007), p. 164.
4 Quoted in D. L. Macdonald, *Monk Lewis: A Critical Biography* (Toronto: University of Toronto Press, 2000), p. 206.
5 See H. L. Malchow, *Gothic Images of Race in Nineteenth-Century Britain* (Stanford, CA: Stanford University Press, 1996), pp. 10 and 38–9.

6   Mary Shelley, *Frankenstein or The Modern Prometheus*, ed. Maurice Hindle (London: Penguin [1818], 2007), p. 78. Subsequent references are made parenthetically in the text.

7   See Allan Lloyd Smith, '"This Thing of Darkness": Racial Discourse in Mary Shelley's *Frankenstein*', *Gothic Studies*, 6:2 (2004), 208–22. For an argument focusing more on the African American slave, see Elizabeth Young, *Black Frankenstein: The Making of an American Metaphor* (New York: New York University Press, 2008), pp. 19–67.

8   See Malchow, *Gothic Images of Race*, p. 16.

9   See Eliza Fenwick, *Secresy; or, The Ruin on the Rock*, ed. Isobel Grundy (Peterborough, Ontario: Broadview [1795], 1994), pp. 18, 10 and 14.

10 See Caroline Bressey and Tom Wareham, *Reading the London Sugar and Slavery Gallery* (London: Museum of London Docklands, 2010), p. 36.

11 Quoted in Madge Dresser, *Slavery Obscured: The Social History of the Slave Trade in Bristol* (Bristol: Redcliffe Press [2001], 2007), p. 209.

12 See Walvin, *A Short History of Slavery*, p. 197.

13 Creole slaves were born locally into slavery and thought to be more tractable than free-born Africans taken as slaves. Because Creoles were thought to be more acclimatised to the condition, their rebellion was all the more unexpected.

14 George Canning, *The Parliamentary Debates*, House of Commons, 16 March 1824, col. 1103, http://www.hansardarchive.parliament.uk/Parliamentary_Debates,_New_Series_Vol_1_(April_1820)to_Vol_25_(July_1830) S2V0010P0.zip. Accessed 5 February 2013.

15 For a summary of the play, see H. Philip Bolton, *Women Writers Dramatized: A Calendar of Performances from Narrative Works Published in English to 1900* (London: Mansell Publishing, 2000), pp. 276–7.

16 Richard Cumberland, *The Wheel of Fortune*, in *The British Theatre or a Collection of Plays*, 25 vols (London: Longman, Hurst, Rees and Orme, 1808), 18, p. 27.

17 *The Letters of Mary Wollstonecraft Shelley*, ed. Betty T. Bennett, 3 vols (Baltimore, MD: Johns Hopkins University Press, 1980–8), vol. 1: *A Part of the Elect*, p. 417.

18 Mary Shelley, letter to Teresa Guiccioli, 20 August 1827, *Letters*, translated by Ricki Herzfeld for Bennett, 1, p. 566.

19 Miranda Seymour, *Mary Shelley* (London: Picador, 2001), p. 335.

20 See Bressey and Wareham, *Reading the London Sugar and Slavery Gallery*, p. 36.

21 I am grateful to Nora Crook for this clarification.

22 See Nigel Sadler, *The Slave Trade* (Oxford: Shire Publications, 2009), p. 42.

23 Quoted in James Bieri, *Percy Bysshe Shelley: A Biography - Youth's Unextinguished Fire, 1792-1816* (Newark, DE: University of Delaware Press, 2004), p. 389.

24 Percy Bysshe Shelley, *The Complete Poetical Works of Percy Bysshe Shelley*, ed. Thomas Hutchinson (London: Oxford University Press, 1935), p. 33.

25 See H. L. Malchow, 'Frankenstein's Monster and Images of Race in Nineteenth-Century Britain', *Past and Present*, 139 (1993), 95–6.

26 See Seymour, *Mary Shelley*, p. 162. Here she notes that summaries of *The Times* were made available for travellers on the Continent through *Galignani's Messenger*. This seems to suggest that the report was read by the Shelleys, who were travelling there at the time, but there is no evidence for this. They would have known of the Sierra Leone colony.

27 See Emily Sunstein, *Mary Shelley: Romance and Reality* (Baltimore, MD: Johns Hopkins University Press, 1991), p. 285.

28 See Chris Baldick, *In Frankenstein's Shadow: Myth, Monstrosity and Nineteenth-Century Writing* (Oxford: Clarendon Press, 1987), p. 10.

29 In addition, Mary Shelley made passing remarks on slavery elsewhere. During her travels around Europe, she comments that 'the Swiss', being 'a people slow of comprehension and of action', has made them 'unfit for slavery'; *History of a Six Weeks' Tour through a Part of France, Switzerland, Germany, and Holland; with Letters Descriptive of a Sail round the Lake of Geneva and of the Glaciers of Chamouni* (London: T. Hookham Jun. and C. and J. Ollier, 1817), p. 50.

30 Quoted in Nora Crook, 'Counting the Carbonari: A Newly Attributed Mary Shelley Article', *Keats-Shelley Review*, 23 (2009), 49. This is from a piece of political journalism recently attributed to the Mary Shelley canon by Nora Crook, where Shelley writes: 'Mr Cobbett says: "The treatment of the Jews has been a subject of great outcry with English Protestant visitors at Rome. But if we are to judge by the vicious example of this people, in all that relates to dealings between man and man, how could the Roman government justify itself for placing them on a footing with their Christian subjects?"'; Mary Shelley, 'Review of J. P. Cobbett, *Journal of a Tour in Italy*', *Westminster Review*, 14 (January 1831), 179. Mary Shelley's attitudes towards Jews are also discussed in Chapter 4.

31 Some doubt has been cast on the extent of Paine's abolitionist stance; see James V. Lynch, 'The Limits of Revolutionary Radicalism: Tom Paine and Slavery', *Pennsylvania Magazine of History and Biography*, 123 (July 1999), 177–99.

32 John Thelwall, *The Daughter of Adoption: A Tale of Modern Times*, ed. Michael Scrivener, Yasmin Solomonescu and Judith Thompson (Peterborough, Ontario: Broadview, 2013), p. 484.

33 See Malchow, *Gothic Images of Race*, p. 14.

34 Wil Verhoeven, *Gilbert Imlay: Citizen of the World* (London: Pickering & Chatto, 2008), p. 93. See also his chapter 4, 'Slave Trader', pp. 83–91. In his novel *The Emigrants* (1793), like Wollstonecraft, Imlay makes use of the

discourse of enslavement in relation to tyranny in marriage; see Verhoeven, *Gilbert Imlay*, pp. 130–1.

35 Quoted in Verhoeven, *Gilbert Imlay*, p. 83.

36 Anon., *Cuffy the Negro's Doggrel Description of the Progress of Sugar* (London: E. Wallis, 1823).

37 Her journal for that period is lost. Having left Torquay where she had been lodging with P. B. Shelley until the end of June, it is probable that Mary stayed in Bristol for the month of July and a few days into August. This was while P. B. Shelley was away house-hunting. She would have been worried that he might have met up with Claire Claremont, with whom an affair has been suspected. Her anxiety over their long separation is evident in the letter she wrote to him from Clifton on 27 July. Had she remained in Torquay it is likely that she would have referred to the landing of Napoleon on 24 July in Devon, which she does not. I owe these observations to Nora Crook.

38 In May 1814, the Treaty of Paris, which had come out of the Napoleonic War, contained a resolution to abolish the French slave trade, though not slavery itself, over a five-year period. Five months later, French traders were striving to reinstate their trading rights. British people reacted by sending 806 petitions of protest to the House of Commons.

39 See *Felix Farley's Bristol Journal* for 2, 9 and 16 July 1815.

40 Quoted in Sadler, *The Slave Trade*, p. 54.

41 I am indebted to Madge Dresser for this point. By 1834, the year of emancipation, there were 70 slaves-owners living in Bristol, 58 of whom garnered £829, 205 compensation for the loss of their slaves, the equivalent of £70.1 million in today's money. http://www.bristolpost.co.uk/FAMILY/story-26892102-detail/story.html. Accessed 14 July 2015.

42 See E. J. Clery, *Women's Gothic: From Clara Reeve to Mary Shelley* (Tavistock: Northcote House, 2004), p. 47.

43 Quoted in A. A. Markley, *Conversion and Reform in the British Novel in the 1790s: A Revolution of Opinions* (London: Palgrave Macmillan, 2009), p. 103.

44 See Bryan Edwards, *The History, Civil and Commercial of the British West Indies*, 5 vols (Boston, MA: Elibron Classics [1819], 2005), 2, p. 143.

45 See Anne K. Mellor, *Mary Shelley: Her Life, Her Fiction, Her Monsters* (London: Routledge, 1988), p. 77.

46 John Milton, *Paradise Lost: A Poem* (London: S. Simmons, 2nd edn, 1674), Book I, ll. 65–7.

47 Quoted in Seymour, *Mary Shelley*, p. 138.

48 Edwards, *History*, 2, p. 78.

49 Quoted in Adam Hochschild, *Bury the Chains: The British Struggle to Abolish Slavery* (London: Macmillan, 2005), p. 261.

50 This forms a parallel with Matthew Lewis' description of how a fifteen-year-old black servant girl, who claims to be innocent, is executed for a murder. See

Journal of a West India Proprietor, ed. Judith Terry (Oxford: Oxford University Press [1834], 1999), p. 111. For a discussion of the possible influence of this work on *Frankenstein*, see the next section of this chapter.

51 Thelwall, *The Daughter of Adoption*, p. 24.

52 See Edwards, *History*, 3, pp. 73–4.

53 Quoted in Edwards, *History*, 3, p. 99.

54 See Hochschild, *Bury the Chains*, p. 276.

55 Quoted in Hochschild, *Bury the Chains*, p. 257.

56 See Christopher Z. Hobson, *The Chained Boy: Orc and Blake's Idea of Revolution* (London: Associated University Presses, 1999), p. 111.

57 Edwards, *History*, 3, p. 67.

58 Mary Shelley, *The Journals of Mary Shelley 1814–1844*, ed. Paula K. Feldman and Diana Scott-Kilvert (Baltimore, MD: Johns Hopkins University Press [1987], 1995), p. 52. Quotations from the original journals have been corrected. The reference to 'prejudice' alludes to religion rather than to race in this context.

59 See Malchow, *Gothic Images of Race*, pp. 14–21.

60 Mungo Park, *Travels in the Interior of Africa* (Ware: Wordsworth Editions [1799], 2002), p. 111.

61 Lewis includes a Negro poem about a penitent fugitive called 'The Runaway'. See *Journal*, pp. 76–7.

62 France abolished the slave trade in 1818, the same year that *Frankenstein* was first published.

63 Park, *Travels*, p. 74.

64 Quoted in Hochschild, *Bury the Chains*, p. 257.

65 See Park, *Travels*, p. 296.

66 This took place in Grenada in 1795. See Hochschild, *Bury the Chains*, p. 275.

67 Lewis, *Journal*, pp. 102–3.

68 Ellen Malenas Ledoux, *Social Reform in Gothic Writing: Fantastic Forms of Change, 1764–1834* (Basingstoke: Palgrave Macmillan, 2013), p. 196.

69 See Bieri, *Percy Bysshe Shelley*, p. 389.

70 See M. G. Lewis, letter to William Wilberforce, 16 October 1817, *The Correspondence of William Wilberforce*, ed. Robert Isaac Wilberforce and Samuel Wilberforce, 2 vols (London: John Murray, 1840), 2, p. 383.

71 Shelley, *Journals*, p. 130.

72 Quoted in Macdonald, *Monk Lewis*, p. 56.

73 Lewis, *The Castle Spectre*, p. 196.

74 See Ledoux, *Social Reform in Gothic Writing*, p. 162.

75 Edwards, *History*, 2, p. 101.

76 Malchow, *Gothic Images of Race*, p. 21.

77 Lewis, *Journal*, p. 92.

78 This had taken place during 15–26 March 1816.

79   See Lewis, *Journal*, p. 137.
80   See Macdonald, *Monk Lewis*, p. 23, n.
81   See Macdonald, *Monk Lewis*, p. 209.
82   Matthew Gregory Lewis, *The Life and Correspondence of M. G. Lewis*, 2 vols (London: Henry Colburn, 1839), 2, p. 161.
83   See Thomas Medwin, *Conversations of Lord Byron* (London: Henry Colburn, 1824), p. 293.
84   Edwards, *History*, 2, p. 176.
85   Edward Long, *History of Jamaica*, 3 vols (London: T. Lowndes, 1774), 2, p. 335.
86   See Kenneth F. Kiple, *The Caribbean Slave: A Biological History* (Cambridge: Cambridge University Press, 1985), pp. 120–34.
87   See Lewis, *Journal*, p. 79.
88   See Macdonald, *Monk Lewis*, p. 57.
89   See Walvin, *A Short History of Slavery*, p. 203.
90   'It very frequently happens that the lowest White person, considering himself as greatly superior to the richest and best-educated Free man of Colour, will disdain to associate with a person of the latter description [...]. To the Negroes they are objects of envy and hatred; for the same or a greater degree of superiority which the Whites assume over *them*, the free Mulattoes lay claim to over the Blacks'; Edwards, *History*, 2, pp. 23–4.
91   See Malchow, *Gothic Images of Race*, p. 30.
92   Mary Shelley, 'Modern Italian Romances', *The Monthly Chronicle*, 2 (July–December 1838), 547.
93   As Nora Crook pointed out to me, Mary Shelley's essay indicates that the 'whole race' of Medici was detested by Florentines and therefore we should not infer from this that she disapproved of miscegenation or regarded black people as 'brutish'.
94   Thelwall, *The Daughter of Adoption*, pp. 20 and 208.
95   See Malchow, *Gothic Images of Race*, p. 26.
96   Lewis, *Journal*, p. 169.
97   Lewis, *Journal*, p. 178.
98   Lewis, *Journal*, p. 173.
99   Kerry Sinanan explored miscegenation in 'Beauty and the Breast: Contextualising Matthew Lewis "Isle of Devils"', presented at the University of the West of England, Bristol, Staff Research Seminars in April 2010.
100 See Ellen Malenas, 'Reform Ideology and Generic Structure in Matthew Lewis' Journal of a West India Proprietor', *Studies in Eighteenth-Century Culture*, 35 (2006), 45.
101 See Lewis, *Journal*, p. 251.
102 Macdonald, *Monk Lewis*, p. 199.
103 Lewis, *Journal*, p. 46.

104 Lewis, *Journal*, p. 229.
105 Quoted in Lisa Nevárez, ' "Monk" Lewis' "The Isle of Devils" and the Perils of Colonialism', *Romanticism and Victorianism on the Net*, 50 (May 2008), www .erudit.org/revue/ravon/2008/v/n50/018147ar.html. Accessed 3 May 2013.
106 Malchow, *Gothic Images of Race*, p. 18.
107 Seymour, *Mary Shelley*, p. 139. See also Anne K. Mellor, '*Frankenstein*, Racial Science, and the Yellow Peril', *Nineteenth-Century Contexts*, 23 (2001), 1–28.
108 Quoted in Trevor Burnard, 'The Planter Class', in Gad Heuman and Trevor Burnard (eds), *The Routledge History of Slavery* (London: Routledge, 2011), p. 195.
109 Maria Nugent, *Lady Nugent's Journal of Her Residence in Jamaica from 1801 to 1805*, ed. Philip Wright (Kingston: Institute of Jamaica, 1966), p. 12.
110 Nugent, *Lady Nugent's Journal*, p. 29.
111 Shelley, *Journals*, p. 58.
112 This pamphlet was Joseph Marryat's *More Thoughts Still on the State of the West India Colonies and the Proceedings of the African Institution with Observations on the Speech of James Stephen Esq.* (1818). The author was a Member of Parliament and agent for the island of Grenada.
113 For example, a Quaker lies flat on the floor with his mouth open, into which a black footman vomits (see Figure 4), and a white sailor is mistreated by a black one. The thrust of the caricature's invective was the plight of the labouring poor, which had been sidelined by the campaign against slavery. See Marcus Wood, *Blind Memory: Visual Representations of Slavery in England and America 1780–1865* (Manchester: Manchester University Press, 2000), p. 166.
114 See Long, *History of Jamaica*, 2, p. 335.
115 Lewis, *Journal*, p. 106.
116 Quoted in Peter Kitson, *Romantic Literature, Race, and Colonial Encounter* (Basingstoke: Palgrave Macmillan, 2007), p. 18.
117 Shelley, *Journals*, pp. 20–1. Punctuation corrected.
118 See Walvin, *A Short History of Slavery*, p. 164.
119 Quoted in Jenny Sharpe, *Ghosts of Slavery: A Literary Archaeology of Black Women's Lives* (Minneapolis, MN: University of Minnesota Press, 2003), p. 12.
120 Quoted in Sharpe, *Ghosts of Slavery*, p. 27.
121 Quoted in Sharpe, *Ghosts of Slavery*, p. 27.
122 He shares his name, William Cuffee, with the compliant slave of the juvenile engravings printed by Mary Shelley's neighbour.
123 Baartman's brain had been used in an argument about Negro emancipation in the United States. See Rachel Holmes, *The Hottentot Venus* (London: Bloomsbury, 2008), p. 156. Zachary Macaulay, a founding member of the African Institution, argued that she was being treated as a slave. See Holmes, *The Hottentot Venus*, pp. 92–3.

124 See Holmes, *The Hottentot Venus*, p. 15.

125 Holmes, *The Hottentot Venus*, p. 184. The *Journal général de France* criticised Réaux, her new 'owner', for not having 'his monster vaccinated' against smallpox; quoted in Holmes, *The Hottentot Venus*, p. 160.

126 Holmes, *The Hottentot Venus*, p. 164.

127 See Kitson, *Romantic Literature*, p. 83.

128 The results were written up initially by Henri Ducrotay de Blainville. See Sander L. Gilman, *Difference and Pathology: Stereotypes of Sexuality, Race, and Madness* (Ithaca, NY: Cornell University Press, 1985), p. 85.

129 Quoted in Holmes, *The Hottentot Venus*, p. 164.

130 Lawrence has also been discussed in relation to *Frankenstein* over his position as a materialist as opposed to the vitalism of John Abernethy, a debate that has been seen as pertinent to the novel. See the introduction to *Frankenstein*, ed. Marilyn Butler (Oxford: Oxford World's Classics, 1993), pp. xv–xxi.

131 See Kitson, *Romantic Literature*, p. 100.

132 William Lawrence, *Lectures on Physiology, Zoology and the Natural History of Man* (London: Benbow [1819], 1822), pp. 108 and 211.

133 See Walvin, *A Short History of Slavery*, p. 164.

134 See Lewis, *Journal*, p. 76.

135 Quoted in Hochschild, *Bury the Chains*, p. 260.

136 See Gilman, *Difference and Pathology*, p. 88.

137 See Elizabeth Young, 'Here Comes the Bride: Wedding Gender and Race in *Bride of Frankenstein*', in Barry Keith Grant (ed.), *The Dread of Difference: Gender and the Horror Film* (Austin, TX: University of Texas Press, 1996), pp. 310 and 321.

138 See Dora Apel, *Imagery of Lynching: Black Men, White Women and the Mob* (New Brunswick, NJ: Rutgers University Press, 2004), p. 142.

139 See Young, 'Here Comes the Bride', p. 322.

140 The film is *Fury* (1936), dir. Fritz Lang. See Young, 'Here Comes the Bride', p. 322.

141 This links to the end of *Frankenstein* where revenge for the monster's attempt to kill his maker is exacted when he is thrown from the top of an old mill.

142 See Michael Grant, 'James Whale's "Frankenstein": The Horror Film and the Symbolic Biology of the Cinematic Monster', in Stephen Bann (ed.), *Frankenstein, Creation and Monstrosity* (London: Reaktion Books, 1994), p. 128.

143 This was directed by Danny Boyle and performed at the National Theatre, London in 2011. The actors playing Victor and the monster were white, while those playing his family members were black.

3

Death by orgasm: sexual surgery and Dracula

> She was found dead, and with every evidence of having expired during a paroxysm of abnormal excitement.[1]
>
> Isaac Baker Brown, *On the Curability of Certain Forms of Insanity* [...] *in Females* (1866)

> Let us suppose the case of a young man, intellectual, talented and perhaps, with great aptitude in surgery, but nevertheless at heart a sexual pervert. He begins practice and soon acquires a reputation as a skilful surgeon. But he feels, stirring within him, sadistic tendencies which he cannot or will not repress. He looks about him for a means of gratification that will be well within the law, and his search is soon rewarded. He becomes a gynecologist [*sic*] [...] never so happy as when cutting out ovaries.[2]
>
> Norman Barnesby, *Medical Chaos and Crime* (1910)

The most sinister reason for carrying out sexual surgery on men and women is to control sexuality. Female genital mutilation is the most obvious example. A practice dating back to ancient times, it continues to this day. Currently around 140 million women worldwide, mainly from African countries, have undergone this mutilating procedure. Less well known is the fact that it was carried out in Britain during the nineteenth century on white British women and continued in America until the middle of the twentieth century. Unnecessary sexual surgery was performed even more extensively on men and boys during the same period, subjecting many to painful procedures, such as attempts to cauterise the bladder for the prevention of spermatorrhea.[3] In regard to women, it has not been sufficiently recognised that unethical experimental sexual surgeries performed by leading surgeons coincided with developments and key events in the history of women's rights. According to obstetrician and general practitioner, Augustus Kinsley Gardner, who wrote an article on the 'Physical Decline of American Women' (1860), the putative 'deterioration' of women brought gynaecology into existence.[4] I will argue that details of unnecessary and punitive operations on female sexual and reproductive organs were known to Bram Stoker and are encoded in *Dracula*. Here vampirism will be read as a trope for an invented female pathology, believed to require a surgical solution. Throughout the decade in which the novel was written, female castration was 'an epidemic, a rage, a thriving industry'.[5]

Stoker certainly knew about ill health first-hand, having suffered a prolonged life-threatening childhood illness that prevented him from standing upright until about the age of seven.[6] The precise nature of his ailment remains mysterious, but it might have contributed towards his abiding interest in medicine. In 1849–50, Stoker delivered a paper to the College of Physicians in Dublin, in which he compared aspects of mesmerism with epidemics of nervous diseases in Medieval Europe, assumed to have a divine or diabolical origin.[7] The combination of medicine, mesmerism and the demonic re-emerge in *Dracula*. Stoker came from a medical family, going back generations. His uncle Edward Alexander Stoker, whose five sons all became doctors, was a surgeon and chief examiner for the Royal College of Surgeons, Ireland.[8] The physician, medical reformer and writer, Dr William Stoker, who was a professor of surgery at the Royal College of Surgeons in Ireland, was a more distant relative whose three brothers, father and grandfather had all been physicians. William Stoker published on the value of therapeutic phlebotomy and had Bram read his work, it might have supplied him with an indirect source for the vampiric bleeding and blood transfusions taking place in *Dracula*. Three of Bram's four brothers were doctors. The eldest, Sir William Thornley Stoker, was a celebrated surgeon, whose gynaecological operations have never before been considered in relation to the novel. Thornley provided Stoker with a model for his fictional physicians, Professor Abraham Van Helsing and Dr John Seward. Van Helsing is a consulting physician brought in by his favourite former pupil Seward to assist with the mysterious symptoms of his patient Lucy Westenra. This chapter will look at the ways in which Van Helsing's destruction of the sexualised Lucy, along with Dracula's three vampire women, parallel surgeries to destroy aspects of female sexuality and reproduction, which were performed by Thornley and other nineteenth-century surgeons. These include Dr Robert Battey and Dr Lawson Tait, advocates of normal ovariotomy; Dr James Marion Sims, known as the 'Architect of the Vagina'; and Isaac Baker Brown, the father of clitoridectomy, who was convinced that his castrating surgeries helped preserve marriage. *Dracula* was written at a time when the New Woman movement was challenging traditional marital roles. While this social change is reflected in the novel, the treatment of the roles of husband, wife and betrothed are, in many respects, consistent with the agenda of certain castrating surgeons. Even though it should not be forgotten that these doctors were pioneers who did a great deal of surgical good, it is the more questionable aspects of their practice that will be examined here.[9]

SURGERY, MASTURBATION AND HYSTERIA

Dracula is a medical novel, dealing with the diagnosis and treatment of illness, doctors and patients, who include Lucy, Jonathan Harker and R. M. Renfield, Count Dracula's disciple.[10] Zoophagous Renfield is the inmate of a lunatic asylum, run by Dr Seward, where he undergoes cranial surgery after Dracula fractures his skull. Thornley, who was an expert on neurosurgery and trepanning, provided his younger brother with a memo and illustration, detailing the effects of an injury to the side of the head.[11] Stoker's merging of medicine with the supernatural is most apparent when he applies the discourse of surgery to the occult pathology of vampirism. The staking of Lucy by Van Helsing and his team can be seen as a sublimation of the castrating surgeon and his assistants operating on a hysterical female patient. This reading chimes with the widely accepted view of the text as mirroring the Victorian pathologising of femininity and Freudian hysterisation of women's bodies.[12]

By the time of *Dracula*'s publication in 1897, sexual surgery had been used to remedy a wide variety of ailments. Many of these were related to the correction of moral behaviour, such as masturbation, hypersexuality or the mind–body state of hysteria. Hysterectomy proved to be a kind of sexual lobotomy for Victorian women. It has been claimed that 90 per cent of hysterectomies carried out in the United States, up to the late twentieth century, have been unnecessary and driven by non-clinical factors, such as medical sexism.[13] Other superfluous castrating surgeries include male circumcision, clitoridectomy and normal ovariotomy, more commonly known in Britain as oophorectomy. The procedure involved cutting out healthy ovaries and was popularised by the American surgeon

Robert Battey from 1872 onwards. The surgery was believed to cure a host of female maladies, including menstrual disturbances, insanity and epilepsy, along with the now discredited and discarded diseases of ovariomania, hysteria and nymphomania. By 1906, around 150,000 women mainly of childbearing age had been subjected to the unnecessary extirpation of these organs. The first woman to qualify in medicine in the United States was Bristol-born Elizabeth Blackwell, who referred to these procedures as 'the castration of women'.[14] The operation was more prevalent in America than Britain, where it was thought by many gynaecologists to de-sex women. The leading voice opposing this view was the English gynaecologist Lawson Tait, who devised a more drastic variation, known as 'Tait's Operation', involving the removal of the ovaries and Fallopian tubes. The surgeon Thomas Spencer Wells was against the operation and marvelled at the tolerance of women for agreeing to these 'mutilations'.[15] He condemned the operation as castration or 'spaying', a term used for the sterilisation of pre-pubescent animals.[16] One of his opponents, Dr David Gilliam, while comparing women to farm animals, declared in 1898 that female castration ought to be more widespread, since it made women docile: 'Why do we alter our colts and calves?', he asked: 'Not that we expect to abate strength or endurance, not yet to render them less intelligent: but that we may make them tractable and trustworthy, that we may convert them into faithful, well-disposed servants.'[17]

Gynaecological operations, made possible by anaesthesia and the adoption of aseptic and antiseptic methods of hygiene, literally opened up new opportunities for surgical practice, exploration and experimentation. There was little shortage during the late nineteenth century, owing to a plethora of invented abnormalities. Amongst them was menstrual epilepsy and the condition of the backward-facing womb. As this perfectly normal positioning occurs in one-third of all women, it provided surgeons and their trainees with ample cases for bogus corrective surgery. Van Helsing's expertise lies in the field of obscure diseases. In the case of Lucy Westenra, who presents symptoms of the classic hysteric, his diagnosis of vampirism, along with its surgical cure, is in keeping with the nosology of imaginary diseases, fallacious deformities and mistaken malfunctions that prevailed during the Victorian period.

Since *Dracula* sits on the cusp of the old world of superstition and the new world of scientific enterprise, it is hardly surprising to find Stoker making use of Thomas Joseph Pettigrew's *On Superstitions Connected with the History and Practice of Medicine and Surgery* (1844). Here an alchemist, Van Helmont, is mentioned, and it has been suggested that his name might have inspired that of Van Helsing, a character who is prepared to use folk remedies alongside the latest medical advances.[18] Besides drawing on Eastern European folklore connected with the vampire, *Dracula* reflects a preoccupation with modernity from the invention of the phonograph to innovations in medicine. The period when Stoker was writing the novel, generally regarded as being from 1890 up to 1897, coincided with a 'golden age' of surgical advancement. In 1895, the first radical hysterectomy was performed through the abdomen, involving the removal of glands and surrounding tissues.[19] As Stoker's brother Thornley had already pointed out, 'the treatment, by surgical means, of no other part of the human frame has undergone such a complete improvement and revolution of late as has that of the uterus and its appendages'.[20] Given his medical connections and interest in medicine, Stoker must have been aware of such surgical landmarks, especially since his brother made gynaecological history by performing the first successful abdominal hysterectomy in Ireland. The patient was a slim, dark-haired woman of sallow complexion, who was twenty-six years old and the mother of a six-year-old child. She was suffering from a large uterine tumour, which, by the time of her operation, had grown to the size of the head of a nine-month-old foetus. In Dublin on 6 June 1878, Thornley removed her uterus and one of the ovaries. The procedure was risky and the patient could easily have died had it not been for his skill and the dedicated aftercare she received. For her seven-week hospital stay, Thornley declared that the post-operative stimulant that agreed with her best was champagne. After being discharged, he observed that she had grown ruddy and plump and was capable of fulfilling her household duties as of old. Thornley had operated on her to great acclaim. His illustrious career as a surgeon culminated in his appointment in 1894 as President of the Royal College of Surgeons in Ireland, a position he held up to 1896, the year before *Dracula* appeared. At an earlier stage in his career, Thornley was a demonstrator at the Royal College and taught surgery to medical students at the Richmond Hospital in Dublin. He went on to hold the Examinership in Surgery at the Royal University of Ireland. The scene in which Professor Van Helsing instructs Arthur Holmwood on how to open up the body of his fiancée Lucy can be seen to parody an operation conducted by a trainee surgeon, under the supervision of a distinguished Professor of Medicine just like Thornley, who was also the Professor of Practical Anatomy at the Royal College of Surgeons, Ireland.

A further analogy can be made with post-mortem anatomical dissection, in relation to Dr Seward's question put to Van Helsing: 'Must we make an autopsy?' His reply is, 'Yes and no. I want to operate' (p. 202). The professor's conundrum is that the patient is paradoxically both dead and alive. In abdominal surgery, the issue of 'life or death' was ever present, for as Thornley pointed out: 'Even the momentous question of opening joints wanes in significance beside that of laying open the abdomen.'[21] While his abdominal hysterectomy proved to be of national importance, as the first to restore a patient to health, in *Dracula* the old adage that the operation was a success, though the patient died, proves true in Lucy's case and bears out the sentiment quoted in one of Stoker's sources: 'Death is the cure of all diseases.'[22]

Before her ultimate demise, Dr Seward describes the opening of Lucy's coffin in language analogous to the surgical entry into the body. He refers to Van Helsing using a turnscrew, a tool that has a semantic link with the myoma screw used in uterine surgery. In the novel, the turnscrew makes an incision large enough to admit the point of 'a tiny fret-saw' (p. 235). As pointed out in the surgeon's guide, *Abdominal Surgery* (1896), the surgical saw could be used during anatomical dissection for making an abdominal section when a cadaver was frozen.[23] Thornley kept an eye on the accuracy of surgical instruments in *Dracula* and, shortly before the novel went to press, corrected his brother's references to operating knives by changing them to post-mortem knives.[24] Autopsical knowledge is also demonstrated through Seward's expectation that the coffin will contain an emission of gas from Lucy's week-old decomposing body, as when he explains: 'We doctors, who have had to study our dangers, have to become accustomed to such things' (p. 235). Van Helsing takes the edge of the loose flange and bends it back, using a light to peer into the aperture. This is not dissimilar to the way in which a surgeon turns back a flap of membrane in order to inspect the body's interior during a laparotomy. But, as the doctors discover, the enclosure is empty. On a subsequent visit, when Lucy is firmly ensconced in her coffin, another incision is made, only this time directly into her body rather than her coffin and using a wooden stake rather than a turnscrew. Delivered by her fiancé Arthur, under the direction of Van Helsing, it is aimed, not at her abdomen, but in the direction of her heart.

According to ancient belief, the uterus was a movable organ that, in the case of hysterics, rose upwards through the abdominal cavity to the throat where it caused a sense of suffocation. This folklore belief is referred to in Stoker's Pettigrew source in a short section on hysteria, a word deriving from the Greek for 'womb'.[25] Lucy's malady has been seen by critics to encode the case history of a hysteric.[26] The condition was associated with a wide range of ailments, many of which relate to female sexuality, such as menstrual disorders, nymphomania, frigidity and onanism.[27]

The eighteenth century saw a hysterisation of masturbation that continued into the following century, to become what Jean Stengers and Anne Van Neck refer to in the subtitle of their book as *The History of a Great Terror*.[28] According to one French physician, quoted in a New Orleans medical journal for 1855: 'In my opinion, neither the plague, nor war, nor smallpox, nor a crowd of similar evils, have resulted more disastrously for humanity, than the habit of masturbation: it is the destroying element of civilized society.'[29] In nineteenth-century America, boys caught masturbating were sometimes confined to lunatic asylums where they could be castrated, circumcised or shackled in cells.[30] Tailor-made surgical responses were developed, which included spermectomy, in which spermatic ducts were removed, and neurectomy, a popular procedure in the 1890s for permanently destroying penile sensitivity by severing the dorsal nerves. There were plenty of non-surgical tortures applied to the penis of the masturbating boy, often dispensed by quacks, such as blistering, flaying and enclosing the beleaguered member in spiked rings or metal cages.[31] But by far the most popular and persistent method of treatment for boys was circumcision. A major incentive was the widely held belief that onanism for both sexes led to illness, which included the deadly and much-feared disease tuberculosis (phthisis). Stoker kept a cutting from the *New York World* (2 February 1896) reporting on a nineteenth-century belief in vampires in New England, where symptoms of consumption were sometimes mistaken for vampirism.[32] In suffering from a wasting disease of the blood brought about by a vampire, the pale patient Lucy brings the two conditions together since her bloody mouth resembles that of an emaciated pulmonary consumptive coughing up blood. The figure of the nocturnal blood-sucker is conjured up by William Fox in a book directed to the working man subtitled, *Every Man His Own Doctor* (1884), in which consumption is figured as a disease that 'enters into our dwellings unseen and unlooked for, pursuing the noiseless tenor of its way, and, *like a vampire*, drinks the vital stream, and then fans with his wings the never-dying hopes that perpetually flutter in the hectic breast.'[33]

Lucy's appearance not only characterises the symptoms of phthisis but also resembles the related condition of chronic masturbator. This conflation is made in Nicholas Francis Cooke's *Satan in Society* (1870), which lists symptoms for girls committing the 'crime' of masturbation, which present as:

> A general condition of languor, weakness and loss of flesh; the absence of freshness and beauty, of colour from the complexion ... livid physiognomy, a bluish circle around the eyes which are sunken, dull, and spiritless; a sad expression, dry cough, oppression and panting on the least exertion, [and] the appearance of incipient consumption.[34]

Lucy's 'weakness' is brought about by the 'horror' (p. 161) of Count Dracula, leaching her life-force during the night, a time when the chronic onanist was most susceptible to temptation. It is only when watched over by a doctor that she awakes more refreshed the next morning. The peak of masturbation anxiety was reflected in the proliferation of warning literature from the 1880s onwards. Its zenith was not, as commonly believed, during the mid-Victorian period but in the wake of the campaign against the Contagious Diseases Acts, repealed in 1886, and through to the Edwardian period.[35] The writing and publication of *Dracula* takes place within this time-frame. Robert Mighall argues that Victorian novelists did not use fictional vampirism as a device to symbolise masturbation, but employed it instead as a means of approximating how onanism was represented at the time. This relates to the idea of a somatic economy which is common to both discourses. While the vampire was depleting a sanguinary economy, the onanist sapped nervous energy. Both systems were thought to have a finite capacity relating to theories of degenerative disease and reflex neurosis. The assumption was that the stimulation of sensitive tissue, particularly relating to the sexual organs, disrupted the balance of nerves thus creating disease. Mighall suggests that 'the medico-moral discourse on masturbation somehow contributed to Victorian fiction's refashioning of the vampire' and that 'authors adapted vampirism to the model of morbidity found in the literature on self-abuse'.[36] The legend of the vampire presented in *Dracula* provides a fictional counterpart to the medical mythologising of the morbid effects of masturbation.

In common with many other physicians, Isaac Baker Brown considered the pathogenesis of onanism to be a leading cause of insanity, along with alcoholism and hereditary disease. Victorian lunatic asylums admitted patients who practised so-called self-abuse or suffered from masturbatory insanity, an invented disease believed to afflict both sexes.[37] For women, the offending organ was the clitoris. Brown's solution was simple – excision. This surgical assault on female onanists helped address concerns that they were breaking down the gender divide by becoming more like men, with whom masturbation was more widely associated. Amongst the many symptoms detected, Barker-Benfield noted that the most prevalent was sexual appetite, another indicator that women were becoming more masculinised. This could be extended to food, since 'eating like a ploughman' was yet another onanist trait.[38] After having had 'a capital "severe tea"' tea with Lucy at Robin Hood's Bay, Mina Harker comments: 'I believe we should have shocked the "New Woman" with our appetites' (p. 123). Evidently, the New Woman, who had been linked to manliness, had come to be associated with hearty eating. Later, Lucy compares herself to a voracious seabird by telling Mina that she has 'an appetite like a cormorant' (p. 142). In addition, Lucy is taking plenty of exercise, an activity more compatible with a masculine lifestyle than that of a late Victorian young lady. For males, vigorous exercise and circumcision was demanded by the social purity movement, which was intent on deterring 'self-pollution' and its attendant maladies. At its height, during the latter part of the nineteenth century, the penises of 30 to 40 per cent of boys in Britain were cut. A class bias operated in favour of this practice, since the absence of a foreskin was seen as the mark of a gentleman. For public school boys, the statistics reached two-thirds or more.[39] The removal of the foreskin was aimed to prevent irritation from the accumulation of accretions, believed to incite onanism. As recently as 1970, circumcision was recommended as a preventative for masturbating males in a standard textbook on urology.[40] For both sexes, surgery was employed to deter masturbation, an activity that was thought to feminise men and masculinise women. Stoker drew attention to the demarcation between the sexes in one of his novels, where he wrote: 'the ideal man is entirely or almost entirely masculine, and the ideal woman is entirely or almost entirely feminine.'[41] Obligingly, sexual surgery served to reinforce the polarisation of these gender roles.

The medical justification for surgical intervention, however, was made primarily on the grounds of halting disease than on the politics of gender. Brown subscribed to the orthodox view that masturbation, which he regarded as 'peripheral excitement of the pubic nerve' (p. vi), led to a lack of nerve power. In turn, this gave rise to a number of nervous disorders, amongst other conditions. His prognosis for the self-abuser advanced through eight stages of decline. Beginning with hysteria, the sufferer deteriorated into spinal irritation, hysterical epilepsy, cataleptic fits, epileptic fits, idiocy and mania. Finally, Brown pronounced, rather aptly: 'Death is indeed the direct climax of the series' (p. 8). For him, the surgical excision of the clitoris, which he identified as 'the source of evil' (p. 10), was a procedure nothing short of lifesaving. Parallels can be seen with Van Helsing staking Lucy in order to save her spiritual life from the 'evil' (p. 167) with which she has been afflicted/infected. One of Brown's case histories in his book, *On the Curability of Certain Forms of Insanity*, documents a vampire-like hysteric, a twenty-three-year-old woman from Ireland who had been training in Paris as a governess. He diagnosed her paroxysms as the result of 'peripheral irritation' (p. 79), for which his solution was clitoridectomy. Before the operation, the patient not only attacked the surgeon but also wanted to bite off the matron's hand. In the manner of the undead, she refused food, preferring blood. Following a seizure, she fell into a death-like comatose state. On regaining consciousness, her lips quivered with the words: 'I want blood!' (p. 80). She confessed: 'I have wanted a child's blood. I have had it sometimes by sucking the wounds of a child' (p. 81). In a prelude to her impaling, Lucy, with blood-stained lips, approaches her tomb holding a child in her arms. Van Helsing warns: 'Those children whose blood she suck [*sic*] are not as yet so much the worse; but if she live [*sic*] on, Un-Dead, more and more they lose their blood, and by her power over them they come to her; and so she draw [*sic*] their blood with that so wicked mouth. But if she die in truth, then all cease; the tiny wounds of the throats disappear' (p. 253). Earlier in the novel, the three vampire women in Dracula's castle, wanting to feed off a young child, demonstrate a warped maternal instinct. Rather than nurturing the child, they use it as nurture for themselves. Masturbation was thought to impair or destroy the capacity of a woman to bear children.[42] The related condition of hysteria was also blamed on rendering women unfit for motherhood. In the eyes of Brown, both perversities could be remedied by clitoridectomy. As for his vampire-like patient, he documented that following the operation, she recovered sufficiently well enough to take up knitting and get 'legally married' (p. 83), which was really all the evidence he needed to attest to her cure.

Another malady that Brown linked to masturbation was epilepsy. Again he insisted that for women, the cure was clitoridectomy. As Dr Forbes Winslow pointed out, since epilepsy was in the head, Brown had patently started 'at the wrong end'.[43] But he was by no means alone in persisting with this wrong-headedness. Amputation of the foreskin was recommended in some quarters to cure hysteria and epilepsy in men and boys, whether or not it was connected to masturbation.[44] John Harvey Kellogg, who introduced the health cereals, corn flakes, granola and shredded wheat as 'masturbatory inhibitors', was an advocate of clitoridectomy and male circumcision.[45] Directing most of his advice concerning self-abuse to men and boys, he insisted that masturbation-related deaths demonstrated how 'a victim literally dies by his own hand'.[46] Contained within his long list of resulting maladies is epilepsy, 'a horrible disease', which, he claimed, was 'frequently the result of this pernicious practice'.[47] The reasoning behind his assertion was as follows:

> The practice of self-abuse is particularly prone to produce epilepsy, as venereal excitement itself partakes very much of the character of an epileptic convulsion, the state of the nervous system at the moment of greatest excitement being almost identical with that during an epileptic fit, only in less degree. It is not strange, then, that such a powerful excitement, frequently repeated, and particularly in immature individuals, should ultimately result in the production of this grave and sometimes incurable disorder.[48]

Kellogg was convinced that youthful masturbators, who indulge in repeated sexual climaxes, unwittingly brought about their own punishment. This involved being doomed to replay the forbidden and private pleasure of orgasm through involuntary fits, sometimes in public. He compared the convulsions of an epileptic fit to shocks from a powerful electrical current coursing through a patient. This is similar to the appearance of Lucy, when staked through the heart by her fiancé:

> The Thing in the coffin writhed; and a hideous, blood-curdling screech came from the opened red lips. The body shook and quivered and twisted in wild contortions; the sharp white teeth champed together till the lips were cut, and the mouth was smeared with a crimson foam. But Arthur never faltered [...]. And then the writhing and quivering of the body became less, and the teeth ceased to champ, and the face to quiver. Finally it lay still. (p. 254)

There are resemblances here to the characteristics of an epileptic seizure. Attacks are sometimes ushered in by a shrill cry similar to Lucy's blood-curdling scream. In the tonic phase, there is a stiffening of the limbs and breathing can cease, resulting in a corpse-like state, similar to Lucy's undead status. This is followed by the clonic phase of the fit, during which breathing resumes, albeit irregularly, and the limbs jerk and twitch. For the climactic grand mal seizure, the entire brain and body is affected, rather like how, for Lucy, 'The body shook and quivered and twisted in wild contortions'. It is common for epileptics to bite their tongue and lips, rather like the way in which Lucy's 'sharp white teeth champed together till the lips were cut'. Kellogg's description of blood and froth issuing from the mouth corresponds to how, in Stoker's words, her 'mouth was smeared with a crimson foam'. The facial gesticulations made by her gnashing teeth resemble his description of an epileptic's face during a fit distorted by the most frightful grimaces. The convulsion ends with unconsciousness and the cessation of any motion. Lucy's wild contortions terminate in the ultimate stillness of death: 'Finally it lay still'. The tonic and final appearance of the epileptic is a contracted version of the catatonic state, which bears a physical resemblance to the undead. Catatonia was another condition that Brown believed was caused by masturbation and could be cured by clitoridectomy. Along with other diseases, he lists it in the title of his book, *On the Curability of Certain Forms of Insanity, Epilepsy, Catalepsy, and Hysteria in Females*. In *Idols of Perversity: Fantasies of Feminine Evil in Fin-de-Siècle Culture* (1986), Bram Dijkstra argues that representations of sleeping women in *fin-de-siècle* paintings have a kinship with the sexual exhaustion of the self-abuser. He also shows how female mortality was regarded as a source of aesthetic pleasure, enacted through the eroticisation of dead and dying women in art.[49] Lucy, while resting in her coffin, is another such picture of sleep (or seductive slumber) and death.

Lucy's dying convulsions bring together the epileptic convulsion, the climactic hysterical paroxysm and the orgasmic *petit mort*. The eroticised pathology of the late nineteenth-century hysteric was studied by Freud's mentor, Jean-Martin Charcot, who exhibited his hysterical patients at the Salpêtrière Hospital in Paris to an audience of medical students. The sexualised conditions of hysteria and epilepsy coalesce in Brown's category of hysterical epilepsy. The climaxes of these illnesses were perceived as having a peculiar relationship with the physiology of orgasm. Dr Robert Barnes, the Victorian obstetrician who worked at St George's and St Thomas' Hospitals in London, opposed marriage for epileptics on the grounds that 'marital intercourse' could trigger a fit.[50] Confusion between the two is known to have existed even between married couples. In the early twentieth century, a husband wrote to Marie Stopes, expressing his alarm after mistaking his wife's orgasm for 'some sort of fit'.[51] But the real danger of orgasm, as far as most physicians and writers of popular medical texts were concerned, was when it was reached through masturbation, for, as Kellogg claimed: 'Of all forms of nervous disease, none are more appalling in their aspect, and few more dreadful in ultimate results,

(a)

Figure 6a The harmful effects of masturbation in an illustration from Seth Pancoast's *Boyhood's Perils and Manhood's Curse* (1858).

Note: This was on display at the Museum of Sex in New York.

than this.'[52] In his chapter on 'Sexual Sins and their Consequences' from *Man the Masterpiece or Plain Truths Plainly Told, about Boyhood, Youth and Manhood* (1894), Kellogg describes the effect on men and boys of such 'venereal excitement' as a 'mind-destroying vice', which could cause a sufferer to sit, 'staring vacantly into space, with an open, drooling mouth (Figure 6a), and a senseless, idiotic smile upon his face.'[53] Onanism was also thought to bring about premature aging (Figure 6b). Female auto-eroticism was thought by many Victorian physicians to interfere with conjugal duty by over-sexing or de-feminising women, as it was believed that masturbation enlarged the clitoris. Hypertrophy was a popular justification for amputation, being a condition related to masturbation, hermaphroditism, tribadic behaviour, sapphism or sexual inversion. Nuances of lesbianism between Lucy and Mina can be read into the scene in which they undress one other. If seen as studies in sexual deviancy then Lucy's vampirism overlays a case history of hysteria and aetiology of self-abuse, while Mina, with her 'man's brain' (p. 274), corresponds to the manly woman, who was associated with the New Woman.

According to Thomas Laqueur in *Making Sex* (1992), a doctrine of the one-sex model predominated from the ancients up to the eighteenth

(b)

At 16.   At 21.

At 50.   At 70.

Figure 6b The unhealthy and prematurely aged masturbator contrasted with the healthier and more youthful looking abstainer in 1875.

Note: Dr E. C. Abbey, *The Sexual System and Its Derangements* (Buffalo: NY, n.p., 1875), taken from pp. 14 and 16.

century, which maintained that a woman, as a lesser male body, possessed an internal set of male genitalia. The belief facilitated a greater erotic confluence between the sexes, through which conception was assumed to be the result of mutual orgasm. This notion was discarded once it was recognised that in order to conceive a woman did not need to be orgasmic, or even conscious. To illustrate this, Laqueur drew on a disquisition of 1749 by Jacques-Jean Bruhier, which contains an anecdote about a young monk assigned to watch over the dead body of a beautiful young girl.[54] Overcome with lust at the sight of her, he commits necrophilia. Later, it transpires that she was not, in fact, dead and had been impregnated by the amorous monk. This bringing of life from the supposedly dead is analogous to the creation of a vampire. Contained in a vault like Bruhier's young girl, Lucy is also seen as sexually enticing, as are Dracula's three vampire sisters, referred to by Van Helsing as 'the wanton Un-dead' (p. 411). Bruhier's tale serves as a parable for the death of the one-sex model in favour of an alternative, which emphasised the fundamental differences, rather than similarities, between the sexes. The theory of the two-sex model was first hypothesised in 1595.[55] It may be no coincidence that during the 1590s in Britain, debate on divorce reached crisis point, leading to the family becoming an internalised instrument for greater social control.[56] In the paradigm shift from one-sex to two-sex model, confusion reigned over the genital correspondences between the sexes. The male foreskin was invariably matched to the hood of the clitoris and labia, while the clitoris was compared with either the glans on its own or the penis in its entirety. As Robert Darby indicates: 'These analogies might seem scholastic, but they became critical in the 1860s, when doctors were debating whether it was legitimate to treat masturbation by excision of the clitoris in women and the foreskin in men.'[57] It is obvious which side of the debate Brown favoured when he revived the ancient custom of removing the female organ.[58]

At the height of his career, Brown was hailed as a brilliant and innovative surgeon, who specialised in female diseases and founded a women's hospital. In 1865, he became the President of the Medical Society of London. His less illustrious moments included performing ovariectomies on three women who subsequently died, though his fourth attempt at this heroic surgery on his sister proved successful. In 1854, he wrote the first book specifically on surgical gynaecology. It was followed by J. Marion Sims' *Clinical Notes on Uterine Surgery* in 1866, the year before Brown was expelled from the Obstetrical Society of London. This disgrace had been triggered not so much by the suffering he had inflicted on his victims, but for a number of other reasons including his self-publicity that smacked of quackery. Brown had disseminated all too widely for the likes of his fellow physicians the notion that British womanhood was masturbating en masse and in need of his surgical solution. From 1860 to 1866, it has been estimated that 600 of these operations were performed and, during one month alone, forty to fifty 'middle aged practitioners' watched Brown operating.[59] Lawson Tait, who claimed to have performed the operation successfully, expressed regret that the surgeon's excesses had brought the procedure into disrepute, since he believed that it benefited inveterate female onanists.[60] Brown had aroused controversy by operating without the full knowledge or consent of his patients. Quite obviously, Van Helsing gives Lucy no advance warning of the drastic procedure he is about to undertake. He also has to convince Dr Seward to assist in the operation. As an ex-suitor, Seward shuddered at the thought of '*mutilating* the body of the woman whom I had loved' (p. 239; emphasis added). In the end, it is Lucy's fiancé who wields the stake, which, within this context, can be seen to represent a scalpel. With a hand that 'rose and fell' (p. 254), Arthur's penetration of her body, with his 'mercy-bearing stake' (p. 254), on what would have been their wedding night, also resembles sublimated rape.[61]

In the light of this reading, Lucy's restoration from sexual vamp to virginal purity seems contradictory. As a representative of the classic hysteric, she is already contained within a diagnostic category full of paradoxes. Hysteria was a condition associated with sexual excess, yet believed by many to have been brought about by sexual deprivation. In order to satisfy her desire, Lucy tries enticing her fiancé with the words 'Come, my husband, come!' (p. 250). Arthur's phallic stake provides an ambiguous response by representing both the satiation and destruction of her sexual urges. The reader is informed that his exertions had taken a tremendous toll upon him: 'He reeled and would have fallen had we not caught him. The great drops of sweat sprang out on his forehead, and his breath came in broken gasps. It had indeed been an awful strain on him' (p. 254). Diane Mason suggests that this 'sweat can be seen to encode another bodily fluid' and that Arthur, along with Lucy, 'displays similarly climactic or orgasmic behaviour after the almost rapacious destruction of his "undead" fiancée'.[62] A link between male sexual exertion and female vampirism was made by a doctor who was head of a department of genito-urinary diseases in New York. This was William J. Robinson, author of the popular guide, *Married Life and Happiness* (1922), where he refers to the 'excessive sexuality' of the hypersensual woman, whose demands for intercourse more than once every two weeks or ten days, which was considered normal, were a danger to her husband.[63] Revamping hysteria into hypersensuality, Robinson describes such women as vampires and explains: 'Just as the vampire sucks the blood of its victims in their sleep while they are alive, so does the woman vampire suck the life and exhaust the vitality of her male partner – or victim. And some of them – the pronounced type – are utterly without pity or consideration.'[64] American gynaecologist and obstetrician, Augustus Kinsley Gardner, warned against the dangers during intercourse for the male partner of a sexually aroused woman. As a form of protection, Gardner 'fenced "the act" around with rules and defined copulation as religious duty and holy work'.[65] One can almost see a kindred spirit in Stoker's Van

Helsing, who sanctions Arthur's quasi phallic penetration of Lucy's body as 'blessed' (p. 253).

ARCHITECT OF THE VAGINA AND THE 'FINGER OF GOD'

The anxiety that unrestrained female sexuality could drain a man of his 'life' and 'vitality' is epitomised by Lucy's voluptuous and 'wicked mouth' (p. 253). Lucy expresses her sexual hunger for her fiancé Arthur by declaring: 'My arms are hungry for you' (p. 250). Gardner and his fellow American physician, Sims, referred to the vagina as a hungry mouth. The food needed to satisfy this hunger was semen, for only that could restore a woman to 'perfect calm', claimed Gardner in his *Conjugal Sins* (1870).[66] After being staked, Lucy's body is bathed in a 'holy calm' (p. 255). Prior to that, the imagery of ejaculation is evoked when Van Helsing approaches Lucy's coffin, holding his candle at such an angle that 'the sperm dropped in white patches which congealed as they touched the metal' (p. 235) coffin plate.[67] Sims did not restrict himself in his *Clinical Notes* to equating only the mouth with the vagina. He went on to show how other parts of a woman's nether regions corresponded with the higher ones, so that 'the womb [has] a "neck" and a "throat," and the cervix is compared to the "tonsils."'[68] He once described the uterus, while in a state of readiness for impregnation, as a 'gaping, graceful form'.[69] This was indicative of the nineteenth-century perception that a woman's entire being was contained within her pelvic region. Dr Sims' feminised gynaecological discourse bears comparison with Dr Seward's observation that Lucy, while attempting to seduce her fiancé, exudes a 'languorous, voluptuous grace' (p. 250), the very symptom of her somatic and spiritual disorder.

Hailed as the father of modern gynaecology, Sims was dubbed 'Architect of the Vagina' and acclaimed by Gardner as 'The great apostle of vaginal surgery', whose medical gaze was that of a 'God-inspired eye'.[70] A brilliant surgeon, he was acclaimed for remedying vesico-vaginal fistulas caused by tears to the vaginal wall during protracted childbirth. But at the start of his dazzling career, Sims admitted: 'if there was anything I hated, it was investigating the organs of the female pelvis.'[71] Barker-Benfield suggests that 'Cutting into the organs' to enhance his standing amongst his male peers and pave the way for modern gynaecology enabled Sims to deal 'with the horror they aroused'.[72] Sims' remark gives added weight to Dr Seward's words on seeing the 'livid' colour of Lucy's face with the 'folds of the flesh' and 'blood-stained mouth', when he declares: 'There can be no horror like this' (p. 250). After the procedure, Seward observes: 'There, in the coffin lay no longer the foul Thing that we had so dreaded and grown to hate' (p. 255). Sims stated that vaginas were as 'variegated as faces' and it is the transformation of Lucy's face that confirms that the operation has been a success.[73] She no longer wears a 'wanton smile' (p. 249), but instead has a look of 'unequalled sweetness and purity' (p. 255). Her demeanour is indicative of her having attained the ideal of Victorian womanhood in shifting from an active, libidinal and masculinised sexuality to a passive and womanly model. This transformation evokes Dr William Acton's often-quoted remark that 'the majority of women (happily for them) are not very much troubled with sexual feeling of any kind'.[74] Even though this can hardly be taken as a consensual view, it did reflect that of a minority. This included the influential sexologist Richard von Krafft-Ebing, who, in 1871, asserted: 'Woman, however, if physically and mentally normal, and properly educated, has but little sensual desire'.[75] From having been lascivious, diseased, demonic and undead, Lucy undergoes an angelic transformation through the destruction of her body. This process is an accelerated version of the way in which, according to Dr Gardner, a woman's final illness could enhance her spiritual well-being at the expense of her bodily functions:

> the most marked evidence of the benefits to the whole character is seen in those early afflicted by that disease of lingering suffering […]. [T]hose weeks and months of persistent agony have purified the whole nature, have seemingly eliminated every grain of gross alloy, and left the fine gold, purified as by fire […]. [T]his baptism of pain and privation has regenerated the individual's whole nature, and as the physical creature has been weakened and destroyed, the spiritual being, in humble, submissive resignation to the loss which it has sustained, has been nurtured and strengthened by resignation, and beautified.[76]

Over the dead Lucy lay a 'holy calm' that was 'like sunshine over the wasted face and form' (p. 255). Restored to purity, her corpse is a statement of the ultimate passivity in feminine quiescence.

According to Barker-Benfield, the assertiveness of women calling for collective female emancipation catalysed the science of gynaecology. In 1848, an early Woman's Rights Convention took place at Seneca Falls, New York, out of which emerged a resolution for women's suffrage. The same year, Dr Charles Meigs famously declared in his book, *Females and Their Diseases* (1848), that woman had 'a head almost too small for

intellect but just big enough for love'.[77] He steered post Civil War gynaecologists towards treating female genitalia for moral and psychological
maladies. While the market economy of the Industrial Revolution opened
up new opportunities for working women, the traditional female profession of midwifery was being squeezed out by male practitioners. In 1852,
Dr Gardner inveighed against 'disorderly women, lumping together fem-
inists, Bloomer wearers, and midwives'.[78] The Woman Question, which
fundamentally questioned the role and rights of women, gained momentum during the second half of the nineteenth century in Britain and
America. In an article appearing in a medical journal for 1890, entitled
'Sexual Hunger as a Factor in Diseases of Women', physician Ralph Perry
seems to suggest that, if women had sufficient sexual pleasure in marriage, 'there would be less talk of women's rights at the ballot-box and less
violation of the civil code'.[79] Surgery on the clitoris, in the 1890s, was used
in the United States to improve sexual relations between husband and
wife by removing the hood to increase sensitivity. This is a more accu-
rate description of the term 'female circumcision', since the removal of
the prepuce, rather than the entire organ, corresponds to the excision of
the foreskin in males. In Britain, the first clitoridectomy was performed
two years after the passing of the Divorce Act (1857), a reform making it
easier for women to dissolve unhappy marriages. Brown boasted that his
surgical interventions saved five marriages. Surgery was thus a political
act for preserving or encouraging marriage by subduing women who had
rebelled against traditional femininity.

Stoker's Lucy is such a woman. Her unsuitability as a mother is evident
from her drinking of children's blood, while her credentials as a future
wife are compromised by her tendency towards polyandry, as when
she expresses the desire for three husbands. This is symbolically satis-
fied through the blood transfusions she receives from male donors, who
include her suitors. The impaling of Lucy, masterminded by Van Helsing
as an act of redemption, is clearly punitive. The destruction of her sexuality is couched in a language of surgical horror. In advance of the operation, Van Helsing explains to his protégé, Seward: 'I want to operate, but
not as you think. Let me tell you now, but not a word to another. I want
to cut off her head and take out her heart. Ah! you a surgeon, and so
shocked' (p. 202). The final comment could just as well be addressed to
those doctors who disapproved of the mutilating operations carried out
by castrating surgeons. Indeed, decapitation is equated with castration in
Freud's essay, 'Medusa's Head' (1922). Apart from the hammer and stake,

which form an essential part of the vampire slayer's kit, Seward records in his diary how Van Helsing

> took out a soldering iron and some plumbing solder, and then a small oil-lamp, which gave out, when lit in a corner of the tomb, gas which burned at fierce heat with a blue flame; then his operating knives, which he placed to hand [...]. To me, a doctor's preparations for work of any kind are stimulating and bracing, but the effect of these things on both Arthur and Quincey was to cause them a sort of consternation. (p. 252)

Several of these tools are similar to the surgical instruments used for excising the clitoris. Van Helsing uses the soldering iron to reseal the coffin, which can be seen as a surrogate for the surgical body of Lucy who, as a femme fatale, is also a signifier of death.[80]

In *A Dark Science* (1986), on women and psychiatry during the nineteenth century, Jeffrey Moussaieff Masson provides case studies of castrating doctors that were published in French and German medical journals between 1865 and 1900. One of the physicians mentioned in the book is Dr Jules Guérin, who insisted that 'when all else had failed, he had cured young girls suffering from masturbation by burning the clitoris with a hot iron'.[81] Another practitioner was Démétrius Alexandre Zambaco, who, like Brown and Van Helsing, was a renowned medical authority. He studied medicine in Paris and was awarded amongst other honours that of Commander of the French Legion of Honour for his work. His medical research involved the torture of children for masturbating, which he refers to as 'horrors'.[82] In a case study of 1882 documenting the genital mutilation of a ten-year-old girl called X and her younger sister, who was about six years of age, called Y, he employs a moral discourse of disobedience and punishment using the language of religious atonement:

> September 16: A new cauterization. I burned her three times on both labia majora, and once on the clitoris, and to punish her for her disobedience I cauterized her buttocks and loins with the dreaded large iron. She swore to me that she will not fail again, and confessed that she feels very guilty because since the first cauterization she has not had as much desire to excite herself: 'I see that this method will work, because I have been able to go more than twenty-four hours without doing any horrors.'[83]

Van Helsing cauterises Mina's forehead with a consecrated communion wafer to expunge the impurity of her contact with Dracula. The harrowing procedure is described in the journal of Jonathan Harker: 'There was a fearful scream, which almost froze our hearts to hear', when the Eucharistic host 'seared it' and 'burned into the flesh as though it had been a piece of white-hot metal' (p. 336). Mina's response is to cry out: 'Unclean! Unclean!' (p. 336). The word 'nosferatu', rightly or wrongly, has been traced to the Romanian word '*necuratu*' meaning 'unclean spirit', which has associations with the devil. Certainly, Mina's outburst is that of a moral leper. In view of this, it is ironic that Zambaco was praised for his 'profound compassion' for lepers and eunuchs.[84] In his article, 'Sexual Perversion in the Female' (1894), Dr A. J. Bloch refers to female masturbation as 'moral leprosy' and in one of his case histories recorded how a teenage girl was cured of her nervousness and pallor once her clitoris was released from its adhesions.[85] In his campaign to eradicate self-abuse, Zambaco even excised the clitoris of a girl as young as two-and-a-half years of age. Prior to his treatment of X, he contrives to frighten her as much as possible by placing an iron axe on top of red-hot coals and blowing on it until it glowed red, pretending that he was going to use the axe for the surgery. Zambaco then presents himself as merciful, by explaining: 'I only cauterized her clitoris with a tiny stylet, three millimeters in diameter, that had been heated red-hot by an alcohol lamp.'[86] To cure her recidivism, he warned her that, if she masturbated again, he will burn her with the large iron axe, and show no mercy. From this sadistic experiment, Zambaco concluded that 'fear at the sight of the instruments of torture, and the image that a red-hot iron produces in the imagination of children, should also be counted among the beneficial effects of electrical cauterization'.[87] Like a penitent sinner tormented by the instruments of torture, X succumbs to her physician redeemer/ torturer, insisting: 'I deserve to be burned, and I will be. I will bravely submit to the operation; I won't scream.'[88] Similarly, Mina implores her husband, Jonathan: 'When you shall be convinced that I am so changed that it is better that I die that I may live [*sic*]. When I am thus dead in the flesh, then you will, without a moment's delay, drive a stake through me and cut off my head; or do whatever else may be wanting to give me rest' (pp. 371–2). In 1904, the bodybuilder and influential writer on health, Bernarr Macfadden, stated that children 'would be far better off dead rather than undergoing the *living death* that follows on the practice of secret sensuality'.[89] It is sinister to reflect that as a married woman during this period, Mina had the same legal rights as a child. The shame made visible by the stigmata of her burn mark prompts her to declare: 'Even the Almighty shuns my polluted flesh! I must bear this mark of shame upon my forehead until the Judgement Day' (p. 336). In Zambaco's case history, X, who witnesses the torture of her sister when hearing the Angelus Bell, shouts: 'The ringing bells remind me of the Last Judgment.'[90] Indeed the teleological task undertaken by Van Helsing with his hell-fire rhetoric and team of redemptionists is to save Lucy's soul for the Day of Judgement through the sacrifice of her body. In Stoker's novel, the doctor turns into a secular version of the exorcist. The legend of the vampire has now been transformed into a clinical case history, and the daytime resting place for the undead remodelled into a surgeon's operating table.

In the nineteenth century, the roles of physician and priest converged to form a medico-religious discourse. In 1889, *The Lancet* compared doctors to 'the old type of priests who combined moral and medical functions.'[91] While Arthur is staking Lucy, Van Helsing reads from his missal. When her dead body is bathed in a 'holy calm', Arthur thanks him for having restored her soul. Likening himself to a hierophant or priest, twentieth-century surgeon Richard Selzer, on opening up a body, finds himself to be in a place of 'holy dread' where he sees 'surgery as a Mass served with Body and Blood, wherein disease is assailed as though it were sin.'[92] To defeat vampirism, a disease of the body as well as of the soul, Van Helsing arms himself with holy water and the Eucharist, along with the implements of incision: a hammer and stake. This is the point of entry for a gynaecological reading of the novel culminating in the staking of Lucy. Van Helsing is intent on defeating the power of Dracula, a type of anti-Christ figure. Conversely, messianic aspirations were mockingly attributed to Brown 'as a kind of second Christ', in a contemporary satire of 1867, the year of his expulsion from the Obstetrical Society.[93] His disgrace, however, did not extend to the United States, where his operation formed the basis of a lucrative industry around the amputation of the clitoris, until at least 1927.[94] So dismayed was the editor of the Philadelphia-based *Medical Record* at the momentum of the anti-clitoridectomy movement in Britain that he lamented: 'What now will be the chances of recovery for the poor epileptic female with a clitoris?'[95] The operation was endorsed by the influential American surgeon Sims, who demonstrated before Brown in London his own speciality vaginal operation. 'A blessed instrument in the hands of God for the accomplishment of good' was how Sims regarded himself.[96] Here the deity is figured as a divine surgeon, guiding his mortal counterpart. Sims referred

113

to 'the finger of God' as being visible in all human afflictions, which he set out to counteract through the power and skill of his own healing hands.[97]

As the start of his career, it was standard practice for male physicians to carry out examinations of the female pelvic region purely by touch rather than through direct observation, as this would have further compromised female modesty. But it is unlikely that Sims would have heeded any such decorum in regard to the female slaves he owned and on whom he experimented to repair vesico-vaginal fistulas. This debilitating condition could reduce a woman to the permanent misery of chronic incontinence. Sims was determined to rectify the damage. But one of the difficulties was that he was unable to observe high enough into the vagina to see where surgery was needed. After bending a pewter spoon into a U shape, he used it to examine the vagina of one of his patients. The result was the double-ended duckbilled speculum, which he went on to patent.[98] This instrument, combined with the Sims Position, enabled him to explore more fully hidden female parts, the physiological equivalent of Freud's psychological approximation of female sexuality to 'a dark continent'.[99] In his journal, Sims makes use of the rhetoric of scientific and geographical discovery, saying: 'I felt like an explorer in medicine who first views a new and important territory' seeing everything 'as no man had ever seen before'.[100] His sentiments are echoed by Stoker's Dr Seward, who records in his diary: 'I trust, shall such ever be seen again by mortal eyes' (p. 250). Here he is referring to the sight of Lucy as both vampire and Medusa: 'The beautiful colour became livid, the eyes seemed to throw out sparks of hell-fire, the brows were wrinkled as though the folds of the flesh were the coils of Medusa's snakes, and the lovely, blood-stained mouth grew to an open square' (p. 250). Sims, who famously compared the vagina to a face, had now gazed upon it through the reflecting surface of the speculum. For this modern-day Perseus breaking medical taboo, it was the equivalent of the life-preserving shield, deflecting the gaze of the gorgon. According to ancient Greek myth, those who looked directly upon her were turned into stone, and, as Seward declared of Lucy: 'If ever a face meant death – if looks could kill – we saw it at that moment' (p. 250). According to Freud, the decapitated head with its writhing snakes symbolises the castrated female genitals, while petrification represents a stiffening of the penis, as defence against the fear of castration. By decapitating Lucy, Van Helsing (albeit with the help of Seward) turns into a version of Perseus, beheading the Medusa. While

Stoker does not describe the bloody mess in cutting off her head, he does depict the blood welling up from Arthur's buried stake and spurting up around it. Although this effect is associated more with a live body than a living corpse, one of Thornley's post-mortem case histories describes him opening a cadaver containing a large quantity of blood.[101] Copious blood loss is, of course, more commonly found in operations, like the hysterectomy described earlier which was performed by Thornley. Karen Halttunen makes a connection between Gothic fiction and blood lost in childbirth from Dr Gardiner's graphic description: 'Startling and fearful as may be the sight of streams of blood and clotted gore in various scenes, there are none found more appalling than [those] in the obstetrical chamber.'[102] Discourses of medicine and horror also converge in a description by a leading neurologist from Philadelphia who, in 1891, compared the inexperienced surgeon to a novice blood-drinker, noting: 'A first successful abdominal section seems to have the same effect upon an operator as the taste of blood upon the Indian tiger. A thirst insatiable is aroused, and life is spent in looking for new victims.'[103] This analogy with the blood-thirsty tiger presents another way of looking not only at the surgeon but also at the physician and vampire hunter, Van Helsing, who is instrumental in shedding the blood of five vampires, beginning with Lucy.

As the undead, Lucy's liminal status means that her lack of consent to the 'cure' prescribed by her doctor was never an issue. Like Van Helsing, Sims did not always seek patient consent from his slaves or the destitute Irish emigrants upon whom he also operated. Stoker's mother, Charlotte, as it happens, was more concerned with the rights of these disempowered women since she had been an advocate for female paupers emigrating from Irish workhouses to America.[104] While Sims was cavalier about consent from women who were marginalised on the grounds of race and class, he was also negligent about anaesthesia and was by no means the only surgeon of that persuasion. Charles Meigs too was known for his opposition to obstetrical anaesthesia. In this context, the staking of Lucy literalises the comparison between gynaecology and vivisection made by Robert Barnes in the *British Gynaecology Journal* for 1890, where he noted: 'Gynaecology is largely surgical [...]. It is vivisection of the noblest kind.'[105] The two are brought together in the experiments carried out by Spencer Wells on living animals, in his efforts to improve the surgical techniques involved in ovariotomy.[106] In 1879, Stoker's brother, Thornley, took up the position of Inspector of Vivisection for Ireland and remained in the post for nearly thirty years. He granted licences to permit experiments on live animals and initially supported vivisection, but later became an advocate for the cause of antivivisectionism.[107] Stoker's Dr Seward speaks up in its favour by declaring: 'Men sneered at vivisection, and yet look at its results today!' (p. 104). By contrast, the New Woman, with whom Lucy shares characteristics, tended to be a vociferous opponent of this cruelty and parallels were made between the lack of rights for women and the need for animal welfare.[108] In *Dracula*, the staking of Lucy, without numbing her pain, resembles a vivisectionist's experiment, particularly as she is represented as an animal. Her feline nature is in evidence, for example, when she is confronted in the tomb by her assailants. They hear 'an angry snarl, such as a cat gives when taken unawares' (p. 249). H. G. Wells' novel, *The Island of Doctor Moreau* (1896), appeared the year before *Dracula* and describes a female puma being vivisected for the purpose of being surgically transformed into a woman. In common with Lucy, the puma has been identified by literary critics as a New Woman figure.[109] In Stoker's novel, a sick puma in a monkey house hearkens back to Dr Moreau's operating theatre, known as the House of Pain. There could be no better name for the shed Sims built in his yard for the gynaecological experiments he carried out on his slave women, one of whom was operated upon over thirty times without anaesthetic.

While Sims did not always anaesthetise his patients for gynaecological surgery, he was willing to dope wives with ether for having resisted their husbands' sexual advances, to achieve what he called 'ethereal copulation'.[110] This expression conjures up a vision of heavenly conjugality of the angel in the house with her divine bridegroom. Lucy, the bride of Dracula, when drained of blood on her sick bed or especially while lying in her coffin, is a parody of the ultimately supine and passive woman. This contrasts with her explosive reaction when staked by her fiancé under the direction of Van Helsing. Many doctors believed that the symptoms of hysteria could be alleviated by bringing the 'disease' to a crisis, known as a 'hysterical paroxysm', which some physicians viewed as synonymous with orgasm. In 1883, the French physician, Auguste Tripier, described how his colleague Pierre Briquet 'was treating hysteria with masturbation, practiced [sic] more or less systematically by his interns'.[111] This kind of vulvular massage had been discussed in medical circles over twenty-five years earlier. As Mary Lynn Stewart points out, 'medical masturbation' had been attempted on hysterics, but was regarded as a 'dubious therapy'.[112] Such therapies, including the 'uterine massage' reported in *The Lancet* in 1881, had arisen in the first place, albeit minimally, owing to the association between hysteria and the overly sexualised woman.[113] Within Victorian society, both conditions were deemed in need of eradication. In the light of this, the slaying of Lucy dramatises the vanquishing of hysteria and the eradication of overt female sexuality with its orgasmic excesses. Her crypt, by having shape-shifted into an operating theatre and dissecting room, furnishes the ideal setting for the staging of her death.

WILLIAM THORNLEY STOKER AND *DRACULA*

Bram Stoker would have known about the various sexual surgeries carried out on women, since the increase in gynaecological operations in the second half of the nineteenth century accompanied a proliferating discourse on sex and sexuality.[114] This circulated amongst members of the medical profession and in the form of popular medical texts for the wider public. Stoker is likely to have had insider knowledge since three out of the five Stoker brothers were surgeons. In 1874, he went to live with his older brother William Thornley at 16 Harcourt Street, where he stayed for the next three years. Thornley was a celebrated physician who was knighted in 1895 for his services to medicine.[115] He was a surgeon in a string of Dublin hospitals in the 1879s: the Whitworth, Hardwicke and the Richmond, where he worked with his friend William Thomson, who became Surgeon-in-Ordinary to Queen Victoria in Ireland.[116] Thomson's research into blood and arteries may have been of interest to Stoker, in view of the preoccupations of his most famous fictional character. In 1878, he witnessed the marriage of his sister Margaret to Thomson, who was knighted in 1897, the year in which *Dracula* was published. Thornley and Thomson founded the school of nursing at the Richmond Hospital and rebuilt its surgical block. Thomson also collaborated with Stoker's youngest brother, George, over equipping the Irish Hospital in South Africa during the Boer War. George, who was also a surgeon, published a book on the treatment of wounds. Specialising in diseases of the throat, he became the consulting physician for the Lyceum Theatre in London, where Bram was business manager.[117] His position had come about through the influence of Dr Henry Maunsell who, like George's eminent brother Thornley, was a member of the Royal College of Surgeons in Ireland. Stoker's other brother Richard was another surgeon, who had entered the Indian medical service and served with the Indian army in Nepal, Tibet and Afghanistan.

Apart from family members, Stoker knew a number of physicians including Sir William Wilde, the eminent ophthalmic specialist and father of the famous wit and playwright, Oscar Wilde. Another acquaintance, also qualified in medicine, was Irish poet and playwright, John Todhunter.[118] But the greatest medical influence on the writing of the novel is generally accepted to have been that of his brother, Thornley. Being an ardent critic of writing style, he had a keen interest in literature, welcoming literary figures to his home at Ely House in Dublin. Stoker brings the arts and sciences together in the person of his brother's fictional counterpart, Professor Van Helsing, who is not only a doctor of medicine but also a doctor of literature.

Thornley graduated in medicine in 1866, the year in which Brown's infamous book was published, which brought his surgical malpractices to public attention. This became the biggest scandal in the history of Victorian medicine and was reported at length in the *British Medical Journal*. Thornley and his brother George were regular contributors. There can be no doubt that they knew about Brown. In view of his medical interests, connections and the dissemination of the fallen surgeon's notorious book amongst the medical laity, Stoker must also have known of the furore over Brown's infamous operation. Not only was Stoker's friend Richard Burton in favour of clitoridectomy, but his brother had actually performed the operation himself.[119] It is a little-known fact that around June 1885 in a Dublin asylum, Thornley excised the clitoris of a lunatic woman, after she confessed to being a masturbator. This was nearly two decades after clitoridectomy had been discredited as an operation in Britain following Brown's downfall, though it was still being carried out in lunatic asylums. While performing the operation on lunatic women as a cure for onanism and even coercing sane women into having their clitorises removed as a prophylactic against insanity, Brown's big mistake was in claiming that the operation cured madness. In the hearing against him, leading psychiatrists Dr Henry Maudsley and Forbes Winslow testified that masturbation was not a cause of insanity, but the other way round.[120] Yet it appears that Thornley subscribed to a diagnosis of masturbatory insanity for his patient, describing her as, 'as mad as could be, and who was a persistent victim to the habit', observing that she had 'lost flesh, and had all the symptoms of hopeless insanity'.[121] After excising her clitoris, he recorded that she was 'now perfectly sane', having returned to her work as a governess and 'earning her living respectably'.[122] Thornley was also an advocate of the widespread 'castration of the male subject' for lunatics since, in his view, 'It corresponded with ovariotomy in the female, and was quite as justifiable.'[123]

Thornley was an authoritative figure to pronounce on such subjects. As well as being a member of the medico-psychological society, he was the visiting surgeon to St Patrick's Hospital (Dean Swift's Hospital for the Insane), where the clitoral surgery had taken place. From 1873, he held the position of surgeon at the Richmond Hospital, whose asylum was under the stewardship of a certain Dr Stewart. Paul Murray suggests that this may be where Stoker acquired the name of the alienist, Dr Seward, who runs the asylum close to Dracula's house on the Carfax estate near Purfleet, Essex.[124] One of his patients, Renfield, has an injury to his cranium, which Seward treats with trepanning. Thornley was an acclaimed pioneer in brain surgery in Ireland and, in 1888, published an article, 'On a Case of Subcranial Haemorrhage Treated by Secondary Trephining'. Seward is praised as a surgeon for his steady hand by Van Helsing, who tells him: 'You, whom I have seen with no tremble of hand or heart, do operations of life and death that make the rest shudder' (p. 202). Most likely, this characterisation was inspired by Thornley, who was renowned as one of the finest surgeons of his generation and particularly lauded for his hernia operations, which invariably involved abdominal surgery. As the surviving manuscript notes reveal, Stoker consulted his brother over medical and surgical details in the novel. In turn Thornley, who edited the clinical records for the Dublin hospitals and wrote articles for medical journals, may have discussed with his younger sibling contentious medical topics, including the rationale for controversial sexual surgery.

In the 1880s, Thornley entered into the debate over whether some gynaecological operations were necessary or not, arguing that clitoridectomy could be an effective deterrent for masturbation and 'the relief of a mental condition'.[125] For him, this treatment was preferable to normal ovariotomy, especially for women of childbearing age. The removal of healthy ovaries was endorsed by the eminent surgeons Sims and Tait and used widely in the treatment of lunacy. Even though Thornley appears to concur with these views, he refused to advocate such treatment unless others were tried first. The question Dr Seward raises in regard to Lucy, 'Why mutilate her poor body without need?' (p. 202), is one that Thornley might have put to fellow surgeons about to perform normal ovariotomy, particularly since he opposed the routine removal of ovaries in gynaecological operations. But he was certainly willing to countenance normal ovariotomy if a cure for mental disturbances by way of clitoridectomy had failed to cure a patient's condition. Medical opinion advocating surgical intervention for masturbation and its treatment was divided. Thornley's brother-in-law William Thomson, who edited the proceedings for the Royal Academy of Medicine in Ireland which recorded these discussions, had opposed the use of ovariotomy in such cases, insisting that other methods be explored first, such as restraint. Unlike Thornley, he expressed scepticism over the link between masturbation and insanity, although he was in no doubt as to the baleful effects of 'the terrible habit'.[126] Disturbingly, it was Thornley's argument that clitoridectomy would halt masturbation, rather than his insistence that it cured insanity, which was challenged by Dr W. K. M'Mordie, a gynaecologist from Belfast whose case history had initiated the debate.[127] This involved a double ovariotomy performed on a woman whose insanity, M'Mordie claimed, resulted from the habit of masturbation. For her, this was scarcely the solitary private activity indicated by Diane Mason in the title of her book, *The Secret Vice*, since the patient used to masturbate openly in front of her husband and children. Although M'Mordie agreed with the incontrovertible fact that Thornley's removal of his patient's clitoris precluded sexual stimulation of that particular erogenous zone, he warned that masturbation might still persist if the patient 'had been in the habit of operating on her person by using a blunt instrument in the vagina, even to the extent of gentle drumming against the cervix uteri'.[128] He used this speculation to defend his own castrating surgery that, he claimed, had 'completely cured' his patient 'of the pernicious habit' of masturbation, even though removing her ovaries had done little to alleviate her insanity.[129] While clitoridectomy was generally frowned on by this time, other forms of female castration as a cure for hysteria and insanity were being questioned during the 1890s by physicians who saw them as a fashionable craze.

Clearly Thornley Stoker was at the forefront of medical practice and debate. Like Brown, Sims and Tait, he was a surgical pioneer. Just like them, he had carried out sexual surgery for sound clinical reasons to alleviate the suffering of women, but he also misguidedly succumbed to bogus theories, justifying surgical mutilation and unnecessary castration. Clearly, there were many aspects of the mind–body relationship in the field of female medicine that were still poorly understood. Thornley's aplomb in the following statement is indicative of the self-assuredness of the Victorian surgeon, who believed that he held the surgical keys to women's health and well-being by operating on female sexual and reproductive organs:

It is but a few years since a host of diseases of these parts, which were imperfectly understood if understood at all, have been explored, explained, and illuminated – have had their pathology made clear, their causation defined, their symptoms and treatment correctly laid down – have been, in fact, removed from the regions of obscurity and uncertainty, and placed in the realms of reasonable observation and intelligent treatment.[130]

The progress outlined above by Thornley is commendable, but the 'host of diseases' in receipt of 'intelligent treatment' would have included hysteria, the pathologising of masturbation and the link between insanity and female reproductive organs. It was not until the 1950s that hysteria, as a diagnostic category, was finally discarded and the last clitoridectomy carried out in the United States for the prevention of masturbation.[131] The pseudo-scientific epistemology of Stoker's fictional professor of medicine gives us a glimpse into the proliferating knowledge of pathology and its experimental surgical cures to which Thornley and his contemporaries contributed. Van Helsing's declaration that 'we must be brave of heart and unselfish, and do our duty' (p. 208) precedes the sentiments expressed in Thornley's obituary, where he is extolled as a man who had 'the courage born of strong conviction and a high sense of duty'.[132] Professor Van Helsing and Dr Seward, who succeed in eradicating the disease of vampirism, unite to form a literary homage in *Dracula* to the medical and surgical prowess of William Thornley Stoker.[133]

NOTES

1 Isaac Baker Brown, *On the Curability of Certain Forms of Insanity, Epilepsy, Catalepsy, and Hysteria in Females* (London: Robert Hardwicke, 1866), p. 8.

2 Quoted in Ann Dally, *Women under the Knife: A History of Surgery* (London: Hutchinson Radius, 1991), p. 199.

3 Although instances of male circumcision in Britain waned by the 1950s, it continues today in the United States for over 50 per cent of newborns.

4 Quoted in J. Barker-Benfield, *The Horrors of the Half-Known Life: Male Attitudes towards Women and Sexuality in Nineteenth-Century America* (New York: Harper & Row, 1976), p. 88.

5 Quoted in G. J. Barker-Benfield, 'The Spermatic Economy: A Nineteenth-Century View of Sexuality', *Feminist Studies*, 1 (Summer 1972), 60.

6 See Bram Stoker, *Personal Reminiscences of Henry Irving* (London: William Heinemann [1906], 1907), p. 20.

7 See Paul Murray, *From the Shadow of Dracula: A Life of Bram Stoker* (London: Jonathan Cape, 2004), p. 26.

8 See Carol A. Senf, *Science and Social Science in Bram Stoker's Fiction* (Westport, CT: Greenwood Press, 2002), p. 50.

9 See James V. Ricci, *The Development of Gynaecological Surgery and Instruments: A Comprehensive Review of the Evolution of Surgery and Surgical Instruments for the Treatment of Female Diseases from the Hippocratic Age to the Antiseptic Period* (San Francisco, CA: Norman Publishing [1949], 1990).

10 For a useful overview of how the novel relates to medicine, the mind and the body, see William Hughes, *Bram Stoker Dracula: A Reader's Guide to Essential Criticism* (Basingstoke: Palgrave Macmillan, 2008), pp. 46–76.

11 See *Bram Stoker's Notes for Dracula: A Facsimile Edition*, ed. Robert Eighteen-Bisang and Elizabeth Miller (Jefferson, NC: McFarland, 2008), pp. 178–85.

12 See Stephanie Moss, 'The Psychiatrist's Couch: Hypnosis, Hysteria, and Proto-Freudian Performance in *Dracula*', in Carol Margaret Davison (ed.), with the participation of Paul Simpson-Housley, *Bram Stoker's Dracula: Sucking through the Century, 1897–1997* (Toronto: Dundern Press, 1997), pp. 123–46.

13 See Stanley West, MD with Paula Dranov, *The Hysterectomy Hoax: The Truth about Why Many Hysterectomies Are Unnecessary and How to Avoid Them* (New York: Doubleday, 1994). In 1971, the gynaecologist Ralph W. Wright's lack of respect for the womb when no longer needed for childbearing is evident from his dismissal of it as 'a useless, bleeding, symptom-producing, potential cancer-bearing organ' that ought to be removed. Wright is quoted in the aptly named chapter 'When in Doubt, Take It Out' by John Robbins, in *Reclaiming Our Health: Exploding the Medical Myth and Embracing the Source of True Healing* (Tiburon, CA: H. J. Kramer, 1996), p. 125.

14 Quoted in Ann Dally, *Fantasy Surgery 1880–1930* (Amsterdam: Rudopi, B.V., 2006), p. 26.

15 Quoted in Ornella Moscucci, *The Science of Woman: Gynaecology and Gender in England 1800–1929* (Cambridge: Cambridge University Press [1990], 1993), p. 158.

16 See Moscucci, *The Science of Woman*, p. 158.

17 Quoted in Hanny Lightfoot-Klein, *Secret Wounds* (Bloomington, IN: 1stBooks, 2002), p. 28.

18 See *Stoker's Notes for Dracula*, ed. Eighteen-Bisang and Miller, p. 283. Here the book title has been cited incorrectly, using the word '*Nature*' instead of '*Practice*'.

19 This was performed by John G. Clark at the Johns Hopkins Hospital in Baltimore, Maryland, which had been preceded by the first, less radical abdominal extirpation of the uterus in 1878. See Dally, *Women under the Knife*, p. 141.

20 William Thornley Stoker, 'Successful Removal of the Uterus and One Ovary for the Relief of a Subperitoneal Uterine Tumour', *The Dublin Journal of Medical Science*, 69:2 (1880), 87.

21 Thornley Stoker, 'Successful Removal of the Uterus', 87–8.

22 Quoted in Thomas Joseph Pettigrew, *On Superstitions Connected with the History and Practice of Medicine and Surgery* (London: John Churchill, 1844), p. 2. The quotation is from Sir Thomas Browne's *Religio Medici* (1642), which Stoker admired.

23 See James Greig Smith, *Abdominal Surgery*, 2 vols (London: Churchill, 1896), 1, p. 64.

24 See Bram Stoker, *The New Annotated Dracula*, ed. Leslie S. Klinger (New York: W. W. Norton, 2008), p. 248. I am grateful to Elizabeth Miller for drawing my attention to this reference.

25 See Pettigrew, *On Superstitions*, p. 62.

26 See William Hughes, *Beyond Dracula: Bram Stoker's Fiction and Its Cultural Context* (Basingstoke: Macmillan, 2000), pp. 154–5. Elisabeth Bronfen traces a hysterical discourse relating to Lucy and Mina in *Over Her Dead Body: Death, Femininity and the Aesthetic* (Manchester: Manchester University Press, 1992), pp. 313–23.

27 The term 'onanism' originates from the Book of Genesis, chapter 38, in relation to the *coitus interruptus* of Onan and is thought by scholars to have been wrongly applied to masturbation. This usage was popularised through the publication of the highly influential anonymous tract, *Onania; or, The Heinous Sin of Self-Pollution, and All Its Frightful Consequences, in Both Sexes*, probably published some time around 1712.

28 See Jean Stengers and Anne Van Neck, *Masturbation: The History of a Great Terror*, trans. Kathryn Hoffman (New York: Palgrave, 2001).

29 Quoted in John Duffy, 'Masturbation and Clitoridectomy: A Nineteenth-Century View', *Journal of the American Medical Association*, 186:3 (October 1963), 246.

30 See Frederick Hodges, 'A Short History of the Institutionalization of Involuntary Sexual Mutilation in the United States', in George C. Denniston and Marilyn Fayre Milos (eds), *Sexual Mutilations: A Human Tragedy* (New York: Plenum Press, 1997), p. 20.

31 See Hodges, 'A Short History', pp. 20–1. See also Lesley A. Hall, 'Forbidden by God, Despised by Men: Masturbation, Medical Warnings, Moral Panic, and Manhood in Great Britain, 1850–1950', *Journal of the History of Sexuality*, 2:3 (January 1992), 365–87.

32 See Murray, *From the Shadow of Dracula*, p. 174.

33 This was first published in 1852 in Sheffield under the title, William Fox, *Working-Man's Family Botanic Guide*, quoted in Diane Mason, *The Secret Vice: Masturbation in Victorian Fiction and Medical Culture*

(Manchester: Manchester University Press, 2008), p. 41. She has added the emphasis.

34 Quoted in Mason, *The Secret Vice*, p. 36.

35 See Hall, 'Forbidden by God', 371.

36 Robert Mighall, '"A pestilence which walketh in darkness": Diagnosing the Victorian Vampire', in Glennis Byron and David Punter (eds), *Spectral Readings: Towards a Gothic Geography* (Basingstoke: Palgrave Macmillan, 1999), p. 117.

37 The existence of such an illness was endorsed by the leading psychiatrist of his day, Henry Maudsley, in 1867. See Julie Peakman, *The Pleasure's All Mine: A History of Perverse Sex* (London: Reaktion Books, 2013), p. 66. Maudsley later retracted this medical opinion. See also E. H. Hare, 'Masturbatory Insanity: The History of an Idea', *Journal of Mental Science*, 108 (January 1962), 1–25.

38 Barker-Benfield, 'The Spermatic Economy', 60.

39 See Robert Darby, *A Surgical Temptation: The Demonization of the Foreskin and the Rise of Circumcision in Britain* (Chicago, IL: University of Chicago Press, 2005), p. 288.

40 See Robert Darby, 'The Masturbation Taboo and the Rise of Routine Male Circumcision: A Review of the Historiography', *Journal of Social History*, 36:3 (Spring 2003), 750.

41 This is taken from Stoker's novel *Lady Athlyne* (1908) and quoted in Daniel Farson, *The Man Who Wrote Dracula: A Biography of Bram Stoker* (London: Michael Joseph, 1975), p. 215.

42 See Mason, *The Secret Vice*, p. 8.

43 Quoted in Ornella Moscucci, 'Clitoridectomy, Circumcision, and the Politics of Sexual Pleasure', in Andrew H. Miller and James Eli Adam (eds), *Sexualities in Victorian Britain* (Bloomington, IN: Indiana University Press, 1996), p. 74.

44 Other diseases that allegedly could be cured by circumcision in the male included 'hip-joint disease (tuberculosis of the hip joint), hernia, bad digestion, inflammation of the bladder, and clumsiness'; Hodges, 'A Short History of the Institutionalization of Involuntary Sexual Mutilation', p. 22.

45 Ladelle McWhorter, *Racism and Sexual Oppression in Anglo America: A Genealogy* (Bloomington, IN: Indiana University Press, 2009), p. 174.

46 J. H. Kellogg, *Plain Facts for Old and Young or the Science of Human Life from Infancy to Old Age* (Battle Field Creek, MI: Good Health Publishing Company [1877], 1910), p. 383.

47 J. H. Kellogg, *Man the Masterpiece or Plain Truths Plainly Told, about Boyhood, Youth, and Manhood* (Battle Creek, MI: Modern Medicine Publishing Co. [1885], 1894), p. 384.

48 Kellogg, *Man the Masterpiece*, pp. 384–5.

49 See Bram Dijkstra, *Idols of Perversity: Fantasies of Feminine Evil in Fin-de-Siècle Culture* (New York: Oxford University Press, 1986), pp. 50–63.

50 Robert Barnes and Fancourt Barnes, *A System of Obstetric Medicine and Surgery*, 2 vols (London: Smith, Elder and Co., 1884), 1, p. 376.

51 Quoted in Lesley A. Hall, *Hidden Anxieties: Male Sexuality 1900–1950* (Cambridge: Polity Press, 1991), p. 104.

52 Kellogg, *Man the Masterpiece*, p. 384.

53 Kellogg, *Man the Masterpiece*, pp. 384 and 390. The figure number is not part of the quotation.

54 See Thomas Laqueur, *Making Sex: Body and Gender from the Greeks to Freud* (Cambridge, MA: Harvard University Press [1990], 1992), pp. 1–4.

55 See Gary Taylor, *Castration: An Abbreviated History of Western Manhood* (London: Routledge, 2000), p. 113.

56 See Robert Muchembled, *Orgasm and the West: A History of Pleasure from the Sixteenth Century to the Present*, trans. Jean Birrell (Malden, MA: Polity, 2008), p. 55.

57 Darby, *A Surgical Temptation*, p. 25.

58 A few years earlier in 1862, the *San Francisco Medical Press* reported that clitoridectomy had been performed on two young girls who, as compulsive masturbators, were otherwise doomed to 'hopeless insanity or an early grave'. The operation was declared a 'perfect success', even though the faculty of memory was not fully restored; Hodges, 'A Short History of the Institutionalization of Involuntary Sexual Mutilation', p. 21. The practice of removing the clitoris is believed to be ancient, and the word 'infibulation', referring to another form of female genital mutilation, has been traced to the piercing of the labia of Roman slaves with a '*fibulae*' (Latin for 'brooches') to prevent pregnancy.

59 Susan Kingsley Kent, *Sex and Suffrage in Britain 1860–1914* (London: Routledge [1987], 1990), p. 47; Darby, *A Surgical Temptation*, p. 155.

60 See Duffy, 'Masturbation and Clitoridectomy', 248.

61 See Elaine Showalter, *Sexual Anarchy: Gender and Culture at the Fin de Siècle* (London: Virago, 1992), p. 181.

62 Mason, *The Secret Vice*, p. 157, n.

63 Quoted in Dijkstra, *Idols of Perversity*, p. 334.

64 Quoted in Dijkstra, *Idols of Perversity*, p. 334.

65 Barker-Benfield, *The Horrors of the Half-Known Life*, p. 275.

66 Quoted in Barker-Benfield, *The Horrors of the Half-Known Life*, p. 272.

67 The literal meaning refers to spermaceti, which is the wax most commonly taken from the head of the sperm whale.

68 Barker-Benfield, *The Horrors of the Half-Known Life*, p. 94.

69 Quoted in Barker-Benfield, *The Horrors of the Half-Known Life*, p. 113.

70 Quoted in Barker-Benfield, *The Horrors of the Half-Known Life*, p. 250.

71 Quoted in Barker-Benfield, *The Horrors of the Half-Known Life*, p. 93.

72 Quoted in Barker-Benfield, *The Horrors of the Half-Known Life*, pp. 95–6.
73 Quoted in Barker-Benfield, *The Horrors of the Half-Known Life*, p. 112.
74 William Acton, *The Functions and Disorders of the Reproductive Organs in Childhood, Youth, Adult Age, and Advanced Life: Considered in Their Physiological, Social, and Moral Relations* (London: John Churchill, 4th edn [1857], 1865), p. 112.
75 Richard von Krafft-Ebing, *Psychopathia Sexualis with Especial Reference to the Antipathic Sexual Instinct: A Medico-Forensic Study* (New York: Arcade Publishing [1871], 1998), p. 8.
76 Quoted in Barker-Benfield, *The Horrors of the Half-Known Life*, p. 283.
77 Charles D. Meigs, *Females and Their Diseases: A Series of Letters to His Class* (Philadelphia, PA: Lea and Blanchard, 1848), p. 47.
78 Barker-Benfield, *The Horrors of the Half-Known Life*, p. 84.
79 Quoted in Sarah W. Rodriguez, 'Rethinking the History of Female Circumcision and Clitoridectomy: American Medicine and Female Sexuality in the Late Nineteenth Century', *Journal of the History of Medicine and Allied Sciences*, 63:3 (July 2008), 344, n.
80 See Rebecca Stott, *The Fabrication of the Late-Victorian Femme Fatale: The Kiss of Death* (Basingstoke: Palgrave Macmillan, 1992).
81 Quoted in Jeffrey Moussaieff Masson, *A Dark Science: Women, Sexuality, and Psychiatry in the Nineteenth Century* (New York: Farrar, Straus and Giroux, 1986), p. 80.
82 Quoted in Masson, *A Dark Science*, p. 84.
83 Quoted in Masson, *A Dark Science*, pp. 82–3.
84 Quoted in Masson, *A Dark Science*, p. 89.
85 Quoted in Duffy, 'Masturbation and Clitoridectomy', 248.
86 Masson, *A Dark Science*, p. 81.
87 Quoted in Masson, *A Dark Science*, p. 88.
88 Quoted in Masson, *A Dark Science*, p. 84.
89 Quoted in Mason, *The Secret Vice*, p. 43. Emphasis added by Mason.
90 Quoted in Masson, *A Dark Science*, p. 83.
91 Quoted in Lesley Hall, '"The English Have Hot-Water Bottles": The Morganatic Marriage between the British Medical Profession and Sexology since William Acton', in Roy Porter and Mikulas Teich (eds), *Sexual Knowledge, Sexual Science: The History of Attitudes to Sexuality* (Cambridge: Cambridge University Press, 1994), p. 353.
92 Selzer, *Confessions of a Knife*, p. 17.
93 Quoted in Robert Darby, 'The Benefits of Psychological Surgery: John Scoffern's Satire on Isaac Baker Brown', *Medical History*, 51 (2007), 533.
94 See Rodriguez, 'Rethinking the History', 325, n.
95 Quoted in Rodriguez, 'Rethinking the History', 26.
96 Quoted in Barker-Benfield, *The Horrors of the Half-Known Life*, p. 107.

97 Quoted in Barker-Benfield, *The Horrors of the Half-Known Life*, p. 107.

98 There are several versions of this story. It should be noted that Sims was not the inventor of the speculum. See Dally, *Women under the Knife*, pp. 126–8.

99 Sigmund Freud, 'The Question of Lay Analysis: Conversations with an Impartial Person', *Standard Edition of the Complete Psychological Works*, 24 vols (London: Hogarth Press (1926), 20, pp. 183–250.

100 Quoted in Barker-Benfield, *The Horrors of the Half-Known Life*, p. 95.

101 See William Thornley Stoker, 'Extensive Rupture of Liver and One Kidney, Followed by Attempts at Repair, Showing the Possibility of Recovery in Such a Case', Proceedings of the Pathological Society of Dublin, *The Dublin Journal of Medical Science*, 69:2 (1880), 62–4.

102 Quoted in Karen Halttunen, *Murder Most Foul: The Killer and the American Gothic Imagination* (Cambridge, MA: Harvard University Press [1998], 2001), p. 190.

103 This physician was Wharton Sinkler, who is quoted by Andrew Scull in *The Insanity of Place/The Place of Insanity: Essays on the History of Psychiatry* (Abingdon: Routledge, 2006), p. 166.

104 See Charlotte Stoker, *On Female Emigration from Workhouses* (Dublin: Alexander Thom, 1864).

105 Quoted in Dally, *Women under the Knife*, p. 145.

106 See Moscucci, *The Science of Woman*, p. 242, and a letter by T. Spencer Wells, 'Vivisection and Ovariotomy', *The British Medical Journal*, 2 (November 1879), 794.

107 See Anne Stiles, *Popular Fiction and Brain Science in the Late Nineteenth Century* (Cambridge: Cambridge University Press, 2012), pp. 61–2.

108 See Sarah Grand, *The Beth Book*, ed. Sally Mitchell (Bristol: Thoemmes Press [1897], 1994), pp. xvi–xviii. This New Woman novel draws attention to these issues. The antivivisection movement was identified with proto-Victorian feminism and the campaign for women's suffrage.

109 See Showalter, *Sexual Anarchy*, p. 179.

110 Quoted in Barker-Benfield, *The Horrors of the Half-Known Life*, p. 113.

111 Quoted in Rachel Maines, *The Technology of Orgasm: Hysteria, the Vibrator, and Women's Sexual Satisfaction* (Baltimore, MD: Johns Hopkins University Press, 1999), p. 39. The French author A. Sigismond Weber describes 'vulvular massage' in his 1889 book on massage and electricity. See Maines, *The Technology of Orgasm*, pp. 70–1.

112 Mary Lynn Stewart, *For Health and Beauty: Physical Culture for French Women, 1880s–1930s* (Baltimore, MD: Johns Hopkins University Press, 2001), p. 88. Not least for reasons of its doubtful success, there is no convincing evidence to indicate that this was the widespread practice that Maines claims. See Lesley Hall, 'Doctors Masturbating Women as a Cure for

Hysteria/"Victorian Vibrators"', *Victorian Sex Factoids*, www.lesleyahall.net/factoids.htm#hysteria. Accessed 9 September 2011.

113 See Iwan Rhys Morus, *Shocking Bodies: Life, Death and Electricity in Victorian England* (Stroud: The History Press, 2011), p. 154.

114 See Foucault, *The History of Sexuality*, p. 69.

115 See Hughes, *Bram Stoker Dracula: A Reader's Guide*, p. 47.

116 See Murray, *From the Shadow of Dracula*, p. 76.

117 See Senf, *Science and Social Science*, p. 51.

118 See Hughes, *Bram Stoker Dracula: A Reader's Guide*, p. 47.

119 '"Ovariotomy" in Obstetrical Section, in William Thomson (ed.), *Transactions of the Royal Academy of Medicine in Ireland*, 5 (December 1887), 477.

120 See Elaine Showalter, 'Victorian Women and Insanity', in Andrew Scull (ed.), *Madhouses, Mad-Doctors and Madmen* (London: Athlone Press, 1981), p. 328.

121 'Ovariotomy', Thomson (ed.). *Transactions* 477.

122 'Ovariotomy', Thomson (ed.). *Transactions* 477.

123 'Ovariotomy', Thomson (ed.). *Transactions* 477.

124 See Murray, *From the Shadow of Dracula*, p. 175.

125 'Ovariotomy', Thomson (ed.). *Transactions* 477.

126 'Ovariotomy', Thomson (ed.). *Transactions* 479.

127 This had taken place on 4 February 1887.

128 'Ovariotomy', Thomson (ed.). *Transactions* 479.

129 'Ovariotomy', Thomson (ed.). *Transactions* 477.

130 Thornley Stoker, 'Successful Removal of the Uterus', 87.

131 See Darby, 'The Masturbation Taboo', 747.

132 'Obituary. Sir William Thornley Stoker, Bart., M.D., Dublin', *The British Medical Journal* (June 1912), 1400.

133 As Eighteen-Bisang and Miller point out, there are a number of candidates on whom Stoker might have based the character, though 'the Notes champion Bram's brother William Thornley'; *Stoker's Notes for Dracula*, p. 283. In 1879, Stoker named his only son Irving Noel Thornley Stoker, after his celebrated brother and Henry Irving.

4
Nazis, Jews and Nosferatu

[*Dracula*] anticipates the mass destruction of both European Jews and sexual deviants at the hands of Nazi racial hygienists. The teutonic Dr. van Helsing's surgical assault on the supine, immobile, and vulnerable form of Dracula, in a ritual murder outside conventional morality, without the sanction of law and due process, for the sake of the health of the nation, its youth, and its womenfolk, found a kind of realization 45 years later in the operating theater of Dr. Joseph Mengele.[1]

H. L. Malchow, *Gothic Images of Race* (1996)

The Jewish body has been represented as that of blood-sucker and carrier of diseases from plague to syphilis. Even the very body parts of Jews, such as eyes, nose and feet, have been demonised and pathologised. One of the most damaging conflations of monstrosity and race has been that of vampire and Jew. This anti-Semitic association goes back to the Middle Ages and has been perpetuated through folklore, literature and cinema, reaching its nadir as a tool of Nazi propaganda. The most well-known literary vampire, Count Dracula, can be seen to resemble a negative stereotype of a Jew.[2] It will be argued that Jewish influences relating to Stoker's contemporaries, Henry Irving and Richard Burton, may have helped inspire his fictional character, along with various anti-Semitic sources. It is important, however, to note that Stoker does not identify Dracula specifically as Jewish. This may be because he did not want to come across to his reader as overly anti-Semitic, even though he exploits the stereotype of a Jew in the novel through the character of Immanuel Hildesheim. Undeniably a specifically Semitic identification would detract from the versatility of Count Dracula in embodying myths of colonial discourse or as a general racial and political Eastern Europe menace, as discussed in the next chapter.[3] But even though Dracula identifies his racial origins as Szekely, boasting that his veins contain the blood of Attila the Hun, it is difficult to deny that the most prominent racial marker of his ethnically multilayered and composite character is Jewish.

This chapter takes this negative representation further by charting its transmission into the novel's first surviving film adaptation, *Nosferatu: A Symphony of Horror* (1922), directed by F. W. Murnau. As a seminal and much-loved film, it is not surprising to find anti-Semitic interpretations being brushed aside. Its release fed into a resurgence of anti-Semitism in Germany stoked by conspiracy theory and Artur Dinter's best-selling novel, *The Sin against the Blood* (1918). In the 1920s, anti-Jewish discourses, exacerbated by mass immigration, political factions and the economic consequences of the First World War, were rapidly being assimilated into Weimar culture. This is apparent from the shorter fiction of Hanns Heinz Ewers, although his novel *Vampire* (1920) presents a more positive approach to the Jew. Murnau's anti-Jewish stereotype is reflected in E. Elias Merhige's *Shadow of the Vampire* (2000), a dramatisation about the making of *Nosferatu*. Set in the aftermath of the First World War, Merhige's film anticipates the rise of German fascism. Towards the end, a white-coated film-maker addressed as *Herr Doktor* becomes the uncanny double of a Nazi doctor projecting onto a Jew his own diseased ideology. Drawing on Derrida's hauntology, the spectre of anti-Semitism within fascist cinema will be seen shadowing Merhige's film. Negative representations of Jews in German Expressionist cinema, including *Nosferatu* and Paul Wegener's Golem films (1915–30), provided Nazis with ready-made images of horror for their 1940 propaganda films, *The Eternal Jew* and *Jew Süss*, associations that have disturbing implications for the Gothic. Even though the vampire trope has been applied to both Nazi and Jew, the most persistent blood-sucker is undeniably the pestilence of anti-Semitism, which has infected the world for over a millennium.

WANDERING JEWS

The Nazis were not the only nationalist group to harness Jewish otherness for consolidating national identity and economic and political power. Eastern Jews (*Ostjuden*), particularly Ashkenazi, were maligned by their assimilated brethren wanting to distance themselves from the more easily recognisable orthodox Jew.[4] In the absence of a homeland, the Jewish diaspora has been reviled as feeding off the body politic of other nations. Debarred from entering numerous professions and trades by national laws, many Jews went into the practice of usury, especially where the profession was forbidden for Christians. This resulted in them being stigmatised as blood-suckers. Rather ironically the word '*neshech*', the biblical Hebrew for lending with interest, has another meaning of 'to bite', which provides an unfortunate connection with the vampire.[5] In Mary Shelley's historical novel *Valperga* (1823), Castruccio accuses Pepi: 'Thou vile Jew [...]. A usurer, a bloodsucker! [...] No, thou art not human.'[6] Even though these words are uttered by a fictionalised version of a historical personage, they leave a disturbing residue, especially when considered alongside an unfinished essay written by Mary Shelley, between 1814 and 1816, called 'A History of the Jews'. According to Jane Blumberg: 'It seems to represent a systematic anti-semitic diatribe in that it goes beyond a mere critique of religion to evoke racial stereotypes current in Shelley's day.'[7]

By the early 1880s, the term 'anti-Semitic' had gained currency in Britain.[8] Between 1881 and 1900, the number of foreign Jews residing in England had multiplied by 600 per cent.[9] The upsurge related to financial market disasters in Germany during the 1870s, which set in motion a stream of anti-Jewish measures. Repressions there and elsewhere in Europe, particularly Russia, led to mass migration. Literature of the *fin de siècle*, such as *Dracula*, saw the rise of invasion narratives. Fears of miscegenation penetrated British culture, arousing anxieties over the crypto-Jew, whose assimilation into mainstream society was seen as a threat to ideals of racial purity. Pogroms and persecutions, which kept the Jewish race in an endless peripatetic cycle of disappearance and reappearance for centuries, contributed to the notion of the so-called Hebrew as an eternal revenant. This process has been particularly conducive to representations of the Jew as a vampire or ghost. Leon Pinsker's pro-Zionist essay of 1882 describes the Jewish people as the 'ghostlike apparition of a living corpse', who, after having ceased to exist as an 'actual state' or 'political entity', still manage to resist 'total annihilation'.[10] As Sander Gilman points out in *The Jew's Body* (1991), the pseudo-science relating to race secularised religious prejudice against Jews.[11] The eugenic theories of the *fin de siècle* applied discourses of degeneration to constructions of the Jewish body, rendering it both pathological and criminal. These discursive practices were intent upon establishing the difference between Gentile and Jew, as well as emphasising the dangers and differences of the latter.

The most familiar anti-Semitic representation of the Jewish people is the nationless Wandering Jew, who has traversed European literature and myth since the later Middle Ages. His plight, however, has received sympathetic treatment by some writers and poets.[12] The Wandering Jew enters Gothic fiction by way of Matthew Lewis' *The Monk* and reappears in different guises in Godwin's *St Leon*, Maturin's *Melmoth the Wanderer* and Stoker's *Dracula*.[13] In *The Monk*, a burning cross on his forehead is concealed by a black velvet band. He is looked upon with 'terror and detestation' and his eyes hold 'an expression of fury, despair, and malevolence' capable of inspiring 'horror' (p. 163) in the very souls of those who look upon him. The journey of this Gothic immortal allegorises the history of the Jews as one of perpetual return. According to legend, the Wandering Jew, commonly known as Ahasver, was cursed by Christ for taunting him on the way to Calvary. His punishment was to wander the earth until the Second Coming of Christ. Robert Michael in *Holy Hatred* (2006) suggests that a Lutheran pamphlet of 1602 prompted the modern revival of this myth.[14] Bram Stoker was certainly familiar with the legend, as he wrote about the Wandering Jew in his book *Famous Impostors* (1910).

DRACULA AND THE JEW

The Wandering Jew shares with the vampire an extended span of life. For Stoker's vampires, this is of course brought about by drinking blood. The incantation of Dracula's disciple, Renfield, 'The blood is the life' (p. 178), parodies the Christian message of eternal life through the resurrection of Christ. The life-giving blood of the vampire can be read as a perversion of transubstantiation. This is central to the Catholic sacrament of Holy Communion, which is when the priest turns wine into Christ's blood for the congregation to drink. In certain respects, Dracula is a Christ-like figure, since his blood bequeaths perpetual life. In the light of this chapter, he can be seen as a blasphemous Jewish messiah, especially since, as the enemy of Christianity, Jews were accused of desecrating Christian sacraments. The year after *Dracula* was published, the Vatican newspaper, *L'Osservatore Romano*, launched an attack against Jews as vampires thirsting for Christian blood and plotting to destroy Christianity.[15] The egregious Blood Libel, dating back to the twelfth century, accused

Jews of murdering Gentiles, especially children. It was claimed that their blood was used for ritual purposes in the baking of matzot (unleavened bread) eaten during the Feast of Passover or to replenish blood lost by circumcised males and through menstrual bleeding, which also applied to Jewish men. In the novel, vampire women satiate their thirst with the blood of children. Hampstead Heath is Lucy's hunting ground for preying on children, while in Transylvania, Dracula tosses a bag to the three vampire women in his castle, which has something living inside it: 'There was a gasp and a low wail, as of a half-smothered child' (p. 71). Outside the castle walls, a distressed mother shouts out: 'Monster, give me my child!' (p. 77). As Anthony Julius points out: '*Dracula* was published just as the modern ritual-murder accusation in Central and Eastern Europe was at its most intense, and when comparing Jews to vampires was practically commonplace.'[16] There were a number of well-publicised Blood Libel trials in late nineteenth-century Europe, ending in acquittal. Exploited to incite racial hatred against Jews, the trials incited anti-Semitic agitation but also aroused widespread indignation on behalf of Jewish communities. The most well-known Blood Libel trial was the Tiszaeszlár Affair in Hungary, which was reported in the British press.[17]

Jewish persecution prompted a process of dejudaisation. Some Jews converted to Christianity as a means of concealing their Semitic origins and this gave rise to the anti-Semitic view of the Jew as a master of disguise. The Transylvanian Count Dracula attempts to pass as an Englishman when in London and is a shape-shifter, who turns into mist, a bat and a wolf. Another slur was to see the Jew as skilled in cupidity, paralleled by Dracula's hoarding of gold coins gathered from different countries. A connection with money, 'Christ-killing' and Jews has been made through the figure of Judas, described by Edgar Rosenberg as the 'apostle of the cash nexus', whose betrayal of Jesus for thirty pieces of silver is a precursor of Shylock's loan of three thousand ducats, with the forfeit of a pound of Antonio's flesh in Shakespeare's *The Merchant of Venice*.[18] Dracula is said to have had 'a smile that Judas in hell might be proud of' (p. 82). The early Church Father Jerome made his mark on anti-Semitic theology by identifying Jews with Judas. This aspersion fed into the myth of Jewish deicide, even though it was actually the Romans who executed Christ, mocking him as 'King of the Jews'. Father Jerome deepened the fissure between Christianity and Judaism by predicting the rise of a Jewish anti-Christ, who would become king through fraud and succeed in persecuting Christians. 'King-Vampire' (p. 412) is Van

Helsing's name for Dracula, who, through stealth and disguise, penetrates English society in order to harm its citizens and puts the wealth he has accumulated towards his master plan for invasion.

In 1892, American politician Tom Watson declaimed against 'red-eyed Jewish millionaires'.[19] His reference to the red-eyed monster 'Moloch, into which soulless Commercialism is casting human victims – the atrocious sacrifice to an insatiable god', has connotations of the Blood Libel.[20] Dracula's red eyes reoccur throughout the novel and Lucy responds to their uncanny repetition when reporting to Mina: 'His red eyes again! They are just the same' (p. 128). Mina catches sight of a stranger on the East Cliff at Whitby whose 'great eyes [are] like burning flames' (p. 129), the same 'red gleaming eyes' (p. 125) that she witnessed three days earlier. 'His eyes flamed red with devilish passion' (p. 322), as he forces Mina to drink his blood.

Within English anti-Semitism, there was a popular myth that Jews were prone to eye disease.[21] Charles Dickens makes use of the red-eyed Jew in *Great Expectations* (1860) and *Oliver Twist* (1838), which contains the following passage: 'The Jew sat watching in his old lair, with face so distorted and pale, and eyes so red and bloodshot, that he looked less like a man than some hideous phantom, moist from the grave, and worried by an evil spirit'.[22] This portrait of master thief Fagin resembles the criminal Count Dracula, whose three vampire women are described as 'Un-Dead *phantoms*' (p. 411; emphasis added). The eye of the Jew has been stigmatised as red, mesmeric and demonic through its association with the Evil Eye, a superstition referred to in *Dracula* and used in traditional depictions of the devil, an embodiment of evil that was also associated with Jews.

Anti-Semitism tells us, in the words of Judith Halberstam, 'nothing about Jews but everything about anti-Semitic discourse, which seems able to transform all threat into the threat embodied by the Jew'.[23] There is a fine line between explicating the processes involved in the demonisation of a people, religion or race and reinscribing it, as in the identification between vampire and Jew. As Halberstam argues, the markers of monstrosity are constructions of alterity projected onto the monstrous body, so that 'Othering in Gothic fiction scavenges from many discursive fields and makes monsters out of bits and pieces of science and literature. The reason Gothic monsters are over-determined – which is to say, open to numerous interpretations – is precisely because monsters transform the fragments of otherness into one body'.[24] With his 'peculiarly arched nostrils', 'peculiarly sharp white teeth' (p. 48), mesmeric gaze and long sharp fingernails, Count Dracula's physiognomy encodes a negative Jewish stereotype. The nose has been 'one of the central loci of difference in seeing the Jew'.[25] Its nostrility is usually associated with the Jewish or hawk nose described as having the convexity of a bow throughout its length.[26] Joseph Jacobs argued in 1886 that the defining characteristic of the Jewish nose was the accentuation of the nostrils, which Dracula most certainly has.[27] Stoker describes Dracula as having 'a strong – a very strong – aquiline' (p. 48) nose with a high bridge that is hooked and 'beaky' (p. 209). While the aquiline nose is not synonymous with the Semitic nose, the crucial point picked up by Carol Margaret Davison is that Stoker himself regarded the aquiline nose as Jewish.[28] In his *Personal Reminiscences of Henry Irving* (1906), he describes his employer, the redoubtable Henry Irving, applying stage makeup for the role of Shylock, commenting

> Though I have seen it done a hundred times I could never really understand how the lips thickened, with the red of the lower lip curling out and over after the manner of the typical Hebraic countenance, how the bridge of the nose under his painting [maquillage] – for he used no physical building-up – rose into the *Jewish aquiline.* [emphasis added][29]

For twenty-seven years from 1878, Stoker served as Irving's devoted manager. He had originally intended the character of Count Dracula to be a theatrical showcase for his idol and also discussed with Thomas Henry Hall Caine, to whom the novel is dedicated, the possibility of Irving playing the role of the Wandering Jew. Even though Caine was an active Jewish sympathiser, he still managed to perpetuate negative stereotypes through his writing.[30] Stoker describes a meeting between Caine and Irving in which he comments on the latter's distaste for a recent oppression, which had precipitated a Jewish 'Exodus' from Poland.[31] Irving's most well-known role was his highly sympathetic portrayal of Shylock in *The Merchant of Venice*. Nevertheless, this staging could not escape the danger of naturalising public perceptions of the grasping and avaricious Jew. First performed at the Lyceum Theatre in London in 1879, Irving went on to play the role over a thousand times. The drama was staged during the 1880s, when anti-Semitism was rife in Britain, exacerbated by the mass emigration of Eastern Jews into the East End of London. The actor's biographer, John Davis, was at pains to separate character from actor by pointing out that Irving 'has nothing Jewish in him by nature – a little narrowness about the eyes perhaps, but that is due to short sight'. He goes on to quote from a 'very able criticism' of the performance published in the *Daily News*, which insisted that Irving does not portray 'the decrepit nor the grotesque Jew', for 'malignant by nature he scarcely seems to be'. These remarks betray an endemic racism.[32]

Representations of the 'grotesque Jew' most certainly appear in *The Jew, the Gypsy and El Islam* (1898) written by Stoker's friend, Sir Richard Burton, whose research was carried out while serving as British Consul in Damascus. Excoriating the Jew as evil, Burton insisted on the authenticity of the Blood Libel, along with other racist myths. As Davison has noted, Burton's scathing, anti-Semitic depiction of the Jew in the following passage could have provided Stoker with a model for Dracula:

> His fierce passions and fiendish cunning, combined with abnormal powers of intellect, with intense vitality, and with a persistency of purpose which the world has rarely seen, and whetted moreover by a keen thirst for blood engendered by defeat and subjection, combined to make him the deadly enemy of all mankind, whilst his unsocial and iniquitous Oral Law contributed to inflame his wild lust of pelf, and to justify the crimes suggested by spite and superstition.[33]

The book was published the year after *Dracula* appeared, with the most objectionable parts relating to 'Human Sacrifice amongst the Sephardim, or Eastern Jews' removed. Since Burton completed the manuscript over ten years earlier in 1885, it is certainly possible that Stoker had read it and derived inspiration for his own ferocious, orally fixated, bloodthirsty fiend.[34] The year 1885 was also when Henry Irving met Burton. Irving had wanted to find out about the death of his schoolfriend, Edward Henry Palmer, who had been killed in the Sinai Desert, for it was Burton who had brought the murderers to justice. Prior to his death, before the British invasion of Egypt, Palmer had been working undercover, dressed in Arabic costume, as part of a secret reconnaissance mission. While serving as Consul of Trieste, Burton brought Palmer's body back home for burial at St Paul's Cathedral in London. Indeed, a corpse carried by ship from the East would play a pivotal role in Stoker's novel. Burton, who '*knew* the East […] its romances; its beauty; its horrors', might have provided Stoker with a model for the Count.[35] Stoker's first sight of Burton in 1879 riveted his attention as 'dark, and forceful, and masterful, and ruthless', leading him to conclude: 'I have never seen so iron a countenance.'[36] These qualities were in keeping with Burton's account of having murdered a young Arab on a hajj to Mecca, while disguised as a Muslim pilgrim. After telling Stoker the tale, he lifted his top lip and 'his canine tooth showed its full length like the gleam of a dagger'.[37] Had this gesture given Stoker a snapshot of his own fictional murderous traveller?

Certainly, Burton shared with Dracula forays into the worlds of sexual adventure, murder and foreign travel.[38]

Views about Jews, similar to those expressed by Burton, appear in a book that Stoker is known to have read. This is Major E. C. Johnson's *On the Track of the Crescent: Erratic Notes from the Piraeus to Pesth* (1885), which has a section on 'the Hungarian branch of that race "against whom is every man's hand", and who returns the compliment with compound interest'.[39] Accusing them of the commercial exploitation of the peasantry and accumulation of most of the world's wealth, Johnson stereotypes the racial characteristics of these particular Jews, claiming that 'The oval face; the "parrotty" [sic] beak' was 'out of all proportion to the other features', and he remarks on their 'shrewdness in driving bargains'.[40] These characteristics are brought together in an incident involving Stoker's Immanuel Hildesheim, a character identified by Jonathan Harker in theatrical terms as 'a Hebrew of rather the Adelphi Theatre type, with a nose like a sheep, and a fez. His arguments were pointed with specie [coined money] – we doing the punctuation – and with *a little bargaining* he told us what he knew' (p. 390; emphasis added). After helping Dracula flee his pursuers, Hildesheim betrays him to his enemies, thus reinforcing a negative stereotype of the treacherous mercenary Jew.

Another possible Jewish source for Stoker's 'Shylock of the Carpathians'[41] is the mesmeric Svengali, a Jew with big yellow teeth, who corrupts a young girl in George du Maurier's *Trilby* (1894). Barbara Belford points to distinct similarities between the two novels in that 'both deal with the fear of female sexuality and the loss of innocence, and with brave men who rescue the mother figure from a foreigner's embrace'.[42] Du Maurier was completing *Trilby* in Whitby during the summer of 1890, a time when the Stoker family were staying there too. A few years earlier, Du Maurier had sketched them in a country house setting for a *Punch* cartoon (11 September 1886).[43] There can be little doubt that Stoker would have read a novel as popular as *Trilby*, which sold over two hundred thousand copies in its first year. Impressive as these sales figures were, they would be surpassed by *Dracula*. In view of its wide readership, it is all the more disturbing that *Trilby* contains a blatant anti-Semitic discourse. For example, an elderly, fat woman is described as a Jewess 'of rather a grotesque and ignoble type',[44] while the evil impresario Svengali forms a Jewish caricature, whose mesmeric influence transforms the impoverished artist's model Trilby O'Ferrall into a diva. Vying for her affections, Little Billee punches his rival Svengali on the nose, causing a nosebleed, and, in so doing, attacks a signifier of racial difference. Later, Billee's friend Taffy experiences 'a fierce unholy joy' after violently tweaking Svengali's nose, after which he 'had for hours, the feel of that long, thick, shapely Hebrew nose being kneaded between his gloved knuckles, and a pleasing sense of the effectiveness of the tweak he had given it' (p. 201). 'The Nose', as a metonym for the Jew, was familiar enough, in 1892, to be used in the socialist newspaper, *The Clarion*.[45] 'Trilby-mania' led to stage and film adaptations that 'played up Svengali's Jewishness and further demonized the mesmerist'.[46] Described as an 'Oriental Israelite Hebrew Jew' (p. 205), Svengali's 'bold, black, beady Jew's eyes' (p. 35), like those of a rat, emit a 'very ugly gleam' (p. 13). He is compared to a supernatural bringer of nightmares by the young girl Trilby, who dreads him as a 'powerful demon, who [...] oppressed and weighed on her like an incubus' (p. 75). The novel anticipates Dracula's bloodthirst for Lucy and the sight of her dead body in the tomb, when Svengali taunts Trilby with the idea of looking at her lying in a 'little mahogany glass case' (p. 74) and making her feel 'as though he were taking stock of the different bones in her skeleton with *greedy* but discriminating approval' (p. 75; emphasis added). Following Trilby's death, the wooden packing case containing Svengali's personal belongings arrives at his home. Like the Wandering Jew and his descendants forced to wander from country to country, it 'seemed to have travelled all over Europe to London, out of some remote province in eastern Russia – out of the mysterious East! The poisonous East – birthplace and home of an ill wind that blows nobody good' (p. 239).

Similarly Dracula, who is originally from the East, arrives in London. On the cover of the 1902 edition of the novel, published by Doubleday, he resembles the Wandering Jew with his gleaming eyes and wrapped in a rough-looking cloak on his travels. Dracula comes to the attention of the Dutch doctor, lawyer and vampire slayer, Professor Abraham Van Helsing, whose first name doubles that of the author. Abraham is the name of the Old Testament patriarch, a founding father of Judaism, whose lifespan of 175 years pales before that of the Wandering Jew. Van Helsing records admiringly that Dracula in his life was an alchemist with 'a learning beyond compare' (p. 342), attributes often associated with Jews as Faustian dabblers in the occult and 'people of the book'. According to Van Helsing, Dracula 'dared even to attend the Scholomance, and there was no branch of knowledge of his time that he did not essay' (pp. 342–3). This was a place of forbidden learning situated in Transylvania, where the devil was the schoolmaster. Only ten scholars were granted access to his teaching and once the course ended, as Stoker reveals in the novel, the tenth had to remain behind as the devil's servant.[47] Davison suggests that Dracula might have been that tenth scholar.[48] Stoker's source for this folklore is Emily de Laszowska Gerard's essay 'Transylvanian Superstitions' (1885), where it is revealed that the tenth scholar was mounted upon an *ismeju* (dragon) in his capacity as the devil's aide-de-camp.[49] A coiled dragon was the family insignia for the fifteenth-century Eastern European figure from Wallachia, Voivode Dracula, also known as Vlad Tepes or Vlad the Impaler.[50] Stoker read a brief account of him while researching the novel and recorded that the word 'Dracula' means devil in the Wallachian language.[51] Jews were believed to be controlled by the devil and, for Van Helsing, the battle against Dracula is synonymous with that waged against the devil and acolytes like Lucy, who are 'the devil's Un-Dead' (p. 255). On realising that Dracula had left him a prisoner in his castle, Jonathan bewails 'this cursed land, where the devil and his children still walk with earthly feet!' (p. 85). This could be an allusion to the Jewish foot, which, as Gilman points out, 'has analogies with the hidden sign of difference attributed to the cloven-footed devil of the middle ages'.[52] As he indicates, this superstition was transformed by modern science into a signifier of disease. Jonathan condemns the sexualised vampire women in Dracula's castle as devils and disassociates them from his wife, saying: 'I am alone in the castle with those awful women. Faugh! Mina is a woman, and there is nought in common. They are devils of the Pit!' (p. 85). On drinking the blood of Dracula, Mina too becomes 'tainted […] with that devil's illness' (p. 396).

Vampirism, a site of contagion, has been interpreted in *Dracula* as a metaphor for the transmission of sexual disease, which resonates with anti-Jewish inferences of pathology and contamination. Towards the end of the nineteenth century, discourses of infection relating to sexuality were especially cognisant of syphilis and its spread through prostitution. The Contagious Diseases Acts of the 1860s implemented draconian measures of containment. Suspect women, mainly prostitutes, found to be infectious were interned in lock hospitals for protracted periods. Parallels can be made with the three seductive women in Dracula's castle infected with the disease of vampirism. This unpopular legislation was repealed in 1886. A connection between prostitution and Jews appears in the fraudulent Russian document called *Protocols of the Elders of Zion* (1903) and later in a defamatory statement by Adolf Hitler: 'Jews were the arch pimps; Jews ran the brothels; but Jews also infected their prostitutes and caused the weakening of the German national fibre.'[53] For centuries, Jewish people were maligned for spreading diseases such as syphilis, and yet mysteriously not succumbing to it themselves. At the start of the twentieth century, John Foster Fraser complained in the *Yorkshire Post* that England was powerless to prevent the transmission of 'smallpox, scarlet fever, measles, diphtheria', along with the migration of 'unwashed verminous alien[s]' from Eastern Europe and Russia.[54] Centuries earlier, Jews had been expelled from Germany for importing the Black Death.

PLAGUE, *NOSFERATU* AND JEWISH IMMIGRATION

The persistence of this plague-bringing stigma informs the plot of the German film *Nosferatu*, in which Stoker's Dracula, renamed Count Orlok, replays this Jewish menace. His arrival by ship imports two sources of pestilence, plague and vampirism. Not long after, there is a long shot of a line of coffins containing the bodies of plague victims being carried through the town of Wisborg in Germany. The film, set in 1838, probably drew on an actual cholera epidemic in 1830s Europe, in which hundreds of thousands died.[55] In Eugène Sue's novel, *The Wandering Jew* (1844), the curse of the Eternal Jew is linked to the spread of cholera, a notion that struck Stoker as one that 'seemed to be a dramatic inspiration and had prehensile grasp'.[56] The etymology of 'nosferatu' spells out another link with contagion. Stoker would have come across the word in Gerard's article 'Transylvanian Superstitions'. From this context, it is logical to assume that this word is the Romanian for an undead blood-sucker,[57] but it does not actually belong to that language. Its association with plague most probably derives from the Old Slavonic word *'nesufur-atu'*, borrowed from the Greek *'nosophoros'* meaning 'disease bearing'.[58] In Murnau's film, when Count Orlok arrives at the port of Wisborg, plague rats climb out of the hold. The Black Death was transported to many countries by vessels containing disease-carrying rats. The vampire's kinship with his fellow travellers is underscored by his appearance. The claw-like fingers, hairless cranium, bat-like ears and pointed front teeth resemble a rodent, as opposed to the canine fangs of Stoker's Dracula. The implications of Orlok's physiognomy bear the unmistakable stamp of the Jew, particularly since the actor Max Schreck wore a prosthetic to achieve an exaggerated hooked nose.[59] Orlok's rat-like appearance marks him out as the source of contagion. In Stoker's novel, the vampire hunters penetrate Dracula's lair at Carfax, where he keeps his boxes of earth, and discover it to be full of rats: 'They seemed to swarm over the place all at once, till the lamplight, shining on their moving dark bodies and glittering, baleful eyes, made the place look like a bank of earth set with fireflies [...]. The rats were multiplying in thousands' (pp. 291–2). The correlation between Jews and rats, stretching back to the medieval period and up to the twentieth century, has been perpetuated through caricature and cinema. In Murnau's *Nosferatu*, close shots of rats swarming off the ship resemble images in Fritz Hippler's anti-Semitic film *The Eternal Jew*, where shots of Jews are cut with those of teeming rats to generate revulsion over the spread of the 'Jewish plague'.[60] Hippler's graphic delineation of the international routes of Jewish immigration, as comparable to the global spread and transmission routes of plague rats, point to both as sources of contagion and instigators of mass death. A Nazi review of the film was headed: '*The Eternal Jew*: The Film of a 2000 Year Rat Migration'.[61]

Anti-Semites assumed that Jewish immigrants were incapable of assimilation within another country, believing that they took their own cultural soil with them for taking root in the 'host' nation. Count Dracula brings boxes to England containing his own native earth. One of the carriers transporting the boxes to the Count's Carfax residence complains that 'yer might 'ave smelled ole Jerusalem in it' (p. 266). A particularly fetid body odour (*foetor judaicus*) was historically associated with Jews, which medieval sources claimed could only be disguised by the sweet smell of Christian blood.[62] As Jonathan Harker discovers, Dracula has his own distinctly unpleasant smell: 'It may have been that his breath was rank, but a horrible feeling of nausea came over me' (p. 48). An anti-Semitic legend dating back to the Middle Ages tells of a Jew falling into a privy and was retold in John Foxe's *Book of Martyrs* (1570). The incident was used to illustrate the Jew's excremental nature. The 'malodorous air' in Dracula's Carfax lair is as 'stagnant and foul' as a sewer and, like disease, is 'composed of all the ills of mortality' (p. 290).[63] Joseph Banister, in claiming that Jews in London's East End were unhygienic, denied that 'the Jewish exile's smell' was an 'anti-Semite libel'.[64] Dracula sent six boxes of his native soil to Whitechapel in the East End, known as Mile End, New Town. The specific location was 197 Chicksand Street, a street that had at that time around 93 per cent Jewish occupancy.[65] Shop signs in the street were in both Yiddish and English, signifying an uncanny and alien culture. As an area associated with degeneration, crime, disease and prostitution, it provided a suitable resting place for a vampire as a further source of contamination. The boxes of earth being sent out to various locations were part of Dracula's master plan for invasion, which included the deracination of British women. By disguising himself as an Englishman, he was able to conceal his true nature as an enemy alien. Read as a sub-narrative of Jewish assimilation linked to infection and plague, Stoker tells a familiar story and one that would continue into the twentieth century. Hitler publicly announced that the 'opinion that it is possible to co-exist or come to some sort of compromise with this ferment of decomposition among peoples [the Jews], is like hoping that the human body might in the long run assimilate plague bacilli'.[66] In representing Jews as embodying a state of living decay, Hitler was drawing on the discourse of the vampire (Figure 7). He also refers to the Jewish people as blood-suckers in his autobiography *Mein Kampf* (1925–6), which was published three years after the release of *Nosferatu*.

Even though the film can be seen to exploit the association between Jews and vampires, there is no evidence that the director was an anti-Semite. For the part of Knock the estate agent, Murnau hired the most well-known Jewish actor in Berlin, Alexander Granach. Yet his film, like Stoker's novel, was susceptible to the contagion of anti-Semitism exacerbated by a scientific approach to race and widespread negative reactions to the influx of Eastern Jews. In Stoker's novel, the east to west progression of Dracula's journey to Britain marks the start of a vampire invasion as a kind of reverse colonisation, at a time when the British Empire was in decline.[67] Malchow points out that at the turn of the century nearly 90 per cent of emigrants from Romania were Jewish.[68] In the 1890s, political campaigners set out to limit the number of immigrants to Britain, particularly Jews. By 1900, they had even won support from members of the Jewish community. Writing in the *Jewish Chronicle*, Nathan Joseph, Chairman of the Jewish Board of Guardians, declared that helpless Jewish paupers posed 'a grave danger to the community' since they were 'mere dead weight' and 'useless parasites' and to admit them would be tantamount to 'homicide'.[69] These were the kind of immigrants that the Aliens Act, passed in 1905, set out to deter. While the Aliens Bill was being debated, an anti-Semitic question appeared in the London East End newspaper, the *Eastern Post*: 'Are our people ... still to have his fangs fastened in their throats? Is the life-blood of the nation to be sucked by the human vampires?'[70]

Before the making of *Nosferatu*, Jews from Semitic Transylvania had migrated in large numbers to Berlin, where the film would premiere. In the middle of the First World War, Romania's invasion of Transylvania

Der Vampyr

Figure 7 Cartoon of the Jew as vampire by Fips [Philipp Rupprecht], which appeared in the anti-Semitic newspaper *Der Stürmer*, no. 31 (1934). There is a German caption below, '*Vom Teufel in die Welt gesetzt er stets die Völker quält und hetzt*', which translates as 'Brought into the world by the devil he incessantly harrows and chases the people', i.e. the Gentiles.

Note: Reproduced in Randall L. Bytwerk, *Julius Streicher* (New York: Cooper Square Press [1983], 2001), figure 9.

had expedited this mass exodus of Eastern Jews. Their numbers swelled to around 45,000, with the added influx of Russian and Polish Jews fleeing government-sanctioned pogroms. Their traditional black attire gave them a timeless quality. Murnau's vampire wears clothes associated with Jews, such as his box-like Jewish cantor's hat and 'the tight-fitting cassock-like garment'[71] worn by Eastern Jews and mentioned in Johnson's book on Transylvania, which Stoker used as a source for *Dracula*. Between 1881 and 1914, over two-and-a-half million Jews emigrated from Eastern Europe to the West. Dracula's own trajectory in that direction is underscored by the surname of his victim Lucy Westenra, which has occidental connotations. Emigrants who moved to Germany found themselves in the heartland of Martin Luther, the father of the Protestant Reformation, who had been instrumental in expelling Jews from the state of Saxony and many German towns. In his rabidly anti-Semitic treatise entitled *On the Jews and Their Lies* (1543), Luther wrote that Jews contained 'the devil's feces ... which they wallow in like swine', and that the synagogue was an 'incorrigible whore and an evil slut'.[72] Luther advocated that synagogues and schools be set on fire, rabbis forbidden to preach or else face execution and Jewish houses be razed to the ground. He spread fears of Jews harming the wives and children of Germany. Employing a vampiric image, Luther warned that they would drain the wealth of the nation by sucking the marrow from the bones of its people. His treatise was paraded by the Nazis during the Nuremberg Rallies and a first edition was presented to Julius Streicher, editor of the Nazi newspaper *Der Stürmer*. It was hailed as the most radically anti-Semitic tract ever printed. Hitler declared, 'Luther, if he could be with us, would give us his blessing', and identified him as 'the mighty opponent of the Jews'.[73]

By stirring up past hatreds, Hitler was laying the ground for future persecution. Nonetheless anti-Semitism was already well established within Weimar culture. In 1922, the very same year in which *Nosferatu* was released, one of many anti-Semitic groups, the *Schutz und Trutz Bund* (the Protection and Defiance Federation), had recruited over 200,000 members with 530 local groups.[74] One of its members was the rabidly anti-Semitic Julius Streicher, whose poisonous propaganda would pave the way towards genocide. In 1921, he wrote: 'If we solve the Jewish question soon and thoroughly, then our rise and the happy future of our children is secured.'[75] Later he would be more explicit, declaring that Russian Jews 'must be exterminated root and branch', an injunction that he eventually extended to Jewry.[76] The instrument of liquidation was the Nazi Party, whose Nuremberg branch was founded in October 1922 by two thousand of Streicher's followers.[77] A few months earlier, Streicher had spoken out against Jews at a mass meeting held in Nuremberg. During the previous spring of 1921, he stirred up accusations of the Blood Libel by claiming that local children had been victims of this Jewish ritual murder.[78] The cumulative effects of his malicious campaign fed into a milieu of anti-Semitism that was mounting around the time of the making of *Nosferatu* and permeating Expressionist cinema. Yet these cinematic representations proved to be relatively mild compared to the highly dangerous and offensive stereotyping of Jews that had already appeared in a German novel written by Artur Dinter. His intention was to warn against the dangers of cultural assimilation and miscegenation by capitalising on the anti-Jewish feeling emerging out of the First World War.

RASSENSCHANDE

Artur Dinter, *The Sin against the Blood* and Hanns Heinz Ewers, *Vampire*

The Jewish population received an unjustifiable share of the blame for Germany's humiliating defeat in the First World War. Even though propaganda claiming that Jews had either not enlisted or shirked their duty was proved false by the publication of statistics, the damage was already done. In the final year of the war, a spate of anti-Jewish pamphlets, along with literary and historical publications, appeared. A leading anti-Semite was the English-born Houston Stewart Chamberlain, who had married the step-daughter of composer Richard Wagner. Chamberlain was the author of a work on German nationalism regarded as the gospel of the Nationalist Socialist movement, through which he promoted Aryan elitism and pontificated on the Jewish Question. In 1918, German novelist Dinter dedicated to Chamberlain his book, *The Sin against the Blood*, which is widely considered to be the 'first race novel' (*Rassenroman*).[79]

Anxieties over patterns of Jewish migration were gradually eclipsed by fears of assimilation. The mixing of different races, particularly miscegenation, draws on a discourse relating to the mingling of bloods, as does *Dracula* and *Nosferatu*. Dinter's *The Sin against the Blood*, in condemning interracial marriage between Gentile and Jew, provided the Nazis with an insidious tool for propaganda. By demonising such unions within a contemporary novel, Dinter paved the way for how miscegenation might be perceived by German cinema audiences through the conventions of horror film, as in *Nosferatu*.

The plot of Dinter's novel concerns the scientist Hermann Kämpfer (German for 'the fighter') and his relationship with two women. The first is with his wife Elisabeth, who is half-Jewish. She gives birth to his baby, who resembles her father, a Jew. This is imparted to the reader as Hermann's punishment for committing race defilement (*Rassenschande*). After her death, he marries a nurse called Johanna. Despite her pure German bloodline, she produces a Jewish-looking baby. The bogus explanation for this is because of her earlier sexual relationship with a Jewish man. The rationale for this racist plot was corroborated by pseudo-science, authoritatively

145

cited in the text, which asserted that Jewish sperm polluted pure German blood, thereby condemning Aryan mothers to hybrid offspring. Hermann seeks out his wife's Jewish former lover and murders him. On returning home, he discovers that his wife has killed their baby and committed suicide. Tried for his crime by a prosecutor who is a Jew, Hermann defends his actions, at length, insisting that he had helped defend Germany from the Jewish threat by 'defanging the Jewish vampire that sucks [the German people's] unsuspecting heart's blood'.[80] The fear of Jewish blood being mixed with the supposedly racially pure is expressed in a Nazi pamphlet, whose title draws on the discourse of infection and invasion: 'The Jewish World Parasite in the Bloodstream and Organs of the People'.[81] Dinter's dangerous novel was read by an estimated one-and-a-half million readers and provided the Nazis with a sinister mandate: 'If the German people do not succeed' in their endeavour 'to throw off and exterminate the Jewish vampire which it nursed with its heart's blood ... then it will die in the not-too-distant future'.[82]

These sentiments are given visual resonance in *Nosferatu* through a mise-en-scene of surrogate sexual consummation, within which Count Orlok feeds on a young German woman Ellen, as she lies on her bed. It is ironic that his bald head resembles that of a baby being nursed by its mother, at the same time as Ellen is bringing about his destruction. So intent has this creature of darkness been on drinking her blood that he inadvertently exposes himself to the daylight, which destroys him. Clutching his heart, Orlok's undead flesh fades from the screen. As Hitler noted in *Mein Kampf*, in sentiments similar to those of Dinter expressed above, 'After the death of his victim, the vampire [*der Vampir*] sooner or later dies too'.[83] German audiences, having read Dinter's best-selling novel, were primed to view Murnau's scene as a warning against interracial unions leading to racial death and 'bloodless murder'.[84] According to Dinter's racial allegory, Johanna, like Ellen, has to die because her blood has been contaminated, thus precluding her from producing Aryans for the Fatherland. By 1935, *Rassenschande* had become a criminal offence with the passing of the Nuremburg Laws. At the end of the war, Dinter was convicted by a denazification court in Offenburg and fined 1,000 Reichsmarks for being one of the architects of this racist legislation.

Another German novel dealing with sexual relations between a German and a Jew is *Vampire* by Hanns Heinz Ewers, published in 1920, two years before the release of *Nosferatu*. The following decade, the author would join the Nazi Party. Ewers' fascination with decadence, race and blood is evident from his novels and collection of short stories, *Blood* (1930), which contains incidents of drinking blood. The narrator of the title story is rumoured to be a *loup-garou* or blood-drinking werewolf, who targets sleeping children.[85] Ewers' *Alraune* (1911), the second of a fictional trilogy, is about a corrupt woman, who has been created by artificially inseminating a prostitute with the semen of a hanged man. She drinks the blood of the hero Frank Braun, based on the author himself, who, by the third novel, is transformed into a vampire.[86] This is *Vampire*, set during the First World War, which tells of how German patriot Frank goes to New York to garner support for Germany. Stricken by a mysterious illness, he finds himself revitalised following sexual contact with a former lover, Lotte Lewi. She is half-Jewish, as was Ewers' mistress, Adele Guggenheimer-Lewisohn, on whom she is based. It turns out that Frank, while falling into a trance during their love-making, had been drinking her blood. At first, Lotte allows him to imbibe only small amounts. After revealing to him that he has become a vampire, she allows him to drink deeper. Frank's knowledge of his transformation into the otherness of vampire coincides with American involvement in the war in Europe, which leads to his internment as an enemy alien. This event paralleled Ewers' arrest as a German spy in the United States in 1917. On his release, Frank ceases to be a vampire. Once free and in a healthy economy, he no longer needs to be a parasite. But his blood-drinking permanently damages Lotte's health who, like Ellen in *Nosferatu*, has willingly sacrificed herself for the greater good of others. For Lotte, this is for the purpose of uniting Jews and Germans through Frank in order to build a strong Germany. Drinking her Jewish blood enables Frank to acknowledge his German nationalism and acquire a sense of patriotic destiny, spurring him on as a fundraiser for his country. Here the connection with Jewishness and the accumulation of money is put to more positive use, in spite of Ewers' exploitation of a racial stereotype.

Conversely, 'Gold', according to Richard Burton, 'is the master of the world, and the Jewish people are becoming masters of the gold. By means of gold they can spread corruption far and wide, and thus control the destinies of Europe and of the world.'[87] This calumny anticipated the conspiracy theory expounded by the *Protocols of the Elders of Zion*, warning of a global takeover by Jews and the spectre of Jewish bankers controlling world economies. Van Helsing identifies Dracula as an alchemist, an art with an allegedly strong Jewish lineage, which involved the super-natural ability to transmute base metal into gold.[88] The legend provided anti-Semites with a convenient analogy for how they saw Jews manipu-lating the wealth of the world (Figure 8). In monetary terms, the threat of Dracula reverts back to 'the tyranny of feudal monopoly', which, as Franco Moretti explains, threatens the circulation of capital in a free British mar-ket.[89] In fact he is his own repository for wealth, since his cupidity is for blood, as well as money. When his coat is slashed by Jonathan Harker, Dracula appears to bleed a stream of gold coins. This might have been inspired by a story in the book written by his brother George Stoker about his war experiences in Europe and Asiatic Turkey, concerning a Jew who sews coins into his coat.[90] As Jimmie E. Cain explains, George vilified Jews as greedy and had targeted Jewish money lenders and bankers as more intent on accumulating wealth than caring for their families. In a similar vein, Bram picked up on Jewish usurers and merchants in his *Personal Reminiscences of Henry Irving*. Embracing a different fiscal model, Stoker's 'good brave men' (p. 351) are generous with their money in the cause of hunting the count and willingly donate their blood to vampire victim Lucy in a series of blood transfusions.[91] As mentioned earlier, Lotte allows Frank to drink her blood so that he can raise money for public good, by uniting German and Jew to defeat a common enemy. Lotte believes that her Jewish blood has magical properties that will enable Frank to speak charismatically and in such a way as to move the masses, 'the will of the war-spirit'.[92] Ironically, this attribute is prescient of Hitler as demagogue and war hawk. A German drawing on Jewish blood reserves, by sucking the veins of his girlfriend, in order to raise money for the kaiser, would prove to be a grim harbinger of the next world war, when Nazis would drain not only Jewish coffers but also Jewish blood.

Ewers oscillated between pro- and anti-Jewish sentiments. In his essay 'Why I Am a Philo-Semite' (1916), he proclaimed: 'I love the Jews and am obliged to love them, because I belong to the Germanic race and because I am an artist.'[93] Yet, Ewers exploits anti-Semitic stereotypes in 'The Dead Jew' (1930), a short story concerning the corpse of a Jewish man killed in a duel, who comes back to life, echoing Semitic legends of necromancy. Before his death, he is described in terms that are adversely racially inflected: 'God in heaven, but he was ugly! His baggy pants sagged over dirty shoes, whose crooked heels were turned inwards. An impressive pince-nez which dangled from a black cord sat topsy-turvy on a hor-rible nose that nearly eclipsed the bluish, chapped lips. His jaundiced,

Das größte Getreide-Wucherthier der Welt.

Neueste zoologische Entdeckung des Kikeriki.

Figure 8 Cartoon of the Jew as world-devouring vampire (1862). The German heading translates as 'The largest grain-speculating animal on earth', and below it is the caption: 'Most recent zoological discovery of the Kikeriki'. The *Kikeriki* (German for 'cock-a-doodle-doo') was an anti-Semitic Viennese cartoon paper.

Note: 'Anti-Semitism', *Encyclopedia Judaica*, 16 vols (Jerusalem: Keter Publishing House, 1971–2), 3, p. 153.

pockmarked and terribly unclean complexion was of an even more retiring disposition.[94] The representation of Jews as dirty and badly dressed had been widely disseminated through Gustav Freytag's popular novel, *Debit and Credit* (1855), read by millions of Germans.[95] Described as 'a lamb to the slaughter', the Jew is a victim in death, as he was in life.[96] While transporting the corpse back from the duel in a coach, the drunken men irreverently play cards with the dead man's hand. During his lifetime, the Jew had been afflicted by a speech impediment, which is analogous to the Jewish voice as a marker of difference.[97] This is Gothicised at the end of Ewers' story when the dead Jew breaks the silence of death with utterances, the effects of which terrify his drunken companions.

On his sixtieth birthday in 1931, Ewers was inducted into the Nazi Party by Hitler himself. He claims that he was invited by the Führer to write the biography of a member of the SA, a Nazi paramilitary group. Ewers' authorship of this semi-official novelisation of Nazi martyr Horst Wessel met with Hitler's approval, yet this did not prevent his name from being entered on a death list after the 'Night of the Long Knives' in June 1934, on account of his homosexuality and refusal to support the persecution of the Jews. Ewers survived and started writing satires about the Nazi era that remain unpublished. His books were banned, including *Vampire*. Since Ewers' blood-drinker is a German rather than a Jew, the novel failed to serve the ideological purposes of the Nazi Party, unlike Dinter's *The Sin against the Blood*. Its popularity is sure to have tainted how contemporary cinema audiences viewed *Nosferatu*. Appropriately, the film appeared in the same year as the first English translation of *Vampire*, which was published in America.

THE DANGER OF CINEMA AND NAZI VAMPIRISM

The power of cinema was recognised and deployed by the Nazis as a vehicle for more overt forms of anti-Semitism than those lurking in the shadows of Weimar Expressionist film. Gothic elements contained within films such as *Nosferatu* and *The Golem: How He Came into the World* (1920),[98] relating to the portrayal of Jewish characters, haunt the Nazi propaganda films, *Jew Süss*, directed by Veit Harlan, and Fritz Hippler's *The Eternal Jew*. Cinema constitutes a form of spectralisation populated by what Friedrich Kittler describes as the 'celluloid ghosts of the actors' bodies'.[99] This parallels the way in which Jews have been envisaged as a spectral people, inhabiting the uncanny space between life and death. Expressionist film, with its characteristic use of shadow as a cinematic and thematic device, was denounced by the Nazis as a decadent Jewish art form.

As he walks through the German town of Wisborg, Murnau's vampire from the 'land of phantoms'[100] merges with the spectrality of the European Jewish stereotype, appearing to the viewers as an apparition, unseen by locals. Film is a medium for the ghostly, moving backwards and forwards through time in line with Derrida's hauntology: 'Given that a *revenant* is always called upon to come and to come back, the thinking of the specter, contrary to what good sense leads us to believe, signals toward the future. It is a thinking of the past, a legacy that can come only from that which has not yet arrived – from the *arrivant* itself.'[101] Murnau's *Nosferatu* returns through Merhige's *Shadow of the Vampire*. As he wanders through German streets, Count Orlok is carrying with him the baggage of anti-Semitism, not least through his re-enactment of the Wandering Jew, condemned to wander the earth for millennia until the Second Coming. The character of Murnau in Merhige's millennial film replays Christ's curse on this legendary figure: 'May the weight of the centuries venge you', only here it is directed against a vampire. In turn, it also serves as a reply to Stoker's Count Dracula countermanding the Wandering Jew's eternal damnation: 'My revenge is just begun! I spread it over centuries' (p. 347). Nazi cinema constituted a type of vengeance against the mythic crimes of Jewry. *Der ewige Jude*, translated from the German into *The Eternal Jew*, is another name for 'The Wandering Jew'. This film lurks in the shadows of Merhige's recreation of the Weimar period in *Shadow of the Vampire* which points towards Derrida's ghosts of the future in 1940 and beyond. Another shadow of fascist cinema falling across Merhige's film is the historical drama, *Jew Süss*. An early script contains a ballad in which Süss is described as the 'great vampire' and Jews are presented as 'drain[ing] [German] blood'.[102] For these propaganda films intended to prepare German audiences for the Holocaust, Nazi film-makers vampirised the anti-Semitic images permeating German Expressionism. The artificially enlarged ears of Max Schreck, the actor playing the role of the nosferatu, reappear in an illustration from a Nazi propaganda book for children warning of 'Those dirty, standing-out ears!'[103] Enormous ears characterise Fips' cartoon of the Jew as a vampire bat (see Figure 7). From the pseudo documentary, *The Eternal Jew*, and the historically distorted drama, *Jew Süss*, the image of the monstrous Jew was projected outwards onto the world of National Socialism. The consequences of the breakdown between the image and the actual appear in film critic Lester Friedman's comparison of the horrors of the Nazi death camps with imagery derived from horror film:

> Photographs and films taken in concentration camps grasp the strikingly sad resemblance between the tortured inmates and the walking dead of so many vampire movies. What demonic power could match Hitler's feat of turning members of the most humane professions into murderers and supporters of a totally immoral regime? Hitler and his followers transformed the world into a vast and terrifying horror movie in which good and evil battled to the death for mankind's soul.[104]

Friedman's alignment of Jew with the 'walking dead' creates a sympathetic link between Jews and vampirism.[105] Through the double time frame of 2000, when Merhige's film was made, and its 1920s setting, *Shadow of the Vampire* not only shadows *Nosferatu* in its recreation of Weimar cinema but also foreshadows the horrors lying ahead. Its release date at the beginning of the new millennium was an invitation for a retrospective on the twentieth century's two greatest spectacles of horror – the world wars.

In Merhige's film, vampirism is a multivalent metaphor, representing not just blood-lust, but another type of addiction, morphine. This *Todestraum* (dream of death) served as an antidote for the traumas of war. Morphine was utilised by war veterans in post-war Berlin and became a literal opiate of the people. Another analgesic was the cinema screen. Films produced by Weimar culture functioned as a means of numbing the effects of war, but could also be cathartic, and this was most certainly true of *Nosferatu*. In 1920, another distraction from the ignominy of defeat arrived in the form of fears of a worldwide Jewish conspiracy, aroused by the most important German publication of the *Protocols of the Elders of Zion*, which warned of the infiltration and takeover of European societies by Jews. While the paranoia it fomented targeted 'the enemy within', the furore reignited latent war-inspired anxieties of invasion and occupation. In the light of this, the narrative of the nosferatu's arrival in Germany, as the representative of a blood-sucking race bringing death and destruction, takes on a more sinister hue. Two months after the premiere of *Nosferatu* on 4 March 1922, the Jewish German foreign minister was assassinated on the grounds that he was an elder of Zion.[106] Conspiracy theory and immigration anxiety had seamlessly inter-twined. The Jewish indicators in Stoker's original novel, which was translated into German and published in Leipzig in 1908, provided contemporary cinema audiences with further incentive to conflate Murnau's vampire with a Jew in *Nosferatu*.

Merhige, however, makes no mention of Jews in his director's commentary, even though his film can be seen to replay the death of the eternal Jew, immortalised anew through the endless repetition of cinema.[107] By splicing eighty-year-old film from *Nosferatu* with new footage, Merhige demonstrates how 'film is capable of non-linear time' forming 'a seamless psychological space'.[108] His modern talkie literally vampirises the old silent movie that, in turn, is a cinematic re-vamp of Stoker's novel. As Derrida explains, 'a specter is always a *revenant*. One cannot control its comings and goings because it *begins by coming back*'.[109] Like the Eternal or Wandering Jew, the vampire is associated with return and inhabits a marginalised shadow world or liminal space. Hitler regarded Jews as 'that race which shuns the sunlight',[110] and, at the end of *Nosferatu*, the intertitle explains that the shadow of the vampire vanished as if overcome 'by the victorious rays of the living sun.'[111] Count Orlok has now dissolved into light and the shadow of the vampire vanquished.

The title *Shadow of the Vampire* is a reference to shadow as a communicative metaphor, relating to the chiaroscuro of German Expressionist cinema. In *Nosferatu*, the hero Hutter, who is based on Stoker's Jonathan Harker, enters the 'land of phantoms', shown in photographic negative to illustrate the juxtaposition of the living and the dead. Albin Grau, the producer, co-scriptwriter and set designer of *Nosferatu*, was a practicing occultist, who would have agreed with Murnau's claim that the cinematographer's use of shadow is more important than light.[112] In Expressionist cinema, film is the language of shadow through which dark forces are made visible. Film served a similar purpose for fascism. By seeking to make visible the supposed menace surrounding the Jewish question, the Nazis inadvertently exposed the darkness of their own totalitarian vision. *Shadow of the Vampire* replays the most iconic shadow of Expressionist cinema, which is when the nosferatu creeps up the stairs towards his victim's bedchamber. Even though he has a shadow, Merhige's vampire has no mirror image, except as metaphorical Other. This contrasts with *The Student of Prague* (1913), written by Ewers and later remade by Henrik Galeen, who wrote the screenplay for *Nosferatu*. Here the hero's reflection steps outside a mirror to haunt him. This doubling is an obvious metaphor for the haunting effects of the motion picture as a doppelgänger for external reality.

In *Shadow of the Vampire*, the shadow of cinema is captured in a scene playing on the title of the film, which serves as a homage to the birth of the motion picture. This is when the character of Max Schreck, who is performing the role of a real vampire being passed off as a method actor by Murnau, comes across a projector for the first time and starts turning the handle. As he witnesses the shadow of his own hand across the screen, he becomes simultaneously the projection and the projectionist. His encounter with the projector not only permits him to see film for the first time but also to observe once again the daylight of the outside world, only this time through the medium of cinema. As Murnau reminds us, film is 'not life but the shadow of life'.[113] The flickering ghostly images serve as revenants from the original silent movie of 1922, depicting trees, water, sky and the sun, either setting or rising over shimmering water.[114] In the making of *Nosferatu*, he departed from his fellow Expressionist directors by making use of natural light rather than the artificial light of a studio. For aeons, Schreck had not set eyes on daylight. For him, this is a world of dangerous looking, leading inexorably to the death of the vampire. Turning away from the screen, he gazes directly into the light of the projector (Figure 9). The lamplight from the projector merges with the mesmeric gaze of the vampire. According to Gilman, the Jewish 'cold, scanning gaze' was a signifier of racial difference, demonstrating a 'pathognomonic physiognomy', since it was 'in the Jews' gaze that the pathology can be found'.[115] The goggle-eyed Jew, going back to Richard Burton's *Anatomy of Melancholy* (1621), is evoked by the bulging eyes of Count Orlok. In the original storyboard for Murnau's *Nosferatu*, Albin Grau depicted light beams emitting from the eyes of Count Orlok onto his female victim. Streicher, for whom race defilement was the most odious of Jewish crimes, insisted that Jewish men were able to seduce women by hypnotising them.[116] In the film, the hypnotic stare of the vampire is also a prelude to death, and the Jew, according to Luther, 'kills people merely by fastening his eyes on them'.[117] *Shadow of the Vampire* demonstrates a different kind of danger, that of the unprotected gaze for silent movie makers. This was due to toxic fumes emitted from the arc lights and mercury lamps that could cause permanent retinal damage, making it necessary for camera crews to wear goggles (Figure 10). A far greater danger for the vampire is sunlight. For Schreck, safety lies in the simulated world of film with its artificial light, but this too turns out to be part of the illusion of cinema.

In 1896, the year before the publication of *Dracula*, the first vampire film, George Méliès' *The Haunted Castle*, was shown in London. Bram's widow, Florence Stoker, feared that the transition from text to screen, in

Figure 9 Count Orlok looking into a cinema projector for the first time in *Shadow of the Vampire*. The image captures the mesmeric gaze of both vampire and Jew.

the case of *Nosferatu*, would make her husband's book redundant and reduce her royalties. She obtained a court order against the film-makers, Prana-Film (Sanskrit for 'breath of life'), to destroy all prints and nega-tives.[119] The making of *Nosferatu* proved to be the first and last gasp of the company, forcing it to dissolve into bankruptcy, as surely as Count Orlok dissolves before the camera. For Stoker's widow, the vampiric nature of film threatened to drain the life from the book. Other threats were on the horizon. Kittler saw psycho-analysis and cinema join forces in their first hundred years to kill a common enemy – literature and the liter-ary author, who is 'literarily murdered'.[119] In Merhige's film, Schreck, after killing the cinematographer, is on the lookout for another victim and slyly hints to the furious Murnau: 'I do not think we need the writer.' This sounds an alarm bell signalling the potential redundancy of the written word and the mastery of film over text. The subsequent massacre of the film crew is parodic of Florence Stoker's attempts to protect author and book by destroying copies of of *Nosferatu* and serves as a reminder of how she very nearly succeeded.

Along with the typewriter, phonograph and wax cylinders, which are mentioned in the novel, film represents the eternal repetition of

Figure 10 John Malkovich playing F. W. Murnau with his film crew wearing protective goggles as they film *Nosferatu*, in *Shadow of the Vampire*.

mechanical inscription. According to Kittler: 'Under the conditions of technology, literature disappears (like metaphysics for Heidegger) into the un-death of its endless ending.'[120] The anxiety of Stoker's widow that the new technology of the motion picture would vampirise static versions of the arts is echoed by John Malkovich. Playing the role of Murnau in *Shadow of the Vampire*, he proclaims that 'because we have the moving picture our paintings will grow and recede, our poetry will be shadows that lengthen and conceal. Our light will play across living faces that laugh and agonise [...]. We are scientists engaged in the creation of memory, but our memory will neither blur nor fade'.

Film functions as a theatre of memory. Yet in terms of Derrida's hauntology and how it relates to the spectrality of cinema, *Shadow of the Vampire* is Janus-faced, looking back to the Weimar period and ahead to the Third Reich and 'The Final Solution'. A challenge for the Nazis lay in rooting out those of Jewish origin once they were assimilated into the general population, particularly since the Jew was vilified as a master of disguise. Within Nazi cinema, a motif of Jewishness and masquerade emerges in response to the crypto or secret Jew. An analogy can be made with the fanatical quest of Merhige's Murnau to achieve authenticity, which drives him to hire an actor who is a *real* vampire. A self-conscious play on representation and reality is also apparent in Hippler's pseudo-documentary, *The Eternal Jew*, with its spurious depictions of contemporary Jews. This takes the form of a compilation documentary, sometimes known as a 'parasitic genre', whereby footage is taken from other films and edited to produce different meanings.[121] The process of masquerade enacted by Nazi film-makers included treating clips of fictional film as factual. The rolling titles of *The Eternal Jew* claim to show Jews as they really are 'before they conceal themselves behind the mask of the civilized European'. This message set out to exploit racial fears over the crypto-Jew.[122] Material from another Nazi propaganda compilation film, significantly entitled *Jews without Masks* (1938), was based on a travelling exhibition peddling negative Jewish stereotypes. Material from this was integrated into *The Eternal Jew*. Here the cinematic technique of the dissolve exposes what lies beneath the mask to demonstrate how the Eastern Jew without kaftan, beard and ringlets could easily pass as a Westernised citizen.

The anti-hero of *Jew Süss* is Joseph Ben Issachar Süsskind Oppenheimer, who morphs from dark ghetto Jew in traditional costume with beard and ringlets into a sophisticated, powdered European courtier. The motif of disguise recurs at a masked ball, though it is only when he is without a mask that he is faced with the admonition: 'Unmask yourself Hebrew.' When in the dock, where he is being prosecuted for his sexual crime with a Christian woman, Süss, while still wearing the costume of a courtier, reverts back to his Jewish appearance. The court scene foreshadows the time after the war when the film itself would be on trial. Joseph Goebbels, maestro of the dark arts of Nazi propaganda, insisted that *Jew Süss* showed the true face of the Jews, thus reinforcing the anti-Semitic idea of the Jew as adept at disguise.

This notion is played out in *Shadow of the Vampire* when, in a humorous moment of self-reflexivity, Schreck asks for makeup, only to have his request refused by Murnau.[123] It is not until the end of the film that his true face is revealed and he is exposed publicly as a genuine vampire. At that point, the director's own mask drops as he hysterically barks out '*Schweinhund*', a racial invective commonly used by brutalised concentration camp guards to insult imprisoned Jews. His stream of abuse – 'Die you fucking rat, bastard, vampire, pig, *Schweinhund*, shit' – contains

157

insults that have an anti-Semitic resonance.[124] These may be related to the linking of Jews with the plague rat, the vampire, the religious prohibition of pork along with the stories of Jewish women giving birth to pigs,[125] and the medieval association with excrement. The word 'Jew', however, is never mentioned. It remains as unuttered as it inevitably does in the original silent movie. Even though Schreck strangles the producer and breaks the neck of the cameraman, it is Murnau, rather than the nosferatu, who turns out to be the true villain and ultimate vampire. In the final scene, the director vampirises his actors and film crew in a frenzied feeding of their lifeblood for the life of his film. An ironic real-life equivalent of Murnau's deception was when the director of *Jew Süss* was expelled from the Nazi Party for masquerading as an Aryan, following the discovery that one of his grandparents was Jewish. The derogatory term '*Mischling*' ('cross-breed') was used to apply to those without full Aryan ancestry.

In *Specters of Marx*, Derrida considers the authenticity of the specular: 'The "proper" feature of specters, like vampires, is that they are deprived of a specular image, of the true, right specular image (but who is not so deprived?). How do you recognize a ghost? By the fact that it does not recognize itself in a mirror'.[126] It is precisely what the actress Greta Schroeder, playing the role of Ellen, does not recognise in the mirror that signals to her, in the closing scenes of *Shadow of the Vampire*, that something is terribly wrong. While preparations are under way to film the death scene of vampire and victim, Greta notices that the cadaverous Max Schreck, whose name means 'terror' in German, has no reflection in the mirror next to her bed.[127] Her reaction to that void is one of sheer terror when she realises that it is actually reflecting her impending death, soon to be played out in a macabre parody of a love scene. Using a visual quotation from *Nosferatu*, the shadow of Schreck's elongated fingers creeps towards her heart to extinguish her life. It is death by celluloid, the point at which life has been overtaken by shadow. Like the character she plays, Greta too is sacrificed, only this time for a cinematic performance, after having been effectively killed into art.[128] At the start of the movie, Merhige's Murnau persuades her to forgo a theatrical role in order to act in his film. He ominously predicts that this will be her sacrifice for art. Indeed, the original Murnau retained continuity between stage and screen in *Nosferatu* by recreating on film the 'pictorial aesthetic of light, shadow and spectacle' derived from his work with theatrical producer, Max Reinhardt.[129] As Greta insists to Murnau's character: 'A theatrical audience gives me life while that thing [as she points to the camera] merely takes it from me.' Her eventual demise is, in a sense, death by camera in a process that Merhige, as a film director, would have recognised as intrinsic to the vampiric nature of film-making, for as he notes: 'Camera reduces subject to a mere shadow – takes the flesh and the blood away.'[130] By filming the actual rather than the simulated death of Schreck, Murnau strives for authenticity, even in death. The shadow of the vampire is vanquished ultimately by daylight.

The madness of Merhige's Murnau stems from his collapsing of distinctions between representation and reality so that eventually nothing exists for him beyond the frame of the camera. His insanity is a replay of the last days of the Führer, buried in an underground bunker. This location was the concrete actualisation of the ghettoised subterranean psychic habitat projected by Nazis onto Jews. In Merhige's film, demented director morphs into demented dictator. In view of this conflation, it is appropriate that the final scene of *Shadow of the Vampire* was shot in a Second World War bunker. Camera shots have an affinity with those of a gun, audibly realised in the film by the recording of actual gunshot on the soundtrack.[131] Kittler makes comparisons between the movie camera as a means of creation and the machine gun as a mode of destruction, indicating the overlap between the discourses of filming and military engagement.[132] For *Nosferatu*, Murnau decided to depart from Expressionist convention and 'shoot' on location. This followed a process of 'reconnaissance', before 'zooming' in on his 'targets'. The cinematographer in Merhige's film shoots literally in the final scene by firing a pistol at the vampire. As Paul Virilio has noted in *War and Cinema: The Logistics of Perception* (1984), there are similarities between the camera operator and the marksman, who both operate in a closely circumscribed field of vision to 'shoot' their target, directed by the film-maker's 'armed eye'.[133] On the set of Merhige's version of *Nosferatu*, the staged death scene becomes one of actual slaughter. This concretising of metaphor is analogous to the way in which cinematic representation in the hands of the Nazis was intricately connected to real-life mass death. Malkovich takes charge of the lethal weapon of the camera, the very same one used by Murnau for the filming of the original silent movie (Figure 10). Earlier in *Shadow of the Vampire*, his character describes film making in terms of the discourse of warfare, declaring that 'our battle [is] to create art. Our weapon is the moving picture.' Three years after the making of *Nosferatu*, the historical Murnau pioneered innovative ways of deploying the moving camera. Before becoming a film director,

159

Murnau acted as an observer for a *Luftwaffe* squadron in France during the First World War.[134] As this required observational skills from different vantage points, it was especially conducive to the art of cinematography. Murnau survived several crashes. These accidents are likely to have contributed to the kidney damage he was left with after the war, for which he took opiates. In the scene where the character of Murnau is lying in bed in a laudanum-induced stupor, on an adjacent wall is inscribed a swastika. This symbol, along with the Star of David, has the tropological force of the revenant. In terms of hauntology, the latter looks ahead to its reappearance on the yellow armbands Jews were forced to wear in countries under National Socialism. Fascist Germany's war on Old Europe included the sweeping away of what it regarded as cultural decadence and the esoteric, which primarily involved eradicating Jewry. In Murnau's original film, the symbols contained in Orlok's letter to Knock appear to include letters from the Hebrew alphabet, along with the Star of David. As such, they are redolent of a hidden or cryptic language of the Jews, the most mysterious being the secret scripts of the Cabbala, whose magic power words were reputed to bring the dead back to life.

A form of Jewish necromancy is practised in *The Golem* (1915), which Paul Wegener wrote and directed with Galeen, the scriptwriter for *Nosferatu*. The film draws on the rabbinical legend of the Golem, a giant clay monster played by Wegener, which had saved the Jewish citizens of Prague from the wrath of an emperor, accusing them of the Blood Libel. Only fragments of the film survive, but that is more than what remains of the next Golem film, *The Golem and the Dancing Girl* (1917), now considered to be entirely lost. The only complete film in the trilogy is *The Golem: How He Came into the World* (1920), which Wegener, who played the title role in all three films, co-wrote with Galeen. Here, the lifeless clay of the Golem is animated by a life-giving word placed in a hollow Star of David on the statue's chest. The Golem, like the body of the Jew, is inscribed in ways which support Halberstam's thesis that 'European anti-Semitism and American racism towards black Americans are precisely Gothic discourses given over to the making monstrous of particular kinds of bodies'.[135] Similarly, the tattooing of Holocaust victims with numbers not only dehumanised them but also marked them out as different. In Wegener's 1920 Golem film, a decree issued by the Holy Roman Emperor calls for the expulsion of all Jews from the city on the grounds that they are endangering the lives of fellow citizens and practising black magic. Jewish characters appear in dimly lit scenes as settings for diabolical and magical incantations. Even though the Golem is a powerful symbol of resistance to enemies of the Jews, its presence did not prevent the films from exploiting negative stereotypes. An association between Jewishness and money appears in the 1920 film when the Knight Florian, sent by the emperor, uses bribery to enter a Jewish ghetto for the purpose of consorting with the rabbi's daughter, Miriam. The camera lingers in close-up on the upturned palm of a Jewish warden, receiving coin after coin. Miriam is a Jewish femme fatale, who responds sexually to Florian. Mary Shelley reinforced this stereotype by intimating in 'A History of the Jews' that the Jewish lady does not easily resist sensual temptation.[136] Wegener went on to act in Nazi propaganda films for which he won approbation from Goebbels, who appointed him 'Actor of the State' in 1941. The kind of negative representations of Jews disseminated in his films would one day escalate into the blatant anti-Semitism promulgated by film-makers of the Reich.

This escalation is shadowed in the climax of Merhige's film, which foreshadows the treatment of Jews by Nazis. Preparing to shoot the final scene, the white-coated Murnau, consumed by the madness of science and art, resembles a Nazi concentration camp doctor, as he leads his leading lady to her deathbed to be filmed in a deadly experiment. Tellingly, she refers to him as '*Herr Doktor*'. Her fellow actor Schreck is also tricked into co-operating in a death scene, not realising that Murnau plans to film him actually dying.[137] Similarly, Jews in the old Jewish quarter in Lodz in German-occupied Poland were gulled into co-operating with the Nazis filming *The Eternal Jew*, unaware that their Hebraic culture was being depicted as corrupt and barbaric for the purpose of justifying genocide.[138] Merhige's Murnau bribes Schreck into playing the title role of the film with the promise of the leading lady as prey. The sight of the vampire feasting on his victim as his reward and draining the life out of her acts as a metaphor for the parasitical nature of cinema, its film stars and its minions. Director, producer, actors and film crew feed off the insatiability of Schreck's desire. At the same time, viewers voyeuristically gather around Greta's bedside to witness the playing out of sex, death and desire through the dying of the old order under the glare of scientific modernity, transfixed by the hypnotic gaze of cinema.

The scene on which it is based can be read as the sacrifice of a German woman who has brought about the destruction of a Jewish predator in order to preserve the purity of her race. This theme feeds into a traditional narrative prototype defined by Patrick Hogan as triggered typically by the devastation of the dominant group, whether it be from drought, famine or disease, usually plague.[139] The catalyst sometimes involves a sexual sin relating to a tempter from an enemy group. Atonement comes through the sacrifice of an innocent individual who, in national narratives, redeems the nation. According to Hitler, Jews were incapable of making sacrifices for others. In *Nosferatu*, Ellen betrays her promise to her husband not to read *The Book of the Vampire* from which she discovers that only 'a woman with a pure heart' can end the terror. By resolving to 'offer her blood to Orlok' and keeping him next to her until daybreak, Ellen's rendering of Christian sacrifice acts as a counter to the Blood Libel. She survives Count Orlok after he evaporates into sunlight, only to die in the arms of her husband. In *Shadow of the Vampire*, Greta succumbs to the insatiable bloodthirstiness of the nosferatu, who in turn is destroyed by her sacrifice for cinema. In *Jew Süss*, Dorothea gives herself sexually to the vampiric Jew in order to save her husband from torture. For his defiance of an edict criminalising a Jew mingling flesh with a Christian woman, Süss is executed. What is imparted to the contemporary cinema audience is that the contaminated female victim cannot be allowed to live. Similarly, Stoker's Mina, on whom Ellen is loosely based, implores her husband Jonathan to kill her if she ever succumbs to the enemy. This can be seen in sexual terms for, as Dracula expresses it in his parodic wedding vows to her, she was to him 'flesh of my flesh; blood of my blood; kin of my kin; my bountiful wine-press' (p. 328). In his anti-Semitic book, Richard Burton was emphatic that, in England, Jews and Christians should never marry.

Forbidden sexual desire leading to miscegenation is the narrative propulsion of *Nosferatu*, *Shadow of the Vampire*, *The Golem* and *Jew Süss*. When coded Jewish, the male protagonists of these films reinforce the myth of the Jew as having an excessive sexual appetite.[140] This notion of uncontrollable potency was graphically exploited two years after the making of *Nosferatu* in a drawing of a Jew raping an Aryan woman with religious impunity (Figure 11). Streicher's increasing obsession with Jewish sexual depravity was reflected in his *Der Stürmer*, the most virulently anti-Semitic newspaper of all time, founded in 1923, the year after *Nosferatu* was first shown. He firmly believed that the defilement of Gentile women was a holy act in line with Talmudic teaching.[141] An even more distorted reading of this sacred Hebrew text claimed that Jews could rape non-Jewish women after the age of three. At a public meeting in 1924, Streicher called for the execution of Jews engaging in sexual relations

TALMUD:

Figure 11 Karel Relink's anti-Semitic drawing of the Jew according to the Talmud dated 1924. This was reprinted in the German anti-Jewish pamphlet *Judenspiegel* (1926), in which the Talmud is misinterpreted as saying that Jews do not regard themselves as sinning if they abuse a Christian woman.

Note: The image first appeared in Karel Relink, *Zrcadlo Zidu* (Prague: Nakladem vlastnim, 1925), p. 6 and is reproduced in 'Anti-Semitism', *Encyclopedia Judaica*, 3, p. 133.

with Gentiles.[142] It was claimed that such 'race defilement' would leave victims looking 'dead and empty',[143] language similar to that used to describe the victim of a vampire when drained of blood. In 1929, Jewish rapists were said to have ruined the bodies of women and girls and destroyed their souls,[144] accusations that have been levelled at the fictional vampire. In the light of this, the bed on which Ellen dies resembles an altar of sexual sacrifice for Murnau's quasi Jewish vampire. With his hooked nose and erect body, almost ejaculating out of its coffin, Murnau's nosferatu has been described as 'a walking phallus' or 'phallambulist'.[145] The size of his highly prominent nose is exaggerated even more when in shadow. The image is not dissimilar to hideous representations of Jews in cartoons in late nineteenth-century Vienna and Berlin. As Gilman has pointed out: 'These extraordinary caricatures stressed one central aspect of the physiognomy of the Jewish male, his nose, which represented that hidden sign of his sexual difference, his circumcised penis.'[146] The Jewish phallus has been interpreted as a sign of damage and deformity. The association between the nose and the genitals had found its way into medical science. Freud's German Jewish colleague, the otolaryngologist Wilhelm Fliess, endeavoured to change the pathology of the genitalia by operating on the nose. Another case of medical misalignment may be found in Freud's misreading of 'Dora's Case', which he published in 1905. Gilman argues that this misapprehension was prompted in part by Freud's own Jewishness.[147] The patient, whose real name was Ida Bauer, was an Eastern European Jewess whose family moved to Vienna from Bohemia shortly after it became legal for Jews to live in the city.[148] Hers was an important case history since Freud used it to formulate his theory of the Oedipus complex. He interpreted Dora's symptoms of hysteria as part of an unconscious desire to commit fellatio on her syphilitic Jewish father, who had been treated by Freud for the disease. As Gilman points out, one way of interpreting the case is to see a hypersexed Jewish father passing on the disease of hysteria to his daughter. While Freud gendered the syphilitic condition '*tabes dorsalis*' as male, he labelled the equivalent in the female as hysteria. Dora's foot-dragging conformed to the hallmarks of the disease and, as Gilman argues, corresponds to the defective gait of the Jew, at that time seen as a racial sign in Vienna. Similarly, Count Orlok's peculiar way of walking can be identified as a pathognomonic Jewish marker for sexual disease, degeneration and masculine inadequacy. This deficiency was believed to be why Jews were unsuitable for the military in supposedly being flat-footed and, therefore, unable to march.[149] According to Gilman, the malformation of the Jew's foot was seen to reflect the structure of the Jewish mind, signifying the concept of inherent difference.[150] A key indicator of this was the circumcised penis. Dora's sensation of a blockage in her throat was diagnosed by Freud as the *globus hystericus*. From a Jewish perspective, this ties in with circumcision and the ritual of *metsitsah*, the sucking of blood from a newly circumcised infant. Like fellatio, this oral–genital act has been associated with the transmission of syphilis and has nuances of the vampiric.

As Freud and his family would discover, the true and most dangerous of vampires were the Nazis. Four of Freud's five sisters died in concentration camps. The Third Reich released upon the world not only the vampire of anti-Semitism but also one of war, the theme of the next chapter. Hitler set out to create a master race, based on a blood ideology, that drained the lifeblood of nations and provided the blueprint for a blood-drinking monster, which would turn global. His super-race idealism challenged the biblical notion of the Jews as the chosen race. At the same time, the Nazis projected their own monstrosity onto Jews, as a demonised ethnicity. For instance, the historical counterpart for Süss was misrepresented in the 1940 film as a totalitarian who, like the Nazis, had instigated secret police, torture and military domination. Hitler justified the expulsion and extermination of Jews by blaming them for the outbreak of the Second World War. These penalties are paralleled in the ending of Harlan's *Jew Süss*, when the hero is executed and his fellow Jews expelled from Württemberg. The film was an effective propaganda tool for acclimatising Germans to the Final Solution. One in three citizens of the Reich went to screenings and it was compulsory viewing for SS officers and concentration camp guards. It was reported that viewings increased the levels of cruelty inflicted on prisoners in the camps.[151] Following its premiere in September 1940, *Jew Süss* was widely distributed throughout Nazi Europe for the purpose of paving the way for the mass deportations starting in 1942. *The Eternal Jew*, released the same year, also had a wide distribution, though women and children were not permitted to watch the final section on the ritual slaughter of animals for kosher meat (*shechita*), as these involved graphic scenes of blood-draining. The image of a Jewish butcher draining the lifeblood from a living body fed into the anti-Semitic discourse of Jews as vampires and parasites. As Davison has noted, Dracula can be seen as a *shochet* or Jewish ritual slaughterer when comparing his assailants to a line of sheep lined up for slaughter, saying: 'You think to baffle me, – you with your pale faces all in a row, like sheep in a butcher's. You shall be sorry yet, each one of you!' (p. 347).[152] The slaying of Dracula, whose throat is sheared with Jonathan's 'great knife' (p. 417), can be likened to the killing of a beast at a kosher slaughterhouse, which involves draining the blood of a living animal. The separation of blood from flesh has vampiric connotations, although, according to Levitical law, the consumption of blood is taboo. To represent the Jew as a blood-drinking vampire, in view of this religious prohibition, is the ultimate insult. For anti-Semitic opponents of *shechita*, it could serve as a perverse reminder of the Blood Libel. Hippler's abattoir scene would have unquestionably offended the sensibilities of the vegetarian Hitler and fed his racial hatred.

One intriguing question is whether Hitler ever saw *Nosferatu*, since it is not listed amongst the films he is known to have viewed. From the time of his early days in Vienna and Munich, Hitler, like Goebbels, was a keen movie fan. A favourite was the horror film, *King Kong* (1933), which recreates the scene from *The Golem* in which the monster carries Miriam down from a tower. For relaxation, Hitler liked to watch films at the private cinema he constructed at his Berghof mountain retreat. According to Nicholas Tucker, he 'preferred watching many of those titles banned for public performance, in the Chancellory's private projection room'.[153] Might *Nosferatu* as a banned horror film with its anti-Semitic undertones have piqued his curiosity?

The inference Merhige makes between political dictator and film director in *Shadow of the Vampire* leads to a misrepresentation of Murnau, but it does correspond more closely to another German film director, Werner Herzog, who directed a version of *Nosferatu* in 1979. Stories circulated about this allegedly idiosyncratic, demanding and even dangerous director, who apparently threatened to kill anyone who got in the way of his film-making. This even included Klaus Kinski, the actor playing the title role of *Nosferatu*, who once said of Herzog that 'he creates the most senseless difficulties and dangers, risking other people's safety and even their lives'.[154] Herzog grew up with the 'echo of Nazism'[155] and, according to Patrick Day, 'the movie is partly an historical allegory about the infection of romantic idealism passed on to the fascists of the twentieth century' and contains apocalyptic images linked to the horrors of the Second World War and the Holocaust.[156] To the strains of Richard Wagner's prelude in *The Rhine Gold*, the first in his opera cycle *The Ring of the Nibelung*, Jonathan Harker approaches Dracula's castle.[157] Day notes that Herzog uses the music for 'recalling the Nazi affinity for Wagner and linking the vampire to Albrecht [sic]', the dwarf told by three Rhine maidens that if he renounces love, his reward will be mastery of the world.[158] There are similarities here with Stoker's Dracula as a member of a 'conquering race' (p. 60), intent on domination, to whom one of his vampire women declaims: 'You yourself never loved; you never love!' (p. 70). Fritz Lang's two-part silent fantasy film, *The Nibelung* (1924), like Wagner's opera cycle, draws on German and Norse epics. It has been argued that both Wagner and Lang associate Alberich the dwarf with a negative Jewish stereotype, whose villainy is even more racially inflected in the light of the contrasting Teutonic heroism.[159] Theodor Adorno sees the gold-snatching Alberich as a Jewish caricature, a view contested by other critics.[160] Whilst the extent of Wagner's anti-Semitism and its impact on Hitler is a matter debated by historians, the influence of Wagner on National Socialism was by no means limited to the Jews. Bayreuth, the home of the Wagner Festival, provided a spiritual crucible for forging the drama and spectacle of the Nazi rallies, as well as cultivating the almost operatic, histrionic and theatrical body language gesticulated by Hitler, a Wagnerian devotee, during his speeches. Where this would lead is evident from Herzog's opening sequence in which the camera passes over mummified bodies, some with their mouths open as if in a rictus of petrification, like gruesome reminders of concentration camp victims.[161] At the end of Herzog's *Nosferatu the Vampyre*, Jonathan drives a stake through the vampire's heart. This follows the sacrifice made by his wife Lucy in allowing the monster to drink her blood until daybreak.[162] In a final twist, Jonathan turns into a vampire. This has been seen as a transformation into a death's head or *Totenkopf*, the insignia of the SS.[163] The alignment of vampirism with Nazi oppression, rather than Jewish victimhood, points to the versatility of the trope and underlines Halberstam's argument that the figure of the monster is an insignia of horror with 'infinite interpretability'.[164]

Nosferatu, *The Golem* and *The Nibelung* are amongst the Expressionist films that reinforced associations between Jewishness, monstrousness and the occult. During the year in which he wrote the screenplay for *Nosferatu*, Galeen was running a Berlin theatre showcasing Jewish plays. He also directed and wrote scripts for films on subjects relating to Jews. Coming from a Jewish family, this key figure of Weimar fantasy cinema went into exile in response to the rise of the Nazi Party in 1933. According to the Nazis, classic Weimar cinema had been Judaised by 'wheeler-dealer[s] and bloodthirsty Nosferatus',[165] polluting the purity of German cinema. Nevertheless, they seemed willing enough to exploit such images for the racist ideology fuelling their anti-Semitic films. The true purpose of the Nazi Party was concealed from the public for as long as possible. As their Minister for Propaganda, Joseph Goebbels revealed: 'Propaganda becomes ineffective the moment we are aware of it.'[166] He was able to build on the anti-Jewish feeling deeply engrained within the pre-Nazi gestalt, where it had been naturalised through contemporary cinema. In 1920s Europe, anti-Semitism rose to fever pitch. Even though prejudice against Jews was mirrored rather than promoted in Weimar films, it still had the effect of reinforcing racial stereotypes, especially through the Expressionists' trademark penchant for distortion and exaggeration, characteristics shared with Nazi cinema.

The once highly popular *Homunculus* (1916) shows how Expressionism can anticipate Nazism. Directed by Otto Rippert, the film charts the progress of an artificially made man, who becomes a cruel dictator intent on wholesale destruction. Despite the film title, the creation has more in common with the Golem than with the alchemist's relatively innocuous homunculus, another supernatural creature linked to Jewish myth. The making of a homunculus from a mandrake is the method used in Ewers' novel *Alraune*, which means 'mandrake' in German. The novel led to several film adaptations. In Dinter's *The Sin against the Blood*, the blonde Aryan hero's experiments to create synthetic life are taken over by a Jew. In view of this link with Jewish folklore and alchemy, it is ironic that Hitler was identified with Rippert's man-made man.[167] In *From Caligari to Hitler*, Siegfried Kracauer uses this film, amongst others, to claim that Weimar cinema foreshadowed German fascism, through which its fantastical monsters were animated into the horrors of Nazism.[168]

> Since Germany thus carried out what had been anticipated by her cinema from its very beginning, conspicuous screen characters now came true in life itself. Personified daydreams of minds to whom freedom meant a fatal shock, and adolescence a permanent temptation, these figures filled the arena of Nazi Germany. Homunculus walked about in the flesh. Self-appointed Caligaris hypnotized innumerable Cesares into murder. Raving Mabuses committed fantastic crimes with impunity, and mad Ivans devised unheard-of tortures. Along with this unholy procession, many motifs known from the screen turned into actual events.[169]

The cumulative effect of Expressionist cinema reinforced a social and political message against the Jews, which was propounded more blatantly and deliberately by authors like Dinter and by Nazi propaganda films. Gothicised images of Jews on screen, as well as on the page, inadvertently fed the anti-Semitism of the gestalt. Kracauer's view of Weimar film-making as anticipating the rise of the Third Reich has been challenged by Anton Kaes as an 'overarching teleology' and over-simplification of a complex culture. In *Shell Shock Cinema* (2009), he argues that in many Weimar films, 'The double wound of war and defeat festered beneath the glittering surface of its anxious modernity', which was a trauma 'unspoken and concealed, implied and latent, repressed and disavowed'.[170] Kaes explains how, in the interim period between world wars, film functioned in Germany to mitigate the buried pain of a defeated nation and resurrect the war dead. There is no better example of this than *Nosferatu*. Hauntology, which is so applicable to the spectrality of cinema, demonstrates how these two approaches are able to complement one another. While Kaes looks to the victims of the First World War and Kracauer to those of the Second World War, Derrida reminds us to pay heed to the ghosts of injustice in the future, as well as from the past. These include the Jews, denigrated as a spectral people, who were blamed by Hitler for Germany's defeat in 1918 and the outbreak of war in 1939. Contributing to the propaganda was the defamatory equation of vampire and Jew, which had tainted popular consciousness well before the Nazis. But, as the following chapter indicates, it is really war itself, rather than the Jews, which has a natural kinship with the vampire.

NOTES

1 Malchow, *Gothic Images of Race*, p. 166.
2 See Jules Zanger, 'A Sympathetic Vibration: Dracula and the Jews', *English Literature in Transition*, 34:1 (1991), 33–44; Ken Gelder, *Reading the Vampire* (London: Routledge, 1994), pp. 16–23; Halberstam, *Skin Shows*, pp. 95–9; and Carol Margaret Davison's authoritative study, *Anti-Semitism and British Gothic Literature* (Basingstoke: Palgrave Macmillan, 2004), pp. 160–5.
3 See William Hughes, 'A Singular Invasion: Revisiting the Postcoloniality of Bram Stoker's *Dracula*', in William Hughes and Andrew Smith (eds), *Empire and the Gothic: The Politics of Genre* (Basingstoke: Palgrave Macmillan, 2003), pp. 88–102.
4 See Sander L. Gilman, *Jewish Self-Hatred: Anti-Semitism and the Hidden Language of the Jews* (Baltimore, MD: Johns Hopkins University Press, 1986), which examines the construction of the Eastern Jew, pp. 270–85. Many Jews resisted assimilation. A book endorsing this was 'hanged' by Jews before being burnt. See Bosmajian, *Burning Books*, p. 22.

169

5   See James Shapiro, *Shakespeare and the Jews* (New York: Columbia University Press, 1996), p. 110.

6   Mary Wollstonecraft Shelley, *Valperga: or, The Life and Adventures of Castruccio, Prince of Lucca*, ed. Stuart Curran (Oxford: Oxford University Press [1823], 1997), p. 216.

7   Jane Blumberg, *Mary Shelley's Early Novels* (Basingstoke: Macmillan, 1993), p. 11. Nora Crook suggests that these views might have been influenced by P. B. Shelley's dealings with a notorious money-lender known as John 'Jew' King. In later years, Mary Shelley took a progressive position on the question of Jewish emancipation. See Crook, 'Counting the Carbonari', 45.

8   The word first appeared in 1879 in a pamphlet by Wilhelm Marr.

9   See Davison, *Anti-Semitism*, p. 192, n.

10 This is from Leon Pinsker's 'Auto-Emancipation' (1882), quoted in Davison, *Anti-Semitism*, p. 1.

11 See Sander Gilman, *The Jew's Body* (New York: Routledge, 1991), p. 235.

12 See, for example, Aloys Schreiber's poem, 'Der ewige Jude' (1817).

13 See Tyler R. Tichelaar, *The Gothic Wanderer: From Transgression to Redemption – Gothic Literature from 1794–present* (Ann Arbor, MI: Modern History Press, 2012), pp. 43–58; Marie [Mulvey-] Roberts, *Gothic Immortals: The Fiction of the Brotherhood of the Rosy Cross* (London: Routledge, 1990), pp. 72–81; and Davison, *Anti-Semitism*, pp. 87–157.

14 See Robert Michael, *Holy Hatred: Christianity, Antisemitism, and the Holocaust* (London: Palgrave Macmillan, 2006), p. 118.

15 See Michael, *Holy Hatred*, p. 28.

16 Anthony Julius, *Trials of the Diaspora: A History of Anti-Semitism in England* (Oxford: Oxford University Press, 2010), p. 219.

17 It involved the disappearance of a young girl from a Hungarian village who was believed to be the victim of Jewish ritual murder. Over a dozen Jewish men were rounded up and put on trial between 1882 and 1883. Even though they were acquitted and released, the case led to other trials in Europe.

18 Quoted in Davison, *Anti-Semitism*, p. 43. In the 1830s, banking magnate Nathan Rothschild was accused of having the blood of Shylock and Judas running through his veins by the governor of Mississippi.

19 Quoted in Eliza R. L. McGraw, *Two Covenants: Representations of Southern Jewishness* (Baton Rouge, LA: Louisiana State University Press, 2005), p. 23.

20 Quoted in C. Vann Woodward, *Tom Watson: Agrarian Rebel* (Oxford: Oxford University Press [1938], 1987), p. 351.

21 See Maud Ellmann, 'The Imaginary Jew: T. S. Eliot and Ezra Pound', in Bryan Cheyette (ed.), *Between 'Race' and Culture: Representations of 'the Jew' in English and American Literature* (Stanford, CA: Stanford University Press, 1996), p. 86.

22 Charles Dickens, *Oliver Twist: or, The Parish Boy's Progress*, ed. Philip Horne (London: Penguin [1838], 2003), p. 390. The novel was serialised from February 1837 to April 1839.

23 Halberstam, *Skin Shows*, p. 92.

24 Halberstam, *Skin Shows*, p. 92.

25 Gilman, *The Jew's Body*, p. 180.

26 See Gilman, *The Jew's Body*, p. 179.

27 See Anon., 'Nose', in *Jewish Encyclopedia* (1906), www.jewishencyclopedia.com/articles/11598-nose. Accessed 1 September 2012.

28 See Davison, *Anti-Semitism*, p. 135.

29 Stoker, *Personal Reminiscences of Henry Irving*, p. 90.

30 Hall Caine's *The Scapegoat* (1890) is a pro-Jewish novel, though as Malchow points out, it perpetuates racial stereotypes in which 'the majority of the Jewish community, if not evil, are represented as intolerant, unforgiving, and "absorbed in getting and spending" '; *Gothic Images of Race*, p. 157.

31 See Stoker, *Personal Reminiscences of Henry Irving*, p. 320.

32 John Davis, *Henry Irving: A Short Account of His Public Life* (New York: William S. Gottsberger, 1883), p. 105.

33 Quoted in Davison, *Anti-Semitism*, p. 129.

34 See 'Sir Richard Burton's Manuscripts: Alexander v. Manners Sutton', *The Times*, 28 March 1911, 3.

35 Stoker, *Personal Reminiscences of Henry Irving*, pp. 230–1.

36 Stoker, *Personal Reminiscences of Henry Irving*, p. 350.

37 Stoker, *Personal Reminiscences of Henry Irving*, p. 229.

38 These interests are reflected in the titles of the books Burton produced, which include eleven Hindu vampire tales, *King Vikram and the Vampire* (1870), a complete edition of *The Book of the Thousand Nights and a Night* (1885–8), along with editions of the erotic texts, *The Kama Sutra* (1883) and *The Perfumed Garden* (1886).

39 Quoted in Clive Leatherdale, *The Origins of Dracula: The Background to Bram Stoker's Gothic Masterpiece* (London: William Kimber, 1987), p. 100.

40 Quoted in Leatherdale, *The Origins of Dracula*, pp. 99–100.

41 M. Bouvier and J. L. Leutrat first use this designation, which is cited by Gelder, *Reading the Vampire*, p. 96.

42 Barbara Belford, *Bram Stoker: A Biography of the Author of Dracula* (London: Weidenfeld & Nicolson, 1996), p. 228.

43 Reproduced in Belford, *Bram Stoker*, p. 227.

44 George du Maurier, *Trilby*, ed. Leonee Ormond (London: J. M. Dent, 1992), p. 218.

45 See the issue for 1 September 1892.

46 Elaine Showalter, *Hystories: Hysterical Epidemics and Modern Culture* (London: Picador, 1977), p. 36.

47 'The Draculas were, says Arminius, a great and noble race, though now and again were scions who were held by their coevals to have had dealings with the Evil One. They learned his secrets in the Scholomance, amongst the mountains over Lake Hermanstadt, where the devil claims the tenth scholar as his due' (*Dracula*, p. 280).

48 See Davison, *Anti-Semitism*, p. 128.

49 See Leatherdale, *The Origins of Dracula*, p. 117. The essay is reproduced here, pp. 108–26.

50 Vlad's father, who is mentioned in Stoker's William Wilkinson source (see note below), belonged to the Order of the Dragon, 'that would lend him the epithet Dracul, his faction the Draculestis, and his son the title Dracula'; Gavin Baddeley and Paul Woods, *Vlad the Impaler: Son of the Devil, Hero of the People* (Hersham: Ian Allan, 2010), p. 58.

51 Stoker acquired this from William Wilkinson's *An Account of the Principalities of Wallachia and Moldavia* (1820), while researching the novel in Whitby during the summer of 1890. See *Stoker's Notes for Dracula*, ed. Eighteen-Bisang and Miller, pp. 244–5.

52 Gilman, *The Jew's Body*, p. 39.

53 Quoted in Gilman, *The Jew's Body*, p. 97.

54 Quoted in Jimmie E. Cain Jr., *Bram Stoker and Russophobia: Evidence of the British Fear of Russia in Dracula and The Lady of the Shroud* (Jefferson, NC: McFarland, 2006), p. 139.

55 See Anton Kaes, *Shell Shock Cinema: Weimar Culture and the Wounds of War* (Princeton, NJ: Princeton University Press, 2009), p. 93. Their numbers included Carl von Clausewitz, who is mentioned in the conclusion to this book. He was a Prussian general, whose greatest work, *On War* (1832), was never completed because of his death from cholera.

56 Quoted in Malchow, *Gothic Images of Race*, p. 156.

57 See Leatherdale, *The Origins of Dracula*, p. 124.

58 This is translated as 'plague carrier' in 'Nosferatu', in J. Gordon Melton, *The Vampire Book: The Encyclopedia of the Undead* (Detroit, MI: Visible Ink Press, 1999), p. 496.

59 A photograph of the actor without the prosthetic is reproduced in David J. Skal, *Hollywood Gothic: The Tangled Web of Dracula from Novel to Stage to Screen* (New York: Faber & Faber [1990], 2004), p. 99. I am indebted to Christopher Frayling for drawing my attention to this.

60 Kaes, *Shell Shock Cinema*, p. 109.

61 'Der ewig Jude', *Unser Wille und Weg*, 10 (1940), 54–5. This was the Nazi Party's monthly propaganda publication.

62 See Irven M. Resnick, 'Medieval Roots of the Myth of Jewish Male Menses', *Harvard Theological Review*, 93:3 (2000), 244.

63 According to miasma theory, cholera was caused by inhaling a noxious vapour. This belief was disproved in 1854 by John Snow, who traced the cause to contaminated water.

64 Joseph Banister, *England under the Jews* (Boston, MA: Elibron Classics [1907], 2007), p. 58.

65 Linda Friday has made this calculation, drawing on the 1891 Census, which reveals that over 88 per cent of Chicksand Street was occupied by Jewish families. Many were of Russian or Polish birth. Judging from their names and dates of birth, the remainder seems to have been second-generation Jewish immigrant families, which would have created a greater sense of Jewish occupation in the street, where an Egyptian rabbi also resided. Friday delivered most of these research findings in a conference paper, 'Exhuming Dracula's Coffin via E-learning: A Case Study', International Gothic Association Conference, University of Surrey, 7 August 2013.

66 Quoted in Davison, *Anti-Semitism*, p. 162.

67 See Stephen D. Arata, 'The Occidental Tourist: *Dracula* and the Anxiety of Reverse Colonization', *Victorian Studies*, 3:4 (1990), 621–45.

68 See Malchow, *Gothic Images of Race*, p. 162.

69 Quoted in Mordechai Rozin, *The Rich and the Poor: Jewish Philanthropy and Social Control in Nineteenth-Century London* (Brighton: Sussex Academic Press, 1999), p. 140.

70 Quoted in Colin Holmes, 'The Ritual Murder Accusation in Britain', in Alan Dundes (ed.), *The Blood Libel Legend: A Casebook in Anti-Semitic Folklore* (Madison, WI: University of Wisconsin Press, 1991), p. 113.

71 Quoted in Leatherdale, *The Origins of Dracula*, p. 99.

72 Quoted in Michael, *Holy Hatred*, pp. 112–13.

73 Quoted in Michael, *Holy Hatred*, p. 169.

74 See Randall L. Bytwerk, *Julius Streicher* (New York: Cooper Square Press [1983], 2001), p. 73.

75 Bytwerk, *Julius Streicher*, p. 161.

76 Bytwerk, *Julius Streicher*, p. 138.

77 See Bytwerk, *Julius Streicher*, pp. 15–16.

78 See Bytwerk, *Julius Streicher*, pp. 12–13.

79 See Richard S. Levy, 'Dinter, Artur (1876–1948)', in Richard S. Levy (ed.), *Antisemitism: A Historical Encyclopedia of Prejudice and Persecution* (Santa Barbara, CA: ABC-Clio, 2005), p. 180.

80 Quoted in David Biale, *Blood and Belief: The Circulation of a Symbol between Jews and Christians* (Berkeley, CA: University of California Press, 2007), p. 144.

81 *The Jew as World Parasite* (1943), Part 4, German Propaganda Archive, www.calvin.edu/academic/cas/gpa/weltparasit.htm. Accessed 31 December 2012.

82 Quoted in Kaes, *Shell Shock Cinema*, p. 112.

83 Adolph Hitler, *Mein Kampf*, ed. D. C. Watt, trans. Ralph Manheim (London: Pimlico [1925–6], 2007), p. 296.

84 This expression is used in Fritz Fink's pamphlet, 'The Jewish Question in Education' (1937) quoted in Biale, *Blood and Belief*, p. 139.

85 See Hanns Heinz Ewers, *Blood* (Rockville, MD: Olympia Press, 2009), p. 38. In this story, blood-drinking is also part of voodoo ritual in Haity [*sic*]. Another story, 'Tomato Sauce', involves a blood sport with human prey, witnessed by a blood-intoxicated priest.

86 See Hanns Heinz Ewers, *Alraune*, trans. Joe E. Bandel (Newcastle-upon-Tyne: Side Real Press, 2010), pp. xvi and 353.

87 Richard Burton and W. H. Wilkins, *The Jew, the Gypsy and El Islam* (Kila, MT: Kessinger Publishing Co. [1898], 2003), p. 63.

88 The association between alchemist and Jew tends to be overstated and is not well documented.

89 See Franco Moretti, *Signs Taken for Wonders: Essays in the Sociology of Literary Forms*, trans. Susan Fischer, David Forgacs and David Miller (London: Verso, 1983), p. 93.

90 Cain, *Bram Stoker and Russophobia*, p. 115. George Stoker's book, *With 'The Unspeakables;' or Two Years' Campaigning in European and Asiatic Turkey* (London: Chapman and Hall, 1878), is discussed in the next chapter.

91 See Davison, *Anti-Semitism*, pp. 141–2.

92 Karin Elizabeth Wikoff, 'Hans Heinz Ewers' Vampir', MA dissertation (Cornell University, 1995), http://siderealpressxtras.blogspot.co.uk/2010/02/hanns-heinz-ewers-vampir-thesis.html.

93 Hanns Heinz Ewers, *Nachtmahr: Strange Tales*, ed. John Hirschhorn-Smith (Newcastle-upon-Tyne: Side Real Press, 2009), p. xxiii.

94 Ewers, *Nachtmahr*, p. 146.

95 See Bytwerk, *Julius Streicher*, p. 70.

96 Ewers, *Nachtmahr*, p. 148.

97 See Gilman's chapter on the Jewish voice in *The Jew's Body*, pp. 1–37. In *Trilby*, du Maurier writes: 'And here let me say that these vicious imaginations of Svengali's, which look so tame in English print, sounded much more ghastly in French, pronounced with a Hebrew-German accent, and uttered in his hoarse, rasping, nasal, throaty rook's caw, his big yellow teeth baring themselves in a mongrel canine snarl'; p. 75.

98 Future references to *The Golem* are to this version, unless stated otherwise.

99 Quoted in Nicholas Royle, *The Uncanny* (Manchester: Manchester University Press, 2003), p. 78.

100 *Nosferatu*, directed by F. W. Murnau, Prana-Film, 1922, onscreen intertitle, translated from the German..

101 Derrida, *Specters of Marx*, p. 245.

102 Quoted in Susan Tegel, *Nazis and the Cinema* (London: Hambledon Continuum, 2007), p. 150.

103 Quoted in Brenda Gardenour, 'The Biology of Blood-Lust: Medieval Medicine, Theology and the Vampire Jew', *Film and History*, 42:2 (Fall 2011), 59–60.

104 Lester D. Friedman, 'The Edge of Knowledge: Jews as Monsters/Jews as Victims', *MELUS*, 11:3 (Autumn 1984), 56.

105 Jack Dann's short story, 'Down among the Dead Men' (1982), is set in a concentration camp where Jewish prisoners are blood-drinkers.

106 See Kaes, *Shell Shock Cinema*, p. 111.

107 Count Orlok's Jewishness is not specifically brought out in Steven Katz's screenplay or in the haunting musical score written by Dan Jones, who told me: 'I was looking for an Eastern European sound that matched the ancient qualities of Orlok himself. Something that sounded like it might have been locked up in an ancient castle vault waiting for a passer by'; email to Marie Mulvey-Roberts, 6 January 2012.

108 See E. Elias Merhige, 'Director's Commentary', *Shadow of the Vampire*, Saturn Films, DVD, 2001.

109 Derrida, *Specters of Marx*, p. 11.

110 Adolph Hitler, *Mein Kampf*, trans. Alvin Johnson and John Chamberlain (New York: Reynal and Hitchcock [1925–6], 1941), p. 116.

111 This is a translation from the German.

112 See Lotte H. Eisner, *Murnau* (London: Martin Secker & Warburg [1964], 1973), p. 62. Grau wrote a treatise on lighting for black-and-white films.

113 Quoted in Kaes, *Shell Shock Cinema*, p. 125.

114 Murnau's much later film was called *Sunrise: A Song of Two Humans* (1927)

115 Gilman, *The Jew's Body*, pp. 64, 68 and 76.

116 See Bytwerk, *Julius Streicher*, p. 146.

117 Quoted in Bosmajian, *Burning Books*, p. 31.

118 See Skal, *Hollywood Gothic*, p. 98.

119 Friedrich Kittler, 'Dracula's Legacy', *Stanford Humanities Review*, 1:1 (1989), 171; and see Thomas Elsaesser, 'No End to *Nosferatu* (1922)', in Noah Isenberg (ed.), *Weimar Cinema: An Essential Guide to Classic Films of the Era* (New York: Columbia University Press, 2009), p. 92.

120 Kittler, 'Dracula's Legacy', 172.

121 See Tegel, *Nazis and the Cinema*, p. 151.

122 In du Maurier's *Trilby*, Taffy Wynne paints Algerian Jews, 'just as they really are'; p. 124.

123 This could be a tongue-in-cheek reference to the times when Klaus Kinski was having a tantrum on the set of *Nosferatu* (1979) and the director Werner Herzog would threaten him with having to undergo another four-hour makeup session. The film is discussed later in this chapter.

124 Julius Streicher published a storybook for children, which made connections between Jews and unpleasant animals. See Bytwerk, *Julius Streicher*, p. 60.

125 See Bytwerk, *Julius Streicher*, p. 66.

126 Derrida, *Specters of Marx*, p. 195.

127 There were rumours that Schreck was a real vampire. The suggestion is made in Ado Kyrou, *Le Surréalisme au cinéma* [*Surrealism in the Cinema*] (1953). See Elsaesser, 'No End to *Nosferatu* (1922)', p. 90.

128 Carol Margaret Davison made this eloquent point in a conference paper, 'Modernity's Fatal Addictions: Death/Undeath by Technology in E. Elias Merhige's *Shadow of the Vampire* (2000)', International Gothic Association conference, University of Surrey, 7 August 2013.

129 Quoted in Skal, *Hollywood Gothic*, p. 83.

130 Merhige, 'Director's Commentary', *Shadow of the Vampire*.

131 The camera and the Gatling gun, an early rapid-fire gun dating back to the American Civil War, pre-dating the machine gun, were invented at the same time. See Erik Butler, *Metamorphoses of the Vampire in Literature and Film: Cultural Transformations in Europe 1732–1933* (Rochester, NY: Camden House, 2010), p. 153.

132 Kittler points out that Remington, the machine gun factory, marketed the first mass-produced typewriters in 1871. See 'Dracula's Legacy', 155. The typewriter in the hands of Stoker's Mina Harker proves to be an important weapon in bringing about the destruction of Dracula.

133 Paul Virilio, *War and Cinema: The Logistics of Perception*, trans. Patrick Camiller (London: Verso [1984], 1989), p. 20.

134 See Ian Roberts, *German Expressionist Cinema: The World of Light and Shadow* (London: Wallflower Press, 2008), p. 40.

135 Halberstam, *Skin Shows*, p. 4.

136 See Blumberg, *Mary Shelley's Early Novels*, pp. 27, 191.

137 In Merhige's version, it is ironic that Murnau directs Count Orlok to respond to his realisation that his victim had tried deceiving him by bringing along a wooden stake with which to destroy him. Murnau has been exploited in death as the director of the most celebrated vampire film when his grave in Stahnsdorf was opened in July 2015 and his skull stolen.

138 The quarter later became absorbed into the Litzmannstadt Ghetto.

139 See Patrick Colm Hogan, 'Narrative Universals, Nationalism, and Sacrificial Terror: From *Nosferatu* to Nazism', *Film Studies*, 8 (Summer 2006), 93–105.

140 Davison compares Süss' rape of Dorothea Sturm with Count Dracula's 'symbolic acts of miscegenation in Britain'; *Anti-Semitism*, p. 163.

141 See Bytwerk, *Julius Streicher*, p. 143.

142 See Bytwerk, *Julius Streicher*, p. 154.

143 Bytwerk, *Julius Streicher*, p. 145.

144 See Bytwerk, *Julius Streicher*, p. 152.

145 Quoted in Skal, *Hollywood Gothic*, p. 86. Gardenour points out that, according to medieval humoral theory, women and Jews were coded as cold and

damp, like vampires. The uncontrollable lust of the vampire and the thirst of imaginary Jew for warm Christian blood was believed to lead to excessive warmth associated with concupiscence. The males were believed to be incapable of erection, since both were in essence regarded as female and therefore without the necessary male fire. Thus sexual desire is fed through blood-drinking in an endless cycle of lust that remains unsatiated. See 'The Biology of Blood-Lust', 61.

146 Gilman, *The Jew's Body*, p. 189.

147 This relates to male circumcision and hysteria. See Gilman, *The Jew's Body*, pp. 81–96, and also the section on 'Penises and Noses' in Sander L. Gilman, *The Case of Sigmund Freud: Medicine and Identity at the Fin de Siècle* (Baltimore, MD: Johns Hopkins University Press, 1994), pp. 93–106.

148 Previously only a select few had been allowed to reside in the city. See Hannah S. Decker, *Freud, Dora, and Vienna 1900* (New York: The Free Press, 1992), p. 21.

149 See Gilman's chapter on the Jewish foot in *The Jew's Body*, pp. 38–59.

150 See Gilman's chapter on the Jewish foot in *The Jew's Body*, p. 49.

151 See John Abbott, *Another Comment on Jud Süss* (Chicago, IL: International Historic Films, 2007), p. 22.

152 See Carol Margaret Davison, 'Blood Brothers: Dracula and Jack the Ripper', in Davison (ed.), *Bram Stoker's Dracula*, p. 155.

153 Nicholas Tucker, 'Third Reich and Third Rate', *New Society*, 17:447 (April 1971), 682.

154 Quoted in Hadley Freeman, 'The Dark Comedy of Werner Herzog', *The Guardian*, 5 March 2011, www.guardian.co.uk/film/2011/mar/05/werner-herzog-cave-of-forgotten-dreams. Accessed 23 January 2012. See also Klaus Kinski, *Kinski Uncut: The Autobiography of Klaus Kinski*, trans. Joachim Neugröschel (London: Bloomsbury, 1996), p. 214.

155 Quoted in Freeman, 'The Dark Comedy of Werner Herzog'.

156 William Patrick Day, *Vampire Legends in Contemporary American Culture: What Becomes a Legend Most* (Kentucky, KY: The University Press of Kentucky, 2002), pp. 85–7.

157 *Das Rheingold* was first performed in 1869 against Wagner's wishes.

158 Day, *Vampire Legends in Contemporary American Culture*, p. 85.

159 See David J. Levin, *Richard Wagner, Fritz Lang and the Nibelungen: The Dramaturgy of Disavowal* (Princeton, NJ: Princeton University Press, 1988), pp. 9–10.

160 See Theodor Adorno, *In Search of Wagner* (London: Verso [1952], 2005), p. 13.

161 They are actually cholera victims from an 1833 cholera epidemic in Guanajuato in Mexico.

162 This departs from the book where, of course, Mina rather than Lucy is Jonathan's wife.

163 See Day, *Vampire Legends in Contemporary American Culture*, p. 85.

164 Halberstam, *Skin Shows*, p. 31.

165 Quoted in Davison, *Anti-Semitism*, p. 161.

166 Quoted in Tegel, *Nazis and the Cinema*, p. 19.

167 See Siegfried Kracauer, *From Caligari to Hitler: A Psychological History of the German Film* (Princeton, NJ: Princeton University Press, 1947), p. 32.

168 This argument formed part of Kracauer's wider agenda relating to the post-war reconstruction of Germany and prevention of another Hitler.

169 Kracauer, *From Caligari to Hitler*, p. 272. Doctor Mabuse, the mad German scientist, the subject of three Fritz Lang films, starting in 1922, was such a megalomaniacal misanthrope that rather than rule the world, he preferred destroying it.

170 Kaes, *Shell Shock Cinema*, pp. 5 and 2.

5

The vampire of war

Our lads crucified, babies spiked
On bayonets by vampire Aryans.[1]
Robert Greacen, 'Hun' (1995)

In all men's hearts it is.
Some spirit old
Hath turned with malign kiss
Our lives to mould.

Red fangs have torn His face.
God's blood is shed.
He mourns from His lone place
His children dead.

O! ancient crimson curse!
Corrode, consume.
Give back this universe
Its pristine bloom.[2]
Isaac Rosenberg, 'On Receiving
News of the War' (written in 1914)

War is the ultimate horror and supreme blood-sucker, yet little attention has been paid to its representation in literature and film through the metaphors, images and rhetoric of vampirism.[3] An exception has been made by Terry Phillips, who argues that the cultural figure of the vampire influenced First World War fiction.[4] This final chapter will make a wider and deeper foray into the relationship between vampire and war in novels, films and short stories from the Crimean War (1853–6), through to the Russo-Turkish conflict (1877–8), First World War (1914–18) and up to the Vietnam War (1959–75).

In the act of parasitically feeding off a living body, the vampire functions as an appropriate trope for the draining effects of war on the body politic. Just as war lends itself to Gothicisation, as an over-determined signifier, vampirism is applicable to representations of the enemy, men-at-arms, officers, politicians, patriots, men and women on the home front and returning soldiers. Like the vampire, war replicates itself through blood. According to Barbara Ehrenreich: 'However and wherever war begins, it persists, it spreads, it propagates itself through time and across space with the terrifying tenacity of a beast attached to the neck of living prey. This is not an idly chosen figure of speech.'[5] Such perpetuation is evident from the way in which the Crimean War propagated the Russo-Turkish war, which ended with the unsatisfactory Berlin Treaty and helped trigger the global conflict of 1914 to 1918, leading to the Second World War. As Michel Foucault sees it, 'a battlefront runs through the whole of society, continuously and permanently.'[6] It is curiously apt that a particularly volatile cradle of war, the Balkans, should be a region notorious for nurturing legends of the vampire.[7] *Dracula* is the obvious starting point. Not only is it the quintessential vampire fiction, but it can also be read as a war novel. Stoker's most celebrated work went on to inspire a series of adaptations, from the film *Nosferatu* to contemporary novelist Kim Newman's recreation of the First World War, populated by vampires and humans. Newman's postmodern pastiche of history, literature and film highlights the vampiric nature of genre to reveal how the fantastic can be just as effective as the military memoir in exposing the truth, myths and horror of war. This chapter will indicate the ways in which the literary treatment of war and vampirism has been deployed to convey an anti-war message.

CAPTAIN VAMPIRE AND COUNT DRACULA

A novel combining war with a vampire theme appeared eighteen years before *Dracula*. This was *Captain Vampire* (1879), written in French by the twenty-year-old Belgium-born author Marie Nizet. Forgotten for over a century, the novel was rediscovered by Romanian scholar Radu Florescu, whose successor Matei Cazacu considered it as a possible source for *Dracula*.[8] Brian Stableford, who produced the first English translation in 2007, is sceptical, preferring to see the novel instead as significant in its own right as an early exposé of the horrors of war and one of the finest examples of vampire fiction.[9]

Captain Vampire takes place during the Russo-Turkish war of 1877–8. At its core lies a political message decrying the betrayal of Romanian soldiers sent to their deaths by their Russian allies. Nizet, who had never visited Romania, heard about the war from the daughters of the vehemently anti-Russian Romanian political writer, journalist and politician, Ion Heliade Rădulescu. The conflict was sparked by the rise of nationalism amongst various European nations, including Romania and Bulgaria where the novel is set. Both countries had been under the rule of the ailing Ottoman Empire. In 1877, Romania declared independence and along with the Eastern Orthodox Coalition and various Baltic countries, led by Russia, joined in a war against the Turks. Nizet draws on an incident which had arisen from the Romanians granting the Russian army permission to cross their territory in order to launch an attack against the Turks. The novel opens with an image of the Russians 'descending like locusts upon the magnificent country of Rumania [sic], which had been surrendered to them as prey' (p. 19). The parasitic nature of Russian imperialism is personified by the cadaverous-looking Boris Liatoukine, known as Captain Vampire, who exudes a malign influence. Boris insults the Romanian hero, Ion Isacescu,[10] by attempting to seduce his fiancée, Mariora Slobozianu, with his menacing hypnotic gaze. Ion gets his revenge on the battlefield by killing Captain Vampire, who is wearing Mariora's engagement ring; Ion recovers the ring by severing part of his enemy's finger. After the couple are reunited, they catch sight of Boris, who is still alive and about to remarry, with the tell-tale top of his finger missing. At the end of the novel, Captain Vampire is promoted to General by the Tsar. 'The suspicious old dowagers' remain convinced that he died at the siege of Gravitza, leaving just a 'cadaver, temporarily reanimated by a breath of infernal life' (p. 150).

Nizet might have acquired the idea for her undead soldier from accounts in 1727 of a vampire called Arnold Paul. Five years earlier, Arnold complained that he was being 'tormented by a vampire', while serving as a 'heyduke' or militiaman at Cassovia on the frontiers of Turkish Serbia. Dracula mentions 'the shame of Cassova [sic]' (p. 60) in a lecture to Jonathan Harker on the warring history of his people. In his research notes for the novel, Stoker refers to the defeat of the Wallachians led by the fifteenth-century Voivode Dracula, at the Battle of Cassova in Bulgaria. This is the country in which *Captain Vampire* is partly set.[11] After his defeat, the Voivode, also known as Vlad the Impaler, escaped into Hungary, the very same country in which Arnold Paul ravaged the village of Madreyga, killing four people.[12] The villagers retaliated by driving a stake through his heart, beheading him and then burning the body. The story first appeared in *The London Journal* of 1732 and was repeated by John Polidori in his introduction to *The Vampyre* (1819), which was translated into French.[13] It might easily have been relayed to the French-speaking Nizet along this route. Another possible source for her military vampire is James Malcolm Rymer's *Varney the Vampire; or The Feast of Blood* (1847), which started as a Penny Dreadful in 1845. Fifteen chapters of this protracted saga concern a villainous protagonist posing as a wealthy colonel in the Indian Army, who uses the tell-tale sobriquet of Colonel Deverill. He reinforces the deception with tales of his military exploits, and succeeds in draining his victims of money, as well as blood, before being exposed as a vampire.[14]

While it is generally accepted that Stoker was influenced by Polidori and Rymer, *Captain Vampire* has been overlooked as a likely source. That it was written in French should be no obstacle since it is assumed that Stoker, whose parents moved to France in 1872, had a reading knowledge of the language.[15] Both novels have tall, thin and pale aristocratic protagonists, who attempt to seduce a fiancée using mesmeric powers.[16] A crucial difference picked up by Stableford is that there is no evidence of Boris being a blood-drinker. This makes Nizet's understanding of a vampire rather different from that of Stoker since hers rests primarily upon his mesmeric gaze and ability to rise from the dead. Nevertheless, a novel with a vampire protagonist would surely have given Stoker an incentive to read Nizet's novel as part of his research for writing *Dracula*. But there was a still more pressing and personal reason for propelling him towards the book. This is because Nizet writes about the very same war and specific battle in which Stoker's younger brother George served as a surgeon in the Imperial Ottoman Army and medical officer for the Bulgarian Relief Fund in 1877. This young, energetic field surgeon was in charge of twenty purpose-built Red Crescent ambulances for transporting the wounded from the front line. Fellow surgeon Charles Snodgrass Ryan describes how George rescued forty wounded men from Plevna in 1877, a battle central to Nizet's novel (Figure 12).[17] The Turkish army suffered considerable losses with around four thousand dead or wounded. George was decorated for his valour by the Turks, and, in 1881, went to live with Bram's family for several years at their London home in Cheyne Walk.[18] Stoker's biographer, Harry Ludlam, imaginatively recreates George relaying the horrors of war to his brother:

THE WAR: FIELD AMBULANCE BEFORE PLEVNA—WAITING FOR THE WOUNDED.
SKETCH BY ONE OF OUR SPECIAL ARTISTS.

Figure 12 Sketch by war artist, *The War: Field Ambulance before Plevna – Waiting for the Wounded* (1877). Bram Stoker's brother George was in charge of Red Crescent ambulances on the Turkish side of the battle.

Note: The drawing appears in the *Supplement to the Illustrated London News*, 8 December 1877, 553.

To Bram he recounted stark scenes such as that he saw after a hilltop battle, when the dead lay thickly in every conceivable position, stretched out, doubled up, on their faces, with their hands tightly clenched in the grass, on their backs, or propped up against a tree or caught in the bushes which had stayed their downward course after being struck. He described the dreadful sight before him as he entered one town where the wounded, dead and dying lay so thickly together in the streets that it was not possible to ride along; where a good many of the unfortunate soldiers had been struck in the head and were rolling about in the mud, groaning and shrieking, covered with filth and gore, some, exhausted, lying stretched out on the pavement almost lifeless, others propped up against the walls – and bullock carts arriving every minute with more loads of pitifully crying men.[19]

George Stoker wrote an account of his experiences entitled *With 'The Unspeakables;' or Two Years' Campaigning in European and Asiatic Turkey* (1878), providing further evidence of his involvement in the siege

of Plevna in Bulgaria. The following year, Marie Nizet published her fictionalised account of the same battle, only this time from the vantage
point of the opposing side. Even though claims made by biographers
that Bram helped George with the book cannot be substantiated, he
did record his brother's exploits at Plevna in *Personal Reminiscences of
Henry Irving*, where he notes how he 'had brought to Philippopolis all the
Turkish wounded from the battle at the Schipka [*sic*] Pass, and so had had
about as much experience of dead bodies as any man wants'.[20] In turn,
George may well have provided his brother with details of the Balkans
and Asia Minor, which crop up in Stoker's two novels about Eastern
Europe, *Dracula* and *The Lady of the Shroud* (1909).[21] In Stoker's original
plans for the earlier novel, his vampire protagonist was called Count
Wampyr and came from the region of Styria in Austria.[22] Some critics
claim that Stoker altered the name to Count Dracula and location to
Transylvania because of the influence of his brother. This has been rightly
contested by Elizabeth Miller, who points out that George's book 'is about
Bulgaria, not Transylvania, and not even Romania'.[23] Nizet's novel, however, does takes place in Romania, the name given at that time to the
union of the principalities of Moldavia and Wallachia. Furthermore, her
hero is a Wallachian, as was Voivode Dracula, Prince Vlad.[24] While the
Voivode was born in Transylvania, he did not live there, unlike Stoker's
Dracula, whose castle is located near the Borgo Pass. The region would
not be incorporated into Romania until the end of the First World War.
Historically the biggest concern for that part of the world had been fend-
ing off the Ottoman Empire, with which George Stoker had joined forces.
By contrast, the fictional Dracula, a native Szekely, is an implacable foe of
the Turk, as was the formidable warrior Prince Vlad. Through her novel,
Nizet takes up their cause in opposing the Turks.

By weighing up evidence for an influence on *Dracula*, Stableford identifies Captain Vampire as 'a symbolic evil genius of the Russian army;
effective in different ways in different places – including different places at
the same time – and not a mere person at all' (p. 154). He goes on to point
out: 'It is worth remembering that [Boris] Liatoukine first appears in direct response to a formal curse uttered by [Ion] Isacescu's father against
the Russian invaders' (p. 154). Stableford uses this argument to support
his contention that 'it is unlikely that Bram Stoker ever read *Le Captaine
Vampire* –and, more importantly, that even if he did, he did not take any
substantial influence specifically therefrom' (p. 155). But it was precisely
these anti-Russian sentiments and their embodiment in the figure of

Captain Vampire that would have attracted Stoker to Nizet's novel, at a time when Russia was posing a threat to British imperialism. As war between the two countries loomed, the writer T. Pearce described the Russian army as a 'horrid image' that was 'dragging its enormous bulk like some reptile, towards that noble, that devoted band of paladins'.[25] This figurative language is paralleled by a scene early on in Stoker's novel. This is where Dracula is compared to a reptile when seen going head first down his castle wall by Jonathan Harker, who is described as having a 'noble nature' (p. 221) by Van Helsing, the leader of a 'devoted band of paladins' who are determined to resist the Count's plans for invasion.[26] The 'project of imperial Gothic desire',[27] started in *Dracula* and completed in *The Lady of the Shroud*, represents a fictional buttressing of the British Empire to shore up its decline. For the later novel, Stoker invents the Land of the Blue Mountain in the Balkans and a new Balkan federation called Balka. As Victor Sage has noted, Stoker's fictional rearrangement of the Balkans was designed to protect British interests and help curb the ambitions of Turkey and Austria.[28] In keeping with his prerogative as a novelist, Stoker rewrites history and recreates geography, a presumption also made by conquering nations.

As Jimmie E. Cain explains in his persuasive study, *Bram Stoker and Russophobia*, Stoker's formative years were spent in an atmosphere of anxiety over the threat of Russian imperialism to Britain's democracy and British colonies, especially India. He listened keenly to his father-in-law Lieutenant Colonel James Balcombe's first-hand accounts of fighting the Russians in the Crimea, for which he was awarded a campaign medal and clasp for every battle fought, which had included Balaclava (1854) and Inkerman (1854) (Figure 13).[29] The most well-known campaign in which he took part was the Siege of Sebastopol (1854–5), a Russian port on the Crimean Peninsula. This is where Captain Vampire, having distinguished himself during the Crimean War, freezes to death. His return from the dead is symbolic of the revival of Russian military power in the Russo-Turkish war. Cain points out that the ongoing threat of Russia to Britain, along with the failures of the Crimean War, which haunted the national conscience, are mitigated somewhat by Stoker's fiction of a British victory over a vampire from the East, intent on conquest of the West. All this is shot through with a significant Russian subtext. Dracula, who 'came to London to invade a new land' (p. 383), enters Britain by way of the north-east coast port of Whitby on a Russian ship called *Demeter*. The name was adapted from the Russian schooner, the *Dimitry*,

Figure 13 Lieutenant-Colonel Shadforth and Officers of the 57th (West Middlesex) Regiment of Foot (1855) photographed by Roger Fenton. Quartermaster James Balcome, Bram Stoker's future father-in-law, is on the far right of the photograph.

which had been shipwrecked at Whitby in October 1885. Both ships set sail from Varna, a port city of Bulgaria, the country in which the most important military action in *Captain Vampire* takes place.[30] Varna had also been associated with cholera and the 'blood disease' scorbutus, which had killed large numbers of British soldiers during the Crimean War. Subsequently, it was given the Turkish name for 'the Valley of Death', making Varna a suitable starting point for the undead, shipping pestilence to Britain. For his eventual retreat from England, the Count boards another Russian ship, called *Czarina Catherine*, the name of which brings to mind Russian imperialism. In hot pursuit are Van Helsing's 'brave men' (p. 397) who, as Cain observes follow in the footsteps of the British troops 'in almost every particular' in their military advance and withdrawal from the Crimea.[31] Stoker is likely to have acquired details from his brother George, who had travelled the very same route and wrote in his travelogue of 1878: 'It was after dark when we arrived in Varna, and I fear the peaceful inhabitants must have thought another Crimean war was about to commence.'[32] In describing how the men take rooms at a hotel, 'the Odessus' (p. 374), Cain teasingly adopts the rhetoric of war by announcing, 'their assault begins with an occupation of Varna'.[33] The identification of the hotel's name with Odessa is symbolic, Cain suggests, of Russian interests in Bulgaria. That may be so, but closer connections with the novel can be found. The Russian port was founded by a decree issued by Catherine the Great, after whom Dracula's ship is named. Furthermore, shortly after arriving at Odessa on 13 April 1854, Vice Admiral Sir Leopold George Heath reported how his men captured an enemy merchant brig, 'but left Russian colours flying as a decoy'.[34] In a comparable episode in the novel, Stoker's band of men use subterfuge to ensure a smoother passage for sailing up the Bistritza river in their steam launch. They fly a Romanian flag so that they will be mistaken for a government ship and, like the allied armies, use land and sea operations to get within reach of the enemy.

The pursuit of Dracula is couched in terms of a military campaign. The paladins hold a 'Council of War' (p. 395). Food provided by their landlady is plentiful enough to supply a 'company of soldiers' (p. 401), in what could be a sly reference to Lieutenant Colonel Balcombe's job in the army, as quartermaster. Van Helsing, having taken on the role of commanding officer, insists that the men are armed. Quincey Morris recommends that they add Winchester rifles to their armament. As an American, he must have been influenced by the reputation of this firearm as 'the gun that won the West' for settlers, admitting, 'I have a kind of belief in a Winchester when there is any trouble [...] around' (p. 365). Van Helsing's response is, 'Winchesters it shall be' (p. 365). Stoker would have been acquainted with these guns through his brother, since they were used by the Turks against the Russians during the Russo-Turkish war and most markedly in the Battle of Plevna. This battle, in which George Stoker was involved, also provides the central action of *Captain Vampire* with the storming of the Gravitza redoubt. Plevna was a major European military engagement that popularised the deployment of Winchesters. Their repeating action mowed down Romanians and Russians within 200 yards.[35] As Quincey recalls to Arthur Holmwood: 'Do you remember, Art, when we had the pack after us at Tobolsk? What wouldn't we have given then for a repeater apiece!' (p. 365). Winchesters were commonly used as a hunting rifle and Quincey imagines their effectiveness against wolves in Siberia. Considering that Dracula can turn into a wolf and wolves were particularly prevalent in Russia, there is additional resonance to his remark: 'I understand that the Count comes from a wolf country'

(p. 365).[36] As the men close in on their prey towards the end of the novel, howling wolves are heard in the distance. Surrounded by mounted men, the cart carrying the great chest containing Dracula's undead body races towards his castle against another enemy, daylight, but his enemies intercept it just in time. In the battle against Dracula and his Szgany, or Roma protectors, snow falls. Cain interprets this as a recreation of the siege of Sebastopol during the Russian winter.[37] Stoker's father-in-law had witnessed the fall of Sebastopol, which proved to be crucial in the defeat of Russia and the ending of the Crimean War. But it was a hard-won victory for little gain, leaving British soldiers either starving or frozen to death. The public were shocked to learn that 'raw recruits', little more than boys, had been enlisted to the front, with minimal chance of survival, whereas more seasoned officers escaped the brutal Russian winter on the grounds of 'urgent private affairs, requiring them to return home'.[38] A *Punch* cartoon was published of a drummer boy futilely making a similar request for himself along with a long file of foot soldiers (Figure 14).

The boy soldier sacrificed for war haunts the story, 'A Vampire', in George Whyte-Melville's episodic novel, *'Bones and I' or, The Skeleton at Home* (1869), told to the narrator by a skeleton called 'Bones'. Here a vampiric aristocratic woman, Madame de St Croix, who never seems to age, seduces and then ruins or destroys a number of men connected with the Crimean War.[39] These include a Hungarian Count, Russian General, French Colonel, British businessman and an English boy, who is a poet. After being seen walking away arm in arm with the vampiric woman, Bones fears that the boy is doomed, saying, 'I recognised the hungry glitter in those dark, merciless eyes, and I knew there was no hope.'[40] Even though he is well-bred, handsome and manly, Bones realises that the boy is 'a fit victim for the altar at which he was to be offered up' (p. 96). A few months later his mother is in mourning for him, as the snow covers 'the grave of him whose opening manhood had been so full of promise, so rich in all that makes youth brightest' (p. 99). The pathos of the death of the boy soldier may be read into Bones' lament for him as one of the victims of Madame de St Croix, when he says: 'The others were bad enough in all conscience, but I think she might have spared the boy' (p. 107). Stuart Currie sees the sinister lady as a personification of the Crimean War and notes how this reading 'throw[s] into relief the interstices of a text liberally scarred by the first modern, mechanised war in history'.[41] Yet, her vampiric nature may also be interpreted as a metaphor for war in general, which can 'enslave generation after generation' (p. 96). The allure of

PUNCH, OR THE LONDON CHARIVARI.—November 24, 1855.

THE NEW GAME OF FOLLOW MY LEADER.

'PLEASE, GENERAL, MAY ME AND THESE OTHER CHAPS HAVE LEAVE TO GO HOME ON URGENT *PRIVATE AFFAIRS*.'

Figure 14 John Leech, *The New Game of Follow My Leader*. The caption reads, 'Please, General, may me and these other chaps have leave to go home on urgent *private* affairs' (1855).

Note: First published in *Punch, or The London Charivari*, 28 (24 November 1855), 209.

war may be the reason why 'so many had succumbed' to the 'power' of her 'spell' (p. 94), which corresponds to the hypnotic lure of the vampire. The tale concludes with a condemnation of Madame de St Croix as 'Insatiate – impenetrable – pitiless' (p. 107), qualities that apply equally well to war. Currie suggests that her name, Madame de St Croix, is a reference to the Cross of St George on the Union Jack. One of her victims is an English man of commerce, who Currie sees as representing a new breed of financial speculator who profited from the war. As such, he surely constitutes another form of vampirism. But within eighteen months, the businessman appears 'very old and careworn setting cabbages' (p. 91) as he eagerly awaits the lady who never arrives. Currie speculates that the man might be based on Lord Cardigan, who was in command of the disastrous charge of the Light Cavalry Brigade during the Battle of Balaclava in 1854. He died after falling from his horse, the year before the novel was published. Cardigan was a keen horseman and on retiring from the army devoted himself to horse racing and indulging his passion for expensive steam yachts. These interests point to similarities with Whyte-Melville's businessman, who is introduced as owning the best horses and a yacht on which Madame de St Croix departs for a Greek island. As it sails away, the yacht is evocative of slaughter, 'hull-down in the wake of a crimson sunset that seemed to stain the waters with a broad track of blood' (p. 91). Cardigan, who led countless British soldiers to their deaths and emerged unscathed himself, was known contemptuously by his troops as 'the noble yachtsman'.[42] This was because, during the campaign, he stayed at night on a luxury steam yacht moored in Balaclava harbour. Cardigan returned to England on the grounds of ill health following the Battle of Balaclava, in which Bram Stoker's father-in-law had fought.

Instead of seeing traces of the Crimean War in Stoker's novel and viewing Dracula as representing Russian imperialism, Matthew Gibson, in his article on Stoker and the Treaty of Berlin (1878), takes the count at face value as an ethnic Szekely, who fought the Turk.[43] Dracula proclaims that the bloodline of his warrior clan 'can boast a record that mushroom growths like the Hapsburgs and the Romanoffs can never reach' (p. 61). Even though his ancestors were defeated by the Ottoman crescent, Dracula is mindful of the time when they were victorious, declaring: 'who was it but one of my own race who as Voivode crossed the Danube and beat the Turk on his own ground? This was a Dracula indeed!' He states proudly: 'and to us for centuries was trusted the guarding of the frontier of Turkey-land' (p. 60). Gibson argues that a reason why Dracula planned to infect London with the scourge of vampirism was reprisal for the betrayal by those who had not valued his efforts in fighting the Turk.[44] As he complains to Mina: 'Whilst they played wits against me – against me who commanded nations, and intrigued for them, and fought for them, hundreds of years before they were born – I was countermining them' (p. 328). Here, Dracula can be seen reflecting the sense of betrayal over the Treaty of Berlin (1878) when Budjak, which had been part of the Black Sea coast, north of Moldavia, one of the principalities of Romania, was ceded to the Russians. In other respects, the treaty had benefited Romanians by ratifying their independence, thus enabling Romania to become a kingdom by 1881. In that year, King Carol I was proclaimed the first Romanian monarch. The following decade, Van Helsing refers to Dracula as 'King-Vampire' (p. 412). The crowned heads of Europe played a decisive role in the power play of war and peace. Although Gibson's political reading of the novel contrasts with Cain's contention that the count represents the Russian invader, both critics demonstrate the extent to which Dracula serves as a focal point for the complex web of alliances and adversaries in Europe. By the time Stoker came to write *The Lady of the Shroud* these had already shifted, making Austro-Hungarian aspirations, rather than the Russian Empire, the greater threat to British colonial interests.

The Treaty of Berlin, which concluded the Russo-Turkish War, was hailed as an achievement in peace, a verdict to prove just as unreliable as the announcement made by foreign invader Count Dracula that 'The warlike days are over. Blood is too precious a thing in these days of dishonourable peace; and the glories of the great races are as a tale that is told' (p. 61). When Benjamin Disraeli returned home triumphant from the Congress of Berlin and gave his well-known 'Peace with Honour' speech, the Liberal Member of Parliament, William Gladstone, denounced it as the 'Peace which passeth all understanding, and the Honour that is common among thieves'.[45] The *New York Times* (21 July 1878) reported that Gladstone decried it as 'our shame' and accused Britain of having 'sold' Romanian Bessarabia (Budjak) to a despotic Russia. Counterbalancing that gain, Russian power was reduced, through the intervention of Disraeli, in favour of the Turks. In his book, George Stoker describes the rape of Turkish women by Bulgarians and Russians. Cain suggests that 'the foul-smelling, rapacious, and licentious Russians' in George's account have an analogue with 'the aromatic count who invades Britain to prey promiscuously on its female population'.[46] In vilifying the Russians, George Stoker played down the massacres of around fifteen thousand Bulgarian men, women and children by the Turks, one of which helped spark the Russo-Turkish War. Gladstone vehemently attacked the Disraeli government for their strategic indifference to Ottoman atrocities. In his pamphlet, *Bulgarian Horrors and the Question of the East* (1876), he referred to the 'murderous harvest' from 'soil soaked and reeking with blood'.[47] Bram Stoker dined with Gladstone on many occasions at the Beef Steak Room in London, where the government's foreign policy and conduct of recent wars would have been discussed. He seems to have stuck to his guns in exonerating the shameful effects of the Treaty of Berlin indirectly through *Dracula* and *The Lady of the Shroud*.[48] The Liberals regarded the settlement as a disaster for the Balkan people. Forty years later, their discontent would be detonated by a Bosnian Serb to become the trigger for the start of the First World War in 1914.[49]

NOSFERATU AND THE SHADOW OF WAR

F. W. Murnau's film adaptation of *Dracula* extends the relationship of the novel with war, only this time through the First World War, that 'dark enigma scrawled in blood'.[50] Four years after the war ended, *Nosferatu* appeared in 1922. This was during the Weimar period, an era criticised by Nazi propagandist and director of German radio, Eugen Hadamovsky, for not seeking 'control over the world' but instead preferring to worship the intellect, 'in a way that nourished itself like a vampire on the will and character'.[51]

The idea for *Nosferatu* was conceived in 1916 by Albin Grau, who became the producer and production designer, as well as co-founder of the studio that made the film. While serving with the German army in Serbia, Grau heard a tale from a Serbian peasant farmer, who claimed to have seen 'an undead or a Nosferatu', in Romania.[52] This was the Serb's own father, who had risen from his grave as a vampire after being buried without the last rites. The subsequent deaths in an isolated Carpathian village were blamed initially on the plague, but when the villagers discovered that the actual cause was a vampire, they laid him to rest by hammering a stake through his heart. To his incredulous audience, the peasant insisted, 'it's here, where we're at in the Balkans, that one finds the cradle of those vampires'.[53] This anecdote appeared in a 1921 article on vampires written by Grau for the magazine *Bühne und Film* (German for *Stage and Film*) and may have been invented to publicise the film. Genuine or not, the tale and its setting create an intriguing link with vampirism and the catalyst for the First World War, since both center on the Balkans, where Arch Duke Franz Ferdinand was assassinated by the Serbian nationalist. When the film's protagonist, Hutter, is about to go to the land of the nosferatu, he traces his finger across a map 'until it comes to rest on the Balkans'.[54] From that starting point, war fanned out to engulf most of Europe, leaving its deepest imprint in Flanders. *Oorlog*, the Dutch word for war, has some similarity with the name of the vampire protagonist, Count Orlok, a progenitor for a blood-sucking form of warfare on mankind.[55] As Kaes notes, the naive Hutter, in being dispatched to a foreign country to confront a vampire by an unscrupulous elder, Knock, is not unlike those young men posted abroad by their cynical superiors to fight the enemy. Just before the estate agent Knock steers him towards the map of Europe and eventually to the bloodthirsty Count Orlok, he remarks: 'And, young as you are, what matter if it costs you some pain – or even a little blood?'[56]

'Blood-Lust' (1926) is the title of Dion Fortune's short story about a First World War veteran, Captain Donald Craigie, who has been possessed by the spirit of a vampire from Eastern Europe. His case is investigated by psychic investigator Dr Taverner, who runs a nursing home for treating unorthodox mental disturbances. The 'spirit parasite', manifesting as a soldier wearing the flat cap and field-grey uniform of the German army, has attached itself to 'a corpse who was insufficiently dead'.[57] Similarly, *Nosferatu* encapsulates the spirit of a war not 'sufficiently dead' and, according to Kaes, provides a prime example of shell shock cinema. It is precisely because he is suffering from shell shock that Captain Craigie is susceptible to psychic possession. The narrator, who joins Dr Taverner as a medical superintendant, explains how his own nerves were shattered while serving as a medic in the army. The cinema screen provided film-makers Grau and Murnau, who had both seen active service, with a medium for exorcising the trauma of combat for themselves and others. Murnau had fought on the Eastern and Western fronts and survived the Battle of Verdun, which had resulted in over 700,000 casualties. As Grau observed: 'One no longer reads the terror of war in the eyes of men; but something of it has remained. Suffering and grief have weakened the heart of man and have bit by bit stirred up the desire to understand what is behind this monstrous event that is unleashed across the earth like a cosmic vampire to drink the blood of millions and millions of men.'[58] Vampire-like, the First World War drank the blood of soldiers, sacrificed to heal 'the vast wound of the world'.[59] As a landscape of Gothic horror, the Western Front formed a vast open grave 'seeded with millions of dead' and scarred by 'disembodied limbs, tattered scraps of uniform, [and] exposed bones'.[60] Exploding soil could bury soldiers alive. The sight of a combatant crawling out from beneath disturbed ground does more than resemble the undead climbing out of a grave as it can also represent the eternal soldier, who literally soldiers on in every nation and in every war.

It is not only war but also peace that can suck dry the lifeblood of a nation. To put it another way, Foucault writes about the importance of having to 'interpret the war that is going on beneath peace' since 'peace itself is a coded war'.[61] He sees the peace brought about by the power and force of politics and inscribed upon institutions, the economy and even the bodies of individuals as the continuation of a silent secret war. An illustration of this can be seen in the *Schandfrieden* (shameful peace), when a defeated Germany was drained by the Treaty of Versailles, which demanded the annexation of German territory and heavy cost of reparation. There is the popular perception that these harsh measures led to the onset of the Second World War.[62] *Nosferatu* was produced in the shadow left behind by the Great War and the post-war influenza pandemic, which took the lives of 400,000 German civilians. The camera shot of coffins containing plague victims being carried through the stricken town of Wisborg must have been a poignant reminder of the incalculable losses brought about by war and disease. When Orlok arrives with his 'coffin' under his arm, he becomes literally a carrier of death. Kaes views *Nosferatu* as a film about mass death and commemoration. As he points out, tens of thousands of the war dead were never properly buried or mourned. Through the ghostly effects of cinema, *Nosferatu* served as a form of bereavement. Cinematic techniques, such as the dissolve, double exposure and filming in negative for the 'land of the phantoms', convey a sense of the ghostly, pertinent to the war dead, while an interest in spirit photography was revived after the Great War.[63] The blood-sucker and the ghostly were brought together for Grau, during his wartime experience, when he was shown an official document referring to the blood-sucking dead as vampire phantoms.[64] Powerful images of soldiers returning from the dead appear in the French silent movie, *J'accuse* (1919), directed by Abel Gance as a protest against the war. Jay Winter describes Gance's spectral soldiers as 'ghost-like' and 'wrapped in tattered bandages, some limping, some blind walking with upraised arms, some stumbling like Frankenstein's monster'.[65] Two thousand of the extras filmed in 1918 were soldiers on leave from the fighting at the Battle of Verdun. Some 80 per cent were killed when they returned to the front a few weeks later. It is ironic that the film, in setting out to remember the dead, became a memorial for the actors, who died shortly after playing the part of the living dead.

Another version of the revenant is the wounded veteran soldier, who had been permanently maimed or disfigured by the war. Orlok can be seen as a returning soldier, ostracised by his hideous appearance. Here the monstrous body becomes the war-damaged body. Even though the mutilated bodies of former combatants were not hidden from view in Britain, they were not explored as a crucial site of revulsion and shame through art, as they were in Weimar Germany.[66] For the horrified onlooker, serious facial wounds could compromise human identity. According to the surgeon Harold Gillies, the sight of horrific injuries following the Battle of the Somme resulted in men being 'burned and maimed to the condition of animals'.[67] Orlok's monstrosity, especially his rat-like features, dehumanises him. As the film progresses and he appears less and less human, his visage becomes increasingly mask-like, thus evoking the prosthetic masks used to provide facially disfigured veterans with only the barest semblance of humanity. In his fantastical recreation of the First World War, Kim Newman recollects 'the old days, when *nosferatu* were hunted like plague rats'.[68] The sight of the rattish Orlok and his accompanying rodents on film must have provoked eerie memories of scampering trench rats for those ex-servicemen who feared them more than the enemy. Soldiers shared their living space with millions of these unwelcome guests. Erich Maria Remarque, in *All Quiet on the Western Front* (1929), refers to the large 'corpse-rats' with their 'horrible, evil-looking, naked faces and the sight of their long, bare tails [that] can make you feel sick'.[69] Not only were these vermin carriers of disease but they were also creatures of horror feeding on the dead, often starting with the eyes.

As the rats, fleas, enemy attacks, trench diseases, body parts, mud, filth, dead horses and interminable noise indicated, there was little that was great about the Great War, apart from the catastrophic numbers of dead, wounded and missing. Yet a battle-weary French infantry soldier, towards the end of Henri Barbusse's novel, *Under Fire* (1916), still managed to wonder: 'After all, what is it that makes the greatness and horror of war?'[70] The reply given him by a compatriot is that the greatness lies in the people. The greatness of war may also be found in the aesthetics of warfare, which for the Greek soldier Stratis Myrivilis was a kind of battlefield sublime. He described a bombardment as 'divinely majestic', and referred to the terrible beauty of the batteries seeking 'mutual annihilation'.[71] This connects to the Gothic through Edmund Burke's analysis of the awe arising from horror and terror and its connections to the sublime. Characterised by greatness, vastness, power and obscurity, as in darkness or the unknown, the Burkean sublime, like the Gothic, is a vehicle of excess, provoking 'delightful horror, a sort of tranquillity tinged with terror; which as it belongs to self-preservation is one of the strongest of all the passions'.[72] For the soldier pinned down in a trench during a bombardment, witnessing seismic regurgitations of earth and gazing into the bowels of hell, this was an opportunity for witnessing, at a relatively safe distance, the perils of annihilation as an instigator of sublimity. Burke's distinction between the beautiful and the sublime is informed by eighteenth-century gender stereotypes. These equate to the beautiful being gendered as female and the sublime as male. Yet for Myrivilis, and soldiers like him, the experience of being overwhelmed by the sublime, as a greater power, must have brought about a feeling of powerlessness more akin to a state of femininity.

Warfare is traditionally regarded as a masculine pursuit, yet war itself has been allegorised as a vampiric woman. In his novel, *L'Inconnu sur les villes: Roman des foules modernes* (1921) (French for *The Stranger in the Towns*), which was published in Paris, Marcello Fabri eroticises the Great War as a seductive female vampire, draining virility from the bodies of men.[73] This imagery was doubtless inspired by the military brothels provided by the French authorities that were implicated in the spread of sexually transmitted diseases. A meeting of the Imperial War Conference in 1917 concluded that venereal disease was seriously impeding the fighting ability of the Allied forces. The French government calculated that there had been over a million cases of syphilis and gonorrhoea from the start of the war to 1917, when 23,000 British military men were admitted to hospitals for treatment.[74]

In his war novel, *Goodbye to All That* (1929), Robert Graves describes a queue of 150 men waiting outside a licensed brothel in France, for the services of just three women. Each woman had a weekly allocation of nearly a battalion of men, 'for as long as she lasted'.[75] Brothels with a blue lamp outside were designated for the use of officers, while red ones were for troops. Graves mused on how this demarcation corresponded to the type of woman employed. Prostitution was the main route of transmission for venereal diseases, as revealed by French military surgeon Dr Georges Thibierge in *Syphilis and the Army* (1918). Syphilis was rife in military zones. To combat its corrosive effects, war was also being waged on a moral front. The prostitute, rather than the soldier, was perceived to be the primary source of danger. The American General John J. Pershing vigorously campaigned to keep his soldiers away from brothels in order to reduce the spread of the disease. To this end, the artist H. Dewitt Welsh created a politically inspired poster produced by a New York company with the message: 'We've fought in the open – bubonic plague, yellow fever, tuberculosis now venereal diseases' (Figure 15).[76] Three macabre figures standing in a trench embody the first three diseases. Towering above them is the triumphant figure of a bare-breasted woman representing venereal disease. She is pouring blood from a wine glass, the colour of which matches her hair, while scarlet robes billow behind her, like great

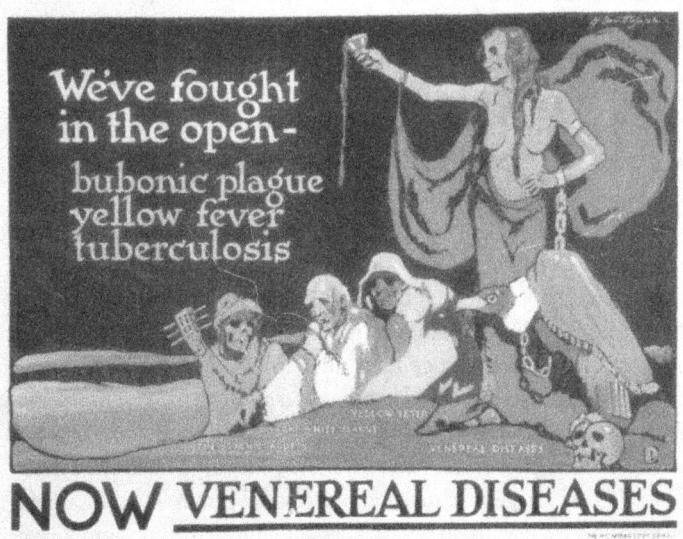

Figure 15 'We've fought in the open bubonic plague, yellow fever, tuberculosis now venereal diseases' by H. Dewitt Welsh (*c*.1918). Here venereal disease is depicted as a female vampire, who is represented as another enemy during the First World War.

wings. Her predatory nature is signified by the vulture perched on a skull and chained to her arm. As a personification of sex and death, the femme fatale literally spills the lifeblood of her military clients. The image was a declaration of war on the female prostitute by identifying her with the blood-drinking vampire as a carrier of death and disease. A French poster of 1916 sent out a similar message, warning soldiers that 'a sickness as dangerous as the war awaits you … It carries its victims to decay and death, without honor, without happiness'.[77] Yet the safety of soldiers could not be assured if they were on guard merely against a prostitute or any other femme fatale. As Thibierge pointed out, there was 'a danger to soldiers in women who are apparently most innocent, and the importance of this cannot be exaggerated'.[78] So, even the most unlikely woman was potentially a source of infection for unsuspecting officers and men. Some military surgeons were of the opinion that 'every woman in the war zone ought to be watched, and that no social position should prevent the suspicion of syphilis from being traced to its lair'.[79]

The use of the word 'lair' is suggestive of an association between women and animals. It appears in the title of Bram Stoker's novel, *The Lair of the White Worm* (1911), which alludes to the snake-like woman, Lady Arabella March. Stoker makes a number of allusions to the vampire's lair in *Dracula*. Here his use of vampirism has been interpreted as a thinly disguised metaphor for syphilis, a disease widely feared by the Victorians.[80] The Contagious Diseases Acts of the 1860s had been instigated by an enquiry into venereal disease in the armed services. As Josephine Butler and her fellow campaigners complained, it was only women and not their clients who were subjected to enforced medical inspections. Similarly, in France during the First World War, regular examinations were carried out on prostitutes rather than on their military clientele. Yet these measures proved inadequate in stemming the disease, described by Thibierge in militaristic terms as having made an 'incessant advance' and in whose vanguard were the prostitutes 'who swarm in the large towns in search of soldiers'.[81] This imagery, associated more with vermin invading urban spaces for food than with street walkers soliciting custom, points to a double irony. The first is that such women, through the infection they transmitted, saved the lives of countless numbers of soldiers by rescuing them from the trenches. Secondly, while soldiers were fighting for their womenfolk, now it was women themselves who were being targeted as an enemy, and even those left at home presented another kind of threat.

When the men went off to war, women filled many of the vacancies that were left in the workplaces of Britain, Austria, Russia and France.[82] Some people regarded this as bringing about a vampiric emasculation of men. As Charles-Noël Renard insisted, the war had empowered women, who, he believed, were on course to destroy civilisation. In the introduction to his fantastical novel, *Les Androphobes* (1930) (French for *The Manhaters*), Renard proclaimed that a saviour was needed to 'destroy the work of women' and that preparations should be made for 'the biggest war that ever drenched the Earth in blood'.[83] He described the First World War as a pack of vampire lesbians whom soldiers found alluring. Indeed many women had started lesbian relationships in response to the shortage of men consumed by the war. In the early 1920s, there were calculated to be around two million single women in Britain, dubbed 'surplus women'. War had robbed many of marriage, children and sexual fulfilment. In the satiric introduction to his war novel, *Death of a Hero* (1929), Richard Aldington suggested that for women, war had become a form of sexual sublimation with vampiric undertones: 'The war did

that to lots of women. All the dying and wounds and mud and bloodiness – at a safe distance – gave them a great kick, and excited them to an
almost unbearable pitch of amorousness. Of course, in that eternity of
1914–18 they must have come to feel that men alone were mortal, and
they immortals.'[84]

In Sarah Smith's short story, 'When the Red Storm Comes' (1993),
an Austro-Hungarian officer identifies himself as a vampire to the heroine, whom he accuses of being fascinated by blood 'more than a woman
should be', telling her:

> You like the uniforms, the danger, the soldiers, but what you truly like, Miss
> Wentworth, is red. When you read about this war in the newspapers, will you
> pretend you are shocked and say *Oh, how dreadful*, while you look twice and
> then again at the pictures of blood, and hope you do not know why your heart
> beats so strong?[85]

The war in question had preceded the First World War. This was the
Russo-Japanese War (1904–5), which was the first major war of the
twentieth century. Smith's story is set in Portsmouth, New Hampshire,
in August 1905, when the plenipotentiaries were negotiating the peace
settlement which, at one point, was in danger of collapse. Here Miss
Wentworth, who is named after the actual hotel where the negotiators
were staying, has been reading Stoker's *Dracula*. After allowing the officer she encountered to drink her blood, she has a vision of the future as
a great red storm of slaughter, which can be seen to portend the First
World War. On losing her virginity to the soldier, she regards herself as
no longer 'respectable' and exults in becoming a vampire.

In 1915, the sexualised word 'vamp' gained wide currency after being
used in the silent movie, *A Fool There Was* (1914), starring Theda Bara,
about a femme fatale who destroys a man and his family.[86] Based on a
Broadway play of 1909, the title was taken from Rudyard Kipling's poem,
'The Vampire' (1897), published in the same year as *Dracula*:[87]

> A fool there was and he made his prayer
> (Even as you or I!)
> To a rag and a bone and a hank of hair
> (We called her the woman who did not care)
> But the fool he called her his lady fair –
> (Even as you and I!).

The playwright was the American writer Porter Emerson Browne, who
supported America's intervention in the First World War and advocated

an anti-pacifist stance through his fiction. In 1916, a year before America entered the war, he published the short story, 'Mary and Marie', about two women with similar names living parallel lives; the first in an affluent American home and the latter as a poor peasant in Belgium. While Marie and her family suffer rape and death at the hands of German soldiers, Mary and her father profit from the war in Europe through the munitions industry. Mary's father makes a 'killing' on the stock market with the manufacture of military cartridges and refers to his booty as 'a war bride'.[88] As Celia Malone Kingsbury expresses it, Mary and her father were 'feeding off the blood of a devastated Europe'.[89]

Marcello Fabri extends the metaphor to those at home who, in urging men to enlist, were 'no longer content to suck at wounds, like a vampire' but demanded 'more victims to pollute'.[90] D. H. Lawrence angrily points the finger at the enemy on the home front in his semi-autobiographical novel, *Kangaroo* (1923):

> We hear so much of the bravery and horrors at the front ... It was at home the world was lost ... At home stayed all the jackals, middle-aged, male and female jackals. And they bit us all. And blood-poisoning and mortification set in.
>
> We should never have let the jackals loose, and patted them on the head. They were feeding on our death all the while.[91]

In her 'War-fairy-tale', *Ashe of Rings* (1926), Mary Butts writes about a khaki-fevered female vampire, who personifies the carnage of the First World War.[92] This is sexual predator Judy Marston, who has a Russian lover, the exiled artist Serge Fyodorovitch. At the same time, she is having a relationship with Peter Amburton, discharged from the army due to war trauma. When she threatens to tell Peter about the affair, Serge warns that she will lose her soul. She responds with a 'vile laugh. Squeezed scarlet gums. Blood down the teeth. Red teeth. Red breath' (p. 79). Judy has a mercenary attitude towards marriage and is dismissive of Peter, the man she intends to marry, describing him as 'a shell-shocked lump of carrion' (p. 116). Terry Phillips notes: 'The term "carrion" strongly suggests the act of feeding; manifesting the disregard for male war victims which commentators like Aldington felt they saw in women of their time'.[93] Even though Serge refuses to fight, he cannot escape the war since it is being replayed through Judy: 'You came with the war – you are inside me, playing its infernal tunes. You are the war's smallest doll. You are the war' (p. 81). This identification is reinforced by the derivation of Judy's surname, Marston, from Mars, the name of the Roman god of war. The milder Vanna Ashe marvels at how Judy manages to embody an erotic and vampiric thirst for war, saying:

> Consider the war. Have you known anyone who loves the war as Judy loves it? *Stoop then and wash.* She dips her tall, white body in the blood and rolls it in her mouth, and squeezes it out of her hair. She is a delicate woman of good family; I know nothing in her history to account for it. Am I clear? There is the war. There is Judy and her kind. The individual state bred the general state, that bred the catastrophe. Oh, I know tribal instincts and heroism, and love of a row, and coal and duty and obedience and too many people made the war; but this is different. Other people conduct a war, and suffer in it; get a man's job out of it or physical death. People like Judy live on the fact of it, and get spirit-nourishing food out of the ruin of so much life. There are no checks on such people now. (p. 149)

Judy thrives on the war in a way not directly exploitative like Browne's Mary and her father, but, as Vanna points out, 'when you touch the property sense in Judy, you touch something as large as the world and as bad as the war' (p. 102). She is a manifestation of 'extreme anti-life' (p. 150), instinctively joining forces with the vampiric impulses of excess, so characteristic of war.

On the home front, women handing out white feathers to men refusing to sign up have been identified as another type of female vampire feeding off the glory of war. According to Chris Baldick, the representation of women as 'fickle and bloodthirsty vampires' appears in masculine war writing, a notable example of which is Siegfried Sassoon's ironically entitled poem of 1917, 'The Glory of Women'.[94] The polarisation of women into vampires or saintly martyrs in literary representations of women and war is a reworking of the binary opposition of Madonna and whore. The ideal woman sacrificed herself for the war effort, often as a nurse or in a munitions factory. Women to emulate would have included Browne's Marie, who heroically risked death warning others of the enemy, or Ellen in Murnau's *Nosferatu*, prepared to sacrifice her life to rid the community of an invading force. The reactionary German philosopher and Jew, Otto Weininger, argued in his controversial and misogynistic *Sex and Character* (1903) that the crisis of masculinity arising from the increasingly feminised world of modernity could only be surmounted by the self-sacrifice of women. His teachings, which aligned women with Negroes and Jews, were taken up, not surprisingly, by the Nazis. After asserting that woman has no soul, Weininger went on to ask, 'Is she, then, still a human being?'[95] It is a question more commonly asked of the female vampire.

KIM NEWMAN, *THE BLOODY RED BARON*

A fictional world in which male and female vampires co-exist with humans is central to Kim Newman's alternative history of the First World War. This is *The Bloody Red Baron* (1995), which focuses on the career of the legendary Manfred Albrecht Freiherr von Richthofen, known as the Red Baron, who was Germany's greatest fighter pilot. His career ended when he was fatally shot down near the Somme River on the Western Front in France on 21 April 1918. This novel is the second volume of a trilogy that serves as a sequel to Stoker's *Dracula*.[96] The point of departure stems from Van Helsing's failure to kill Count Dracula and therefore curtail his plans to invade Britain.

Newman uses vampire metaphors to convey the vampiric nature of war and imperialism. In his creation of a parallel world, vampirism has spread to the crowned heads of Europe, who share a common ancestry in Vlad Tepes through the Dracula bloodline. Arch Duke Franz Ferdinand, nephew of the King and Emperor Franz Joseph, is '*nosferatu*, a provocation' and member of the 'bloodsucking Habsburgs', who will be assassinated by a silver bullet piercing his 'vampire heart' (p. 18). In 1918, another ruling vampire family, the Romanovs, would be destroyed by a stake hammered through the heart and beheaded with the swipe of a sickle. Kaiser Wilhelm II uses the archduke's assassination as an opportunity 'to redraw the map of Europe' (p. 19). After being turned into the undead by Dracula, 'Germany', he declares, 'must turn vampire, and find its place in the moonlight' (p. 16). The kaiser has passed the running of the war to Graf von Dracula, who has been appointed chancellor and commander-in-chief of the armies of the Fatherland in 1914. Vampires found on the side of the Allies include Winston Churchill, whose tipple is a tell-tale cocktail of alcohol and blood.

For his novel, Newman vampirises not only history but also literature and film. By raiding Gothic novels and German Expressionist cinema, he creates a network of intertextuality. In turn, this feeds on itself as a knowingly self-referential genre, navigating a path between parody and pastiche. Newman's intertextual proliferations are counter-fictions self-consciously located alongside established literary texts. Part One, entitled 'All Quiet on the Western Front', is a nod towards Remarque's anti-war novel. Part Two, 'No Man's Land', alludes to John Toland's novel of 1918, which engages rather appropriately with the mysterious death of the Red Baron. The next section, 'Memoirs of a Fox-hunting Man', borrows its title from Sassoon's war novel of 1928. The final part, 'Journey's End', is named after R. C. Sherriff's 1928 play about life in a British officer's dugout at Saint-Quentin, Aisne. Newman draws on Weimar film for some of his characters and conscripts Count Orlok from *Nosferatu*, Dr Caligari from *The Cabinet of Dr. Caligari* (1920), the mad scientist figure Rotwang from Fritz Lang's *Metropolis* (1927) and Dr Mabuse, who appears in the films and novels of Norbert Jacques. Characters based on historical figures associated with horror film include Murnau, the director of *Nosferatu*, and the actor Bela Lugosi, who is referred to obliquely as 'A Hungarian actor. A matineé idol from Lugos' (p. 341). Most well-known for playing the role of Dracula, he turns out to be one of Graf von Dracula's many doubles in a veritable 'plague of *doppelgängers*' (p. 333). In real life, Lugosi also played the vampire Armand Tesla in a film made during the Second World War called *The Return of the Vampire* (1943), which will be discussed later. In *The Bloody Red Baron*, the same Dr Tesla used to be chief of Dracula's secret police. Literary vampires purloined from classical Gothic texts include Lord Ruthven from John Polidori's *The Vampyre*; General Karnstein, whose name is taken from Sheridan Le Fanu's *Carmilla* (1872); Mina Harker and a bride of Dracula from Stoker's *Dracula*; and Dr Moreau from H. G. Wells' *The Island of Doctor Moreau*. Newman also turns Gothic writers into characters, who include Edgar [Allan] Poe; the novelist and journalist Sydney Horler, described as 'a tub-thumper for the *Mail*' (p. 53), whose novel *The Vampire* (1935) is commented upon below; and Hanns Heinz Ewers, the author of *Vampire*.

Ewers is portrayed as a cynic, a characterisation that is likely to have met with his approval for, as he wrote in an early diary: 'How happy it makes me when I can make people believe I'm cold and cruel and cynical, I always think: that suits me! But it's all just a pitiful lie.'[97] Certainly his character in the novel fails to impress Poe, to whom he confides: 'We are truly doubles, mirror images, *doppelgängers*' (p. 38). Here Ewers is referring to the screenplay he wrote for the Expressionist film, *The Student of Prague*, about a student who makes a Faustian pact with a sorcerer and whose reflection, which steps out of the mirror, goes on to commit crimes. Ewers links this to 'William Wilson' (1839), a short story by Poe, who accuses him of plagiarism. This is the tale of a man who, on seeing the blood-stained reflection of himself in a looking glass, realises that he has murdered his own double. The banter on doubles is indicative of why Poe has been summoned to a meeting in Prague, which is rather apt in view of his film title. Here he meets Dr Mabuse, the Director of the Intelligence and Press Department of the Imperial German Air Service, who invites him to be the ghostwriter for the Red Baron's memoirs. He is to be given editorial help from Ewers, who, in real life, had written an essay on Poe, published in 1906. A description of Ewers standing in the shadows is a fitting metaphor, not only for this secretive role but also for his career in Expressionist film, as a language of shadow and light. The book, entitled *Der rote Kampfflieger* (German for *Red Battle Flyer*), is named after the baron's signature red aircraft and corresponds to the autobiography of that name produced by the historical Richthofen in 1917.[98]

The death-defying Red Baron, who racked up a record number of kills and whose survival in the air was nothing short of miraculous, is turned into a deadly flying vampire in Newman's novel. According to Slavoj Žižek, the vampire occupies the place of the thing that cannot be represented and while looking like us still remains 'not one of us'.[99] Consequently, a member of the undead 'retains all the predicates of a living being without being one', unlike a dead person 'who loses the predicates of a living being, yet they remain the same person'.[100] Even though their vampirism armed with technology makes them far more deadly than humans, Newman's flyers are not impervious to death. The baron regards himself and his squadron as men inhabiting the bodies of corpses, who are already dead in the sense of being very unlikely to survive the war. In fact, actual fighter pilots on both sides were expected to last only a few weeks before being shot down. Yet the historical Richthofen and his squadron managed to prolong the duration and number of their aerial attacks against tremendous odds. Newman's description of their vampire equivalents is close to how the actual German pilots were perceived by admiring friends and foes, 'these fliers, were gods and demons and angels' (p. 181). His version of the Red Baron sprouts great leathery bat wings to transform himself into a human triplane fully equipped with guns. Richthofen is now his own weapon, part man, machine and vampire. He is the arrowhead for the mass of giant bats flying in formation. Along with his shape-shifting flying circus squadron, the Bloody Red Baron has been genetically modified 'to literally suck the Allied forces out of the sky!'[101] German scientists have done experiments on Richthofen and his flyers in a cross-breeding programme fertilised by Dracula's blood for the purpose of creating a new breed of

Figure 16 L. J. Jordaan, *De Vampyr* (1940). The vampiric effect of war is depicted by a German soldier draining the blood of a Dutch national.

Note: L. J. Jordaan's cartoon was produced in response to the German invasion of Holland in the Battle of the Netherlands in May 1940. It appeared in an underground edition of the Dutch magazine, *De Groene Amsterdammer* [*The Green Amsterdammer*], which officially ceased publication in 1940 until 1945.

soldier. This is a literalisation of how the enemy is projected as a monster in the Gothicisation of war. L. J. Jordaan's war cartoon, 'De Vampyr' (1945) depicts a hideously clawed and spiky-winged creature wearing a German helmet and squatting over the semi-naked body of a man lying with his arms spread out in a crucifixion position (Figure 16). Under the light of the moon, blood from the heart of the victim is being sucked up by the vampire through the rubber hose of a gas mask. Its huge goggles, emitting a glowing stare, are integral to his face, so that he, like the Bloody Red Baron, resembles part soldier and part blood-drinking vampire.

In the First World War, the enemy was demonised by military propagandists, jingoists, war hawks and instructors for training troops. In what sounds like a drill for an attacking vampire, Robert Graves recalls how one of his trainers, full of 'bullet-and-bayonet enthusiasm', urged soldiers to aim their bayonets at a German's privates with the capitalised injunction: 'BITE HIM, I SAY! STICK YOUR TEETH IN HIM AND WORRY HIM! EAT HIS HEART OUT!'[102] But in spite of the best efforts of the military to represent the enemy as monstrous Other, as Derrida points out in *The Gift of Death* (1995), soldiers on the front line during the First World War were still able 'to identify the enemy and even and especially to *identify with* the enemy'.[103] As Newman's Red Baron wryly reflects: 'The tragedy of war is the pitting of like against like. We fliers have more in common with those we fight than with those for whom we fight [...]. We fall from the sky in flames. Only the plodding dogs will survive' (p. 256). For the flyer, the war is an elemental force: 'Up there, in the night sky, is war. Eternal war. Not only with the British and French, but with the air. The sky does not wish us in it. Us, the presumptuous ones, it kills [...]. We shall never be its creatures' (p. 256). Dracula fails to appreciate the heroism and brilliance of the Red Baron, that 'knight of futurity', because he was more at ease 'with Görings about him, fathead bureaucrats of death' (p. 342).

In *The Bloody Red Baron*, a prediction that Dracula will 'make of this century a killing ground' (p. 46) is an augury of the colossal death toll from both world wars. Poe looks into the future when peering through a crack in a door of a building in a Prague ghetto, 'infested with chattering, chanting Hebrews' (p. 33), and sees a swarm of rats and Semitic children. He ruminates disdainfully that 'degenerate races bred without restraint' and concurs with Dracula's decision to prevent them from turning vampire (p. 35). This is the equivalent of how the Nazis sought to disempower Jews and other sections of the population through their repressive ideology of blood and race. According to Newman's military surgeon Dr Moreau, who works on the side of the Allies: 'Blood, blood, blood. To the Germans, it's all in the blood. It's as if the *corpus* was constituted of nothing but blood' (p. 118). Moreau believes that the German mind has been perverted by the Gothic imagination. In view of his origins in H. G. Wells' novel as a mad scientist, it should come as no great surprise to discover that the illicit experiments which he is carrying out on his patients involve the vivisection of vampires. These anticipate the inhuman medical experiments conducted by Dr Josef Mengele at Auschwitz.

Moreau works for a front-line subterranean hospital in a dugout at the end of a long tunnel with an opening like a mine shaft. Due to the static nature of the First World War, extensive military mining had taken place beneath enemy fortifications in order to break into their lines or plant explosives. Three thousand miles of tunnels were burrowed and the soldiers, who lived and worked underground, led a troglodyte twilight existence, sharing with the dead a habitat below the ground. Dugouts (one of which on the British side in Belgium was known as 'The Vampire Dugout') could be around thirty feet deep and were usually where officers lived. Interiors could be furnished so as to uncannily resemble home. Battlefield underworlds were also accorded a mythic dimension by soldiers believing that they housed a battalion of deserters from all the armies, who had taken refuge underground or in abandoned trenches, grottoes or caves. Allegedly, these fabled renegades emerged at night to pillage corpses and collect food supplies. In his memoir, *The Squadroon* (1920), Ardern Beaman describes how on that 'horrid desolation' of the battlefields of the Somme, in which 'a warren of trenches and dugouts extended for untold miles', they met a salvage company at work: 'They warned us, if we insisted on going further in, not to let any man go singly, but only in strong parties, as the Golgotha was peopled with wild men, British, French, Australian, German deserters, who lived there underground, like ghouls among the mouldering dead, and who came out at nights to plunder and kill.'[104] The legend served as a projection for the guilt of those forced to abandon the wounded in no-man's-land. Wearing unkempt beards and tattered uniforms, these deserters were anathema to military discipline and personifications of anarchy. The idea of an imagined fraternity, illicitly recruited from the warring forces of both sides, provided a far-fetched explanation for the mysterious nightly sounds emanating from the ghastly and ghostly wastes of No Man's Land.

While attempting to traverse this particular zone, Newman's British intelligence agent, Edwin Winthrop, a living warm-blood, is accompanied by the wounded vampire pilot, Albert Ball. They suddenly find themselves 'surrounded by a forest of living scarecrows' when 'darkness swarmed up around them' (p. 184). Unlike many of the war dead assigned to mass graves, these troglodyte deserters sleep underground in coffins. As such, they represent the undead nature of trench warfare and, like infantry troops, are suspended between life and death. In First World War memoirs, it is not uncommon to come across imagery relating to the resurrection from the dead once a bombardment ceased or a soldier could emerge safely from a trench. Stratis Myrivilis entitles his memoir about trench warfare on the Macedonian front between 1917 and 1918 as *Life in the Tomb* (1923–4). The dying trapped between the front lines parallel the in-between state of the living corpse. Not only is No Man's Land a place of interstitiality and abjection, but so too is the wound. The wounded body, which in Newman's novel has either human warmth or vampire coldness, is a microcosm of the battlefield as 'an empire of injury' mapping out 'seas of pale skin, continents of blue-black bruise, islands of red weal, archipelagoes [*sic*] of stitching, national boundaries of scar' (p. 236). The vampire is created through the wound, as is war. When countries are broken open and drained of their populations, blood and capital, they recirculate in the host economy of a foreign body politic. As Kate Reed, a character excised from Stoker's *Dracula* and revamped as Newman's radical vampire journalist, observes: 'All Europe is stark mad with red thirst' (p. 355).[105] Through her reporting, she wants to tell the true story of war and for her voice to drown out 'the drumbeat of jingo and the blather of politicians. She could not be the last priestess of the truth. People would listen. Things would change' (p. 356).

But the 'War to end all Wars' spawned a 'Peace to end Peace'.[106] The various treaties signed between 1919 and 1921 resulted in a series of shaky European national settlements. Shock waves from the Bolshevik Revolution in Russia, starting in 1917, reverberated as far as America, stoking fears of communist take-overs. The League of Nations, founded in 1920, worked towards peace and universal disarmament. But it was not enough to deter the spectre of the warring vampire from stalking the No Man's Land of 1918 to 1939, the troubled interval between world wars.

WAR VAMPIRE, 'THE HORROR UNDYING' AND RETURN OF THE SOLDIER

The American clergyman William Montgomery Brown, known as 'Bad Bishop Brown', was a pacifist and communist who employed the figure of the vampire in his anti-war pamphlet of 1931, 'The War-Vampire and the Churches'.[107] Here he warned of two real vampires far worse than the mythical ones, since they do not confine themselves to attacking individuals in a village, but instead infect and infest entire nations. The first of these is capitalism, which sucks the blood of the workers, for as Karl Marx famously said: 'Capital is dead labor, that vampire-like, only lives by sucking living labor, and lives the more, the more labor it sucks.'[108] The second is war, for bringing about the ruination of numerous civilisations. For Brown, the primer for war was economic competition amongst capitalist countries. In his lecture, 'Why I am a Communist' (October 1932), he explains that the catalyst for his conversion was the outbreak of the Great War, which caused blood to flow across the map of Europe. Brown made history by becoming the first Anglican Bishop since the

Reformation to be tried for heresy (1924–5), resulting in his dismissal by the American House of Bishops.

The equation of war with vampirism may be found in another text from the 1930s. This is Manly Wade Wellman's short story set in the Old West. 'The Horror Undying' (1936) is about Sergeant Stanlas, a vampire and cannibal, who fights on the side of the Americans. The narrator discovers a sheaf of papers hidden under the floorboards of a lonely deserted cabin, which contains a very old booklet entitled, *A True Story of the Revolting and Bloody Crimes of Sergeant Stanlas, U.S.A. Together With His Court-Martial and Execution*. It tells of how Ivan Stanlas, an Eastern European, brought vampirism and lycanthropy from the Old World to the New World. This monster, who feasts on flesh and blood, is symbolic of how an invasionary force saps the resources of an occupied country, draining its defenders. The vampiric connotations of the title, 'The Horror Undying', apply equally well to the perennial horrors of imperial aggression. Ivan's unnaturally extended lifespan as a soldier is indicative of the continuity of war, waged in different countries and on different continents. Born in 1810 during the Napoleonic Wars, near the Polish border of Prussia, with its traditions of militarism, Ivan immigrated to the United States at the age of twelve and in 1827 joined a dragoon regiment. The narrator comes across a woodcut of him in the uniform of a cavalryman dated 1848, which marked the end of the Mexican–American War (1846–8) in which he fought. The ideological driver for this war was the expansionist principle of American imperialism known as Manifest Destiny, which the Democrats were the first to exploit when they tried justifying the annexation by the United States of territory claimed to be Mexican. Sergeant Stanlas was given a citation for bravery at the Battle of Monterey in California, which had taken place in 1846. As a foreigner, he found himself unable to secure an officer's commission, despite the brilliance of his military career. His status as outsider is reinforced by his hidden vampire self, which knows no allegiance. When hunting for prey, like death itself, Ivan makes no distinction between his own side and that of the enemy. At his garrison, sentries die in mysterious circumstances, their bodies mangled and mutilated with the fleshiest parts excised. The blame falls on the Comanche Indians, who have been carrying out raids. But they too fall victim to this supernatural creature, who they refer to as the devil at the fort. On seeing Ivan, they identify him as the perpetrator. Evidence for the murders surfaces literally when the skeletons of two Indians are discovered beneath the floorboards of his quarters. Ivan confesses to these killings, along with 'more than fifty, perhaps a hundred' others.[109] At his court-martial, he pleads for his body to be burnt to ashes so that his soul can be redeemed. As the narrator later discovers: 'A werewolf, if killed and left unburnt, would rise from death, and rise to be a blood-drinking vampire' (p. 143). But since Ivan's remains are not destroyed by fire, he rises from the dead to resume his military career in yet another war. In 1879, under the name of Sergeant Wilfred Maxim, he again faces a court-martial, this time for killing a civilian labourer and drinking his blood. By now, the narrator has reached the conclusion that Ivan and Wilfred are one and the same: 'Ivan Stanlas, shot almost to pieces, could not have rested in his disgraced, unmarked grave. He had struggled up from under that burden of earth, had walked again. He had joined the army under a new name' (p. 142). Terrified, the narrator destroys the booklet just as the vampire soldier enters the cabin, baring 'two pointed teeth' from 'a loose, lipless mouth' (p. 143).

The title, 'The Horror Undying', referring to its vampire protagonist, is redolent not just of the undead nature of warfare but also of how wars feed off each other, often over the vampirisation of territory. This process is illustrated in Wellman's later story, 'The Devil Is Not Mocked' (1943), concerning an encounter taking place near Bistritz in Transylvania, during the Second World War, between German soldiers and Count Dracula.[110] General von Grunn arrives at Dracula's castle, which he intends to commandeer for his headquarters. The locals call it 'Devil's Castle', which is renamed by Grunn with the German equivalent, 'Teufelstoss'.[111] This act of requisition and renaming is typical of the military annexations that have blighted Transylvania's history. As Grunn reflects: 'This country had been Romanian not so long ago. Now it was Hungarian, which meant that it was German.'[112] The Nazi invasion of Hungary took place the year after Wellman's story appeared. The significance of the title, 'The Devil Is Not Mocked', becomes apparent when the Germans are destroyed by wolves, protecting their master against an invading force. By contrast, Count Dracula in Robert Bloch's short story, 'Underground' (1967), also set during the Second World War, assists the Germans. In Sydney Horler's novel, *The Vampire* (1935), a 1930s pastiche of *Dracula*, the lair of the vampire, Baron Ziska, is in the cellars of the Sovranian embassy. Sovrania is an unmistakable reference to Nazi Germany. Tellingly, the ambassador is identified as Bavarian, having 'been reared on stories of were-wolves and vampires'.[113] His compatriot, Captain

Hermann von Zant, is spying on the British government and, as Horler informs the reader, 'True Sovranian that he was, he had all his nation's unreasoning hatred and contempt for the country which was now giving him hospitality.'[114] Jews are identified as among the racial enemies of the country, 'forced to leave their native land because of the foul tortures to which they were subjected on account of their religious beliefs.'[115] Horler's vampires are on the side of the devil and a Teutonic one at that.

Whatever side he may be on, Dracula continues to reappear in literature and film. Bela Lugosi, who first played the role in Tod Browning's *Dracula* (1931), produced repeat performances in the same accent and similar costumes, only with different scripts and sometimes different names. A case in point is Lew Landers' horror film, *The Return of the Vampire*, released in 1944 by Columbia Pictures, in which Lugosi replays the count against the backdrop of the two world wars.[116] Landers had recent experience of making a war film, having directed, two years earlier, *Atlantic Convoy* (1942), about naval patrols battling German U-boats during the Second World War. In his vampire movie, 200-year-old blood-drinker Armand Tesla, played by Lugosi, is revived from the dead by his werewolf servant Andreas Obry. To stop the ensuing vampire attacks, Armand is staked in his coffin. The year is 1918, which not only marked the end of this particular vampire menace but also that of the First World War. But with the Second World War the vampire returns, assisted by the German military machine, rising again when, twenty-three years later, the bombing of a cemetery during the London Blitz reopens his coffin. Actual footage of German bombers and the resulting devastation is spliced into the diegesis. Gravediggers wearing tin helmets are assigned to rebury the disturbed coffins. One of them wryly notes that nowadays: 'It ain't even safe to be dead.' Yet it is their actions that directly cause the living to be no longer safe from the marauding dead. They spot the stake through the corpse's heart and, assuming it to be shrapnel, remove it. This reanimates the vampire, who resumes his blood-drinking. Andreas, under the spell of Armand's hypnotic gaze, is ordered to kill visiting scientist Dr Hugo Bruckner, who has escaped from a Nazi concentration camp. As part of his cover, Armand impersonates Dr Bruckner, who has become his latest victim. Shortly after the deception is discovered, the cemetery where Armand rests by day is again blown up during a German air raid. His werewolf servant, who has now turned against him, drags him unconscious from the tomb and, using bomb debris, hammers a spike through his heart. Released the previous year was *Son of Dracula* (1943), made by Universal

Pictures, which benefited from the talents of European émigrés fleeing Hitler. Both the writer for the original story and director were Polish Jews, the Siodmak brothers. In a sense, they brought Dracula with them by transporting him from Europe into an American setting. *The Return of the Vampire* and *Son of Dracula* were made during the war, but after its ending in 1945, there would be no more serious vampire films for over a decade, prompting film critic David Pirie to declare: 'The vampire movie was pronounced dead.'[117] This demise was undoubtedly a response to the biggest blood-letting in history. After cinema audiences witnessed news-reel footage from the liberated concentration camps, with mountains of cadavers and skeletal walking dead, the appeal of fictional vampires as a source of horror dramatically waned.

Vampirism would reappear during the Vietnam War to bring home an anti-war message. *Deathdream* (1972) is one of the few anti-war films made during the war.[118] The main character is a vampire soldier called Andy Brooks who, on returning from Vietnam, acts strangely, spending time in the local cemetery. When his father says, 'We thought you were dead', his reply is the ironic quip, 'I was.' Andy survives by injecting him-self with a syringe filled with blood from his murder victims. He regards his vampirism as compensation for the sacrifice he made for his coun-try, saying to one of them: 'I died for you, Doc. Now why shouldn't you return the favour?' Andy's emotional passivity indicates that he is dead inside. At the end of the film, he externalises this inner state by climbing into a grave with his name and date of death on the tombstone. As the living dead needing a blood 'fix', Andy is symbolic of the soldiers return-ing from Vietnam who were driven to drug addiction or crime by the traumas of war.

David Drake's vampire short story, 'Something Had to Be Done', also concerns the traumatised returning soldier. The story was published in 1975, the year when Saigon was captured by the North Vietnamese Army, marking the end of the Vietnam War. The author had served as an interrogator with the 11th Armored Cavalry Regiment in Vietnam and Cambodia. The title of the story signals his relief that war ended. For him, 'It was a waste of blood and time and treasure. It did no good of which I'm aware, and did a great deal of evil of which I'm far too aware.'[119] The story centres on Sergeant Morzek, who has spent four years in active com-bat in Vietnam. He notices that his comrade, Private Stefan Lunkowski, suffers no ill effects after being shot five times in the chest with bullets piercing his flak jacket. Shortly afterwards, the platoon suffers a series of deaths unrelated to enemy attack. Convinced that Lunkowski is a vampire and responsible for the killings, Morzek destroys him by tossing a grenade into his bunk. Having escaped suspicion for the murder, he is selected to visit the dead man's family and accompany the coffin home. He insensitively reveals to the relatives that Lunkowski's coffin is actually filled with gravel because the body had been pulverised beyond retrieval. Morzek becomes convinced that the family, with their glittering teeth, are vampires. Although he denies that he is insane, he seems to be suffering from post-traumatic stress disorder, exacerbated by alcoholism. The story concludes with Morzek destroying himself and the family with a white phosphorus incendiary. On a number of levels, he is a signifier of death and, indeed, his name entombs the Latin word for death, 'mors'. Having served his country as a professional soldier for twenty-six years, Morzek turns suicide bomber in the sure knowledge that he is dying. Malignant melanomas cover his face, caused by exposure to the sun. It is a reminder that for the traditional vampire sunlight can be every bit as fatal as the blaze of white phosphorus. While Morzek's homecoming is ostensibly to accompany a coffin, it is his own 'cadaverous figure' that substitutes for the missing dead body. Appropriately, Captain Richmond describes him as a 'walking corpse'.[120] On observing Morzek's long row of service stripes, the captain wonders if he might have served in the Second World War. This linking of the Vietnam War with an earlier war, in which Americans also fought, captures a sense of the oneness of wars and their homogenising effect.

Vampirism is a suitable trope for the bloodthirstiness and perpetuation of warfare, applying equally well to an enemy soldier across No Man's Land as to the might of an imperial military power. War profiteering has been shown to be yet another form of vampirism, along with jingoism and the venereal diseases infecting armies. Many veterans of the Vietnam War, forced to fight in the most unpopular war of the twentieth century, felt vampirised by their government, which had drained them of their youth and vitality. The transformation of civilian into soldier finds an apposite metaphor through the metamorphosis of human into vampire. Bill Compton turns vampire while serving as an American Civil War soldier in Charlaine Harris' Southern Vampire Mysteries series, televised as the HBO series, *True Blood*.[121] In *Being Human*, the BBC Three series, John Mitchell, an Irish soldier fighting in the trenches of the First World War, discovers vampires rifling through the corpses in search of fresh blood.[122] In order to save members of his battalion from being killed,

Mitchell sacrifices himself by allowing the vampire William Herrick to recruit him as one of the undead. After having been satiated by the carnage of war, Bill Compton and John Mitchell are reluctant vampires, who try to abstain from killing humans. Without doubt, the most insatiable of all blood-drinkers, the vampire of vampires, is war itself. Towards the end of Barbusse's *Under Fire*, when soldiers in the trenches reach the conclusion that 'You've got to kill war', they have finally come to recognise the true enemy.[123] Literature, art and film have been enlisted in the campaign to expose the horror and pathos of war, even though the impact of trench warfare was deemed 'too colossal to be dramatic' by American film-maker D. W. Griffith.[124] He persisted, nevertheless, in relaying his pacifism through cinema and is reported to have said: 'If moving pictures properly done of the horrors of war had been innoculated [*sic*] in all the nations of Europe, there would be no bodies of men lying on European battlefields.'[125] War may well be the failure of art. So far, it has not been dissuaded from its *raison d'être* by poem, novel, play or film. The barricade of culture has proved powerless to stem the onslaught of warfare. Resistant to all adversaries, war marches on – undefeated, unquenchable, and very much undead.

NOTES

1 Robert Greacen, 'Hun' (1995), in Jim Haughey (ed.), *The First World War in Irish Poetry* (Cranbury, NJ: Associated University Presses, 2002), p. 228.
2 Isaac Rosenberg, 'On Receiving News of the War', in *First World War Poetry*, ed. Jon Silkin (Harmondsworth: Penguin [1979], 1986), p. 204.
3 Critics who have been looking at the relationship between war and the Gothic include Sarah Wasson, *Urban Gothic of the Second World War: Dark London* (Basingstoke: Palgrave Macmillan, 2010), which investigates literature of the home front, and Terry Phillips, 'The Rules of War: Gothic Transgressions in First World War Fiction', *Gothic Studies*, 2:2 (2000), 232–44. Jarlath Killeen looks briefly at the literature of the First World War in his conclusion subtitled, 'Moving to the Gothic trenches', in *Gothic Literature 1825–1914* (Cardiff: University of Wales Press, 2009), pp. 160–5.
4 See Terry Phillips, 'The Discourse of the Vampire in First World War Writing', in Peter Day (ed.), *Vampires: Myths and Metaphors of Enduring Evil* (Amsterdam: Rodopi, 2006), pp. 65–80. There is a forthcoming essay by Leigh M. McLennon on vampirism and the American Civil War in a collection of essays entitled *War Gothic*, edited by Steffen Hantke and Agnieszka Soltysik Monnet.

5 Barbara Ehrenreich, *Blood Rites: The Origins and History of the Passions of War* (London: Granta [1997], 2011), p. 132.

6 Foucault, *Society Must Be Defended*, p. 51. See also Elisabeth Bronfen, *Specters of War: Hollywood's Engagement with Military Conflict* (New Brunswick, NJ: Rutgers University Press, 2013).

7 The Balkans is a term denoting countries lying in the Balkan Peninsula, but studies of the region can include lands beyond the Danube, which marks the northern border of the territory occupied by Romanian, Croatian, Slovene and Hungarian people. See Barbara Jelavich, *History of the Balkans: Eighteenth and Nineteenth Centuries* (Cambridge: Cambridge University Press, 1983), p. 1.

8 See Marie Nizet, *Captain Vampire*, ed. Brian Stableford (Encino, CA: Black Coat Press, 2007), p. 5.

9 See Nizet, *Captain Vampire*, pp. 151–5.

10 His name probably served as a tribute to the inspiration of Ion Heliade Rădulescu.

11 See *Bram Stoker's Notes*, ed. Eighteen-Bisang and Miller, p. 245.

12 See Margo Collins, ed. *Before the Count: British Vampire Tales, 1732–1897* (Crestline, CA: Zittaw Press, 2007), p. 43.

13 There was also an unauthorised sequel by Cyprien Bérard [Charles Nodier] called *Lord Ruthven ou Les Vampires* (1820) and the theatrical adaptation by Alexandre Dumas, *Le Vampire* (1851).

14 See James Malcolm Rymer, *Varney the Vampire; or, The Feast of Blood*, ed. Curt Herr (Crestline, CA: Zittaw Press, 2008), pp. 493–546.

15 See Moss, 'The Psychiatrist's Couch', p. 142, n. There is a record of Stoker's visit to Paris in 1878, the year before Nizet's novel was published. See Stoker, *Personal Reminiscences of Henry Irving*, p. 36.

16 See Nizet, *Captain Vampire*, p. 151.

17 See Charles Snodgrass Ryan, *Under the Red Crescent: Adventures of an English Surgeon with the Turkish Army at Plevna and Erzeroum, 1877–1878* (London: John Murray, 1897), pp. 292 and 297.

18 See Belford, *Bram Stoker*, p. 128. George Stoker received the Honour of the Medjidie (4th class), which was awarded by the Ottoman Empire, often to non-Turkish nationals. He had taken part in the battles of Erzurum, Plevna and Shipka Pass.

19 Harry Ludlam, *A Biography of Bram Stoker: Creator of Dracula* (London: New English Library [1962], 1977), pp. 53–4.

20 Stoker, *Personal Reminiscences of Henry Irving*, p. 62.

21 See the second half of Cain's *Bram Stoker and Russophobia*. For other sources that Stoker cobbled together for his garbled and contrived history of Eastern Europe, see Leatherdale, *The Origins of Dracula*, pp. 86–126 and Christopher Frayling, *Vampires: Lord Byron to Count Dracula* (London: Faber & Faber, 1991), pp. 317–47.

22 See *Bram Stoker's Notes*, ed. Eighteen-Bisang and Miller, p. 318.

23 Elizabeth Miller, *Dracula: Sense and Nonsense* (Southend-on-Sea: Desert Island Books [2000], 2006), p. 123.

24 See Baddeley and Woods, *Vlad the Impaler*, p. 12.

25 Quoted in Cain, *Bram Stoker and Russophobia*, p. 37.

26 Stoker chose this image of the count for the cover of the British paperback edition of 1901.

27 Cain, *Bram Stoker and Russophobia*, p. 166.

28 See Victor Sage, 'Exchanging Fantasies: Sex and the Serbian Crisis in *The Lady of the Shroud*', in William Hughes and Andrew Smith (eds), *Bram Stoker: History, Psychoanalysis and the Gothic* (Basingstoke: Macmillan, 1998), p. 127 and Matthew Gibson, 'Bram Stoker and the Treaty of Berlin (1878)', *Gothic Studies*, 6:2 (2004), 248.

29 In 1860, Lieutenant Colonel James Balcombe joined the Royal South Down Militia as adjutant and was promoted to major in 1875 and the following year to lieutenant colonel. See Murray, *From the Shadow of Dracula*, p. 77.

30 See *Bram Stoker's Notes*, ed. Eighteen-Bisang and Miller, p. 139.

31 Cain, *Bram Stoker and Russophobia*, p. 146.

32 Quoted in Cain, *Bram Stoker and Russophobia*, p. 184, n.

33 Cain, *Bram Stoker and Russophobia*, p. 146.

34 Admiral Sir Leopold George Heath, *Letters from the Black Sea during the Crimean War 1854–1855* (London: Richard Bentley and Son, 1897), p. 6.

35 See Richard T. Trenk, Sr, 'The Plevna Delay: Winchesters and Peabody-Martinis in the Russo-Turkish War', *Man At Arms Magazine*, 19:4 (August 1997), 29–36.

36 See Will N. Grave, *Wolves in Russia: Anxiety through the Ages* (Calgary, Alberta: Detselig Enterprises, 2007). Stoker had a werewolf in his original plan for *Dracula*. See *Bram Stoker's Notes*, ed. Eighteen-Bisang and Miller, p. 319.

37 See Cain, *Bram Stoker and Russophobia*, p. 147.

38 Quoted in Stuart Currie, 'George Whyte-Melville, Vampirism and the Crimean War', www.victorianweb.org/authors/whyte-melville/currie1.html. Accessed 10 February 2010.

39 Her name in the text contains an italics, as in Madame *de* St Croix.

40 G. J. Whyte-Melville, *'Bones and I' or, the Skeleton at Home* (London: Chapman and Hall, 1868), p. 98.

41 Currie, 'George Whyte-Melville, Vampirism and the Crimean War'.

42 Quoted by Currie, 'George Whyte-Melville, Vampirism and the Crimean War'.

43 See Gibson, 'Bram Stoker and the Treaty of Berlin', 239–41.

44 Gibson, 'Bram Stoker and the Treaty of Berlin', 241–2.

45 Quoted in Gibson, 'Bram Stoker and the Treaty of Berlin', 238.

46 Jimmie Cain, 'Racism and the Vampire: The Anti-Slavic Premise of Bram Stoker's *Dracula* (1897)', in John Edgar Browning and Caroline Joan (Kay)

Picart (eds), *Draculas, Vampires and Other Undead Forms: Essays on Gender, Race and Culture* (Lanham, MD: Scarecrow Press, 2009), p. 133.

47 William E. Gladstone, *Bulgarian Horrors and Russia in Turkistan with Other Tracts* (Boston, MA: Elibron Classics [1876], 2005), p. 66.

48 See Gibson, 'Bram Stoker and the Treaty of Berlin', 248.

49 This was the Serb nationalist, Gavrilo Princip, who assassinated Arch Duke Franz Ferdinand, heir to the Austro-Hungarian throne, and his wife Sophie on 28 June 1914.

50 Quoted in Edmund Blunden, *Undertones of War*, ed. Hew Strachan (London: Penguin [1928], 2010), p. 184.

51 F. Scheffeur is being quoted here by Eugen Hadamovsky in *Propaganda and National Power: The Organization of Public Opinion for National Politics*, trans. Randall Bytwerk (German Propaganda Archive [1933], 2007), www.calvin.edu/academic/cas/gpa/hadamovsky1-2.htm. Accessed 3 March 2010.

52 Albin Grau, 'Vampires', *Nosferatu: A Film by F. W. Murnau*, trans. Craig Keller (booklet accompanying *Nosferatu*, DVD, 2007), p. 60.

53 Grau, 'Vampires', p. 60.

54 Kaes, *Shell Shock Cinema*, p. 102.

55 Kaes makes this observation; see *Shell Shock Cinema*, p. 88.

56 *Nosferatu*, onscreen intertitle, translated from the German.

57 Dion Fortune, *The Secrets of Dr. Taverner* (Columbus, OH: Ariel Press [1926], 1989), p. 21.

58 Grau, 'Vampires', p. 61.

59 Henri Barbusse, *Under Fire*, ed. Jay Winter (London: Penguin [1916], 2003), p. 316.

60 Kim Newman, *The Bloody Red Baron* (London: Simon & Schuster, 1996), p. 170. Subsequent references are made parenthetically in the text.

61 Foucault, *Society Must Be Defended*, p. 51.

62 Historians such as Margaret MacMillan feel that the treaty has been used as an unfair scapegoat for the mistakes of those who came later in the build-up to the Second World War. See *Peacemakers: Six Months That Changed the World* (London: John Murray, 2003).

63 In *Nosferatu*, Stoker's Professor Van Helsing is changed to Professor Bulwer. The name is likely to have been inspired by Edward Bulwer Lytton, the British novelist and occultist, who was keen on German culture. He took part in seances and has been linked to spirit photography.

64 See Grau, 'Vampires', p. 61.

65 Jay Winter, *Sites of Memory, Sites of Mourning: The Great War in European Cultural History* (Cambridge: Cambridge University Press, 1995), p. 15.

66 See Suzannah Biernoff, 'The Rhetoric of Disfigurement in First World War Britain', *Social History of Medicine*, 24:3 (December 2011), 667. German artists included Otto Dix and George Grosz.

67 Biernoff, 'The Rhetoric of Disfigurement', 670. The British artist Henry Tonks recorded facial injury cases of these 'broken gargoyles', as the soldiers called themselves, through his drawings for Harold Gillies, who is widely regarded as the father of plastic surgery.

68 Newman, *The Bloody Red Baron*, p. 4.

69 Erich Maria Remarque, *All Quiet on the Western Front*, ed. Brian Murdoch (London: Vintage [1929], 1996), p. 71.

70 Barbusse, *Under Fire*, p. 310.

71 Stratis Myrivilis, 'The Beauty of the Battlefield', in *The Vintage Book of War Stories*, ed. Sebastian Faulks and Jörg Hensgen (London: Vintage, 1999), pp. 51–5.

72 Burke, A Philosophical Enquiry, p. 136.

73 See Carolyn J. Dean, *The Frail Social Body: Pornography, Homosexuality and Other Fantasies in Interwar France* (Berkeley, CA: University of California Press, 2000), p. 114.

74 See Donald Smythe, 'Venereal Disease: The AEF's Experience', *Prologue: The Journal of the National Archives*, 9:2 (Summer 1977), 65. Philippa Levine, in *Prostitution, Race and Politics: Policing Venereal Disease in the British Empire* (New York: Routledge, 2003), p. 146, states that in the British army infection rates applied to 51.8 per 1,000 troops, which did not exceed the worst pre-war figures.

75 Robert Graves, *Goodbye to All That* (London: Penguin [1929], 2000), p. 104.

76 The cartoon was sanctioned by the Committee on Public Information, Division of Pictorial Publicity, founded in 1917 to promote public acceptance of America's participation in the First World War. Punctuation has been added to the quotation.

77 Herbert A. Friedman, 'Venereal Disease Propaganda', www.psywarrior.com/PSYOPVD.htm. Accessed 1 March 2010.

78 George Thibierge, *Syphilis and the Army*, ed. C. F. Marshall (London: University of London Press, 1918), p. 13.

79 Thibierge, *Syphilis and the Army*, p. 13.

80 See Elaine Showalter, 'Syphilis, Sexuality, and the Fiction of the Fin de Siècle', in Ruth Bernard Yeazell (ed.), *Sex, Politics and Science in the Nineteenth-Century Novel* (Baltimore, MD: Johns Hopkins University Press, 1986), pp. 98–100.

81 Thibierge, *Syphilis and the Army*, p. 13.

82 This was not so applicable to Germany where gender roles were more traditional.

83 Quoted in Florence Tamagne, *A History of Homosexuality in Europe: Berlin, London, Paris 1919–1939* (New York: Alogora Publishing, 2006), p. 392.

84 Quoted in Phillips, 'The Discourse of the Vampire', p. 66.

85 Sarah Smith, 'When the Red Storm Comes: Or, The History of a Young Lady's Awakening to Her Nature', in *Shudder Again: 22 Tales of Sex and Horror*, ed. Michele Slung (Harmondsworth: Penguin, 1993), p. 157.

86 As in the earlier film, *The Vampire* (1913), directed by Robert G. Vignola, early vamps were not blood-suckers but femmes fatales.

87 The verses were written to commemorate the exhibition of a painting, *The Vampire* by Philip Burne-Jones, the cousin of Kipling, who was known to Stoker. See Cain, *Bram Stoker and Russophobia*, p. 88.

88 Porter Emerson Browne, *Scars and Stripes* (New York: George H. Doran, 1917), p. 135.

89 Celia Malone Kingsbury, *For Home and Country: World War I Propaganda on the Home Front* (Lincoln, NE: University of Nebraska Press, 2010), p. 70.

90 Quoted in Dean, *The Frail Social Body*, p. 115.

91 Quoted in Paul Fussell, *The Great War and Modern Memory* (Oxford: Oxford University Press [1975], 2000), p. 90.

92 Mary Butts, *Ashe of Rings and Other Writings*, ed. Nathalie Blondel (New York: McPherson, 1998), p. 232 and see p. 110.

93 Phillips, 'The Discourse of the Vampire', p. 75.

94 Chris Baldick, *1910–1940: The Modern Movement*, in Jonathan Bate (gen. ed.), *The Oxford English Literary History*, 13 vols (Oxford: Oxford University Press, 2004), 10, p. 344.

95 Otto Weininger, *Sex and Character: An Investigation of Fundamental Principles* (Bloomington, IN: Indiana University Press [1903], 2005), p. 262.

96 The first in the series is *Anno Dracula* (1992), taking place during the Victorian period, and the final novel is *Dracula Cha Cha Cha* (1998), set in the 1960s.

97 Ewers, *Nachtmahr*, ed. Hirschhorn-Smith, p. xxvii.

98 Because of Richthofen's importance to German propaganda, the text was heavily censored and edited.

99 Slavoj Žižek, *Interrogating the Real*, ed. Rex Butler and Scott Stephens (London: Continuum, 2005), p. 157.

100 Žižek, *Interrogating the Real*, p. 157. See also Keith Scott, 'Blood, Bodies, Books: Kim Newman and the Vampire as Cultural Text', in Deborah Mutch (ed.), *The Modern Vampire and Human Identity* (London: Palgrave Macmillan, 2013), p. 23.

101 Elizabeth Hardaway, '"Ourselves Expanded": The Vampire's Evolution from Bram Stoker to Kim Newman', in Leonard G. Heldreth and Mary Pharr (eds), *The Blood Is the Life: Vampires in Literature* (Bowling Green, OH: Bowling Green State University Popular Press, 1999), p. 177.

102 Graves, *Goodbye to All That*, pp. 195–6.

103 Jacques Derrida, *The Gift of Death*, trans. David Wills (Chicago, IL: University of Chicago Press, 1995), p. 17.

104 Quoted in Fussell, *The Great War*, p. 123.

105 See *Bram Stoker's Notes*, ed. Eighteen-Bisang and Miller, p. 318.

106 This was the conclusion reached by Field-Marshall Earl Wavell, quoted in Anthony Pagden, *Worlds at War: The 2,500-year Struggle between East and West* (Oxford: Oxford University Press, 2008), p. 407.

107 See William Montgomery Brown, 'The War-Vampire and the Churches', *Bishop Brown's Lectures*, 12 (1932), www.anglocatholicsocialism.org/episcopus.html. Accessed 10 January 2012.

108 Karl Marx, *Capital: A Critique of Political Economy*, ed. Frederick Engels, trans. Samuel Moore and Edward Aveling (New York: Modern Library [1867], 1906), p. 257.

109 Manly Wade Wellman, 'The Horror Undying', in *The Rivals of Dracula: A Century of Vampire Fiction*, ed. Michel Parry (London: Corgi, 1977), p. 139.

110 The vampire hunters in *Dracula* sail up the Bistritza river in Transylvania, mentioned above in the section, 'Captain Vampire and Count Dracula'.

111 Manly Wade Wellman, 'The Devil Is Not Mocked', in *The Mammoth Book of Dracula*, ed. Stephen Jones (London: Constable & Robinson [1997], 2011), p. 51.

112 Wellman, 'The Devil Is Not Mocked', p. 51

113 Sydney Horler, *The Vampire* (New York: Bookfinger [1935], 1974), p. 199.

114 Horler, *The Vampire*, p. 197.

115 Horler, *The Vampire*, p. 196.

116 The copyright date is 1943.

117 David Pirie, *Vampire Cinema* (London: Hamlyn, 1977), p. 9.

118 *Deathdream*, dir. Bob Clark, Impact Films, 1972. The film was also released under the title, *Dead of Night*.

119 David Drake, 'Vietnam', http://david-drake.com/2009/vietnam/#more-1306. Accessed 2 August 2009.

120 David Drake, 'Something Had to Be Done', in *The Rivals of Dracula*, p. 168.

121 Bill Compton is turned into a vampire by a predatory woman who preys on soldiers. This series of novels dates from 2001.

122 The television series was first broadcast in 2008.

123 Barbusse, *Under Fire*, p. 308.

124 Quoted in Andrew Kelly, *Cinema and the Great War* (London: Routledge, 1997), p. 25.

125 Kelly, *Cinema and the Great War*, p. 25.

Conclusion: conflict Gothic

'I is another.'[1]

Arthur Rimbaud, letter to Paul Demeny, 15 Mary 1871

'... a new *modus legendi*: a method of reading cultures from the monsters they engender.'[2]

Jeffrey Jerome Cohen, *Monster Culture: Reading Culture* (1996)

Corporeality has been used by the Gothic to express horror of the Other, whether it be through the body of the Catholic, Caribbean slave, femme fatale, Jew or enemy soldier. The construct of the monster is a declaration of war on individuals, who are demonised for their marginality and whose bodies are overlaid with fear and danger. The title of the final chapter, 'The Vampire of War', echoes the phrase, 'the fog of war', alluding to the difficulty of decision-making in the midst of conflict.[3] This expression goes back to Carl von Clausewitz, the Prussian military analyst, who declared in his monumental book, *On War* (1832): 'War is the realm of uncertainty.'[4] Within the Gothic realms of uncertainty, lack of clarity can extend to determining friend from foe or self from Other. As we have seen, this can manifest in the shifting metaphor of the vampire, applicable not only to the enemy but also to soldiers and their leaders, men and women on the home front, war veterans, those involved in the armament industry, regimental prostitutes and the forces of imperialism. During her keynote at a Gothic conference in Poland, Agnieszka Soltysik Monnet paraded a number of subgenres, including battlefield Gothic, which are contained within the burgeoning genre of War Gothic.[5] It is a banner under which the category of vampirism and war is readily mustered.

Invariably the Gothic arises out of conflict. As the Marquis de Sade observed, the Gothic novel emerged from the horrors of the French Revolution. He expressed particular admiration for Matthew Lewis' *The Monk*, which can be read as a gory map of the Terror and the anti-clericalism blighting France from 1793 to 1794, a process continued by several of his imitators.[6] Yet this was by no means the bloodiest conflict within living memory. A longer-lasting and more global conflict with a much greater death toll was the Seven Years War, which Winston Churchill famously described as the 'first world war'.[7] The year after it ended in 1763, Walpole published *The Castle of Otranto*, in which a castle is haunted by a giant suit of armour, serving as a suitable metonym for war.[8] As Angela Wright points out: '*The Castle of Otranto* is linguistically and generically freighted with the effects of the Seven Years War'.[9] Significantly, the first instance of supernatural terror is the crushing of Manfred's son by a giant helmet, a symbol of how large the recent memory of war loomed. Bearing down on nations, war crushes those in its path, as surely as did Prince Alfonso's helmet.[10] The relationship between war and the Gothic novel has been inextricably linked from the start of this literary tradition and continues in *The Old English Baron* (1778), which its author Clara Reeves regarded as the literary offspring of *The Castle of Otranto*. Her description of the inside of a suit of armour, found to be stained with blood, turns out to be more realistic and abject than Walpole's gigantic spectral version.

The year before his novel appeared, an appeal for Catholics to be allowed to enlist in the British army was rebuffed. Shock waves from Henry VIII's fissure with Rome over two hundred years earlier were still resonating, and indeed the Dissolution of the Monasteries can be seen as the unspoken horror in *Castle of Otranto*. Similarly, *The Monk* is a response to the desecration of the Catholic Church in France. In many ways, the French Revolution and the Henrician English Reformation brought about the destruction of a Gothic world in Britain and France, which Walpole and Lewis sought to recapture imaginatively through Gothic fiction. As a literature dealing with oppression, the Gothic novel is a political genre encrypting the return of the repressed, as well as pointing towards what was to come.

Hauntology, an evocation of the revenant, opens up a way of looking at the spectres lying ahead. Mary Shelley's *Frankenstein* can be read as a warning against future anarchy being unleashed on the world as a result of the man-made monster of slavery. Her scientist hero is increasingly apprehensive that, if his male and female monster were to depart to a remote desert in the New World, they would 'thirst', vampire-like, to propagate 'a race of devils', foment terror and endanger 'the very existence of the species of man' (pp. 170–1). Similarly, fears of rebellion in the New World were not far removed from the minds of Shelley's contemporaries. This prospect of massacres, machetes and dismemberment coalesces in the incipient dangers posed by Frankenstein's female creature as a mother of monsters. The body of the female monster is a cabinet of curiosities, whose body parts, like those of the Hottentot Venus, lend themselves to fragmentation.[11] Once torn apart, Shelley's potentially dangerous female is rendered safe, until reintegrated by later novelists in the form of, for example, Shelley Jackson's Patchwork Girl, Elizabeth Hand's bride of Frankenstein, Pandora, or Fay Weldon's she devil who, in order to take revenge on her unfaithful husband, defies her maker by remaking herself anew, not just psychically but also through plastic surgery.[12]

The use of surgery as an instrument of pacification rather than empowerment, demonstrated by the sexual surgery carried out by Isaac Baker Brown, was symptomatic of the war on women waged in the operating theatre. Bogus medical theory and practice underpin this surgical misogyny. Read as a medical novel, *Dracula* can be seen to mirror some of these attitudes to women, including the construction of the femme fatale, at a time when gender roles were in the spotlight and under the scalpel. While a limited number of contemporary cognoscenti readers might have picked up on this surgical subtext, the general reader is unlikely to have registered it consciously. Likewise, German audiences watching the vampire in F. W. Murnau's *Nosferatu* would not have identified this hairless creature with a Jew in the first instance. But within the context of an anti-Semitic gestalt, the encroaching accumulation of Jewish stereotypes, such as the exaggerated nose, long fingernails, enlarged ears, shuffling gait, black attire and blood-sucking tendencies, are likely to have crept up on them, as stealthily as Count Orlok mounts the stairs on the way to his victim's bedroom.

The body is a potential site of monstrosity for those who do not fit into the body politic. Irregularity and the grotesque have been associated with the architecture of the Gothic and are also indicative of wayward flesh and its deformities. The monstrous body provides a battleground on which good versus evil can play out for perpetuity. Monsters are a rupture in the fabric of society, which can itself become monstrous, imperilling existence or making it merely monotonous, like the lives of the human pistons in Lang's film *Metropolis*. The Gothic has even been co-opted by the forces of oppression, as when George Canning used the monster in *Frankenstein* to sway Parliament from agreeing to the immediate emancipation of slaves. Religious persecution, racism, misogyny and war are responses to bodies considered dangerous by the controlling institutional bodies of the Church, medical profession and state. Throughout history, the body has had to endure being tortured by the Inquisition, enchained by slavery, mutilated by castrating surgeons or victimised by the vampirism of war and persecution. The endangered or dangerous body lies at the centre of the clash between victim and persecutor and has generated tales of terror and narratives of horror, which function to either salve, purge or dangerously perpetuate such oppositions.

NOTES

1 Arthur Rimbaud, letter to Paul Demeny, 15 May 1871, in *Complete Works, Selected Letters*, trans. Wallace Fowlie (Chicago, IL: University of Chicago Press, 1966), p. 304.

2 Jeffrey Jerome Cohen, 'Monster Culture (Seven Theses) (extract)', in *Speaking of Monsters: A Teratological Anthology*, ed. Caroline Joan S. Picart and John Edgar Browning (New York: Palgrave Macmillan, 2012), p. 15.

3 See *The Fog of War: Eleven Lessons from the Life of Robert S. McNamara* (2003), a documentary directed by Errol Morris.

4 Carl von Clausewitz, *On War*, ed. and trans. Michael Howard and Peter Paret (Princeton, NJ: Princeton University Press, 1989), p. 101.

5 This took place during the 'All That Gothic: Excess and Exuberance' conference held at the University of Lodz, Poland, 9–11 October 2014.

6 Musäus' 'The Elopement', which appears to have been Lewis' primary source for his Raymond and Agnes sub-plot in *The Monk*, is set during the Thirty Years War.

7 Quoted by Wright, *Britain, France and the Gothic, 1764–1820*, p. 3.

8 I owe this point to Agnieszka Soltysik Monnet.

9 Wright, *Britain, France and the Gothic, 1764–1820*, p. 8. Wright indicates how Ann Radcliffe's final novel, *Gaston de Blondeville* (1826), reveals an 'enduring fascination' with 'the historical circumstances of the Anglo-French conflict', p. 14.

10 The language of warfare is deployed even in the first preface.

11 I owe this point to Zofia Kolbuszewska.

12 See Fay Weldon, *The Life and Loves of a She-Devil* (London: Hodder and Stoughton, 1983).

Bibliography

~

Abbey, E. C., *The Sexual System and Its Derangements* (Buffalo, NY: n.p., 1875).

Abbott, John, *Another Comment on Jud Süss* (Chicago, IL: International Historic Films, 2007).

Acton, William, *The Functions and Disorders of the Reproductive Organs in Childhood, Youth, Adult Age, and Advanced Life: Considered in Their Physiological, Social, and Moral Relations* (London: John Churchill, 4th edn [1857], 1865).

Adorno, Theodor, *In Search of Wagner* (London: Verso [1952], 2005).

Aikin, Anna L., 'On Monastic Institutions', in *The Works of Anna Laetitia Barbauld*, ed. Lucy Aikin, 2 vols (London: Longman, Hurst, Rees, Orme, Brown and Green, 1825), 2, pp. 195–213.

Anolik, Ruth Bienstock, 'Reviving the Golem, Reviving *Frankenstein*: Cultural Negotiations in Ozick's *The Puttermesser Papers* and Piercy's *He, She and It*', in Lois E. Rubin (ed.), *Connections and Collisions: Identities in Contemporary Jewish-American Women* (Cranbury, NJ: Associated University Presses, 2005), pp. 139–59.

Anolik, Ruth Bienstock, 'The Infamous Svengali: George du Maurier's Satanic Jew', in Ruth Bienstock Anolik and Douglas L. Howard (eds), *The Gothic Other: Racial and Social Constructions in the Literary Imagination* (Jefferson, NC: McFarland, 2004), pp. 163–93.

Anolik, Ruth Bienstock and Douglas L. Howard (eds), *The Gothic Other: Racial and Social Constructions in the Literary Imagination* (Jefferson, NC: McFarland, 2004).

Anon., *Common Sense* (1739), in E. J. Clery and Robert Miles (eds), *Gothic Documents: A Sourcebook 1700–1820* (Manchester: Manchester University Press, 2000), pp. 60–1.

Anon., 'The Bleeding Nun of St Catherine's', in *Romances and Gothic Tales*, ed. Franz J. Potter (Crestline, CA: Zittaw Press [1801], 2006), pp. 25–32.

Anon., *Cuffy the Negro's Doggrel Description of the Progress of Sugar* (London: E. Wallis, 1823).

Anon., 'Der ewig Jude', *Unser Wille und Weg*, 10 (1940), 54–5.

225

Anon., 'Nose', in *Jewish Encyclopedia* (1906), www.jewishencyclopedia.com/articles/11598-nose. Accessed 1 September 2012.

Anon., 'Obituary. Sir William Thornley Stoker, Bart., M.D., Dublin', *The British Medical Journal* (June 1912), 1399–1400.

Anon., 'Ristori as Marie Antoinette', *McBride's Magazine*, 1 (February 1868), 175–85.

Anon., 'Sir Richard Burton's Manuscripts: Alexander v. Manners Sutton', *The Times*, 28 March 1911, 3.

'Anti-Semitism', in *Encyclopedia Judaica*, 16 vols (Jerusalem: Keter Publishing House, 1971–2), 3, pp. 87–159.

Apel, Dora, *Imagery of Lynching: Black Men, White Women and the Mob* (New Brunswick, NJ: Rutgers University Press, 2004).

Arata, Stephen D., 'The Occidental Tourist: *Dracula* and the Anxiety of Reverse Colonization', *Victorian Studies*, 33:4 (1990), 621–45.

Baddeley, Gavin and Paul Woods, *Vlad the Impaler: Son of the Devil, Hero of the People* (Hersham: Ian Allan, 2010).

Baldick, Chris, *In Frankenstein's Shadow: Myth, Monstrosity and Nineteenth-Century Writing* (Oxford: Clarendon Press, 1987).

Baldick, Chris, *1910–1940: The Modern Movement*, in Jonathan Bate (gen. ed.), *The Oxford English Literary History*, 13 vols (Oxford: Oxford University Press, 2004), 10.

Banister, Joseph, *England under the Jews* (Boston, MA: Elibron Classics [1907], 2007).

Bann, Stephen (ed.), *Frankenstein, Creation and Monstrosity* (London: Reaktion Books, 1994).

Barbusse, Henri, *Under Fire*, ed. Jay Winter (Penguin: London [1916], 2003).

Barker-Benfield, G. J., *The Horrors of the Half-Known Life: Male Attitudes towards Women and Sexuality in Nineteenth-Century America* (New York: Harper & Row, 1976).

Barker-Benfield, G. J., 'The Spermatic Economy: A Nineteenth-Century View of Sexuality', *Feminist Studies*, 1 (Summer 1972), 45–74.

Barnes, Robert and Fancourt Barnes, *A System of Obstetric Medicine and Surgery*, 2 vols (London: Smith, Elder and Co., 1884–5).

Bate, Jonathan (gen. ed.), *The Oxford English Literary History*, 13 vols (Oxford: Oxford University Press, 2004).

Belford, Barbara, *Bram Stoker: A Biography of the Author of Dracula* (London: Weidenfeld & Nicolson, 1996).

Biale, David, *Blood and Belief: The Circulation of a Symbol between Jews and Christians* (Berkeley, CA: University of California Press, 2007).

Bieri, James, *Percy Bysshe Shelley: A Biography – Youth's Unextinguished Fire, 1792–1816* (Newark, DE: University of Delaware Press, 2004).

Biernoff, Suzannah, 'The Rhetoric of Disfigurement in First World War Britain', *Social History of Medicine*, 24:3 (December 2011), 666–85, www.ncbi.nlm.nih.gov/pmc/articles/PMC3223959/#FN6. Accessed 23 January 2013.

Blumberg, Jane, *Mary Shelley's Early Novels* (Basingstoke: Macmillan, 1993).

Blunden, Edmund, *Undertones of War*, ed. Hew Strachan (London: Penguin [1928], 2010).

Bolton, H. Philip, *Women Writers Dramatized: A Calendar of Performances from Narrative Works Published in English to 1900* (London: Mansell Publishing, 2000).

Bosmajian, Haig, *Burning Books* (Jefferson, NC: McFarland, 2006).

Botting, Fred, *Gothic* (London: Routledge, 1996).

Botting, Fred (ed.), *The Gothic: Essays and Studies* (Cambridge: D.S. Brewer, 2001).

Bressey, Caroline and Tom Wareham, *Reading the London Sugar and Slavery Gallery* (London: Museum of London Docklands, 2010).

Bride of Frankenstein, dir. James Whale, Universal Pictures, 1935.

Bronfen, Elisabeth, *Over Her Dead Body: Death, Femininity and the Aesthetic* (Manchester: Manchester University Press, 1992).

Bronfen, Elisabeth, *Specters of War: Hollywood's Engagement with Military Conflict* (New Brunswick, NJ: Rutgers University Press, 2013).

Brown, Isaac Baker, *On the Curability of Certain Forms of Insanity, Epilepsy, Catalepsy, and Hysteria in Females* (London: Robert Hardwicke, 1866).

Brown, William Montgomery, 'The War-Vampire and the Churches', *Bishop Brown's Lectures*, 12 (1932), www.anglocatholicsocialism.org/episcopus.html. Accessed 10 January 2012.

Browne, Porter Emerson, *Scars and Stripes* (New York: George H. Doran, 1917).

Browning, John Edgar and Caroline Joan (Kay) Picart (eds), *Draculas, Vampires and Other Undead Forms: Essays on Gender, Race and Culture* (Lanham, MD: Scarecrow Press, 2009).

Bruhm, Steven, *Gothic Bodies: The Politics of Pain in Romantic Fiction* (Philadelphia, PA: University of Pennsylvania Press, 1994).

Burke, Edmund, *A Philosophical Enquiry into the Origin of Our Ideas of the Sublime and Beautiful*, ed. James T. Boulton (Oxford: Basil Blackwell [1757], 1987).

[Burke, Edmund], 'Case of the Suffering Clergy of France: Refugees in the British Dominions', letter to *The Times* (18 September 1792), 3.

Burnard, Trevor, 'The Planter Class', in Gad Heuman and Trevor Burnard (eds), *The Routledge History of Slavery* (London: Routledge, 2011).

Burton, Richard and W. H. Wilkins, *The Jew, the Gypsy and El Islam* (Kila, MT: Kessinger Publishing Co. [1898], 2003).

Butler, Erik, *Metamorphoses of the Vampire in Literature and Film: Cultural Transformations in Europe 1732–1933* (Rochester, NY: Camden House, 2010).

Butts, Mary, *Ashe of Rings and Other Writings*, ed. Nathalie Blondel (New York: McPherson, 1998).

Bynum, Caroline Walker, *Jesus as Mother: Studies in the Spirituality of the High Middle Ages* (Berkeley, CA: University of California Press, 1982).

Bynum, Caroline Walker, *Wonderful Blood: Theology and Practice in Late Medieval Northern Germany and Beyond* (Philadelphia, PA: Pennsylvania University Press, 2007).

Byron, Glennis (ed.), *Dracula* (Basingstoke: Palgrave Macmillan, 1999).

Byron, Glennis and David Punter (eds), *Spectral Readings: Towards a Gothic Geography* (Basingstoke: Palgrave Macmillan, 1999).

Bytwerk, Randall L., *Julius Streicher* (New York: Cooper Square Press [1983], 2001).

Cain, Jimmie E., Jr, *Bram Stoker and Russophobia: Evidence of the British Fear of Russia in Dracula and The Lady of the Shroud* (Jefferson, NC: McFarland, 2006).

Cain, Jimmie E., Jr, 'Racism and the Vampire: The Anti-Slavic Premise of Bram Stoker's *Dracula* (1897)', in John Edgar Browning and Caroline Joan (Kay) Picart (eds), *Draculas, Vampires and Other Undead Forms: Essays on Gender, Race and Culture* (Lanham, MD: Scarecrow Press, 2009), pp. 127–34.

Canning, George, *The Parliamentary Debates*, House of Commons, 16 March 1824, col. 1103, www.hansardarchive.parliament.uk/Parliamentary_Debates,_ New_Series_Vol_1_(April_1820)to_Vol_25_(July_1830)S2V0010P0.zip. Accessed 5 February 2013.

Canuel, Mark, *Religion, Toleration, and British Writing, 1790–1830* (Cambridge: Cambridge University Press, 2005).

Carter, Angela, *The Sadeian Woman* (London: Virago Press, 1979).

Chaplin, Sue, *The Gothic and the Rule of Law 1764–1820* (Basingstoke: Palgrave Macmillan, 2007).

Cheyette, Bryan (ed.), *Between 'Race' and Culture: Representations of 'the Jew' in English and American Literature* (Stanford, CA: Stanford University Press, 1996).

Clausewitz, Carl von, *On War*, ed. and trans. Michael Howard and Peter Paret (Princeton, NJ: Princeton University Press, 1989).

Clery, E. J., *Women's Gothic: From Clara Reeve to Mary Shelley* (Tavistock: Northcote House, 2004).

Clery, E. J. and Robert Miles (eds), *Gothic Documents: A Sourcebook 1700–1820* (Manchester: Manchester University Press, 2000).

Cohen, Jeffrey Jerome, 'Monster Culture (Seven Theses) (extract)', in Caroline Joan S. Picart and John Edgar Browning (eds), *Speaking of Monsters: A Teratological Anthology* (New York: Palgrave Macmillan, 2012), pp. 15–18.

Collins, Margo (ed.), *Before the Count: British Vampire Tales, 1732–1897* (Crestline, CA: Zittaw Press, 2007).

Conger, Syndy M., *Matthew G. Lewis, Charles Robert Maturin, and the Germans* (New York: Arno Press, 1980).

Connor, Steven, *The Book of Skin* (London: Reaktion, 2004).

Cooper, L. Andrew, *Gothic Realities: The Impact of Horror Fiction on Modern Culture* (Jefferson, NC: McFarland, 2010).

Craft, Christopher, 'Kiss Me with Those Red Lips: Gender and Inversion in Bram Stoker's *Dracula*', in Glennis Byron (ed.), *Dracula* (Basingstoke: Palgrave Macmillan, 1999), pp. 93–118.

Crook, Nora, 'Counting the Carbonari: A Newly Attributed Mary Shelley Article', *Keats-Shelley Review*, 23 (2009), 39–50.

Cumberland, Richard, *The Wheel of Fortune*, in *The British Theatre or a Collection of Plays* (London: Longman, Hurst, Rees and Orme, 1808).

Curbet, Joan, '"Hallelujah to your dying screams of torture": Representations of Ritual Violence in English and Spanish Romanticism', in Avril Horner (ed.), *European Gothic: A Spirited Exchange 1760–1960* (Manchester: Manchester University Press, 2002), pp. 161–82.

Currie, Stuart, 'George Whyte-Melville, Vampirism and the Crimean War', www.victorianweb.org/authors/whyte-melville/currie1.html. Accessed 10 February 2010.

Dally, Ann, *Fantasy Surgery 1880–1930* (Amsterdam: Rudopi, B.V., 2006).

Dally, Ann, *Women under the Knife: A History of Surgery* (London: Hutchinson Radius, 1991).

Darby, Robert, 'The Benefits of Psychological Surgery: John Scoffern's Satire on Isaac Baker Brown', *Medical History*, 51 (2007), 527–44.

Darby, Robert, 'The Masturbation Taboo and the Rise of Routine Male Circumcision: A Review of the Historiography', *Journal of Social History*, 36:3 (Spring 2003), 737–57.

Darby, Robert, *A Surgical Temptation: The Demonization of the Foreskin and the Rise of Circumcision in Britain* (Chicago, IL: University of Chicago Press, 2005).

Davis, John, *Henry Irving: A Short Account of His Public Life* (New York: William S. Gottsberger, 1883).

Davison, Carol Margaret, *Anti-Semitism and British Gothic Literature* (Basingstoke: Palgrave Macmillan, 2004).

Davison, Carol Margaret, 'Blood Brothers: Dracula and Jack the Ripper', in Carol Margaret Davison (ed.), with the participation of Paul Simpson-Housley, *Bram Stoker's Dracula: Sucking through the Century, 1897–1997* (Toronto: Dundern Press, 1997), pp. 147–72.

Davison, Carol Margaret, *Gothic Literature 1764–1824* (Cardiff: University of Wales Press, 2009).

Davison, Carol Margaret, 'Modernity's Fatal Addictions: Death/Undeath by Technology in E. Elias Merhige's *Shadow of the Vampire* (2000)', International Gothic Association conference, University of Surrey, 7 August 2013.

Davison, Carol Margaret (ed.), with the participation of Paul Simpson-Housley, *Bram Stoker's Dracula: Sucking through the Century, 1897–1997* (Toronto: Dundern Press, 1997).

Day, Peter (ed.), *Vampires: Myths and Metaphors of Enduring Evil* (Amsterdam: Rodopi, 2006).

Day, Thomas, *The Dying Negro* (London: Flexney, Wilkie and Robson, 1775).

Day, William Patrick, *Vampire Legends in Contemporary American Culture: What Becomes a Legend Most* (Kentucky, KY: The University Press of Kentucky, 2002).

De Sade, Marquis, 'Marquis de Sade (1800)', in Victor Sage (ed.), *The Gothick Novel* (Basingstoke: Macmillan, 1990), pp. 48–9.

Dean, Carolyn J., *The Frail Social Body: Pornography, Homosexuality and Other Fantasies in Interwar France* (Berkeley, CA: University of California Press, 2000).

Deathdream, dir. Bob Clark, Impact Films, 1972.

Decker, Hannah S., *Freud, Dora, and Vienna 1900* (New York: The Free Press, 1992).

Denniston, George C. and Marilyn Fayre Milos (eds), *Sexual Mutilations: A Human Tragedy* (New York: Plenum Press, 1997).

Derrida, Jacques, *The Gift of Death*, trans. David Wills (Chicago, IL: University of Chicago Press, 1995).

Derrida, Jacques, *Specters of Marx: The State of the Debt, the Work of Mourning and the New International*, ed. Bernd Magnus and Stephen Cullenberg, trans. Peggy Kamuf (New York: Routledge, 1994).

Dickens, Charles, *Oliver Twist: or, The Parish Boy's Progress*, ed. Philip Horne (London: Penguin [1838], 2003).

Dijkstra, Bram, *Idols of Perversity: Fantasies of Feminine Evil in Fin-de-Siècle Culture* (New York: Oxford University Press, 1986).

Drake, David, 'Something Had to Be Done', in *The Rivals of Dracula: A Century of Vampire Fiction*, ed. Michel Parry (London: Corgi, 1977), pp. 168–73.

Drake, David, 'Vietnam', http://david-drake.com/2009/vietnam/#more-1306. Accessed 2 August 2009.

Dresser, Madge, *Slavery Obscured: The Social History of the Slave Trade in Bristol* (Bristol: Redcliffe Press [2001], 2007).

Duffy, John, 'Masturbation and Clitoridectomy: A Nineteenth-Century View', *Journal of the American Medical Association*, 186:3 (October 1963), 246–8.

Du Maurier, George, *Trilby*, ed. Leonee Ormond (London: J. M. Dent, 1992).

Dundes, Alan (ed.), *The Blood Libel Legend: A Casebook in Anti-Semitic Folklore* (Madison, WI: University of Wisconsin Press, 1991).

Edwards, Bryan, *The History, Civil and Commercial of the British West Indies*, 5 vols (Boston, MA: Elibron Classics [1819], 2005).

Ehrenreich, Barbara, *Blood Rites: The Origins and History of the Passions of War* (London: Granta [1997], 2011).

Eisner, Lotte H., *Murnau* (London: Martin Secker & Warburg [1964], 1973).

Elbert, Monika and Bridget M. Marshall (eds), *Transnational Gothic: Literary and Social Exchanges in the Long Nineteenth Century* (Farnham: Ashgate, 2013).

Ellis, Markman, *The History of Gothic Fiction* (Edinburgh: Edinburgh University Press, 2000).

Ellmann, Maud, 'The Imaginary Jew: T. S. Eliot and Ezra Pound', in Bryan Cheyette (ed.), *Between 'Race' and Culture: Representations of 'the Jew' in English and American Literature* (Stanford, CA: Stanford University Press, 1996), pp. 84–101.

Elsaesser, Thomas, 'No End to *Nosferatu* (1922)', in Noah Isenberg (ed.), *Weimar Cinema: An Essential Guide to Classic Films of the Era* (New York: Columbia University Press, 2009), pp. 79–94.

The Eternal Jew, dir. Fritz Hipper, Terra Film, 1940.

Ewers, Hanns Heinz, *Alraune*, trans. Joe E. Bandel (Newcastle-upon-Tyne: Side Real Press, 2010).

Ewers, Hanns Heinz, *Blood* (Rockville, MD: Olympia Press, 2009).

Ewers, Hanns Heinz, *Nachtmahr: Strange Tales*, ed. John Hirschhorn-Smith (Newcastle-upon-Tyne: Side Real Press, 2009).

Farson, Daniel, *The Man Who Wrote Dracula: A Biography of Bram Stoker* (London: Michael Joseph, 1975).

Fenwick, Eliza, *Secresy; or, The Ruin on the Rock*, ed. Isobel Grundy (Peterborough, Ontario: Broadview [1795], 1994).

Fisher, Benjamin Franklin, 'Poe and the Gothic Tradition', in Kevin J. Hayes (ed.), *The Cambridge Companion to Edgar Allan Poe* (Cambridge: Cambridge University Press, 2002), pp. 72–91.

Fortune, Dion, *The Secrets of Dr. Taverner* (Columbus, OH: Ariel Press [1926], 1989).

Foucault, Michel, *The History of Sexuality, Vol. 1: An Introduction*, trans. Robert Hurley (Harmondsworth: Penguin [1976], 1990).

Foucault, Michel, *Society Must Be Defended: Lectures at the Collège de France 1975–76*, ed. Mauro Bertani and Alessandro Fontana, trans. David Macey (London: Penguin [1997], 2004).

Frankenstein, dir. James Whale, Universal Pictures, 1931.

Fraser, Antonia, *Marie Antoinette* (London: Weidenfeld & Nicolson, 2001).

Fraser, John Foster, *The Conquering Jew* (New York: Funk & Wagnalls, 1915).

Frayling, Christopher, *Vampires: Lord Byron to Count Dracula* (London: Faber & Faber, 1991).

Freeman, Hadley, 'The Dark Comedy of Werner Herzog', *The Guardian*, 5 March 2011, www.guardian.co.uk/film/2011/mar/05/werner-herzog-cave-of-forgotten-dreams. Accessed 23 January 2012.

Freud, Sigmund, 'The Question of Lay Analysis: Conversations with an Impartial Person', in *Standard Edition of the Complete Psychological Works*, 24 vols (London: Hogarth Press (1926), 20, pp. 183–250.

Friday, Linda, 'Exhuming Dracula's Coffin via E-learning: A Case Study', International Gothic Association Conference, University of Surrey, 7 August 2013.

Friedman, Herbert A., 'Venereal Disease Propaganda', www.psywarrior.com/PSYOPVD.htm. Accessed 1 March 2010.

Friedman, Lester D., 'The Edge of Knowledge: Jews as Monsters/Jews as Victims', *MELUS*, 11:3 (Autumn 1984), 49–62.

Fussell, Paul, *The Great War and Modern Memory* (Oxford: Oxford University Press [1975], 2000).

Gardenour, Brenda, 'The Biology of Blood-Lust: Medieval Medicine, Theology and the Vampire Jew', *Film and History*, 42:2 (Fall 2011), 51–63.

Gardner, Augustus K. 'Physical Decline of American Women', *The Knickerbocker* (January 1860), 37–51.

Gelder, Ken, *Reading the Vampire* (London: Routledge, 1994).

Gibson, Matthew, 'Bram Stoker and the Treaty of Berlin (1878)', *Gothic Studies*, 6:2 (2004), 236–51.

Gilman, Sander L., *Difference and Pathology: Stereotypes of Sexuality, Race, and Madness* (Ithaca, NY: Cornell University Press, 1985).

Gilman, Sander L., *Jewish Self-Hatred: Anti-Semitism and the Hidden Language of the Jews* (Baltimore, MD: Johns Hopkins University Press, 1986).

Gilman, Sander L., *The Case of Sigmund Freud: Medicine and Identity at the Fin de Siècle* (Baltimore, MD: Johns Hopkins University Press, 1994).

Gilman, Sander L., *The Jew's Body* (New York: Routledge, 1991).

Gladstone, William E., *Bulgarian Horrors and Russia in Turkistan with Other Tracts* (Boston, MA: Elibron Classics [1876], 2005).

Glucklich, Ariel, *Sacred Pain: Hurting the Body for the Sake of the Soul* (New York: Oxford University Press, 2001).

Godwin, William, *Caleb Williams*, ed. David McCracken (Oxford: Oxford University Press [1794], 1970).

The Golem: How He Came into the World, dir. Carl Boese and Paul Wegener, Projektions-AG Union, 1920.

Grand, Sarah, *The Beth Book*, ed. Sally Mitchell (Bristol: Thoemmes Press [1897], 1994).

Grant, Michael, 'James Whale's "Frankenstein": The Horror Film and the Symbolic Biology of the Cinematic Monster', in Stephen Bann (ed.), *Frankenstein, Creation and Monstrosity* (London: Reaktion Books, 1994), pp. 113–35.

Grau, Albin, 'Vampires', *Nosferatu: A Film by F. W. Murnau*, trans. Craig Keller (booklet accompanying *Nosferatu*, DVD, 2007).

Grave, Will N., *Wolves in Russia: Anxiety through the Ages* (Calgary, Alberta: Detselig Enterprises, 2007).

Graves, Robert, *Goodbye to All That* (London: Penguin [1929], 2000).

Greacen, Robert, 'Hun' (1995), in Jim Haughey (ed.), *The First World War in Irish Poetry* (Cranbury, NJ: Associated University Presses, 2002), p. 228.

Green, Toby, *Inquisition: The Reign of Terror* (Basingstoke: Macmillan, 2007).

Groom, Nick, *The Gothic: A Very Short Introduction* (Oxford: Oxford University Press, 2012).

Grosz, Elizabeth, *Volatile Bodies: Towards a Corporeal Feminism* (Bloomington, IN: Indiana University Press, 1994).

Hadamovsky, Eugen, *Propaganda and National Power: The Organization of Public Opinion for National Politics*, trans. Randall Bytwerk, German Propaganda Archive [1933], 2007, www.calvin.edu/academic/cas/gpa/hadamovsky1-2. htm. Accessed 3 March 2010.

Halberstam, Judith, *Skin Shows: Gothic Horror and the Technology of Monsters* (Durham, NC: Duke University Press, 1995).

Hall, Lesley A., 'Doctors Masturbating Women as a Cure for Hysteria/"Victorian Vibrators" ', *Victorian Sex Factoids*, www.lesleyahall.net/factoids.htm#hysteria. Accessed 9 September 2011.

Hall, Lesley A., 'Forbidden by God, Despised by Men: Masturbation, Medical Warnings, Moral Panic, and Manhood in Great Britain, 1850–1950', *Journal of the History of Sexuality*, 2:3 (January 1992), 365–87.

Hall, Lesley A., *Hidden Anxieties: Male Sexuality 1900–1950* (Cambridge: Polity Press, 1991).

Hall, Lesley A., ' "The English Have Hot-Water Bottles": The Morganatic Marriage between the British Medical Profession and Sexology since William Acton', in Roy Porter and Mikulas Teich (eds), *Sexual Knowledge, Sexual Science: The History of Attitudes to Sexuality* (Cambridge: Cambridge University Press, 1994), pp. 350–66.

Halttunen, Karen, *Murder Most Foul: The Killer and the American Gothic Imagination* (Cambridge, MA: Harvard University Press [1998], 2001).

Hardaway, Elizabeth, ' "Ourselves Expanded": The Vampire's Evolution from Bram Stoker to Kim Newman', in Leonard G. Heldreth and Mary Pharr (eds), *The Blood Is the Life: Vampires in Literature* (Bowling Green, OH: Bowling Green State University Popular Press, 1999), pp. 177–86.

Hare, E. H., 'Masturbatory Insanity: The History of an Idea', *Journal of Mental Science*, 108 (January 1962), 1–25.

Haughey, Jim (ed.), *The First World War in Irish Poetry* (Cranbury, NJ: Associated University Presses, 2002).

Hayes, Kevin J. (ed.), *The Cambridge Companion to Edgar Allan Poe* (Cambridge: Cambridge University Press, 2002).

Haynes, A. E., *Man-Hunting in the Desert: Being a Narrative of the Palmer Search-Expedition 1882, 1883* (London: Horace Cox, 1894).

Haywood, Ian, *Bloody Romanticism: Spectacular Violence and the Politics of Representation, 1776–1832* (Basingstoke: Palgrave Macmillan, 2006).

Heath, Leopold George, *Letters from the Black Sea during the Crimean War 1854–1855* (London: Richard Bentley and Son, 1897).

Heldreth, Leonard G. and Mary Pharr (eds), *The Blood Is the Life: Vampires in Literature* (Bowling Green, OH: Bowling Green State University Popular Press, 1999).

Heuman, Gad and Trevor Burnard (eds), *The Routledge History of Slavery* (London: Routledge, 2011).

Hise, James Van (ed.), *Stephen King and Clive Barker: The Illustrated Guide to the Masters of the Macabre II* (Las Vegas, NV: Pioneer Books, 1992).

Hitler, Adolph, *Mein Kampf*, trans. Alvin Johnson and John Chamberlain (New York: Reynal and Hitchcock [1925–6], 1941).

Hitler, Adolph, *Mein Kampf*, ed. D. C. Watt, trans. Ralph Manheim (London: Pimlico [1925–6], 2007).

Hobson, Christopher Z., *The Chained Boy: Orc and Blake's Idea of Revolution* (London: Associated University Presses, 1999).

Hochschild, Adam, *Bury the Chains: The British Struggle to Abolish Slavery* (London: Macmillan, 2005).

Hochschild, Adam, *To End All Wars: How the First World War Divided Britain* (London: Macmillan, 2011).

Hodges, Frederick, 'A Short History of the Institutionalization of Involuntary Sexual Mutilation in the United States', in George C. Denniston and Marilyn Fayre Milos (eds), *Sexual Mutilations: A Human Tragedy* (New York: Plenum Press, 1997), pp. 17–40.

Hoeveler, Diane Long, 'Demonizing the Catholic Other: Religion and the Secularizing Process in Gothic Literature', in Monika Elbert and Bridget M. Marshall (eds), *Transnational Gothic: Literary and Social Exchanges in the Long Nineteenth Century* (Farnham: Ashgate, 2013), pp. 83–96.

Hoeveler, Diane Long, *Gothic Feminism: The Professionalization of Gender from Charlotte Smith to the Brontës* (Pennsylvania, PA: Pennsylvania State University Press, 1998).

Hoeveler, Diane Long, *The Gothic Ideology: Religious Hysteria and Anti-Catholicism in British Popular Fiction, 1780–1880* (Cardiff: University of Wales Press, 2014).

Hogan, Patrick Colm, 'Narrative Universals, Nationalism, and Sacrificial Terror: From *Nosferatu* to Nazism', *Film Studies*, 8 (Summer 2006), 93–105.

Hogle, Jerrold E., 'The Gothic Ghost of the Counterfeit and the Progress of Abjection', in David Punter (ed.), *A Companion to the Gothic* (Oxford: Blackwell, 2000), pp. 293–304.

Holmes, Colin, 'The Ritual Murder Accusation in Britain', in Alan Dundes (ed.), *The Blood Libel Legend: A Casebook in Anti-Semitic Folklore* (Madison, WI: University of Wisconsin Press, 1991), pp. 99–134.

Holmes, Rachel, *The Hottentot Venus* (London: Bloomsbury, 2008).

Horkheimer, Max and Theodor W. Adorno, *Dialectic of Enlightenment: Philosophical Fragments*, ed. Gunzelin Schmid Noerr (Stanford, CA: Stanford University Press [1947], 2007).

Horler, Sydney, *The Vampire* (New York: Bookfinger [1935], 1974).

Horner, Avril (ed.), *European Gothic: A Spirited Exchange 1760–1960* (Manchester: Manchester University Press, 2002).

Hughes, Derek, *Culture and Sacrifice: Ritual Death in Literature and Opera* (Cambridge: Cambridge University Press, 2007).

Hughes, William, 'A Singular Invasion: Revisiting the Postcoloniality of Bram Stoker's *Dracula*', in William Hughes and Andrew Smith (eds), *Empire and the Gothic: The Politics of Genre* (Basingstoke: Palgrave Macmillan, 2003), pp. 88–102.

Hughes, William, *Beyond Dracula: Bram Stoker's Fiction and Its Cultural Context* (Basingstoke: Macmillan, 2000).

Hughes, William, *Bram Stoker Dracula: A Reader's Guide to Essential Criticism* (London: Palgrave Macmillan, 2008).

Hughes, William and Andrew Smith (eds), *Bram Stoker: History, Psychoanalysis and the Gothic* (Basingstoke: Macmillan, 1998).

Hughes, William and Andrew Smith (eds), *Empire and the Gothic: The Politics of Genre* (Basingstoke: Palgrave Macmillan, 2003).

Hughes, William, David Punter and Andrew Smith (eds), *The Encyclopedia of the Gothic*, 2 vols (Oxford: Wiley-Blackwell, 2013).

Hurley, Kelly, *The Gothic Body: Sexuality, Materialism, and Degeneration at the Fin de Siècle* (Cambridge: Cambridge University Press, 1996).

Idman, Niilo, *Charles Robert Maturin: His Life and Works* (London: Constable, 1923).

Isenberg, Noah (ed.), *Weimar Cinema: An Essential Guide to Classic Films of the Era* (New York: Columbia University Press, 2009).

Jelavich, Barbara, *History of the Balkans: Eighteenth and Nineteenth Centuries* (Cambridge: Cambridge University Press, 1983).

Jew Süss, dir. Veit Harlan, Terra Film, 1940.

Joshi, S. T. (ed.), *Encyclopedia of the Vampire: The Living Dead in Myth, Legend and Popular Culture* (Santa Barbara, CA: Greenwood, 2011).

Julius, Anthony, *Trials of the Diaspora: A History of Anti-Semitism in England* (Oxford: Oxford University Press, 2010).

Jump, Harriet Devine, 'Monstrous Stepmother: Mary Shelley and Mary Jane Godwin', in Marie Mulvey-Roberts and Janet Todd (eds), bicenntenial special issue on Mary Shelley, *Women's Writing*, 6:3 (1999), 297–308.

Kaes, Anton, *Shell Shock Cinema: Weimar Culture and the Wounds of War* (Princeton, NJ: Princeton University Press, 2009).

Kastan, David Scott (ed.), *The Oxford Encyclopaedia of British Literature* (Oxford: Oxford University Press, 2006).

Kellogg, J. H., *Man the Masterpiece or Plain Truths Plainly Told, about Boyhood, Youth, and Manhood* (Battle Creek, MI: Modern Medicine Publishing Co. [1885], 1894).

Kellogg, J. H., *Plain Facts for Old and Young or The Science of Human Life from Infancy to Old Age* (Battle Field Creek, MI: Good Health Publishing Company [1877], 1910).

Kelly, Andrew, *Cinema and the Great War* (Abingdon: Routledge, 1997).

Kent, Susan Kingsley, *Sex and Suffrage in Britain 1860–1914* (London: Routledge [1987], 1990).

Kilgour, Maggie, *The Rise of the Gothic Novel* (London: Routledge, 1995).

Killeen, Jarlath, *Gothic Literature 1825–1914* (Cardiff: University of Wales Press, 2009).

Kingsbury, Celia Malone, *For Home and Country: World War I Propaganda on the Home Front* (Lincoln, NE: University of Nebraska Press, 2010).

Kinski, Klaus, *Kinski Uncut: The Autobiography of Klaus Kinski*, trans. Joachim Neugröschel (London: Bloomsbury, 1996).

Kiple, Kenneth F., *The Caribbean Slave: A Biological History* (Cambridge: Cambridge University Press, 1985).

Kitson, Peter, *Romantic Literature, Race, and Colonial Encounter* (Basingstoke: Palgrave Macmillan, 2007).

Kittler, Friedrich, 'Dracula's Legacy', *Stanford Humanities Review*, 1:1 (1989), 143–73.

Koenigsberg, Richard A., *Hitler's Ideology: Embodied Metaphor, Fantasy and History* (Charlotte, NC: Information Age Publishing [1975], 2007).

Kracauer, Siegfried, *From Caligari to Hitler: A Psychological History of the German Film* (Princeton, NJ: Princeton University Press, 1947).

Krafft-Ebing, Richard von, *Psychopathia Sexualis with Especial Reference to the Antipathic Sexual Instinct: A Medico-Forensic Study* (New York: Arcade Publishing [1871], 1998).

Kristeva, Julia, *Powers of Horror: An Essay on Abjection*, trans. Leon S. Roudiez (New York: Columbia University Press, 1982).

Kuiper, B. K., *The Church in History* (Grand Rapids, MI: Christian Schools International, 1964).

Laqueur, Thomas, *Making Sex: Body and Gender from the Greeks to Freud* (Cambridge, MA: Harvard University Press [1990], 1992).

Lawrence, William, *Lectures on Physiology, Zoology and the Natural History of Man* (London: Benbow [1819], 1822).

Leatherdale, Clive, *The Origins of Dracula: The Background to Bram Stoker's Gothic Masterpiece* (London: William Kimber, 1987).

Ledoux, Ellen Malenas, *Social Reform in Gothic Writing: Fantastic Forms of Change, 1764–1834* (Basingstoke: Palgrave Macmillan, 2013).

Lee, Debbie, *Slavery and the Romantic Imagination* (Philadelphia, PA: University of Pennsylvania Press, 2002).

Lembcke, Jerry, *The Spitting Image: Myth, Memory and the Legacy of Vietnam* (New York: New York University Press, 1998).

Levin, David J., *Richard Wagner, Fritz Lang and the Nibelungen: The Dramaturgy of Disavowal* (Princeton, NJ: Princeton University Press, 1988).

Levine, Philippa, *Prostitution, Race and Politics: Policing Venereal Disease in the British Empire* (New York: Routledge, 2003).

Levy, Richard S. (ed.), *Antisemitism: A Historical Encyclopedia of Prejudice and Persecution* (Santa Barbara, CA: ABC-Clio, 2005).

Levy, Richard S., 'Dinter, Artur (1876–1948)', in Richard S. Levy (ed.), *Antisemitism: A Historical Encyclopedia of Prejudice and Persecution* (Santa Barbara, CA: ABC-Clio, 2005).

Lewis, Matthew Gregory, *Journal of a West India Proprietor*, ed. Judith Terry (Oxford: Oxford University Press [1834], 1999).

Lewis, Matthew Gregory, *The Castle Spectre*, in *Seven Gothic Dramas 1789–1825*, ed. Jeffrey N. Cox (Athens, OH: Ohio University Press, 1992), pp. 149–224.

Lewis, Matthew Gregory, *The Life and Correspondence of M. G. Lewis*, 2 vols (London: Henry Colburn, 1839).

Lewis, Matthew Gregory, *The Monk*, ed. D. L. Macdonald and Kathleen Scherf (Peterborough, Ontario: Broadview Press [1796], 2004).

Lewis, Matthew Gregory, *Venoni, or the Novice of St Mark's* (London: Longman, Hurst, Rees, and Orme, 1809).

Lightfoot-Klein, Hanny, *Secret Wounds* (Bloomington, IN: 1stBooks, 2002).

Lochhead, Liz, *Blood and Ice* (Edinburgh: The Salamander Press [1982], 1984).

Long, Edward, *History of Jamaica*, 3 vols (London: T. Lowndes, 1774).

Ludlam, Harry, *A Biography of Bram Stoker: Creator of Dracula* (London: New English Library [1962], 1977).

Lupoff, Richard, Richard Wolinsky and Lawrence Davidson, 'A Talk with the King', in James Van Hise (ed.), *Stephen King and Clive Barker: The Illustrated Guide to the Masters of the Macabre II* (Las Vegas, NV: Pioneer Books, 1992), pp. 79–95.

Lynch, James V., 'The Limits of Revolutionary Radicalism: Tom Paine and Slavery', *Pennsylvania Magazine of History and Biography*, 123 (July 1999), 177–99.

Macdonald, D. L., *Monk Lewis: A Critical Biography* (Toronto: University of Toronto Press, 2000).

McGraw, Eliza R. L., *Two Covenants: Representations of Southern Jewishness* (Baton Rouge, LA: Louisiana State University Press, 2005).

MacMillan, Margaret, *Peacemakers: Six Months That Changed the World* (London: John Murray, 2003).

McWhorter, Ladelle, *Racism and Sexual Oppression in Anglo America: A Genealogy* (Bloomington, IN: Indiana University Press, 2009).

Maines, Rachel, *The Technology of Orgasm: Hysteria, the Vibrator, and Women's Sexual Satisfaction* (Baltimore, MD: Johns Hopkins University Press, 1999).

Malchow, H. L., 'Frankenstein's Monster and Images of Race in Nineteenth-Century Britain', *Past and Present*, 139 (1993), 90–130.

Malchow, H. L., *Gothic Images of Race in Nineteenth-Century Britain* (Stanford, CA: Stanford University Press, 1996).

Malenas, Ellen, 'Reform Ideology and Generic Structure in Matthew Lewis's *Journal of a West India Proprietor*', *Studies in Eighteenth-Century Culture*, 35 (2006), 27–51.

Markley, A. A., *Conversion and Reform in the British Novel in the 1790s: A Revolution of Opinions* (London: Palgrave Macmillan, 2009).

Marx, Karl, *Capital: A Critique of Political Economy*, ed. Frederick Engels, trans. Samuel Moore and Edward Aveling (New York: Modern Library[1867], 1906).

Mason, Diane, *The Secret Vice: Masturbation in Victorian Fiction and Medical Culture* (Manchester: Manchester University Press, 2008).

Masson, Jeffrey Moussaieff, *A Dark Science: Women, Sexuality, and Psychiatry in the Nineteenth Century* (New York: Farrar, Straus and Giroux, 1986).

Maturin, Charles, *Melmoth the Wanderer*, ed. Chris Baldick (Oxford: Oxford University Press [1820], 1989).

Medwin, Thomas, *Conversations of Lord Byron* (London: Henry Colburn, 1824).

Meigs, Charles D., *Females and Their Diseases: A Series of Letters to His Class* (Philadelphia, PA: Lea and Blanchard, 1848).

Mellor, Anne K., 'Frankenstein, Racial Science, and the Yellow Peril', *Nineteenth-Century Contexts*, 23 (2001), 1–28.

Mellor, Anne K., *Mary Shelley: Her Life, Her Fiction, Her Monsters* (London: Routledge, 1988).

Melton, J. Gordon, *The Vampire Book: The Encyclopedia of the Undead* (Detroit, MI: Visible Ink Press, 1999).

Michael, Robert, *Holy Hatred: Christianity, Antisemitism, and the Holocaust* (London: Palgrave Macmillan, 2006).

Mighall, Robert, *A Geography of Victorian Gothic Fiction: Mapping History's Nightmares* (Oxford: Oxford University Press, 1999).

Mighall, Robert, '"A pestilence which walketh in darkness": Diagnosing the Victorian Vampire', in Glennis Byron and David Punter (eds), *Spectral Readings: Towards a Gothic Geography* (Basingstoke: Palgrave Macmillan, 1999), pp. 108–26.

Miles, Robert, 'Abjection, Nationalism and the Gothic', in Fred Botting (ed.), *The Gothic: Essays and Studies* (Cambridge: D.S. Brewer, 2001), pp. 47–70.

Miles, Robert, 'Europhobia: The Catholic Other in Horace Walpole and Charles Maturin', in Avril Horner (ed.), *European Gothic: A Spirited Exchange 1760–1960* (Manchester: Manchester University Press, 2002), pp. 84–103.

Miles, Robert, 'The Gothic Novel', in David Scott Kastan (ed.), *The Oxford Encyclopaedia of British Literature* (Oxford: Oxford University Press, 2006), pp. 443–6.

Miller, Andrew H. and James Eli Adam (eds), *Sexualities in Victorian Britain* (Bloomington, IN: Indiana University Press, 1996).

Miller, Elizabeth, *Dracula: Sense and Nonsense* (Southend-on-Sea: Desert Island Books [2000], 2006).

Milton, John, *Paradise Lost: A Poem* (London: S. Simmons, 2nd edn, 1674).

Montague, Edward, *The Demon of Sicily* (Kansas City, MO: Valancourt Books, 2007).

Moretti, Franco, *Signs Taken for Wonders: Essays in the Sociology of Literary Forms*, trans. Susan Fischer, David Forgacs and David Miller (London: Verso, 1983).

Morus, Iwan Rhys, *Shocking Bodies: Life, Death and Electricity in Victorian England* (Stroud: The History Press, 2011).

Moscucci, Ornella, 'Clitoridectomy, Circumcision, and the Politics of Sexual Pleasure', in Andrew H. Miller and James Eli Adam (eds), *Sexualities in Victorian Britain* (Bloomington, IN: Indiana University Press, 1996), pp. 60–78.

Moscucci, Ornella, *The Science of Woman: Gynaecology and Gender in England 1800–1929* (Cambridge: Cambridge University Press [1990], 1993).

Moss, Stephanie, 'The Psychiatrist's Couch: Hypnosis, Hysteria, and Proto-Freudian Performance in *Dracula*', in Carol Margaret Davison (ed.), with the participation of Paul Simpson-Housley, *Bram Stoker's Dracula: Sucking through the Century, 1897–1997* (Toronto: Dundern Press, 1997), pp. 123–46.

Mozley, John, *John Foxe and His Book* (London: SPCK [1940], 1972).

Muchembled, Robert, *Orgasm and the West: A History of Pleasure from the Sixteenth Century to the Present*, trans. Jean Birrell (Malden, MA: Polity, 2008).

Mulvey-Roberts, Marie, 'The After-lives of the Bride of Frankenstein: Mary Shelley and Shelley Jackson', in Maria Purves (ed.), *Women and Gothic* (Newcastle-upon-Tyne: Cambridge Scholars Publishing, 2014), pp. 81–96.

[Mulvey-]Roberts, Marie, *Gothic Immortals: The Fiction of the Brotherhood of the Rosy Cross* (London: Routledge, 1990).

Mulvey-Roberts, Marie, 'Menstrual Misogyny and Taboo: The Medusa, Vampire and the Female Stigmatic', in Andrew Shail and Gillian Howie (eds), *Menstruation: A Cultural History* (Basingstoke: Palgrave Macmillan, 2005), pp. 149–61.

Mulvey-Roberts, Marie and Janet Todd (eds), bicenntenial special issue on Mary Shelley, *Women's Writing*, 6:3 (1999), 297–308.

Murray, Paul, *From the Shadow of Dracula: A Life of Bram Stoker* (London: Jonathan Cape, 2004).

Mutch, Deborah (ed.), *The Modern Vampire and Human Identity* (London: Palgrave Macmillan, 2013).

Myrivilis, Stratis, 'The Beauty of the Battlefield', in *The Vintage Book of War Stories*, ed. Sebastian Faulks and Jörg Hensgen (London: Vintage, 1999).

Nevárez, Lisa, '"Monk" Lewis' "The Isle of Devils" and the Perils of Colonialism', *Romanticism and Victorianism on the Net*, 50 (May 2008), www.erudit.org/revue/ravon/2008/v/n50/018147ar.html. Accessed 3 May 2013.

Newman, Kim, *The Bloody Red Baron* (London: Simon & Schuster, 1996).

Nizet, Marie, *Captain Vampire*, ed. Brian Stableford (Encino, CA: Black Coat Press, 2007).

Nosferatu: A Sympathy of Horror, dir. F. W. Murnau, Prana-Film, 1922.

Nugent, Maria, *Lady Nugent's Journal of Her Residence in Jamaica from 1801 to 1805*, ed. Philip Wright (Kingston: Institute of Jamaica, 1966).

O'Malley, Patrick R., *Catholicism, Sexual Deviance, and Victorian Gothic Culture* (Cambridge: Cambridge University Press, 2006).

Pagden, Anthony, *Worlds at War: The 2,500-year Struggle between East and West* (Oxford: Oxford University Press, 2008).

Park, Mungo, *Travels in the Interior of Africa* (Ware: Wordsworth Editions [1799], 2002).

Paulson, Ronald, *Representations of Revolution (1789–1820)* (New Haven, CT: Yale University Press, 1983).

Peake, Richard Brinsley, *Presumption; or, The Fate of Frankenstein*, in *Seven Gothic Dramas*, ed. Jeffrey N. Cox (Athens, OH: Ohio University Press, 1992), pp. 385–425.

Peakman, Julie, *Mighty Lewd Books: The Development of Pornography in Eighteenth-Century England* (Basingstoke: Palgrave Macmillan, 2003).

Peakman, Julie, *The Pleasure's All Mine: A History of Perverse Sex* (London: Reaktion Books, 2013).

Pearce, Edward, *The Great Man: Robert Walpole: Scoundrel, Genius and Britain's First Prime Minister* (London: Pimlico, 2008).

Pettigrew, Thomas Joseph, *On Superstitions Connected with the History and Practice of Medicine and Surgery* (London: John Churchill, 1844).

Phillips, John, 'Circles of Influence: Lewis, Sade and Artaud', *Comparative Critical Studies*, 9 (2012), 61–82.

Phillips, Terry, 'The Discourse of the Vampire in First World War Writing', in Peter Day (ed.), *Vampires: Myths and Metaphors of Enduring Evil* (Amsterdam: Rodopi, 2006), pp. 65–80.

Phillips, Terry, 'The Rules of War: Gothic Transgressions in First World War Fiction', *Gothic Studies*, 2:2 (2000), 232–44.

Picart, Caroline Joan S. and John Edgar Browning (eds), *Speaking of Monsters: A Teratological Anthology* (New York: Palgrave Macmillan, 2012).

Pirie, David, *Vampire Cinema* (London: Hamlyn, 1977).

Polner, Murray, *No Victory Parades: The Return of the Vietnam Veteran* (New York: Holt, Rinehart and Winston, 1971).

Porter, Roy and Mikulas Teich (eds), *Sexual Knowledge, Sexual Science: The History of Attitudes to Sexuality* (Cambridge: Cambridge University Press, 1994).

Potter, Franz J. (ed.), *Literary Mushrooms: Tales of Terror and Horror from the Gothic Chapbooks, 1800–1830* (Fullerton, CA: Zittaw Press, 2009).

Praz, Mario, *The Romantic Agony* (Oxford: Oxford University Press, 1970).

Punter, David, *Gothic Pathologies: The Text, the Body and the Law* (Basingstoke: Macmillan, 1998).

Punter, David, *The Literature of Terrror*, 2 vols (London: Longman, 1996).

Punter, David (ed.), *A Companion to the Gothic* (Oxford: Blackwell, 2000).

Purves, Maria, *The Gothic and Catholicism: Religion, Cultural Exchange and the Popular Novel, 1785–1829* (Cardiff: University of Wales Press, 2009).

Purves, Maria (ed.), *Women and Gothic* (Newcastle-upon-Tyne: Cambridge Scholars Publishing, 2014).

Quigley, Christine, *The Corpse: A History* (Jefferson, NC: McFarland, 1996).

Radcliffe, Ann, *The Italian, or, The Confessional of the Black Penitents*, ed. Robert Miles (Harmondsworth: Penguin Classics [1797], 2000).

Radcliffe, Ann, *The Mysteries of Udolpho* (Oxford: Oxford University Press [1794], 1992).

Ranke-Heinemann, Uta, *Eunuchs for the Kingdom of Heaven: Women, Sexuality, and the Catholic Church*, trans. Peter Heinegg (New York: Doubleday, 1990).

Rawlings, Helen, *The Spanish Inquisition* (Oxford: Blackwell Publishing, 2006).

Relink, Karel, *Zrcadlo Zidu* (Prague: Nakladem vlastnim, 1925),

Remarque, Erich Maria, *All Quiet on the Western Front*, ed. Brian Murdoch (London: Vintage [1929], 1996).

Resnick, Irven M., 'Medieval Roots of the Myth of Jewish Male Menses', *Harvard Theological Review*, 93:3 (2000), 241–63.

The Return of the Vampire, dir. Lew Landers, Columbia, 1944.

Reyes, Xavier Aldana, *Body Gothic: Corporeal Transgression in Contemporary Literature and Horror Film* (Cardiff: University of Wales Press, 2014).

Ricci, James V., *The Development of Gynaecological Surgery and Instruments: A Comprehensive Review of the Evolution of Surgery and Surgical Instruments for the Treatment of Female Diseases from the Hippocratic Age to the Antiseptic Period* (San Francisco, CA: Norman Publishing [1949], 1990).

Rimbaud, Arthur, letter to Paul Demeny, 15 May 1871, in *Complete Works, Selected Letters*, trans. Wallace Fowlie (Chicago, IL: University of Chicago Press, 1966).

Robbins, John, *Reclaiming Our Health: Exploding the Medical Myth and Embracing the Source of True Healing* (Tiburon, CA: H. J. Kramer, 1996).

Roberts, Ian, *German Expressionist Cinema: The World of Light and Shadow* (London: Wallflower Press, 2008).

Rodriguez, Sarah W., 'Rethinking the History of Female Circumcision and Clitoridectomy: American Medicine and Female Sexuality in the Late Nineteenth Century', *Journal of the History of Medicine and Allied Sciences*, 63:3 (July 2008), 323–47.

Rosenberg, Isaac, 'On Receiving News of the War', in *First World War Poetry*, ed. Jon Silkin (Harmondsworth: Penguin [1979], 1986), p. 204.

Rowling, J. K., *Harry Potter and the Chamber of Secrets* (London: Bloomsbury, 1998).

Rowling, J. K., *Harry Potter and the Order of the Phoenix* (London: Bloomsbury, 2003).

Royle, Nicholas, *The Uncanny* (Manchester: Manchester University Press, 2003).

Rozin, Mordechai, *The Rich and the Poor: Jewish Philanthropy and Social Control in Nineteenth-Century London* (Brighton: Sussex Academic Press, 1999).

Rubin, Lois E. (ed.), *Connections and Collisions: Identities in Contemporary Jewish-American Women* (Cranbury, NJ: Associated University Presses, 2005).

Ryan, Charles Snodgrass, *Under the Red Crescent: Adventures of an English Surgeon with the Turkish Army at Plevna and Erzeroum, 1877–1878* (London: John Murray, 1897).

Rymer, Malcolm James, *Varney the Vampire; or, The Feast of Blood*, ed. Curt Herr (Crestline, CA: Zittaw Press, 2008).

Sadler, Nigel, *The Slave Trade* (Oxford: Shire Publications, 2009).

Sage, Victor, 'Exchanging Fantasies: Sex and the Serbian Crisis in *The Lady of the Shroud*', in William Hughes and Andrew Smith (eds), *Bram Stoker: History, Psychoanalysis and the Gothic* (Basingstoke: Macmillan, 1998), pp. 116–33.

Sage, Victor, *Horror Fiction in the Protestant Tradition* (Basingstoke: Macmillan, 1988).

Sage, Victor, 'Roman Catholicism', in William Hughes, David Punter and Andrew Smith (eds), *The Encyclopedia of the Gothic*, 2 vols (Oxford: Wiley-Blackwell, 2013), 2, pp. 564–9.

Sage, Victor (ed.), *The Gothick Novel* (Basingstoke: Macmillan, 1990).

Scott, Keith, 'Blood, Bodies, Books: Kim Newman and the Vampire as Cultural Text', in Deborah Mutch (ed.), *The Modern Vampire and Human Identity* (London: Palgrave Macmillan, 2013), pp. 18–36.

Scull, Andrew, *The Insanity of Place/The Place of Insanity: Essays on the History of Psychiatry* (Abingdon: Routledge, 2006).

Scull, Andrew (ed.), *Madhouses, Mad-Doctors and Mad-Men* (London: Athlone Press, 1981).

Selzer, Richard, *Confessions of a Knife: Meditations on the Art of Surgery* (London: Triad/Granada, 1982).

Senf, Carol A., *Science and Social Science in Bram Stoker's Fiction* (Westport, CT: Greenwood Press, 2002).

Seymour, Miranda, *Mary Shelley* (London: Picador, 2001).

Shadow of the Vampire, dir. E. Elias Merhige, Saturn Films, 2000.

Shail, Andrew and Gillian Howie (eds), *Menstruation: A Cultural History* (Basingstoke: Palgrave Macmillan, 2005).

Shapiro, James, *Shakespeare and the Jews* (New York: Columbia University Press, 1996).

Sharpe, Jenny, *Ghosts of Slavery: A Literary Archaeology of Black Women's Lives* (Minneapolis, MN: University of Minnesota Press, 2003).

Shelley, Mary, *Frankenstein or The Modern Prometheus*, ed. Maurice Hindle (London: Penguin [1818], 2007).

Shelley, Mary, *Frankenstein or The Modern Prometheus: The 1818 Text*, ed. Marilyn Butler (Oxford: Oxford World's Classics [1818], 1993).

Shelley, Mary, *History of a Six Weeks' Tour through a Part of France, Switzerland, Germany, and Holland; with Letters Descriptive of a Sail round the Lake of Geneva and of the Glaciers of Chamouni* (London: T. Hookham Jun. and C. and J. Ollier, 1817).

Shelley, Mary, 'Modern Italian Romances', *The Monthly Chronicle*, 2 (July–December 1838), 415–28 and 547–57.

Shelley, Mary, 'Review of J. P. Cobbett, *Journal of a Tour in Italy*', *Westminster Review*, 14 (January 1831), 174–80.

Shelley, Mary, *The Journals of Mary Shelley 1814–1844*, ed. Paula K. Feldman and Diana Scott-Kilvert (Baltimore, MD: Johns Hopkins University Press [1987], 1995).

Shelley, Mary, *The Letters of Mary Wollstonecraft Shelley, Vol. 1: 'A Part of the Elect'*, ed. Betty T. Bennett (Baltimore, MD: Johns Hopkins University Press, 1980).

Shelley, Mary, *The Letters of Mary Wollstonecraft Shelley, Vol. 2: 'Treading in Unknown Paths'*, ed. Betty T. Bennett (Baltimore, MD: Johns Hopkins University Press, 1983).

Shelley, Mary, *The Letters of Mary Wollstonecraft Shelley, Vol. 3: 'What Years I Have Spent!'*, ed. Betty T. Bennett (Baltimore, MD: Johns Hopkins University Press, 1988).

Shelley, Mary, *Valperga: or, The Life and Adventures of Castruccio, Prince of Lucca*, ed. Stuart Curran (Oxford: Oxford University Press [1823], 1997).

Shelley, Percy Bysshe, *The Complete Poetical Works of Percy Bysshe Shelley*, ed. Thomas Hutchinson (London: Oxford University Press, 1935).

Showalter, Elaine, *Hystories: Hysterical Epidemics and Modern Culture* (London: Picador, 1977).

Showalter, Elaine, *Sexual Anarchy: Gender and Culture at the Fin de Siècle* (London: Virago, 1992).

Showalter, Elaine, 'Syphilis, Sexuality, and the Fiction of the Fin de Siècle', in Ruth Bernard Yeazell (ed.), *Sex, Politics and Science in the Nineteenth-Century Novel* (Baltimore, MD: Johns Hopkins University Press, 1986), pp. 88–115.

Showalter, Elaine, 'Victorian Women and Insanity', in Andrew Scull (ed.), *Madhouses, Mad-Doctors and Mad-Men* (London: Athlone Press, 1981), pp. 313–16.

Skal, David J., *Hollywood Gothic: The Tangled Web of Dracula from Novel to Stage to Screen* (New York: Faber & Faber [1990], 2004).

Slung, Michele (ed.), *Shudder Again: 22 Tales of Sex and Horror* (Harmondsworth: Penguin, 1993).

Smith, Alan Lloyd, *American Gothic Fiction: An Introduction* (New York: Continuum, 2004).

Smith, Allan Lloyd, '"This Thing of Darkness": Racial Discourse in Mary Shelley's *Frankenstein*', *Gothic Studies*, 6:2 (2004), 208–22.

Smith, Andrew, *Victorian Demons: Medicine, Masculinity and the Gothic at the Fin-de-Siècle* (Manchester: Manchester University Press, 2004).

Smith, James Greig, *Abdominal Surgery*, 2 vols (London: Churchill, 1896).

Smith, Sarah, 'When the Red Storm Comes: Or, The History of a Young Lady's Awakening to Her Nature', in *Shudder Again: 22 Tales of Sex and Horror*, ed. Michele Slung (Harmondsworth: Penguin, 1993), pp. 149–64.

Smythe, Donald, 'Venereal Disease: The AEF's Experience', *Prologue: The Journal of the National Archives*, 9:2 (Summer 1977), 65–74.

Spooner, Catherine, *Fashioning Gothic Bodies* (Manchester: Manchester University Press, 2004).

Stableford, Brian, 'Capitaine Vampire, le', in S. T. Joshi (ed.), *Encyclopedia of the Vampire: The Living Dead in Myth, Legend and Popular Culture* (Santa Barbara, CA: Greenwood, 2011), pp. 36–7.

Stengers, Jean and Anne Van Neck, *Masturbation: The History of a Great Terror*, trans. Kathryn Hoffman (New York: Palgrave, 2001).

Stewart, Mary Lynn, *For Health and Beauty: Physical Culture for French Women, 1880s–1930s* (Baltimore, MD: Johns Hopkins University Press, 2001).

Stiles, Anne, *Popular Fiction and Brain Science in the Late Nineteenth Century* (Cambridge: Cambridge University Press, 2012).

Stoker, Bram, *Bram Stoker's Notes for Dracula: A Facsimile Edition*, ed. Robert Eighteen-Bisang and Elizabeth Miller (Jefferson, NC: McFarland, 2008).

Stoker, Bram, *Dracula*, ed. Glennis Byron (Peterborough, Ontario: Broadview Press [1897], 1998).

Stoker, Bram, *The Lady of the Shroud*, ed. William Hughes (Westcliff-on-Sea: Desert Island Books [1909], 2001).

Stoker, Bram, *The New Annotated Dracula*, ed. Leslie S. Klinger (New York: W. W. Norton, 2008).

Stoker, Bram, *Personal Reminiscences of Henry Irving* (London: William Heinemann [1906], 1907).

Stoker, Charlotte, *On Female Emigration from Workhouses* (Dublin: Alexander Thom, 1864).

Stoker, George, *With 'The Unspeakables;' or Two Years' Campaigning in European and Asiatic Turkey* (London: Chapman and Hall, 1878).

Stoker, William Thornley, 'Extensive Rupture of Liver and One Kidney, Followed by Attempts at Repair, Showing the Possibility of Recovery in Such a Case', *The Dublin Journal of Medical Science*, 69:2 (1880), 62–4.

Stoker, William Thornley, 'Successful Removal of the Uterus and One Ovary for the Relief of a Subperitoneal Uterine Tumour', *The Dublin Journal of Medical Science*, 69:2 (1880), 87–96.

Stott, Rebecca, *The Fabrication of the Late-Victorian Femme Fatale: The Kiss of Death* (Basingstoke: Palgrave Macmillan, 1992).

Strawberry Hill Residents' Association, 'A History of Roman Catholicism in Strawberry Hill', www.shra.org.uk/Catholicism%20in%20Strawberry%20Hill.pdf. Accessed 3 May 2011.

Summers, Montague, *The Gothic Quest: A History of the Gothic Novel* (New York: Russell and Russell, 1964).

Sunstein, Emily, *Mary Shelley: Romance and Reality* (Baltimore, MD: Johns Hopkins University, 1991).

Swan, Beth, 'Radcliffe's Inquisition and Eighteenth-Century English Legal Practice', *The Eighteenth-Century Novel*, 3 (2002), 195–216.

Tamagne, Florence, *A History of Homosexuality in Europe: Berlin, London, Paris 1919–1939* (New York: Alogora Publishing, 2006).

Tarr, Mary Muriel, *Catholicism in Gothic Fiction: A Study of the Nature and Function of Catholic Materials in Gothic Fiction in England 1762–1820* (Washington, DC: The Catholic University of America Press, 1946).

Taylor, Gary, *Castration: An Abbreviated History of Western Manhood* (London: Routledge, 2000).

Tegel, Susan, *Nazis and the Cinema* (London: Hambledon Continuum, 2007).

Thelwall, John, *The Daughter of Adoption: A Tale of Modern Times*, ed. Michael Scrivener, Yasmin Solomonescu and Judith Thompson (Peterborough, Ontario: Broadview, 2013).

Thibierge, George, *Syphilis and the Army*, ed. C. F. Marshall (London: University of London Press, 1918).

Thomson, Douglass H., 'Mingled Measures: Gothic Parody in *Tales of Wonder* and *Tales of Terror*', *Romanticism and Victorianism on the Net* (May 2008), http://id.erudit.org/iderudit/018143ar. Accessed 1 February 2014.

Thomson, William (ed.), *Transactions of the Academy of Medicine in Ireland*, 5 (December 1887).

Tichelaar, Tyler R., *The Gothic Wanderer: From Transgression to Redemption Gothic Literature from 1794–present* (Ann Arbor, MI: Modern History Press, 2012).

Townshend, Dale, *The Orders of the Gothic: Foucault, Lacan, and the Subject of Gothic Writing 1764–1820* (New York: AMS Press, 2007).

Tremlett, Giles, *Catherine of Aragon: Henry's Spanish Queen* (London: Faber & Faber, 2010).

Trenk, Richard T., Sr, 'The Plevna Delay: Winchesters and Peabody-Martinis in the Russo-Turkish War', *Man At Arms Magazine*, 19:4 (August 1997), 29–36.

Tropp, Martin, *Images of Fear: How Horror Stories Helped Shape Modern Culture, 1818–1918* (Jefferson, NC: McFarland, 1990).

Tucker, Nicholas, 'Third Reich and Third Rate', *New Society*, 17:447 (April 1971), 682.

Turner, Ralph V., *Magna Carta* (Harlow: Pearson Education, 2003).

Verhoeven, Wil, *Gilbert Imlay: Citizen of the World* (London: Pickering & Chatto, 2008).

Virilio, Paul, *War and Cinema: The Logistics of Perception*, trans. Patrick Camiller (London: Verso [1984], 1989).

Wagner, Peter, *Eros Revived: Erotica of the Enlightenment in England and America* (London: Paladin, 1988).

Walpole, Horace, *The Castle of Otranto*, ed. E. J. Clery and W. S. Lewis (Oxford: Oxford University Press [1764], 1996).

Walpole, Horace, *The Castle of Otranto*, ed. Michael Gamer (London: Penguin [1764], 2001).

Walpole, Horace, *The Castle of Otranto*, ed. Nick Groom (Oxford: Oxford University Press [1764], 2014).

Walpole, Horace, *The Castle of Otranto and The Mysterious Mother*, ed. Frederick S. Frank (Peterborough, Ontario: Broadview Press [1764 and 1768], 2003).

Walpole, Horace, *The Yale Edition of Walpole's Correspondence*, W. S. Lewis *et al.* (eds), 48 vols (New Haven, CT: Yale University Press, 1937–83).

Walvin, James, *A Short History of Slavery* (London: Penguin Books, 2007).

Ward, Candace, '"Duppy Know Who Fi Frighten": Laying Ghosts in Jamaican Fiction', in Monika Elbert and Bridget M. Marshall (eds), *Transnational Gothic: Literary and Social Exchanges in the Long Nineteenth Century* (Farnham: Ashgate, 2013), pp. 217–36.

Wasson, Sarah, *Urban Gothic of the Second World War: Dark London* (Basingstoke: Palgrave Macmillan, 2010).

Weininger, Otto, *Sex and Character: An Investigation of Fundamental Principles* (Bloomington, IN: Indiana University Press [1903], 2005).

Weir, Alison, *The Six Wives of Henry VIII* (London: The Bodley Head, 1991).

Wellman, Manly Wade, 'The Devil Is Not Mocked', in *The Mammoth Book of Dracula*, ed. Stephen Jones (London: Constable & Robinson [1997], 2011), pp. 50–6.

Wellman, Manly Wade, 'The Horror Undying', in *The Rivals of Dracula: A Century of Vampire Fiction*, ed. Michel Parry (London: Corgi, 1977), pp. 135–43.

Wells, T. Spencer, 'Vivisection and Ovariotomy', *The British Medical Journal*, 2 (November 1879), 794.

West, Stanley, MD, with Paula Dranov, *The Hysterectomy Hoax: The Truth about Why Many Hysterectomies Are Unnecessary and How to Avoid Them* (New York: Doubleday, 1994).

Whyte-Melville, G. J., *'Bones and I' or, the Skeleton at Home* (London: Chapman and Hall, 1868).

Wikoff, Karin Elizabeth, 'Hans Heinz Ewers' Vampir', MA dissertation, Cornell University (1995), http://siderealpressxtras.blogspot.co.uk/2010/02/hanns-heinz-ewers-vampir-thesis.html. Accessed 1 January 2013.

Wilberforce, William, *The Correspondence of William Wilberforce*, ed. Robert Isaac Wilberforce and Samuel Wilberforce, 2 vols (London: John Murray, 1840).

Williams, Anne, *Art of Darkness: A Poetics of Gothic* (Chicago, IL: University of Chicago Press, 1995).

Williams, Anne, 'Lewis/Gounod's Bleeding *Nonne*: An Introduction and Translation of the Scribe/Delavigne Libretto', in Gillen D'Arcy Wood (ed.), *Romanticism and Opera*, Romantic Circles (May 2005), http://rc.ctsdh.luc .edu/praxis/opera/williams/williams_notes.htm. Accessed 12 February 2013.

Winter, Jay, *Site of Memory, Sites of Mourning: The Great War in European Cultural History* (Cambridge: Cambridge University Press, 1995).

Wisker, Gina, *Horror: An Introduction* (New York: Continuum, 2005).

Wollstonecraft, Mary, *A Vindication of the Rights of Woman, A Vindication of the Rights of Men, An Historical and Moral View of the French Revolution*, ed. Janet Todd (Oxford: Oxford World's Classics, 1994).

Wood, Gillen D'Arcy (ed.), *Romanticism and Opera*, Romantic Circles (May 2005), http://rc.ctsdh.luc.edu/praxis/opera/williams/williams_notes.htm. Accessed 12 February 2013.

Wood, Marcus, *Blind Memory: Visual Representations of Slavery in England and America 1780-1865* (Manchester: Manchester University Press, 2000).

Woodward, C. Vann, *Tom Watson: Agrarian Rebel* (Oxford: Oxford University Press [1938], 1987).

Wright, Angela, *Britain, France and the Gothic, 1764-1820: The Import of Terror* (Cambridge: Cambridge University Press, 2013).

Wright, Angela, 'European Disruptions of the Idealized Woman: Matthew Lewis's *The Monk* and the Marquis de Sade's *La Nouvelle Justine*', in Avril Horner (ed.), *European Gothic: A Spirited Exchange 1760-1960* (Manchester: Manchester University Press, 2002), pp. 39-54.

Wright, Angela, *Gothic Fiction: A Reader's Guide to Essential Criticism* (Basingstoke: Palgrave Macmillan 2007).

Yeazell, Ruth Bernard (ed.), *Sex, Politics and Science in the Nineteenth-Century Novel* (Baltimore, MD: Johns Hopkins University Press, 1986).

Young, Elizabeth, *Black Frankenstein: The Making of an American Metaphor* (New York: New York University Press, 2008).

Young, Elizabeth, 'Here Comes the Bride: Wedding Gender and Race in *Bride of Frankenstein*', in Barry Keith Grant (ed.), *The Dread of Difference: Gender and the Horror Film* (Austin, TX: University of Texas Press, 1996).

Zanger, Jules, 'A Sympathetic Vibration: Dracula and the Jews', *English Literature in Transition*, 34:1 (1991), 33-44.

Žižek, Slavoj, *Interrogating the Real*, ed. Rex Butler and Scott Stephens (London: Continuum, 2005).

Index

EU authorised representative for GPSR:
Easy Access System Europe, Mustamäe tee 50,
10621 Tallinn, Estonia
gpsr.requests@easproject.com